ALSO BY K.A. TUCKER

Ten Tiny Breaths

One Tiny Lie

Four Seconds to Lose

Five Ways to Fall

In Her Wake

Burying Water

Becoming Rain

Chasing River

Surviving Ice

He Will Be My Ruin

Until It Fades

Keep Her Safe

The Simple Wild

Be the Girl

Say You Still Love Me

Wild at Heart

Forever Wild

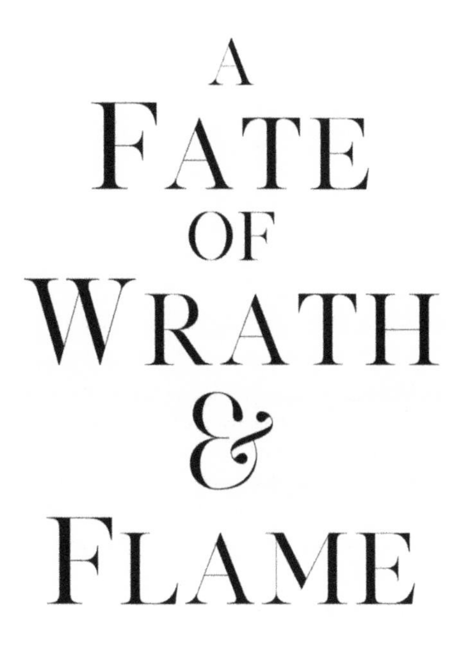

K.A. TUCKER

ISBN 978-1-990105-15-9 (paperback)

Edited by Jennifer Sommersby

Cover design by Hang Le

Published by K.A.Tucker

Manufactured in the United States of America

To Paul, for taking care of "what's for dinner?" every night these past three months.

AUTHOR'S NOTE

I published my first book ten years ago, in May 2011. It was a young adult fantasy called *Anathema,* the first in a series. A few years later, I switched to writing contemporary romance and suspense (two genres I love), but in the back of my mind, I've always known I would dive back into a fantasy world.

In 2015 I began plotting a new fantasy story. Every year, I opened that file, added more, and wondered if that would be the year I actually wrote it. But it was never the right time.

Then 2020 happened, and it rolled into 2021, and this book became my escape from it all when we weren't allowed to go anywhere. For those who read *Anathema,* you will notice a few things plucked from that story—a lot of the magic and world-building, the fates, the non-humans, even some of the names. The first scene has some literal copy-and-paste sections. I wanted to take concepts that I loved from that world and see where I could go with them. That is where the similarities end, though.

This story goes down an *entirely* different path. For those who haven't read *Anathema,* I've removed that series from the market-places. My writing skill has grown tremendously since those early days.

I cannot think of a better way to celebrate a decade of publishing novels than by releasing *A Fate of Wrath & Flame*. It is an adult (not YA, though I don't think there's anything *too* scandalous) passion project, and a wild escape for me, and I hope you enjoy reading it as much as I enjoyed writing it.

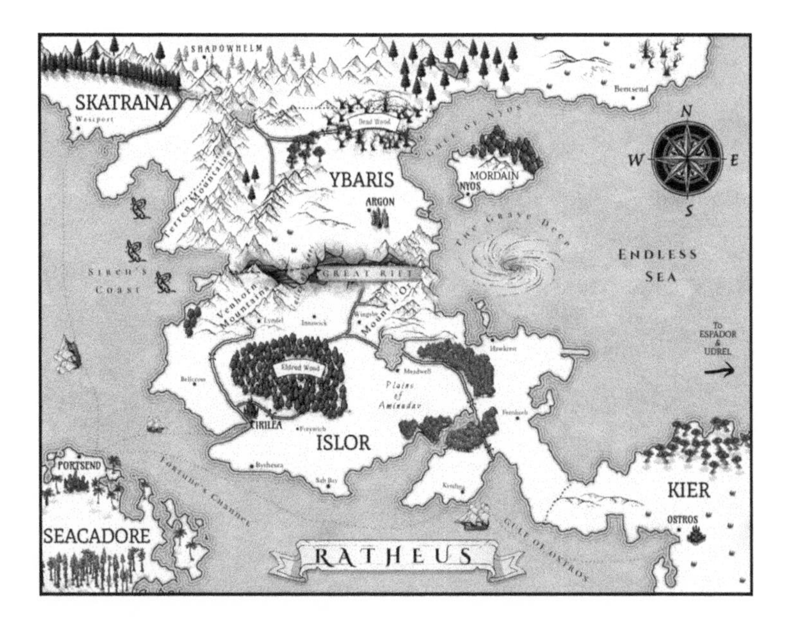
SHADOWHELM
SKATRANA
Westport
Bentsend
Dead Wood
Gulf of Nyos
MORDAIN
NYOS
N
W
E
S
YBARIS
ARGON
Terren Mountains
The Grave Deep
ENDLESS
SEA
Siren's
Coast
GREAT RIFT
Venhorn
Mountains
Lyndel
Mount L'Or
Meadwell
Hawkrest
TO
ESPADOR
&
UDREL
Eldred Wood
Plains
of
Aminadav
Fernbush
CIRILEA
ISLOR
PORTSEND
Salt Bay
KIER
OSTROS
Fortune's Channel
SEACADORE
Gulf of Ostros
RATHEUS

Pronunciations:

Romeria—Row-mair-E-a
Romy—Row-mE
Sofie—So-fee
Elijah—Uh-lie-jah
Zander—Zan-der
Wendeline—Wen-de-line
Annika—An-i-ka
Corrin—KOR-in
Elisaf—El-i-saf
Boaz—Bow-az
Dagny—Dag-knee
Bexley—Bex-lee
Saoirse—Sur-sha
Kaders—Kay-ders
Malachi—Ma-la-kai
Aoife—EE-fuh
Aminadav—Ami-na-dav
Vin'nyla—Vin-ny-la
Ratheus—Ra-tay-us
Islor—I-lor
Ybaris—Yi-bar-is
Cirilea—Sir-il-E-a
Seacadore—See-ka-dor
Skatrana—Ska-tran-a
Kier—KEY-er
Mordain—Mor-day-n
Azo'dem—Az-O-dem
Za'hala—Za-ha-la
Caster—Kas-ter
daaknar—day-knar
caco claws—kay-ko claws

PROLOGUE

1739

"It is time for me to die." Sofie's delicate hands slid up Elijah's chest to slip behind his neck.

"And if you are wrong ..." Unable to finish the sentence, his voice trailed off.

"I am *not* wrong!" she snapped. The copper-haired spitfire was always quick to temper.

He pulled away and moved to stand at a nearby window, to gaze upon the bustling nightlife beyond the castle walls. Rarely did he envy the commoners. Tonight, though, as he watched horse-drawn carriages roll along cobblestone streets, shuttling passengers home from frivolous celebrations and too much ale so they could hump their partners with reckless abandon, his jaw tightened with resentment. Why couldn't his problems be so trivial?

Briefly, Elijah allowed his attention to stray to the square where the pyres beneath the charred remains of three women still smoldered. It had been the largest culling in the region yet, the flames stoked by the bishop in his fervent quest to save humanity from witchcraft. This time, the church cited the plague of vole that ravaged the year's harvest as evidence of these women's guilt. Next time, they would find proof of Satan's wicked hand in a contagion that stole children, or a flood that drowned crops.

There was more truth to it than the portly bishop realized. But Elijah knew the church was motivated not by rooting out the cause of evil as much as its bid to maintain power in a time when a new house of worship was rising.

And this lunacy was spreading.

As Count of Montegarde, Elijah's influence over the church was limited. Still, he could have stopped today's massacre. He could have slipped into the yawning shadows of the bishop's residence and snapped the neck of that sanctimonious prick leading the charge. But his untimely death would only stir inquiry and embolden the masses. Another would quickly ascend into his place, more women would perish atop a bed of flames, and soon attention would turn to these stone walls and the peculiar nobility who arrived overnight, staking claim.

From there, the whispers of heresy and evil would grow legs and teeth. It would be only a matter of time before a frenzied mob congregated outside the gates with pitchforks and swords, and Elijah and Sofie were forced to flee like rodents, to start anew elsewhere.

He knew this pattern well. He had lived it in one form or another many times over.

And so Elijah sat idly by within his comfortable castle and listened to the shrieks of the women as they burned.

Sofie glided over to his side and lifted a finger to push a stray lock of hair off his forehead. "I cannot exist like this anymore, hiding in the shadows and waiting for certain doom."

"Do not worry about those zealots, my love."

"Adele did not worry, and look what happened to her," she reminded him somberly of her dearest friend who relocated to London, whose charred corpse Sofie wept beside last spring. He needed no reminding, though. That night, alight with raw fury,

Sofie had razed the abbey responsible for Adele's death, including its occupants, with nothing more than a flick of her wrist. In all his years on this earth, Elijah had never seen such power. It was both awe-inspiring and terrifying.

He had quickly ferried her sapped body away before too many witnesses could place her at the slaughter. Still, the last messages received from abroad were worrisome. The Casters' Guild knew Sofie was behind the massacre and sought severe penance for her sedition. Meanwhile, the humans hunted for a witch with hair the color of the devil's flame. Already, four victims matching her description had perished for her crime.

He could not fault Sofie for avenging Adele's death. The two shared a childhood of dashing along Paris's narrow passageways between lessons, and later, youthful nights dancing through the streets, enchanting suitors as much with their alluring beauty as their mettle. Sofie's heart was ardent and her loyalty eternal. Unfortunately, when wounded, her emotions engulfed her need for self-preservation.

Elijah sighed. "Adele was not careful. Besides, I would never allow any harm to come to you."

"And what of time? Will you stop that too?" Sofie knew where to aim her words to inflict the sharpest ache. "The madness calls to me even now, at this very moment. I do not know how much longer I can deny answering it."

He flinched, dropping his gaze to the majestic oak in the courtyard garden, dressed for autumn, a scant breeze rustling its golden leaves. Winter's bite hinted in the air. It would arrive within a fortnight, stripping the tree's beauty and imposing rest upon the earth. Sofie despised that long, dreary period, but Elijah found comfort in the visible passage of time.

Beneath that leafy canopy was to be Sofie's burial spot, if their fortunes did not change, though his preference was the crypt under the chapel where he could better guard her remains.

Would she even survive long enough to see the first snowfall?

It was unfathomable to him that this woman, not three

decades old, with the glowing complexion of youth and childish wildness flowing through her veins, would soon slip from his grasp. But he knew this madness she spoke of was true. He had seen it take hold of another like her, many years ago, leaving nothing but a mumbling shell of the impressive elemental she once was, her hair chalk-white and sparse, her eyes worthless, her powers impotent. She passed her days as a prisoner of the guild, reciting nonsensical musings that the scribes recorded as prophecy.

Though he didn't want to admit it, Elijah had begun to see worrisome signs in Sofie—listless stares, volatile mood swings, unintentional incantations that escaped her tongue. He could not bear to see Sofie become a husk of the vibrant woman he adored.

Of course, she had no plan to allow that to happen.

A man stumbled out of a tavern and fell to the ground in a drunken heap, directly in the path of two draft horses. Elijah's eyes widened, the idea of witnessing someone trampled to death lifting his spirits. At least that human's problem might rival his own tonight. He gripped the stone ledge in anticipation, watching the beasts' hooves plodding toward the man's limp body, seconds away from squashing his head as if it were a ripe melon. At the last moment, two men grabbed him by the heels and dragged him to safety. The horses cantered on into the night. *Damn those good Samaritans.*

Elijah scanned the streets for another person in a predicament worse than his own, knowing the chances were slim. His attention landed on a young couple in the midst of a lovers' quarrel, one that quickly escalated from shouts and hand gestures to a swift knee to the man's groin. The growing crowd of spectators erupted in laughter as the young man crumpled, writhing in pain. Despite his bitter mood, Elijah chuckled.

Sofie was not to be deterred, though. "Malachi has answered me, and we *must* act in haste. You have delayed this long enough."

"When the guild finds out, they will kill us on principle," he warned, as he had many times before. They had forbidden such perilous summons for good reason—an accord that had brought about peace after centuries of war between the casters and the immortals.

"What is done is done." Her face was a mask of grim certainty. "*If* they find out, they may punish me. But if we don't do this, I am dead either way."

"And I shortly thereafter." His eyes flickered to the ground beneath the oak tree once again. If she was wrong, the gravedigger would be burrowing two holes in that soil by the morn, for without Sofie, there was no point for Elijah to continue.

But he was not ready to say farewell yet. "One more sunset." Surely, this madness that loomed behind those emerald eyes would allow for that?

Sofie didn't respond immediately. When she did, it was with the sharpness of a well-honed blade. "Very well." The silk layers of her evening gown rustled noisily as she stalked toward the door.

Before she reached it, Elijah was across the room, his hand barring her exit. "You cannot ask it of anyone else." She knew it, and yet the way she stared back at him, her eyes blazing in defiance, he feared she would act foolishly.

She set her chin with determination. "Then you must trust me."

"It is not *you* I don't trust." He could not shake this terrible sense of foreboding. "When has Malachi ever granted anyone what they wanted without demanding *everything* in return?" Of all the fates, the Fate of Fire especially was not known for his compassion, but for his ruthlessness and pride. It had always been this way.

And yet Sofie had decided *he* was the one to beseech.

Elijah was furious when she first revealed that she had bound herself in servitude to him. It could never be undone.

"But I am a chosen one. Malachi's flame runs through *my* veins."

He sighed with forced patience. Sofie was young and arrogant, her faith in those who had given her immense power unwavering. She had not yet felt their wrath.

Her fingertips traced the outline of his jaw, beckoning him to meet her stare. "If we do nothing, then I am soon gone. I would rather die tonight than lose my hold on this world tomorrow. But I *will not* die. *You* will not die. Malachi has assured me of that much," she insisted, smiling up at him. "And we will handle whatever repercussions should arise. *Together.*"

She exuded such confidence. He desperately wanted to believe her. There was a reason she was both revered and reviled within the guild. Her powers were unparalleled in this world.

And while those powers would slip away from her eventually, she was willing to sacrifice them *all* this night for an eternity with him, a truth not lost on Elijah.

"You are insufferable, woman." There was no hint of anger in his tone.

"Yes, but I will be *your* insufferable woman, for always."

He collected her hand in his, bringing it to his mouth to press his lips against the smooth white stone of her wedding ring. He ended the gesture with another sigh, and they both recognized it for what it was—surrender. Elijah would not delay this any longer.

Pulling away from him, Sofie glided to the expansive bed, where they had spent many nights tangled within each other's limbs. A single candle burned on a nearby table, the only source of light in the chamber but one that glowed bright and permeated the air with the sweet aroma of honey.

He watched with growing arousal as she shed her gown and undergarments until only a canvas of bare skin remained. With a mischievous smile, she mounted the bed and knelt provocatively, her ample breasts heaving with each breath. He could sense her pounding heart, the headiness of her exhilaration. She had implored the fate—drawing on her powers until she'd drained every ounce—and he had heeded her call as the foreboding hour chimed.

"Perhaps these humans are right about their Christian beliefs and *you* are their devil, here to tempt them," he teased as he approached her. A nude and eager Sofie was impossible to resist, no matter how dire the circumstance—a fact she well knew.

"Then surely they should never cross me." She reached for his breeches.

"And is *this* a requirement of the invocation?"

"This is *my* requirement. A toll, if you will." Her fingers moved deftly over the hook and eyes, undressing him with haste. Soon, his clothing lay in a heap next to her silk gown.

They made love with their usual fervor, until their skin glistened, and their heavy breaths tangled, and their cries surely carried through the castle for the household to titter about come morning.

When they were both sated, Sofie swept the damp hair away from her neck, beckoning him forward. "May the fates be merciful," she whispered, peering up at him through unguarded eyes. They hinted at the same trepidation that consumed him.

He leaned in to inhale her intoxicating scent of rosewater, more potent after their exertion. "If not here, then in Za'hala." That was a fool's dream, for it was doubtful his kind would ever pass into that hereafter, but it was a dream worth wishing for. He scraped his teeth against her delicate skin—merely a harmless act of seduction in the past. This time, however, she arched her back, enticing him with the rush of blood that surged through her veins.

Sofie blinked away the fog of unconsciousness while staring at the dense velvet canopy draped above. Murky daylight glimpsed through the window, casting shadows in the bedchamber. Church bells tolled, announcing early service in the village. The faint, sweet scent of smoke and honey lingered in the air.

She smiled, the crushing fear of failure lifting from her chest. She had succeeded.

Weakness weighed down her limbs. Elijah said that would be the case. But already, she sensed that she was changed. Within her body a new heart thumped, slow and steady. This was a new dawn for her. Fates willing, she would see countless more with love and friendship at her side.

"Elijah?" she croaked, her throat raw with thirst. She pawed the mattress beside her, searching for his formidable shape. "It worked. We did it."

Silence answered.

She turned to the side and found the bed vacant. It was odd that he would abandon her on this morning of all mornings, but perhaps he had gone to fetch breakfast from the staff. He knew how she enjoyed her first meal in bed, and he was always eager to please her. Though, she supposed her meals might look different, especially in these early days.

She could still sense that innate spark deep within her core flickering in idle wait. Another oddity, given she had tendered her power to Malachi in exchange for this new, immortal form. She tried to call it forth now, but she was too weak, and the magic remained where it was, out of reach. Or perhaps it was now simply a phantom from her past life, a missing limb that tricked its owner by feeling whole.

The burn in her throat was unbearable. Elijah had said she would need to feed quickly to quell the discomfort and build her strength, and that he would be here to guide her through it. So where was he?

She heaved herself out of bed.

The sight of Elijah's naked body in a heap on the rug stole her breath.

She dove for him to give his shoulder a waking shake. "Elijah!" she called out in vain, her dread rising. His skin was chilled beneath her fingertips. Something was not right. His kind did not collapse like this.

Using whatever strength she could muster, she rolled him over.

She gasped at what stared back. "No, no, no …" She cupped his cheeks within her shaky palms. Gone were the soulful brown eyes that reminded her of lush soil after a heavy rainfall. In their place was a vacuous gray haze. "Elijah!" She shook his limp body violently, even though she already suspected it was useless.

On instinct, she closed her eyes and called to her powers again. This time they rose to the surface, uninhibited. Malachi had not taken them after all. She couldn't worry about what that meant at the moment, though, as she sent probing tendrils into Elijah's still form, searching for answers.

Her heart stirred with hope at the image that materialized. He was alive, wandering through a thick, endless fog. "Elijah!"

"Sofie?" His voice echoed in the void, her name laced with fear.

"I see you!" she cried, willing him to hear her.

With a gut-wrenching scream of pain, he crumpled to the misty ground. The image vanished from her mind, slicing off their connection.

"No!" she wheezed, flowing her magic through him once more. This time it recoiled the instant it touched him, fizzling to ash. Again and again, she tried to reach him, until no more would rise to her call, her powers exhausted.

She let her forehead fall against his chest as she wailed in despair. Her time with the guild had taught her of this horror. The oldest texts spoke of a place between the folds of time and dimensions, where the fates would banish souls to wander an eternity alone, a hollow nothingness that was neither Za'hala nor Azo'dem but worse. Most cast it off as more ramblings of the seers. But Sofie knew now that the Nulling was real, and Elijah was trapped in it, far beyond her reach.

This was not supposed to happen. This was not what Malachi had promised! Was he watching? Did they relish her pain? "I do not understand! I am a chosen one!" she cried out, hoping he was listening. Did she not deserve this happiness? She'd been nothing but devoted. Had she not praised him enough? Had she somehow wounded his brittle ego?

Perhaps this was merely a lesson. Perhaps Malachi would free Elijah from this curse yet. She clung to that scant thread of hope as she wept, ignoring her hunger as sorrow overwhelmed her and she longed for yesterday's return.

By nightfall, she shook from weakness and ached from loss. But more than anything else, she burned from regret. It was a mistake to trust Malachi. She saw that now. And yet he had not stripped her of the immense power she had tendered to him. That could only mean one thing—he was not finished with her.

"I will fix this," she promised Elijah's still form, her voice barely a whisper, hoping her words could reach him where her magic could not. "I will never stop." She would feel the warmth of his touch and the tenderness of his kiss once again.

Or she would die trying.

2020

Under the dim glow of lanterns, Sofie's slender figure remained as still as the body in the stone casket, her powers focused in prayer. She spent many hours here each day, on her knees in the crumbling vault beneath the chapel, until the stones cut into her flesh and her blood seeped into the ground.

Nearly three centuries of pleading.

Nearly three centuries of empty promises.

The years had been long, plagued with war and famine, with loneliness as she learned to survive, hiding in the shadows while she embraced her new immortal nature. She'd had to reinvent herself countless times to avoid unwelcome attention—changing identities, fleeing homes in the night, erasing any trails that might suggest to the guild and her other enemies that Sofie Girard had not long since perished.

In all of this, she had remained unwavering in her appeal to Malachi for mercy. The others would never acknowledge her, even though she'd tried to reach them. It was to the Fate of Fire that she was forever bound.

But Sofie had reached the brink.

She rose to her feet, ignoring the trickles of blood that ran down her shins from wounds that would heal within hours as if they'd never existed. With numbing calm, she climbed into the spacious sarcophagus to take her place next to her beloved.

In the early years, she had kept Elijah with her in the bedchamber of her various homes. It was not without difficulty, especially when disobedient servants stumbled upon what appeared to be a fresh human corpse in her bed. Rumors of wickedness and witchcraft followed her wherever she went, and she began to worry that she would not be able to protect him.

Finally, she reclaimed their first home together—the castle atop the hill—and chased the humans away. The decaying undercroft where no one ventured had become their haven.

It was here that she built a new sanctum where she could summon Malachi daily without fear of discovery. Sometimes, like today, her prayers were met with silence. Other times, with an audience. Malachi would arrive in his corporeal form to order her to be patient, for her day with Elijah would come. He had sent her on odd missions that she could not make sense of and was told not to question—part of a web of schemes he was concocting, surely. Occasionally, he would demand she undress and offer herself to him on the altar, so he could use her in ways that made her body and heart ache for different reasons. Those visits were growing more frequent as of late, the requirements bolder.

After three centuries, Sofie no longer believed Malachi had any intention of granting her husband his freedom.

She smiled sadly as she stroked her fingers across Elijah's cheek. He was as handsome now as the day Malachi took him from her. It was callous to preserve him so impeccably. It would have been easier on her had nothing remained of him but dust and bone. That was what the fates dealt, though—cruel tricks for even the most loyal.

"Forgive me, my love." She gripped the smooth obsidian bone handle of the dagger, allowing the fire's light to flicker off the sacred metallic blade. She was not certain the wound she was about to inflict upon Elijah would free him from this curse, but she knew it would release her from hers—the curse of eternal anguish.

"May the fates be merciful," she whispered, knowing they would not. She brought the tip of the blade to Elijah's chest, gathering the courage to drive it through his flesh.

A glimmer caught the metal, stalling her hand. Again it flashed, hinting at movement, and the sound of scraping against stone followed. Rodents lived in these walls and felines hunted them, but she did not sense their heartbeats, and besides, none made such a noise.

Sofie's pulse raced as the glow blossomed within the vault, illuminating the cracks in the stone ceiling and walls with warm, flickering light. Dropping the dagger, she climbed to her knees.

Her mouth dropped in awe at the looming silhouette in the center of the dank vault, his majestic horns alight with flame. She had laid eyes upon him countless times, but never like this.

"The time has come," Malachi's deep voice rumbled. "Are you my loyal servant?"

She scrambled out of the coffin to drop to her knees and press her forehead to the ground before the Fate of Fire. "For eternity." To bring Elijah back, she would do whatever was asked of her.

CHAPTER ONE

"Caviar, miss?" The starchy waiter blocks my path through the milling crowd, thrusting the silver tray forward.

I made the mistake of accepting once. It was my first assignment for Korsakov, and I was nervous, eager to blend into my high-society surroundings, so I accepted the ceramic spoon of tiny black balls that other guests were flocking toward like ducks to strewn bread. It took every ounce of my strength to force the slippery mouthful down my throat.

Offering a curt head shake as I snake past him, I head to the bar in the corner. My heart beats with the steady rush of adrenaline that always accompanies me on these nights. "French 75," I order, settling in to survey the landscape of lavish floral topiaries and designer dresses. Precious jewels wink at me from every angle. For a charity event intended to raise funds to combat hunger, it's ironic that the amount of money hanging off wrists and encircling fingers could likely feed the country's starving for years.

These people have no clue how the other side lives, but they'll take any opportunity to pat themselves on the back for a good deed while sipping their flutes of Moët & Chandon.

My mark stands twenty feet away, the black tuxedo he chose

for tonight flattering on his trim stature, his graying hair freshly cut during his afternoon visit to the gentlemen's club on 57th. He smiles as he watches the violinist draw her needle across the taut string, weaving a haunting tune. To the unaware, it would appear he is merely a connoisseur of fine classical music. I've been casing him for the last few weeks, though, and I know better.

The young musician's eyes are closed, lost in the melody, but in between each piece, she always makes a point of meeting his steady gaze and adjusting herself in her seat, as if she can't bear the wait until she can straddle his lap in the SoHo apartment he rents for her later tonight.

How his wife, standing ten feet away, hasn't picked up on her husband's taste for the doe-eyed college student, I do not understand. Or maybe she has and considers it a fair trade-off for their Upper Eastside life and the digits in her bank account.

"It is a lovely instrument, no?" A female voice laced with a smooth accent fills my ear.

"Hmm." I hum my agreement but otherwise pay the woman no heed. I don't talk to people while I'm working. Conversation leaves a trace, which leads to a trail, and trails that lead to me could end in a visit to the bottom of the Hudson River with a concrete block tied to my ankles.

I collect my drink, noting with disdain the smudge of graphite on my index finger. I did a poor job of washing my hands after my art class, but that is unimportant. What *is* important is moving to a safer vantage spot, one where no one feels compelled to talk to the solo woman by the bar.

"What is it that Viggo Korsakov is paying you to steal from that man?"

I freeze. A sinking feeling hits my gut as I turn to meet the owner of such a careless and dangerous statement. A striking woman with emerald eyes and hair the color of a freshly minted penny watches me intently. She's unfamiliar to me. I've never seen her at one of these events before, and she is someone I'd remember.

It takes me a few heartbeats to gather my wits and plaster on a baffled look. "I don't know what you're talking about."

Her painted red lips twist in a knowing smile, as if she can hear the alarms blaring inside my head. But then she dips her chin. "I must have mistaken you for someone else."

"Yeah. Definitely." I shrug it off with a wooden laugh while I steal a glance around. Whoever this woman is, she's polished and regal, and attracting curious looks from every direction. She's the *last* person I should be standing next to tonight while I'm trying to remain unnoticed. "If you'll excuse me—"

"Was it not you who took that diamond necklace at the gala in the summer?" She leans in to whisper conspiratorially, her eyes flickering with mischief. "I heard you plucked it off that woman's neck without her notice."

My heart hammers in my chest as I struggle to school my expression. That heist made headlines here in Manhattan. She could be guessing. "Sorry, no."

Her brow pinches. "And was it not you who made off with that actress's million-dollar diamond bracelet last spring?"

"Who the hell are you?" I can't keep the shake from my voice. That she would peg me for the Cartier robbery in Chicago is far too coincidental. She can't be a cop. Korsakov has too many of them in his pocket for us to not hear about an investigation.

Her head falls back with husky laughter. "I am not with the authorities, if that is what you are thinking. I am, how do you say … an admirer?"

She's crazy, is what she is. And she speaks oddly, like she belongs in another era. "I'm flattered, but you've got the wrong girl." I down half my drink as I scan the ballroom for the two security guards on Korsakov's payroll. They're supposed to be within a head-nod's reach in case of emergency, but they're nowhere to be seen.

As much as I want to run, I need to know how big a threat this woman is to me. Leaning into the bar, I match her coolness. "Sorry, I didn't catch your name."

"Sofie," she offers without hesitation. Fake, I'm sure. But even fake names can become real if they're used enough. Everyone on the street knows me only as Tee, short for Tarryn—the name of a grifter I met at a shelter when I was fifteen. She took me under her wing and taught me how to steal and not get caught. At first, it was food, books, clothes—necessities. Eventually, that turned to nail polish and hoop earrings, and then wallets stuffed with credit cards and cash. When Tarryn got busted for grand theft auto and locked away, I assumed her identity.

But I'll play along with this act. "So, do you live in New York, *Sofie*?"

"No. My husband and I reside in Belgium presently. It has been some time since I've been here. Almost a decade, I believe." A tiny smirk curls her lips. "Elijah has yet to visit this city of yours, but I imagine he would be *beguiled* by it." She takes a long, leisurely sip of her wine. If she was at all wary or nervous about approaching me tonight, it doesn't show. Every inch of her exudes fearless confidence. Normally, I would envy that.

Now, I'm deeply unnerved.

The violin music has ended. The brunette musician is in the corner, tucking her instrument into its case. Nearby, my mark is in conversation with another man, but the frequent glances at his watch tell me he's trying to cut away. I'm going to miss my window if I don't make a move soon, and I *cannot* miss this one.

"What would you say if I offered you double what your employer is paying you for tonight?"

Sofie startles me yet again, pulling my attention back to her. It's pointless to keep denying that I'm the thief she has pegged me for. Someone has been feeding her solid intel, and I'll get more information out of her if I play along. "And what is it you think I'm going to steal?"

She shrugs, her astute gaze locked on the mirror's reflection behind the bar. "I have no idea, and I care not. But if I were to hazard a guess, I would say those cuff links would be of significant value."

Those cuff links are worth four hundred grand based on what the rich prick forked over at auction last year, not that I'm about to confirm her suspicions. "Thanks for the offer, but I'll have to decline."

Her impeccably sculpted eyebrow arches. "Triple, then?"

I falter. While I didn't start out earning much, now that I've proven my worth, the bundles of cash after a job well done more than pay for my living expenses. *Triple* that amount? Most thieves in my line of work would bite on that lure. But they'd be idiots, because no one crosses a guy like Viggo Korsakov and gets away with it.

Then again, if I don't show up in his office tonight with those diamond-studded cuff links in hand, it'll be my second miss in as many months. My worth to him is already on shaky ground.

"Who sent you?" Everything about this situation screams of a trap. If I weren't *literally* in the middle of a take, I'd think Korsakov himself was behind this, a way of testing my trustworthiness.

Her eyes sparkle with mischief. "Malachi."

"Never heard of him." But I'll definitely be asking around.

She studies my face, as if I'm an object worthy of scrutiny. "I can see that you are terribly wise for your youth. And loyal. I appreciate that."

"More like I like breathing," I mutter through a sip. The drink was meant as a prop, but I'll be ordering another to fill my sweaty palm soon.

"So, it is fear that keeps you with him. A need for self-preservation."

The last decade of my life has been all about self-preservation.

Despite my veil of suspicion, I pity this woman. Whoever Malachi is, he sent her here on a fool's errand. I lower my voice. "Maybe you should take some lessons, then, because dropping Korsakov's name around the city like this? It's a *bad idea*."

"*Mais oui*, I understand he is a dangerous man." She waves her hand dismissively, and my eyes catch the gold ring on her finger.

The band is chunky and ornate, the finish antique, and the sizable white stone held within the claws holds no sparkle. I might dismiss it as a bubblegum-machine prize if this woman weren't wearing it.

"You don't want to get mixed up with him, believe me." Maybe she thinks her beautiful face will buy her grace, but Korsakov is an equal-opportunity killer when someone threatens his empire.

She peers at me again with that measuring stare. "And why are *you* mixed up with him, then?"

"Because I don't have a choice." The words come out unbidden. I quietly chastise myself for allowing them to slip so easily. It makes me appear weak and fearful—nothing more than a pawn, a piece to play in someone else's game. And I suppose I am, to some degree, though I have my own game in play too. An endgame out of this life.

"You have a binding agreement with him." Sofie's eyes don't reflect any pity. If anything, I see genuine interest.

"More like a debt I'll never be able to pay off." I was eighteen when I lifted that diamond bauble off the wrong hand at a nightclub. I took it to the pawnshop the next day, where I hocked everything I stole, knowing Skully would pay me a fraction of its worth, but he wouldn't ask questions. That bulky wad of cash in my pocket had me literally skipping out of the shop. It would keep me afloat for months if I was thrifty.

The next day, three men tracked me down and dragged me into a black SUV. Turns out the ring I stole belonged to Viggo Korsakov's daughter.

I still remember standing in the warehouse office in front of *the* Viggo Korsakov himself, a man with pinched eyes and a cruel smile. One of the fluorescent lights above blinked, ready to give out, making the whole scenario more ominous. It took every ounce of composure to keep my limbs from trembling and my bladder from letting loose as I sang apologies and excuses, begging him not to use the meat cleaver that waited idly on a nearby table. How would I survive without my hands? Stealing was what I was good at—and I was excellent at it.

He offered me a deal instead. Skully had told him about my eye for quality, that the "merchandise" I'd been delivering over the years far outvalued the typical trinkets and trash he bought from others. Korsakov had need of a thief of my talent and profile—young, pretty, unexpected, and most surprising, without fingerprints in the criminal system. If I agreed to work for him, he would forgive me for my grievous mistake.

I'd heard enough whispers on the street about the man to know it wasn't a choice, not if I wanted to walk out of that warehouse with my hands, so I accepted his offer.

That was three years ago, and while I don't have my freedom, my life hasn't been bad. Gone are the days of sleeping in youth shelters and vans, on couches, or tucked into an alcove at the public library when a night guard took pity. I now have a quaint studio apartment in Chelsea, with an exposed brick wall and south-facing window where basil and rosemary grow in pots on the sill, and my fridge is always filled with fresh fruit and meat that I paid for.

Korsakov tasked his daughter—the very one I had stolen the ring from—with transforming me from a scrappy street kid who loitered in dark corners to the pedigreed woman who could stroll into high-society charity events without earning a blink of suspicion. I no longer spend my days in search of valuables left in cars and careless fools who don't guard their wallets and purses. Now, I lead a relatively typical life, relying on my talents only when Korsakov taps my shoulder with a ticket to one of these parties, where I blend in like a chameleon long enough to appropriate well-insured jewels from rich assholes. That's what he calls me: his chameleon.

But in the end, I'm still a thief, one who feels more indebted to Korsakov now than I did three years ago. Short of disappearing into the night and spending the next however many years watching over my shoulder, I don't have options. I'm stuck with him until he's six feet under or he no longer sees value in me—which could mean *I'm* six feet under.

Sofie tips her glass to polish off the last of her wine before gingerly setting it on the counter. "Forgive me. I can sense that you are anxious. I shall not keep you from your *task* any longer. Do not do something silly, like get caught." She winks, and as quickly as she appeared at my side, she vanishes into the crowd, leaving me rattled to my core.

"He's *pissed*." Tony drums his thick fingers against the passenger door to the tune of the sweeping windshield wipers. "Two major screw-ups in a row. My brother's little lizard isn't worth his trouble anymore."

I roll my eyes at the back of the big oaf's head, knowing he's watching me through the side mirror and will catch it. Tony is enjoying my empty hands far too much for someone who's supposed to be on the same team. I'm not surprised, though. He was the one safeguarding Anna the night I stole her ring. It earned him a smashed nose that healed crooked and three broken ribs, as well as a demotion in rank that he hasn't gained back yet. He has despised me ever since, made worse on nights like tonight when he's assigned to babysitting duty.

Tony's opinion doesn't matter, but I know Korsakov will not take lightly to a second miss—especially not this one. He already had a buyer lined up, and he *hates* reneging on a deal.

I've learned not to show fear around these guys, though. Assholes like Tony will feed off it like a rabid coyote until there's nothing left of me but bones. "It's late. Drop me at home and I'll go talk to him tomorrow." Korsakov's temper is scalding, but it cools quickly. It's best not to be around him until it does.

"Nah." Tony's grin is wide and obnoxious. "He called before you came out. Said to bring you in tonight."

"Fine. Whatever." I feign indifference but my stomach roils.

That doesn't bode well for me. He couldn't have known I'd failed by that point. But maybe he'd made a decision about my fate in case I did.

I focus on my breathing as our SUV meanders along the city streets, the hazy glow of brake lights and relentless blast of taxi horns oddly therapeutic. My target left before I could make my move, but it would've been too risky, anyway. I have to assume Sofie is somehow tied to the feds, and if those cuff links went missing tonight, my studio apartment door would be the first they kicked down.

"What's with the souvenir?" Tony asks.

He means Sofie's glass that I swiped off the bar before the bartender could come by to collect, smuggling it out beneath my wrap, careful not to smudge her fingerprints. "You use it to drink wine."

"You know, one of these days, that smart mouth of yours is gonna get you into real trouble. Why'd you lift it?"

"Because I needed a new one."

He snorts. "Idiot."

I took it thinking I'd give it to Korsakov when I told him about her, as a way of buying myself a pass for tonight's failure. But the more I consider that plan, the more I realize it's likely that he'll decide I've been compromised. Last year, when Rolo was caught having a cozy chat with the DEA, Korsakov set him free with a bullet to the back of the skull. At least that's the rumor—Korsakov is not dumb enough to murder with an audience. But no one, including Rolo's wife and kids, have seen him since.

Tony is right. I *am* an idiot, for not slipping out the back of the venue while I still could.

My insides are churning when I spot the familiar vendor cart up ahead. "Stop here for a minute?"

"Seriously?" Tony twists his massive frame around to scowl at me.

"I'm starving," I lie. I doubt I could manage a bite.

"You just left a penguin-suit party full of food!" He groans loudly—he always complains when I ask to stop—but then he nods at Pidge. "Fuck, yeah, *whatever*." He adds under his breath, "Considering it's probably your last meal."

"I'll even eat it outside," I offer, my voice dripping with phony sweetness. The only thing Tony despises more than me is the smell of hotdogs and sauerkraut.

"Yeah, you will. You're not stinking up this leather for the next week." He shakes his head. "Can take the girl out of the street, but can't take the street rat out of the girl."

"There's an umbrella under my seat," Pidge offers as I gingerly set Sofie's glass down.

"Thanks." He's quiet and the nicest of the bunch, but he'd still sell his own sister for the right price. I hop out, my clutch tucked under my arm. The dress I'm wearing is a sleek black satin halter style that pools around my feet—the least flashy of the designer lot the guys procured in their latest heist. Neither it nor my wrap offer any protection against the bone-chilling November air, but in my present state of mind, I barely notice.

I want to believe Korsakov wouldn't end me, not over this. Ironically, the man has shown me more kindness than he does to most, albeit in his own way. Once, one of his goons took the "do not touch my pretty little thief" law as mere guidance and tried to force himself on me. Korsakov had the skin flayed off his back with a whip. I know because Korsakov made me watch the spectacle, smiling as proudly as a cat presenting a massacred bird at its master's feet. Only Korsakov isn't an ordinary cat. He's a tiger who occasionally lunges at those who feed him.

But the phone call, the demand to see me with or without the cuff links …

Does he already know about the red-haired woman sniffing around me?

Or has he somehow learned about the discreet inquiries I've been making into securing a passport? About the cash I've been squirreling away in my vent and the apartment in London that

I've looked at renting? If he has, would he see that as anything other than what it is—an escape plan?

My instincts are telling me to run.

I pick my way along the sidewalk, trying to avoid the puddles as I scramble to devise my strategy. Do I just kick off my heels and bolt? Do I wait until I'm a safe distance away to give myself a head start? I could cut through the park and jump into a taxi on the other side. Going back to my apartment to grab my stash bag would be a risk, but there's no point going to the train station without it. It has money, clothes, a fresh ID—everything I need to disappear.

I'm only partly surprised Tony let me out. He's stupid and arrogant enough to assume I won't take off. Or maybe he wants me to, so he has an excuse to give his brother when he delivers me battered and bruised.

I'm still weighing my best course of action when I reach the stand. Alton is hunched in front of the grill, turning a sausage over the flame. "Yeah?" He grunts before glancing up. Instant recognition touches his face. "Haven't seen you around in a bit." I've come a long way from the gangly kid with heavy kohl-lined eyes and bleached hair who stole a hotdog from him. But he once said that it doesn't matter how much makeup I hide behind or what color my hair is; all he needs to know it's me are my blue eyes. They remind him of his childhood summers by the Adriatic Sea.

It's been a few months. "I've been busy." I dare a glance over my shoulder at the waiting SUV, its blinking hazards earning angry horn blasts from vehicles coming up behind. Tony can't climb a flight of stairs without wheezing by the time he reaches the top; I could probably outrun him, even in my heels. But Pidge is smart enough to drive around and catch me on the other side of the block.

Alton opens his mouth to say something but promptly shuts it. I already know what he's thinking. It's what all my street acquaintances think: that I'm thriving as a high-end prostitute. I've never bothered to correct them. It's more honorable to peddle what you own than what you've stolen. "Glad to see you still kickin' around," he offers.

Not for long, possibly.

If I head for one of the benches in the park to eat, I'll have the best shot at slipping away without immediate notice. It might give me just enough time.

"The usual?" He holds up a foot long in his metal tongs.

I smile. "Yeah."

"One for him too?" Alton nods to his left, his eyebrows raised in question.

I follow his direction to the lump of blankets on the sidewalk fifty yards away, and surprise pushes aside my escape planning for the moment. "Is that Eddie?" Has it been six months already?

"Yup. He's been hanging around here for a few weeks now."

"*And?*"

Alton shrugs. "Hasn't scared away my customers yet. I think his eyesight's gotten worse, though."

Maybe Eddie's time in prison has helped where nothing else ever has. "Give me two dogs. Please." I always buy an extra meal when Eddie's around. Alton has guessed that he's someone to me, but he's never pressed for details.

I tuck a twenty under the napkin dispenser on the counter and wave away the change, as always. I've lost track of the meals the kindhearted street meat vendor has given me over the years, when I was starving and couldn't pay for them.

Gripping both in one hand while I huddle under the umbrella's shelter, I make my way over, ignoring the horn that blares of warning from the curb. The closer I get, the more potent the stench of stale urine and body odor becomes. "Hey, Eddie."

The man peers up from beneath his soiled quilt, squinting against the rain. Or perhaps it's to make out what's in front of his failing eyes. They cut his hair and beard while he was inside, so he doesn't look nearly as straggly as he did when I last saw him, and he's put on a few pounds. He's lost another tooth to decay, though. "Is that you?"

A painful lump stirs in my throat. "Yeah." At least he's aware tonight. "How are things?"

"They won't let me in at St. Stephen's anymore," he grumbles.

"That's because you threatened to kill a volunteer there. That's why you went to prison." It brought me comfort, knowing he had a warm, dry place to sleep and three meals a day, even if it was courtesy of the county jail.

"He tried to poison me. I saw him do it with my own eyes."

I bite my tongue against the urge to remind him that it was fresh parsley that the man—a schoolteacher volunteering at the soup kitchen—sprinkled over the shepherd's pie. Forget his weakening eyesight, Eddie's so far gone to delusion, he won't hear any version of the truth other than his own. "Here. I brought you something." I hold out both hotdogs for him.

His eyes narrow as he studies them, not making a move.

I sigh heavily. "Come on, Dad, it's me, *Romy*. You need to *eat*."

After another long moment, he accepts them with a grimy hand. Tucking one under his quilt for later, he scrapes the toppings off the other with a swipe of his dirty thumb. Sauerkraut and mustard splatters on the sidewalk beside my heel, a few yellow drops hitting my hem.

"So? Things are okay? No aches or lumps or anything that you should get checked out by a doctor?" He's a forty-nine-year-old man who could easily pass for seventy, the decade of living on the street aging him far beyond his years.

"Watch out for the demons. Especially the ones with the twisty horns. They're here, walking among us, wearing our skin."

The foolish shred of hope I held coming over here evaporates. Nothing has changed.

"I will. Definitely." It used to gut me to see this version of my father—perched on milk crates and park benches, ranting about monsters who lurk in the shadows and feed on human souls. That was back when the memories of our old life were still fresh in my mind.

Once, long ago, we lived in a two-bedroom apartment in East Orange, New Jersey. My dad was a line supervisor at a factory that made bolts and screws, and my mom was a grocery store clerk. I took swimming lessons and played soccer. We ate dinner at six p.m. sharp and would drive to a farm every fall where we would spend hours searching for the perfect pumpkins for jack-o'-lanterns.

I lost that version of my father the night he witnessed a woman's brutal murder in the parking lot at work. He claimed a shadowy monster with wings and curly black horns was the culprit, tearing her apart with its talons, and that a witch channeling flames from her fingertips banished it back to Hell.

He was never the same after, spiraling down a tunnel of hallucinations and paranoia that no medications or doctors were able to treat or explain. He lost his job, we lost our apartment, and eventually, it became unsafe to be around him.

We tried to get him help, but we had no money, and the system for people with no money is made from safety nets riddled with holes. My dad slipped through every last one until he landed on the street where he's been ever since.

I spent years angry and pretending he didn't exist, and then years weighed down by guilt and attempts to help him—arranging doctor's appointments he refused to go to, housing he wouldn't stay in, buying clothes he'd lose.

Now, all I have left to give him is a hollow heart, a cheap meal, and a few kind words when I run into him on the street. I have my own problems to deal with.

"I've got to go." A narrow path lies ahead, cutting into the bushes next to a trash can. If I pretend I'm disposing of the wrappers, it should buy me a small lead. Pidge and Tony will go straight to my apartment once I don't return, but if I wait them out a few days, I should eventually be able to slip in, get my things, and run.

"Your mother came by," my father says through a bite. "She asked about you."

Hearing mention of her always stings, but I quickly harden my heart. I know she still looks for me occasionally. "She still with *them*?"

He nods.

My molars gnash against each other. "Stay far away from her." I no longer fault my father for the illness that stole him from us, but my mother *chose* to abandon her own daughter for monsters. I'll never forgive her for that. "Take care of yourself, okay?" I perch the umbrella on the hedge next to him so it will offer some protection. Running will be easier without it, anyway. "Go to St. Vincent's and ask for Sam."

"Sam?"

Sometimes my dad listens to me and seeks out shelter. He never stays long, but it's something. "Yeah. *Sam*. Tell him you're Tee's friend. Okay? *Tee*. Not Romy. He doesn't know Romy." No one knows her. "He's one of the good guys. He won't try to poison you, so *don't* threaten him, okay? I've got to go now—"

My father's hand shoots out, grasping my calf with surprising strength. "Beware of the demon with the flaming hair. She hunts for you," he hisses, bits of bun and meat spraying from his mouth.

A shiver of unease skitters down my spine. I'm used to my father's raving, but they've always been anchored by the same figure—a shadowy monster with black, twisty horns. This is new, and it instantly stirs thoughts of a mysterious red-haired woman in a green dress. "What do you mean by flaming—"

"What the hell?" Tony barks, startling me. I didn't hear him approach. "We're sitting there waiting for you, and you're chatting it up with this *bum*." He sneers at my father.

But Eddie pays him no attention, his eyes boring into mine as if pleading with me to listen. His grip tightens. "The gilded doe has been here. She knows what you are—"

Tony's black boot connects with my father's jaw, sending him tumbling backward with a sickening crack.

"What *the hell*!" I don't think twice; I swing wide. My fist lands squarely against Tony's nose. The feel of bones crunching beneath my knuckles is satisfying.

"You bitch!" He seizes me by my biceps with one hand while cupping his face with the other. Blood trickles down around his mouth.

I kick at his shins, trying to yank myself free so I can check on my father. He's lying on the cold, wet sidewalk, moaning. His jaw is surely broken. "You're hurting me!"

"I haven't *begun* to hurt you." Tony squeezes harder as he tugs me toward the curb where Pidge has edged the SUV forward to collect us. "My brother just called. He wants us there *now*, and he ain't messin' around."

Years on the street have taught me how to defend myself, but none of it will help me break free of Tony's viselike grip. He has at least two hundred pounds on me, and he's too strong. I have no choice. I reach into the slit in my dress and slip the small knife I keep strapped to my thigh from its sheath.

"I don't fucking think so." Tony moves fast for a large and injured man, roping his brawny arm around my body, pinning my back against his chest. "You think I don't know about your little butter knife? What are you gonna do with that? Huh?" He squeezes my wrist with his bloodied hand.

I cry out as pain shoots up my arm, and I lose my grip. The blade falls to the sidewalk, out of reach, leaving me defenseless as Tony hauls me toward the passenger door.

Alton rounds the side of his cart, the baseball bat he keeps tucked away for protection hanging from his grip. "Tee? You need some help?"

Tony snickers. "You'll go back to your hotdogs if you know what's good for you."

Alton pauses, looks at me, conflict in his eyes, and I know what he's thinking: he has a wife and two kids he wants to go home to. But he also can't stand idly by while I'm dragged into the car, kicking and screaming.

Tony isn't posturing—he *will* shoot him with the Glock he has under his jacket.

I go limp and shake my head, warning Alton away. "I'll be fine."

"Wouldn't be so sure about that." Tony shoves me into the back seat of the SUV, climbing in beside me to keep me in place.

The last thing I hear before he slams the door shut is my father's garbled cry: "Find the gilded doe!"

CHAPTER TWO

Korsakov's main import-export operation runs out of a boxy, steel-gray warehouse at the city ports where containers loaded with cargo come and go, and the palms of the port authority are greased so well, everything slides past notice. The property is secured behind fencing, perimeter cameras, and at night, a lot of guys with guns.

I've always hated coming down here, but tonight feels unnervingly similar to three years ago when I was certain I wouldn't be walking out, at least not with all my body parts still attached.

The asshole lumbering ahead of me, whistling an ominous *Kill Bill* tune, isn't helping.

Tony pauses long enough to turn back and flash a vicious grin, though it ends in a grimace of pain that pleases me. His nose has stopped bleeding, but it's red and swollen. If he were smart, he'd head to the hospital and get it set properly this time.

If he were smart.

I ignore him and the throb in my arm where he gripped me too tight, and concentrate on the explanation I crafted on the way over. It's best I keep my story vague and simple, and focus Korsakov on why he values me in the first place. He has always praised me for my gut instincts.

There were eyes on me. It wasn't safe. I would have gotten caught.

I'll only play the Sofie card if I *absolutely* must.

"Who is that?" Pidge frowns at a white SUV parked by the door. Two stone-faced men sit in the front seats, watching us pass. The feel of their eyes on me makes the hair on the back of my neck prickle.

Tony shrugs, unconcerned. Whoever owns that vehicle must be inside, and they wouldn't be there unless Korsakov allowed it. Plus, the armed guards surrounding this warehouse surely have their sights trained on them.

Tony punches in the security code that releases the door lock on the steel door.

I hold my breath, bracing myself for Korsakov's voice. When he's angry, he only has one volume, and you can hear him all the way from the other side of this cavernous space.

Instead, silence greets us.

"Where is everybody?" Pidge's keys jangle from his fingertips as we march along the corridor. On either side of us are aisles of towering pallets full of product, the forklifts sitting idle.

"In the office," Tony says, calling out louder. "We're back, and we brought your little lizard with us!" An echo of his booming voice is the only response. He slows. Finally, the big dumb lout must sense the eeriness that climbed over my skin the second we stepped inside.

Tony juts his chin toward Pidge, and they both draw their guns. Pidge instructs me to get behind him with a nod of his head. I don't argue. I'll happily use him as a shield as I look for any opportunity to run.

My heart pounds in my ears as we proceed to the back of the building, where the door to the office sits ajar. Pidge gives it a push, and it swings open with a moaning creak.

A soundless gasp escapes my mouth.

Korsakov's office is a long, narrow, windowless room, lined with filing cabinets that hold decades of paperwork. Normally it smells of burnt black coffee and smoldering tobacco.

Now, it reeks of death.

Bodies are scattered, their gaping wounds weeping into the cheap blue industrial carpet. Blood splatter decorates the drab beige walls in sweeping arcs like a sinister artwork exhibit. Four men lay dead, including Korsakov himself, sprawled on his back, his neck slashed from ear to ear.

And in the center of the carnage, seated cross-legged in Korsakov's chair, is a woman with copper-red hair, observing us with a taunting smile.

Both Tony and Pidge make to raise their guns.

Sofie moves so quickly, my mind doesn't register the flying objects until the men drop their weapons in unison and grip their forearms, howling in agony.

My eyes widen at the twin daggers that protrude from their wrists.

"Do not," she warns simply.

Do not fight, do not run … Just *do not.*

I couldn't if I wanted to. I am frozen in place.

A feeble groan pulls my eyes to the floor. Korsakov is still alive, though barely, and I doubt for long. He always seemed an unstoppable force, beckoning people to do his bidding with a few commanding words, a threatening squint. Now, he's nothing more than a helpless man, carved by the sword that lies atop his desk, staining stacks of paper in crimson.

People still use swords?

"Who the fuck are you?" Tony manages through gritted teeth. The dagger landed precisely in the center of his right wrist, just below his palm. Severing important nerves, I'm sure.

"Someone your employer was unwilling to negotiate with." As with earlier at the bar, Sofie remains calm and collected, unafraid. She's swapped her emerald gown for head-to-toe black. It amplifies the intensity of her hair color. "I hope you are more intelligent than he was."

Both Tony and Pidge scan the office. I assume they're looking for proof that she didn't slaughter four armed men on her own with nothing other than a sword. Maybe the two men sitting in the SUV out front were the ones to do this. But the speed and precision with which Sofie threw those daggers suggests her fully capable of it, and more.

My insides stir as I survey the bodies more closely, their guns on the floor beside them. All had drawn their weapons, and they're *all* dead.

Even that last shred of life in Korsakov's eyes is now gone.

"What were you negotiating for?" Tony's attention lingers on his older brother. Does he feel any sorrow for the loss?

The weight of Sofie's eyes as they shift to me stalls my heart. "Her."

Beware of the demon with the flaming hair. She hunts for you.

I shove my father's mad rants from my mind.

"You want *her*?" There's disbelief in Tony's voice. "For what?"

"That is none of your concern." A tiny, knowing smile curls her lips as she regards me. "Let's just say it's something only she can help me with."

What could Sofie possibly need me to steal that would be worth *all this*? My mind rifles through our early conversation. Did she leave the charity event knowing she would be coming here to slaughter Korsakov? She must have. If I had accepted her offer and left with her, would she have let them be?

Who *is* this woman?

Tony licks his lips. "How much are you offering me for her?"

Korsakov's Italian suede loafers aren't even cold, and Tony is already trying to jam his sweaty feet into them. With everyone else gone, he's likely to inherit the operation. *If* he makes it out of here alive, and the way Sofie is examining him, I have reason to doubt it.

"For her?" Sofie cocks her head. "She is not a mule for purchase. Clearly, you've misunderstood. I offered to spare your employer's life if he released her from her debt to him, which he foolishly refused. Now he is dead, and she is no longer bound to

him. I am simply giving *you* the choice to either allow us to leave peacefully or forfeit your lives."

Tony glowers at her and for a moment, I think he's going to lunge. A part of me hopes he does.

"Don't be stupid," Pidge pleads under his breath, cradling his injured arm.

"Fine." Tony sneers at me. "She's a worthless bitch, anyway."

Sofie's face hardens, her eyes narrowing as they drop to where dark bruises matching meaty fingers have started to form on my biceps. "Perhaps I should not be the one to choose your outcome." She stands and rounds the desk, her delicate hand curling around the hilt of the bloodied sword. "Should we or should we not leave them breathing, Romeria?"

My stomach drops. She knows my real name. How the hell does she know my *real* name?

"What will it be? Life"—Sofie presses the tip of her blade against Tony's neck—"or death?"

He grimaces as a drop of blood swells against his skin where the sharp point nudges. His blue eyes dart to mine and mixed in with the usual medley of hatred and anger is fear.

I look away, unable to digest the latter. Tony's a degenerate and an asshole. He hurt a helpless man tonight for no good reason. He wanted to see me suffer, even be killed. He deserves to lie in a heap next to the rest of these lifeless bodies.

My attention drifts to them. Irving has a pregnant girlfriend at home. Gavin's twin sons giggle as they hide behind their fence and shoot unsuspecting neighborhood passersby with their water guns. Mark just closed on his first house with his wife. Korsakov leaves behind a daughter who will be devastated. They're men who I would never label "good," but they'll be mourned all the same.

While I may be a thief, I'll never be an executioner. "Let them go."

Sofie waits a few beats but then lowers her blade with a heavy sigh. "She shows mercy where I would not. I'll admit, that's a quality I admire and abhor equally."

Both men release the slowest exhales.

"If you two have an ounce of intelligence, you will remain here until we have departed."

Tony's bearish body shakes from rage but for once, he has the sense to keep his mouth shut.

She strolls past them without a hint of wariness. "Shall we?" It's as if she's inviting me out for a drink. As if she didn't slaughter four men, and there's no need to ask if I'd be willing to work for her now that Korsakov is dead. I guess there isn't, because it's obvious she's intent on getting what she wants.

I have no more of a choice now with Sofie than I did three years ago with Korsakov. I have traded one murderer for another, and I must go along with it until I can get away from her.

We leave Pidge and Tony, daggers jutting from their wrists, standing in the office filled with corpses. My legs feel like they belong to someone else as they propel me forward, step by step. Every few seconds, I steal a glance over my shoulder, expecting to see Tony there, aiming his gun at my back. But the doorway remains empty.

Sofie doesn't look back once. "I did warn them. I wish they had listened." She shakes her head. "But men like them never do."

"Tony is going to call the guys outside," I hear myself say, my voice hollow. "They'll shoot us the second we step out that door."

"My guards will have taken care of them by now. They are no longer an issue."

Right. The two scary men in the SUV. I eye the sword in her grasp and the trail of blood it leaves along the concrete. "And who took care of the guys in the office?"

She flashes me the briefest of looks. "Which answer would you prefer?"

"The truth?"

"I have yet to lie to you."

"How would I know that?"

"You are a clever girl, Romeria. I think you know a great many truths." Quietly, she adds, "More than you realize."

"How do you know my real name? Did Korsakov tell you?" I didn't think even he knew, but there isn't much he can't find out. *Couldn't* find out.

"Malachi told me. He told me many things before he sent me for you."

Do I know this Malachi person? Did I meet him on the street? And why has he sent Sofie for me?

I'm about to ask that question out loud when Sofie says, "I will not harm you, but do not try to run."

There it is, the not-so-subtle threat. I can go willingly—or not —but go with her, I shall.

"Why all this effort? Why didn't you just force me to leave with you from the hotel?"

"I considered it," she admits. "We haven't been given much time to dally. But I would prefer you come with me of your own volition, and it was clear that you felt trapped by that man." She sighs, as if speaking of a daily nuisance that she has gladly put behind her. "I thought if I helped you with your problem, you might be keener to help me with mine."

I wouldn't call this of my own volition.

Maybe it's because my brain is muddled with shock, but none of this makes any sense. I'm a thief. A highly skilled one, sure, but nothing more. I couldn't even defend myself against Tony. Meanwhile, Sofie and her men wiped out a major crime syndicate within minutes, without earning a single scratch. "It's clear you can get your hands on *anything* you want without my help, so what do you want with me?"

"It is not a matter of *want*, but of *need*." Sofie turns to meet my eyes, and that confident veil she hides behind slips for a moment, long enough that I catch a glimpse of the raw desperation behind it. "I *need you* to save my husband."

CHAPTER THREE

"I'm sure there is a suitable change of clothes for you among my things."

"I'm good."

Her eyebrow arches at the mud and mustard splattered on the hem of my dress. I'm sure I wouldn't have to look hard to find smears of Tony's blood too. "Suit yourself." She shifts her attention back to her newspaper. She unfolded it as the plane's engines revved for takeoff and is working her way through, page by page. Korsakov was the only other person I knew who would take the time to read a whole paper like that, rather than skim for interesting headlines.

When we emerged from the warehouse, the armed men were missing from their posts and the two guards with Sofie were waiting in the SUV, their hands drenched in blood. Any thoughts I might still have had about escape evaporated.

They exchanged no words, simply nodding at Sofie when she gave orders to take us to the airport. Now, they huddle in the pod of seats beside us, the sleeves of their black dress shirts rolled up, quietly cleaning and polishing an arsenal of blades with methodical precision.

There are daggers and swords of various lengths and shapes—

some with a simple, functional hilt like the knife I lost tonight, and others with gilding and jewels that gleam under the light and would make Skully salivate. Propped up against the side of the cabin wall is a crossbow, a bundle of sleek quivers next to it.

"You don't use guns." It's an internal thought that I don't mean to blurt out loud.

"Where is the sport in that?" the man on the left says, his voice low and raspy. He pauses to regard me directly for the first time, allowing me to see the predatory gaze in his golden irises.

Though I never witnessed it myself, I know Korsakov killed people. He would rage at their betrayal and blame them for forcing him to exact retribution. But for weeks after someone disappeared, there would be a solemness to his demeanor. Somewhere *very* deep down, despite his justifications, I think ending a life haunted the man.

I see no hint of remorse in the eyes that stare back at me now, and the way they drag over my neck and chest makes me shrink into my wool blanket.

I shift my attention to the small portal window next to me, absorbing the constant hum of the engines. Far below, the city lights fade in the distance. I've never been on a plane before, let alone a private one. I couldn't help the stir of intrigue when the white SUV pulled up beside it. "Where are we going?"

"My home."

Belgium, if what she told me earlier is true. Despite everything, I feel a smile touch my lips.

"This pleases you." Sofie peers over her newspaper again, watching me intently. The sociable, mischievous woman from the bar is gone. She guards her expressions and her tone so well, I can't begin to read her mood.

"I've never been to Europe. I mean, I planned on going, someday." Korsakov demanded that I always be within an hour's reach unless I was robbing someone for him, so escapes to London and Rome weren't an option. Truth be told, I think he worried that if I left, I wouldn't come back.

I can't believe he's dead. I never liked the man, but I cared that he found value in me. Who knows what I'll feel when this shock wears off, if there will be anything beyond relief.

"Fear not. You will see *many* new places, soon enough." Sofie peers out her own window. "I didn't leave my home city of Paris until I was twenty-one. Same age as you are now. That was when I met Elijah. He wanted to show me the world."

And yet he's never been to New York?

She knows how old I am. Or rather, the man who sent her knows. "So, you work for Malachi?" Saying that name out loud doesn't trigger any familiarity.

"I serve him, yes. It will all make sense soon." She pauses. "Romeria is a pretty name. Unique."

I swallow against my unease. It's been years since I answered to my real name, another lifetime ago. "It's Romy."

"I wonder why your parents chose it," she muses, in a way that suggests she already has an idea.

"They never told me," I lie. My mother said it came to her in a dream one night, before I was born.

"Did you know it means 'pilgrimage' in Spanish?"

"No. I'm sure it's coincidence." I doubt my parents could put ten Spanish words together between the two of them.

"'One who journeys to a foreign land,'" she recites as if quoting a definition, her attention still out her window.

"Like Belgium?"

Her lips purse. "Though, the Spanish version would likely refer to the religious connotation. There was a time when humans routinely took long spiritual journeys in search of truth and meaning, and to make offerings to their god." Ridicule touches her tone.

But it's her word choice that makes my eyebrows pop. *"Humans?"*

"It's an interesting thing, what we do in the name of our gods and our own salvation. Did you know they used to burn women at the stake, claiming them to be witches and devil worshippers?"

My stomach constricts.

"Even today, there are still those who search for a truth they cannot see, a truth they fear. Who will kill in the name of their god and in doing their god's work." She peels away from the window to pierce me with her sharp gaze. "But you already know that, do you not?"

I sense where Sofie is so smoothly steering this conversation.

"Your mother—"

"Is dead." My pulse pounds in my ears as I match her stare, daring her to challenge that.

Only the faintest twitch of Sofie's eyebrow hints of a reaction to my lie. "I see I've found a weak spot in your armor. So, you do not support her cause?"

She knows about my mother. Of course, she fucking knows. I school my expression. Losing my temper will only reveal my vulnerability. "You mean, her psychotic *cult's* cause?"

It began harmlessly enough—an invitation to a group grief-counseling session in a church basement, meant to offer solace to people who had suffered a loss. That's what it felt like—the loss of my father, even though he was still physically here, wandering the streets. We'd had our entire world flipped upside down, and I was relieved to see my mom making new friends.

But within weeks, our conversations took an odd turn. She started questioning whether maybe demons and witches *did* exist, and that what my father saw had been real.

Talk soon shifted to whispers of creatures living among us—hiding in plain sight—while the government covered up the truth and witches masquerading as nurses stole newborn babies from maternity wards. She even claimed she had seen proof of magic, though when I pressed, her explanation sounded more like vague riddles than anything resembling fact.

Talk of conspiracies and witchcraft and monsters consumed my mother's every waking moment. I was fourteen and didn't understand what was feeding these growing delusions, but I'd already lost one parent to the demons in his head, and I was afraid I might lose another.

She would leave for days on end, spending her spare hours in the old Baptist church that this group who called themselves the People's Sentinel had purchased. We were barely surviving as it was, relying on food stamps and soup kitchens for meals and secondhand shops for clothes, but still she gave them all our money. I wasn't surprised the day she announced we were moving into a run-down building the Sentinel had purchased for their growing "community," in preparation against the coming war against evil. I screamed and railed, told her I wouldn't go, that I'd run away. She held strong. I'd see the truth, she promised me.

I wanted to believe her.

For weeks, I ate and slept under the Sentinel's roof, listening to these people—all branded with a tattoo of two interlocked crescent moons on the fleshy part of the thumb, the mark of "a disciple"—talk of otherworldly power and the spread of evil, hiding in the skin of the human form.

It was so consuming that a part of me wondered if there was truth to it. It would explain what my father saw, though it wouldn't explain what happened to him afterward.

For her part, my mother was in her element within those walls. She quickly moved up in rank. I didn't know what her role was, but she no longer worked at the grocery store, and everyone referred to her as "Elder" when she spoke.

She'd promised I'd see the truth, and I did, the night she took me to a wooded area outside the city. I witnessed her and the others tie a "witch" to a post on a pile of dry kindling and strike a match.

That's the night I ran.

In some ways, I feel like I've been running ever since, running from what my mother did.

From what I *didn't* do.

I still sometimes hear that woman's screams in my sleep.

"And your father? Is he also *dead*?" Sofie asks, her tone mocking.

Mention of Eddie reminds me of Tony's assault on him. Alton would have called for an ambulance. "No, but he's ill."

"And what ails him?"

"Don't you already know?" What is this game she's playing?

After a moment, she nods, confirming my suspicions. "So, you grew up surrounded by talk of demons, and yet you do not believe in them."

"I guess it's a good thing I have a better grip on reality than both my parents." And a healthy fear of becoming like either of them.

"Perhaps." Again with that curious tone. She doesn't pry further, but she also doesn't offer condolences. "How did you find yourself in this career path?"

I shrug. "One thing led to another." And I like not starving.

"You did not want a new family, a new home? A *normal* life?"

"My life was never going to be normal." I considered going to the police after that fateful night in the church basement, but I didn't have any faith in a system that had already failed my father. I was afraid they wouldn't believe me, or worse, they'd force me to go back to her. I balked whenever the youth shelter workers asked questions—*What's your name, hun? Where did you used to live? What can you tell me about your parents?* I knew they were only trying to help, but anonymity made me feel safer. And then I met the grifter Tarryn. We had big plans to move to LA and live in a van near the ocean, until she got arrested, and I was dragged into the back of an SUV by Korsakov's goons.

These last few years I was on my way toward something that vaguely resembled "normal." I earned my GED and enrolled in art classes. Just last week, I was eyeing programs at the local community college. That's what *normal* twenty-one-year-olds do.

I keep feeding Sofie information about myself—that she somehow already knows—and gathering almost nothing in return. "So, is your husband in prison?"

"Of a sort," she says cryptically.

"I don't know the first thing about breaking a person out of jail, unless you need someone to steal a key, which I'm sure one of *them* can handle." I nod toward her assassin squad.

"Perhaps you should present yourself as *more* useful rather than less? You will find it is in your best interest. People tend to keep those of value alive longer."

I can't tell if that's a lesson or a threat. "I just don't understand why you chose me."

"*I* did not choose you. Malachi did."

"But *why*?" And who is this man!

"I will admit that I do not entirely understand it myself. I am worried. But you have impressed me, especially for one of your age."

"My ability to steal impresses you?"

"Is that the only value you see in yourself?" She cocks her head, her attention drifting over my lengthy black hair. It was as silky as a raven's feather when the night began, but the drizzle has unraveled the stylist's work. "You are proficient in that skill. *So* proficient, in fact, one might say you were blessed with a godly talent for it."

"I'm pretty sure there's a commandment against my *talent*." Though sometimes I've surprised even myself with how effortlessly I'm able to separate people from their belongings.

She smirks. "I see a shrewd young woman who has learned to survive and adapt, despite being betrayed and abandoned by those closest to her, who is acutely aware of her surroundings and suitably wary of dangers, but who has the fortitude to keep her wits about her, even in the most perilous situations, who knows when she has no other choice but to make the best of her circumstances. All these things will serve you well."

My cheeks flush. I'm not accustomed to someone doling out compliments in my direction. I can't remember the last time it happened. But I don't miss her underlying meaning—whatever she has planned for me, there is no escape. "Have I met him? Malachi?"

"You have not, but you may, eventually."

Sofie is evasive, which means she has something to hide. Another question burns for an answer. "What about after I help you free your husband?"

"Your task will be complete."

"And I won't owe you? You'll let me go?" I won't be able to go back to my life in New York. Not with Tony alive. Maybe I should have let Sofie kill him.

Something unreadable flashes in her eyes. "It is *I* who will owe you a debt. One that can never be repaid." It's an echo of what I said to her earlier about Korsakov.

"But I'm not being given a choice."

"You are not." Her voice has turned hard. It's as if the suggestion that I might refuse to help infuriates her. That makes sense, though, if her husband's life is on the line.

The sound of a blade drawing across its scabbard pulls my attention to the yellow-eyed man. He is putting away Sofie's sword after cleaning it, and yet I sense an unspoken warning.

I swallow against my rising nerves. "Can you at least—"

"All will be explained when the time is right. That time is not at present." She shifts her attention back to her paper, giving the pages a shake.

As much as I want to push, the memory of Korsakov and his butchered men still fresh in my mind stays my tongue. I huddle deeper into my wool blanket and watch the world below slip into complete darkness, wondering how long I'll have to bide my time before I can dodge these lunatics.

Somehow, I manage to drift off.

"You *live here?*"

"*Oui.*"

"But it's, like, a *real* castle." Built on top of a hill that overlooks a charming old town, with a stone wall and iron gate to protect it, cobblestones beneath my shoes, and towers scaled with leafless vines and capped with spires soaring high above us.

"Oui. My chateau. Mine and Elijah's."

I know I should be sizing up escape routes, and yet I'm enthralled as I turn slowly, absorbing the vast medieval courtyard, empty of everything but the sleek black car we arrived in and a lone tabby cat that sits on a stair wall, lapping at its paw. The two assassin-guards have disappeared into a separate, smaller building with their duffel bags of deadly weapons.

I note the small door next to the gate that appears to be a walk-through exit to the town. For a place this size, there must be more. I don't see surveillance cameras, but that doesn't mean they're not around.

Beyond the gate, the town bustles with midday activity, but within these walls, it's silent, save for a few withered leaves scuttling across the stone on a breeze. "How old is this place?"

"The original building is from the fifteenth century."

My jaw drops as I quickly do the math. That's over six hundred years of history. And what does a place like this cost? I assumed Sofie and her husband were rich and powerful—the private plane and assassin bodyguards more than hinted at that—but to own a castle …

Sofie's musical laughter carries in the eerie quiet. The simple act softens her features, making her appear less intimidating. "It is refreshing to see your reaction. Mine was much the same when Elijah first brought me to Montegarde and told me this would be our home. We had left Paris rather abruptly and—" She cuts herself off, her smile turning sorrowful. "Well, that was long ago. Hopefully, he will still appreciate its beauty when he finally sees it again."

"How long has he been gone?" I've gathered almost no information since meeting her last night, but she did say she met her husband when she was twenty-one, and she can't be more than thirty.

"Far too long."

Another vague answer that offers me not even a single piece to add to the puzzle that is Sofie.

She squints upward, as if searching for something in the cloudless blue sky. It's early afternoon and colder here than it was when we left New York, the wind carrying a blustering chill that makes me thankful for the sweater and jeans I found folded on the seat next to me when I woke.

"Follow me." She strolls toward a heavy wooden door, her heels skillfully handling the uneven cobblestone.

"So, when are we breaking him out of this sort-of prison?"

Sofie has given me no more hints about what saving her husband means. I can only assume it's not as straightforward as lifting a diamond necklace off a woman's neck.

"Soon. Come, I must prepare you."

"Oui," I mimic under my breath, thankful for these slip-on boots as I chase behind her.

CHAPTER FOUR

"How can you see?" I steady myself with a hand against the stone wall as I trail Sofie down a steep, winding stairwell. The steps are precariously uneven, and the glow from the lantern I carry offers little illumination.

"I've descended these so many times, I could do so blindfolded."

Walking into Sofie's castle felt like traveling back in time, to an era of candlelight and ball gowns, sweeping staircases and elaborate moldings, soaring ceilings and grand reception rooms—all things I've only ever seen dramatized in TV and film and read about in stories, and nothing I imagined anyone living today.

The air was cold and stale as she led me farther in, and our footfalls echoed eerily. My senses were on overload as I absorbed every detail—somber faces painted in oil in gilded frames, suits of armor standing sentry, antique vases on pedestals that looked both ancient and valuable.

I was only treated to a brief glimpse of the vast collection of rooms before Sofie beckoned me to follow her. My disappointment in not getting a guided tour swelled.

Now, the farther we descend, the more apparent it is that we're entering a darker, primeval part of Sofie's grand home where the air smells of damp earth and age. It reminds me that this is not a vacation, and I am here for a specific purpose—one I do not yet understand but should be wary of.

"What's down here?"

"We are going below the main castle where the storerooms and vault are located."

"And the dungeons?" Is she leading me to my waiting cell like a dog following a pork chop?

Her laugh echoes. "If I wished to confine you in such a manner, you would be on your way to the north tower. That is where captives were often imprisoned."

"Sounds hospitable." I've noticed that Sofie has an uncanny ability of answering my unspoken thoughts.

"Better than the gallows or the pyre." I hear the smile in her voice. "Though, important captives were often afforded free rein within the castle walls, and the accommodations *were* quite hospitable. Still, they were held for years, unable to leave unless the lord allowed it."

I'm relieved when my boots touch the floor.

"*This* is the undercroft." One after another, torches ignite in a burst of flame to illuminate a corridor that extends as far as my eyes can see. Massive pillars stand like a line of soldiers on either side to support the great weight of the castle. High above us, the stone ceiling joins in sweeping arches that draw my enthralled gaze.

I study the wrought iron fixtures anchored on each pillar as we pass. There's obviously no electricity down here, and each torch burns with an authentic flame. "How did they light?"

"With fire."

For a woman who insists on not lying to me, Sofie is the master of avoiding the truth.

The floor is hard, packed earth, and it dulls our footfalls as she leads me forward. Every so often, I catch scurrying movement out of the corner of my eye that makes me shudder. I've seen plenty of rats haunting alleyways and city streets, and I've never grown used to them.

"What happened there?" I nod toward a pile of stone rubble.

"These walls are hundreds of years old. They require constant repair. It is one of the downfalls of maintaining such a home." She sighs. "If Elijah didn't love it so, I would have abandoned it long ago."

Every time Sofie talks about her husband, it sounds like she hasn't seen him in an eternity.

"And that?" I point to a patched, uneven wall. "That crumbled too?"

"No. That was a private entry in the first castle, left in ruins after a great battle. Infiltrators scaled the hill and entered through that very spot. When the marquis began to rebuild, he closed off this entry, fearing too many knew of its existence. But he eventually deserted the project in favor of a life elsewhere. This castle as it stands today would not be finished for another six decades."

"And who finished it?"

"The Count of Montegarde, as he was known at that time." She smiles, as if the name brings her fond memories. "It was far grander than the original or even what the marquis's revised designs had in mind."

Awe stretches across my face as Sofie casually dishes out details about the rebuilt castle—the two-level library in the west wing that hosts Elijah's rare-book collection, the grand ballroom where several famous composers once played, the walled garden on the south side that is overtaken by a two-hundred-year-old wisteria vine in the summer.

Despite the dire situation I've found myself trapped in, I can't help but be mesmerized. I feel as though I've stepped into a story of royalty and old-world glamour. In those years between running from my mother and building a life for myself, I spent most days in the public library, where it was safe, and warm, and quiet, escaping my world by getting lost in fictional ones that painted lives like the one these crumbling walls must have entertained.

A gray tabby cat scampers across my path, causing me to stumble a step. It darts through an opening in a small iron gate. "Where does that lead?"

"Out to the garden on one end, but if you climb the narrow passage all the way up, you will find yourself in the lord's bedchamber."

"A secret passageway." There's no missing the thrill in my tone.

"But of course, a thief would be most fascinated by those." She grins. "These castles were always built with plans to flee in mind. The royal chambers often have an escape route. It was usually hidden behind a bookcase or a tapestry, or a statue. Sometimes it is a trapdoor beneath a rug. And occasionally it is quite elaborate. In my chamber, there is a mechanism to open a panel in the wall beside the fireplace."

"That is *so* cool," I blurt, all semblance of calm vanishing. "Can you take me through them all later?"

Her smile wavers. "This way." She marches forward, and I can't help but notice that her enthusiasm for playing tour guide has dulled. "Malachi gave me precious little time to explain, Romeria, so please *listen* carefully. Are you listening?"

"Yes. And it's Romy." Her question makes me feel more like a petulant child than the talented thief she insists everything hinges on.

"You have been tasked with retrieving something of great value. A stone. It is located in a sacred garden where outsiders are not permitted."

So, I need to steal something after all. "What does it look like?"

"You will know when you see it. The sacred garden is guarded, and there is only one way in."

"Guarded by who?"

She hesitates. "Soldiers, of a sort."

My eyebrows pop. "*Soldiers*?" I've only ever dealt with basic security guards and bouncers.

"You will have to earn your way in, and that will take time."

"And you're going to distract them, right?" With her deadly sword and daggers.

"I am able to get you there, but we are unable to go with you. The only aid I can offer is this." She slides the ring off her finger and, with a long, lingering look at it, she seizes my forearm, her nails digging into my flesh as she slips the ring on me. "Do not remove it under *any* circumstances."

The gaudy piece is lighter than I imagined. It must have some sort of tracking device in it, though I don't know how that will help me. "And when am I doing this?"

"Tonight."

My mouth gapes with shock. "Are you insane?" *Tonight*! "I need *at least* a week to case this place, probably more, so I can figure out entries and exits, numbers, shift changes—"

"It must be tonight!" she yells, all semblance of composure vanishing.

That can only mean one thing—that her husband will die otherwise.

I'm beginning to see why she isn't retrieving this stone herself—because it's an idiot's mission that will surely get me killed.

She inhales deeply, and when she speaks again, her calm demeanor has returned. "I wish I could better prepare you, but we do not have time, and I'm afraid no amount of planning would help the situation we both find ourselves in."

She's speaking in riddles again. I need concrete answers if I have a hope in hell of pulling this off. "Where *exactly* am I going?"

"To Cirilea, in Islor."

"I've never heard of it." Not that I'm an expert with European geography.

"Most have not. It is far from here."

"And how are we getting there? Flying, I assume?"

"I will take you there." She stops in front of a broad wooden door strapped with iron bands. "Once you have taken the stone, Malachi will ensure your freedom."

"How?" I don't even know what he looks like.

"You will know when the time comes." Sofie yanks on the handle and the door swings open with a screeching grind. A single torch ignites ahead, bathing the walls in a dim glow.

I promise myself I will figure out how Sofie is lighting those. "What's this room?"

"My sanctum. Where I hold what is most precious to me."

From the threshold, I see only more of the same crumbling walls. Ahead, the dirt floor gives way to cobblestone. An enormous rectangular block plays centerpiece. A much smaller table sits nearby.

Sofie walks to the block. Her fingers smooth across the surface as she slowly walks the perimeter, seemingly lost in thought. "I have waited an eternity for this day," she whispers, her voice taking on a pleading tone. "You must not fail."

It's almost guaranteed I'm going to fail, but she warned me to paint myself more valuable than less, so I keep that thought to myself. What will happen if I do? What will a woman like Sofie—who cut down men like they were errant branches on a sculpted bush in some twisted quid pro quo bid to win me over—do if I don't retrieve this stone for her?

I probably don't need to worry about that, though. These soldiers will kill me before she has a chance.

But even as the weight of my impending doom settles firmly on my shoulders, a familiar excitement thrums in my core. I wish I could say I feel only guilt for my thievery, but there's also a part of me that thrives on the addictive adrenaline that surges with the challenge. It's always been the case.

I could even go as far as convincing myself this is for a noble cause—I'm saving a man's life. How, exactly, I still don't understand. There are major pieces missing from Sofie's plan.

I edge forward. "So, if I get this stone for Malachi, you'll get your husband back?"

"Oui." She reaches out to gingerly touch something. "He will give him back to me."

"*He*'s the one holding him hostage?"

"In a manner."

I'd expect a woman like Sofie would want to kill the person holding her husband hostage, but the way Sofie talks about Malachi, she seems to adore him.

Curious to see what has Sofie's attention so riveted, I close the distance.

A sinking feeling tugs at my insides. A man lies in the hollowed-out center of what I now realize is an enormous coffin. He looks to be in his thirties, tall, with wavy hair the color of black coffee and a clean-shaven, square jaw. He wears a navy-blue suit that looks new and custom fit. "Who is that?" I ask, though I fear I already know.

What I hold most precious.

Sofie skates her knuckles across his lips. "This is my dear Elijah."

"I don't understand," I stammer, even as cold realization washes over me. "He's dead."

"He is *not* dead!" Her green eyes are bright with rage as she glares at me, looking ready to lunge. "He is trapped, and *you* are going to help me free him."

It all becomes clear then—the urgency, the fragmented plan, this mysterious Malachi.

Sofie has lost her bloody mind.

Swallowing my growing panic, I back away slowly.

Her deep, wicked laughter echoes through the chamber. "You truly deem me mad? You think *you* see something I cannot?"

"I honestly don't understand what I'm seeing." Besides the aftermath of a dangerous woman who is grieving and in denial. How long ago did Elijah die? It couldn't have been long. Did she leave his body here while she went to retrieve me?

"But you do." Her eyes narrow. "You've known the truth for years, Romeria. You've simply refused to accept it."

She said something similar last night, in the warehouse. "What are you talking about?"

She rounds the coffin and stalks toward me.

I instinctively shift backward toward the doorway. I need to get out of this crypt now. She's unarmed, and I'm fast. If I start running now—

A thunderous bang sounds behind me, throwing us into darkness save for the single torch.

Sofie lifts a hand, and a flame ignites from the tip of her index finger.

"How did you do that?" I search her palm for a hidden lighter or match.

"You assume it to be some cheap parlor trick, no?"

I stare, dumbfounded, as the flame hops to her middle fingertip, then her ring finger. It moves back and forth like a tide, from finger to finger, the reflection dancing in Sofie's emerald eyes.

"The truth is right in front of you, and yet you *still* search for reasons to not believe. Malachi warned me about you." She casts her hand toward a wall. Just as in the main corridor, every torch erupts with fire.

My eyes widen as I take in the room bathed in light. Where the four pillars surrounding the coffin simply blended into the stone before, now I can see the elaborate carvings on each.

"You are *so sure* that Eddie suffers from delusions, are you?" Sofie rests her palm on the pillar next to her.

The blood rushes in my ears as I gape at the soaring creature etched in stone—a human form, and yet not. It's just as my father described it, right down to the serpent-like eyes and long, twisty black horns protruding from its forehead, each coiling three times before tapering off into pointed ends.

But no ... this is all part of whatever sick game Sofie's playing. She knew about my father. There was nothing to stop her from learning about his hallucinations. He's not discreet about them. I'm sure anyone who has ever walked along Broadway has heard about the demon with the black horns. "He's ill. He doesn't know what he saw—"

"He is not ill. His mind is simply fractured."

"I don't see the difference."

She sighs. "No. The human world does not differentiate."

There she is again, saying *humans* as if there's an option for something else. "What are you trying to convince me of? That this monster is real and my father can see it?"

"*This* is no monster." She gazes up at the horned carving. "This is Malachi, one of four fates who have created all that we have and all that we are. You would call them gods. And I am not trying to convince you of anything, Romeria, because I know it to be a lost cause. The walls you have built around yourself to survive in this world are far too thick. That you don't even realize what you are is fascinating to me. I shouldn't be surprised, though, given you've been immersed in their world. How *could* you know any different?" She sneers.

"Humans are such small-minded creatures. Like little worker ants, breeding and building their little cities and their little lives. They think everything revolves around *them*, that it should exist only if *they* can dominate. They kill in the name of their god, believing it the *only* true god and all others false or evil." She scoffs. "I *could* tell you that humans are in fact the lowliest of creation and that *far* greater beings walk among them. I *could* tell you that this world they have created is a facade for what truly exists. I *could* make flames dance from my fingers and a majestic oak sprout from a seed before your eyes, and *still*, you would doubt." Something dark flashes in her eyes. "But you *will* soon see for yourself, and you will have no choice but to believe."

She is *insane.*

Sofie sounds like my mother. Though, those cultists don't see themselves as weak little ants, toiling away. They think they'll be the world's salvation. Meanwhile, Sofie seems to think she's something *other* than human.

Beware of the demon with the flaming hair. She hunts for you.

I've always denied space for my father's maniacal rants, never allowing them room to fester in my mind. But now I find myself saying them out loud. "Are you a demon?" My voice sounds strained, foreign.

Her lips twitch. "Some have called me that. And others would set fire to me and revel in my screams. As *you* well know."

I squeeze my eyes shut against the memory that stirs. Is Sofie claiming to be a witch? "Why are you doing this to me?" It's like she's dragging out every painful piece of my past and laying them on a table to poke and prod with the tip of her blade.

"You are not asking the right questions." She shakes her head. "I do not have time to convince you of the truth I speak, Romeria, but know that the rules of the world to which you are accustomed are about to change." The flames in the torches flicker and grow, reaching toward the ceiling. "The blood moon is nearly upon us. I have but a small window to take you where you need to go, and I *will not* miss this chance. I have waited too long." She edges closer, like a leopard stalking its prey. "*Please* help bring Elijah back to me. I will be forever in your debt."

Sofie said she can't come with me to this Islor. That's good news, at least. The sooner I'm away from her, the sooner I can clear my mind of these delusions she's trying to force-feed me—and the sooner I can run.

She holds up an object that I didn't see her procure. "We will need this."

"What is it?"

"A gift from Malachi."

It's long and twisted and smooth, like black obsidian. One end is jagged, as if a broken piece of something larger.

I think it's part of an animal's horn.

I edge away, scanning the room for another exit. My heart stops as I take in the intricate carving on another pillar, a creature with the subtle curves of a female human but with a majestic crown of antlers, its form painted in gold and shimmering under the firelight.

"That's … how …" I stammer.

Find the gilded doe.

My father shouted that at me. He started saying something else about her but didn't get to finish because Tony attacked him.

My thoughts spin in so many directions, I can't find purchase on any single one.

"Listen to me carefully, Romeria." Sofie closes the distance, the object in her grip. "You are about to enter a world unlike that which you know. It is imperative that no one in Islor learns of your true identity. They cannot know about Malachi's quest. You must use your skills to blend in, just as you have done up until now." She squeezes my hand, holding it up between us. "And you *must not* remove this ring for *any* reason. It is the only protection I can give, but between it and your wits, I believe you can survive. But if they figure out what you are, I promise, they will not let you live."

She's said that twice. "What am I?"

She hesitates. "It does not matter. All that matters is that you retrieve the stone. Tell me you understand?" she pleads, a touch frantic.

My head bobs numbly, her words anchoring in my mind but not resonating. As soon as Sofie is out of my sight, I will run. I have done it before. It's the only way to get away from this madness before it consumes me like it has my parents. "When do we leave?"

"Now." A gentle smile touches her lips. "And in order to take you there, first, this mortal form must die."

I've barely processed her words when she drives the twisted black horn deep into my heart.

CHAPTER FIVE

Sofie laid Romeria's body next to Elijah, pausing a moment to regard her most precious of possessions, the ring Elijah once slipped on her finger to profess his undying love. Centuries had passed, but the luster of the gold had not dulled in her eyes, for she knew its true value. She felt naked without it, but she would have it back soon enough.

The bloom of blood around where Malachi's horn pierced Romeria's chest remained insignificant. That was a relief. The fate promised this token would keep her mortal form alive long enough for Sofie to complete her task, but while Sofie trusted that Malachi's orders were sound, she was distrustful of the results. The fate never gave without taking. Elijah was proof of that. That he would force Sofie to rely on the success of one so ignorant to the world beyond her own demonstrated once again how cruel he could be.

Sofie may not be able to read minds, but she could read pulses. They all carried a signature—the rush of lust, the race of fear, the plummet of heartbreak—and she knew Romeria hadn't believed a single word. She wouldn't allow herself to. She thought Sofie mad with grief.

Or simply mad.

That is how Malachi intended it. He was explicit in his instruction—Romeria could not know what she was—and Sofie knew better than to question it. She could see now, how all the seemingly random duties he had tasked her with over the years culminated in this gifted mortal before her now. The fate hadn't been ignoring her. He'd been weaving his scheme all along. What he would gain from all this, Sofie was unsure, but she did not care. All she cared was that Elijah was freed from the Nulling, consequences be damned.

She had never enjoyed playing the part of court jester with her powers, but had Malachi granted her more time and freedom, she would have made the stone shake and the sky cry and the wind howl and the flames dance until there was no other option but for the girl to believe. To expel such energy when she needed every ounce for this undertaking was a luxury Sofie did not have. Surely, Malachi intended it that way. He had his reasons. The fates always did.

Perhaps the girl's ignorance would save her. Or, more than likely, it is what would keep her focused on her mission. The little thief was strong-willed and resilient. She was young, but not sheltered to evils. She'd learned how to navigate her cruel world, adapting to survive.

Soon, Romeria would see. She would know the world of vengeful gods and monsters, and the lengths one would go for love. And nothing would ever be the same for her again.

The blood moon was almost upon them. Sofie could not miss this window.

"It is time for your journey, my little pilgrim." She shuttered Romeria's piercing blue eyes and smoothed the tendrils of dark hair to frame her face. She was an adult physically, and yet so young. In some ways, she reminded Sofie of her dear friend, Adele, from long ago. Not so much in looks, but in her feigned swagger, the way she imitated confidence when her little heart thumped like that of a frightened bunny's. Under different circumstances, Sofie might have even enjoyed her company.

"May the fates be merciful."

Sofie dragged the blade across her palm. Blood trickled out in a steady stream to coat Malachi's horn and farther, seeping into the girl's wound, just as the fate had instructed. This was not a ritual she'd ever learned or heard of during her time in the guild.

With that important step completed, Sofie fell to her knees before Malachi's likeness—for it was thanks to him that she might hear Elijah's voice again—and called forth her full power.

Vermin scampered as the ground shook.

CHAPTER SIX

I wake, gasping for air.

A deep throb pains my lungs.

The floor beneath me is soft and dewy, the ceiling above a blanket of darkness. It takes me a moment to realize I'm lying in grass, under a night sky.

And a few more moments to remember Sofie driving that horn into my chest.

My heart races as I draw my hand to where my body aches, expecting to find the object still protruding. Nothing but tenderness remains. "What did you do to me, you crazy bitch?" I mutter, my voice hoarse.

Obviously, I didn't die, but it sure feels like she tried to kill me.

With a wince, I pull myself into a sitting position. And frown at the billow of material around me, confusion scrambling my thoughts. My jeans and sweater are gone, replaced by this enormous *dress,* with layers of silk and a plunging neckline. She stabbed me and then changed me into formal wear?

I hold up my hand. Even in the darkness, I can make out the outline of the ring Sofie slipped onto my finger, the one she believes will somehow protect me.

I don't have time to make sense of this. I need to get the hell out of here.

I heave myself off the wet ground, stumbling a few steps before I regain my balance, my head swimming. Walls of cedar hedge tower over me on either side, forming a long, narrow corridor that gives me only two options—left or right.

Shouts ring in the distance—I can't gauge how far away, but they're definitely coming from my left. They're male in timbre, interspersed with clangs of metal against metal. In the air, the smell of smoke lingers. Something burns.

I take off in the opposite direction of the commotion, sprinting as fast as the darkness and the throb in my chest allows, stumbling in the tangle of bulky material swirling around my legs and a pair of wobbly heeled shoes. By the time the hedge opens into a cobblestone pathway lit with lanterns, I'm panting, my lungs heaving from strain, and I'm ready to tear the skirts from my body.

The moon is full and casting white light where I could not see it before, buried within the cedar. Is this the garden Sofie was talking about? The one with the soldiers, where I'll find the stone? I'm definitely in *a* garden. There are bushes with roses the size of my palm, their potent fragrance melding with the stench of smoke. The air hints at a warm summer night. Wherever Islor is, it must be far south of Belgium.

Blocks of jagged broken stone are strewn across the pathway ahead, as if something was demolished. Among the disarray, a shiny object gleams in the moonlight. Curious, I navigate around the debris to collect it. It's an arrowhead, much like the ones Sofie's guards had in their crossbow, only a brilliant silver.

And it's drenched in someone's blood.

I toss it away in horror, only to find my hands coated. I wipe them across the skirts of my dress as I frantically search for a way out of here. More cedar hedges loom, fanning out around me.

I curse with frustration. Sofie has dressed me like a medieval courtier and left me in a damn labyrinth. The odds of choosing the right path are grim. How long before someone finds me standing next to this bloodied arrow and I have to explain myself?

A female's high-pitched scream snaps my head to the right. I hold my breath and listen. She screams again, and my dread stirs. I've heard that ring of desperation too many times—in dark alleyways, in urine-stained stairwells, in poorly lit parking lots. I've heard it once in my own voice, the night I unwisely took a shortcut through a park to get to the shelter before they locked the doors. If it hadn't been for the bravery of a man out walking his dog, I would have had another horror story to add to my list.

I take off running without much thought about what I'm heading into, instead focusing on the opportunity. If there's any way I can stop what's about to happen to that woman, maybe she will return the favor by helping me escape this place.

My blood pounds in my ears as I race along another narrow cedar corridor, taking turn after turn, until I fear I'm simply running in circles in this rat maze. But then suddenly—thankfully—a stone wall looms before me. It's at least thirty feet high—far too tall to climb—but there's an opening just large enough for a person.

I slip through it.

And stall for a moment upon my first glimpse of the full moon. It's three times the size of any I've ever seen, and it hangs low in the sky, casting a brilliant carpet of light across the land that could almost fool me into believing it to be daytime.

Except, it's not the only one. Another moon glows to my right, this one much smaller and higher—more what I'm used to.

Where the hell has two moons?

The light is a blessing, though—I would surely have tumbled down this steep hill and broken bones had I blindly stepped out. From my vantage spot, I can see clear across the valley below. A long, narrow river serves as a divide between the fields of tall grass and dense forest beyond. A dirt road runs parallel to the river on this side and a wide, arching bridge allows for crossing.

Another bloodcurdling shriek cuts through the night. I spot

movement approaching the foot of the bridge. A man is dragging the woman along, her arms flailing, legs kicking. She's putting up a valiant fight, but for how long?

And what the hell can *I* do except scare him away?

That will have to be enough.

There's no time for stealth. I arm myself with small chunks of stone tumbled from the wall and slide more than run down the hill. Tall, spiky grass pricks at my skin, but I ignore the tiny bites. Eventually, the ground levels and the grass relents to the dirt road. I kick off these wobbly shoes and sprint, surprising myself with how quickly I'm running.

My adrenaline is soaring by the time my feet touch the bridge. A potent energy thrums in my veins, my fear propelling me forward.

The man has stopped at the middle and is hunched over the woman. She's no longer fighting. Am I too late? Is she dead?

"Hey!" With stones gripped in my fist, I muster as much force in my voice as I can. "Leave her alone!"

His head snaps up. I can't make out the finer details of his face from here, but I note his white hair, pulled back in a ponytail. "Are you daft?" he growls. "Why are you not already running toward Ybaris?"

There goes the hope that my presence would scare him off. This degenerate thinks he knows me. But the longer he's mistaken, the closer I can get, the better chance I have of hitting him when I launch these stones at his head. I approach with a touch more stealth, ready to take aim. "What are you going to do to her?"

He returns to his task, winding a silver rope around her ankles. "I was going to enjoy her later, but bringing her across Islor is risky. Too many will recognize her. May as well get some satisfaction from this catastrophe."

A faint sound escapes the woman, confirming she's still alive.

I grip the stones in my right hand tighter. I need to get closer for this to hurt.

"You have failed, Romeria."

My feet falter. I may not know this lunatic, but apparently, he *does* know me. Is he one of Sofie's men? She said they couldn't come. Maybe that was a lie. "I … I didn't have enough time," I stammer.

"You had *weeks*! Weeks to plan, weeks to deceive that fool. You knew it had to be *all* of them, or our efforts would be for naught."

What is he talking about? I only met Sofie last night.

"Your mother will not be pleased when she hears of this."

"*What*?" The word slides out on a gasp. My *mother* is in league with her?

A faint rumble sounds in the distance.

"Here comes the cavalry," he mutters.

I look behind me. The stone wall I escaped through is a looming barrier that stretches across a high ridge. Beyond it, the orange glow of fire disrupts the night sky. Below it, on the dirt road that I took to get here, a dark shadow moves along the path, the distinct whinny of horses carrying in the night.

Those must be the soldiers.

"Leave now, and seek shelter in Lyndel while you still can," the man urges, his gloved hands working furiously. "Before the new king gets hold of you. You cannot defeat him on your own."

The path on the other side of the bridge leads into dense forest. The instinct to listen to him—to run far from this insanity—is overwhelming.

"As for you …" His voice rings with wicked pleasure as he hauls the woman's limp body up. Springy blond tendrils cascade halfway to the ground. She wears a dress much like mine—flowing layers of silk that belong in another century. "Enjoy your death beneath your beloved brother's nose." He hoists her onto the bridge wall to dangle over it.

It's then I notice the sizable boulder by his feet and the other end of the silver rope that's wrapped around it. I watch in horror as he heaves it over the wall, shoving her off to follow. Two loud splashes sound a moment later, one after another.

"Run now, or be damned." The man takes off with remarkable speed, charging for the trees.

It's a delayed reaction, but I whip the rocks at his head. They miss him by a wide margin.

Behind me, the thunderous pounding of hooves grows louder, the sleek, powerful forms more clearly visible as they charge. If I run now, I might be able to hide in the trees.

But dark memories of a forest and an innocent woman set in flames grips my conscience and stalls my legs. If I take off, this woman in the river will drown, and the guilt that I didn't try to help her is something I'll never escape.

I climb onto the bridge wall. I can't judge the distance, but it doesn't appear to be too far a fall. I curse Sofie's name and jump.

Frigid water envelops me, but I'm too fueled with panic to be bothered by its chill. I take a breath and dive, hoping the brilliant moonlight extends into the murky depths, but there is only a bottomless pit of darkness. I swim, groping blindly, until my lungs are ready to burst, and I'm forced to resurface.

"Halt, in the name of the king!" booms a deep, commanding voice above. Two men on horses stand on the bridge. Both wear armor. One holds a blazing torch; the other is aiming an arrow at me.

I swallow against my fear, my heart drumming wildly. "There's a woman in here. She's going to drown! Please, *help* me! I *need* light!"

The man pointing the arrow lowers his weapon a fraction.

I don't wait for an answer, diving back under, though I dread my efforts will be futile.

A beam of light blooms within the shadows. It's coming from the stone in Sofie's ring, intensifying as it expands, stretching out into the darkness like fast-growing vines in search of daylight.

I follow it with bewilderment, all the way to the river bottom, to where long, blond curls float maybe twenty feet below me. The woman is there, motionless, her arms drifting at either side of her lifeless body.

I don't know how the ring is doing this, but I don't waste time, propelling myself deeper. I cut through the water with strong strokes to reach the riverbed and inspect the boulder that anchors her. My dismay swells as I take in the thick, silvery cord, shimmering in the ring's glow. I've never seen rope like this, and the knots are intricate. It will take me hours to unravel, hours she doesn't have, if she isn't already beyond saving. Could it be cut, if a soldier would give me a blade?

I reach out to test it. My eyes widen with surprise as it disintegrates beneath my fingertips, like spun sugar pulled apart. I don't have time to dwell on that miracle. My lungs burn with the need for oxygen. I easily brush away the rest of the binding around her legs and, hooking my arm around her waist, I pull her to the river's surface.

She begins to cough and sputter the moment we reach air, much to my relief.

"You're going to be fine," I promise between ragged breaths. I'm faintly aware of shouting and flaming torches along the bridge and riverbed as I grip her tightly with one arm and use the other to paddle us to shore, thankful the swimming lessons of my youth didn't get lost in my past. By the time we reach the nearest bank, I'm on the verge of collapse from exhaustion, my chest throbbing.

I flop in the mud next to her.

"Annika!" a low male voice filled with anxiety shouts.

"I'm down here!" she cries out before another coughing fit takes over.

Heavy footfalls and the clank of metal approach. A man dressed in black-and-gold armor drops to his knee beside her. His helm covers most of his face, revealing only his mouth and his eyes through a slit.

"You came for me." She looks tiny next to his menacing form until he yanks his gauntlet off, freeing his hand to smooth the sodden curls off her forehead.

"I thought I'd lost you too."

She smiles through her jagged breaths. "You nearly did. The sapling anchored me with *merth*. I doubt you would have discovered me in time. If not for this brave …" Her head lolls toward me and her words fade midsentence. "*You*." Her voice drips with horror.

The relief I felt knowing she was alive, that I'd saved her life, morphs to dread. They all think they know me. But unlike with that man, I already sense it won't be to my advantage this time.

The kneeling soldier turns his attention to me now, and while his face is mostly disguised, the shock is unmistakable. His mouth hangs for a few beats before he gives his head a small shake. "Seize her!" he commands with a roar.

Rough, metal hands grab my arms and haul me to my feet.

The man rises, his gaze never leaving mine. All around us are soldiers gripping swords and waiting quietly. For his next order, I'm guessing. He's someone important.

Where *the hell* am I?

The soldier draws a long dagger from his side and approaches, the blade gleaming in the moonlight. "How are you alive?" There is genuine awe in his voice. "I *saw* your body. I *saw* where the arrow pierced your heart." Lifting the dagger tip to my chest, he ever so lightly grazes my skin above the gown's low neckline. "Your blood is there."

My body trembles as I look down to where his blade scratched me. Torchlight illuminates the brown stains in the pale gray silk bodice that the river did not wash away.

How do I even begin to explain this to myself, let alone to these people?

"I don't know who you think I am or what I've done—"

"You will address the king as Your Highness," the man holding me growls in my ear. His painful grip tightens and makes me wince.

This is the king. Though I can't see much of his face, he looks young. A quick scan of those nearby proves that his suit of armor is more finely made, with elaborate designs carved into the gold breastplate.

"Come now, Captain Boaz," he says with an eerie calm. "We have not yet had time for a coronation, what with Romeria having murdered my father mere *hours* ago."

"*What?*" I gasp, barely a sound escaping. "I didn't … I haven't …" My mind spins. This must be Sofie's doing. What has that devil woman convinced these people I've done? "I didn't murder *anyone*, I swear. I'm only here because—"

"No more lies!" he bellows, his voice bleeding with anguish. He raises his arm and the dagger high above him, the point angled down, his intentions clear.

"Brother! Stop!" The woman I pulled from the river—he called her Annika—cries out, scrambling to her feet. "She saved me!"

"She *killed* Mother and Father! She had plans to kill us too."

Dear God. Apparently, I didn't *only* kill their father. They think I tried to slaughter their entire family? My knees buckle, but the man holding me is strong and keeps me on my feet.

Annika grabs the king's arm, jostling him for attention. "*She saved me*, Zander," she repeats, emphasizing her words. "She *freed* me from the merth. *Raw merth.* With her bare hands."

He blinks, her words seeming to bring with them understanding that I can't comprehend. His eyes drift from my hands to the bloodstains on my dress. Finally, he lowers the dagger, and I allow myself the softest sigh of relief.

"Shall we hunt for the sapling, Your Highness?" a soldier calls from the bridge.

When this king—Zander—speaks again, it's quietly. "No. Atticus and his men are already hunting for those who escaped. I will not risk more of you tonight. We shall return and regroup." His eyes lift to mine, and his jaw—hard and angular—tenses.

"The water, Your Highness," the man he called Boaz says, his voice low and laced with warning.

Zander moves impossibly fast, swiping the tip of his blade across my palm.

I cry out as it bites into my skin, more from the surprise than pain—I'm too shocked to feel much of anything. In the moonlight, I watch my blood seep out in a trickle.

"Bring her," he orders, and then, gathering his sister under his arm, he guides her up the steep embankment.

My trip is nowhere near as gentle. I struggle to keep up with Boaz half dragging me through the mud past mounted, armed soldiers. There must be at least fifty of them, fanned out, their weapons drawn and their eyes on the surroundings as if preparing for an ambush. Any hope of escape is gone.

Boaz locks his arm around my waist and hauls me onto his horse's back along with him. "Attempt to flee, and I will gladly cut you down," he warns, adding quietly, "again." Whoever they think I am, they believe they killed me once. They won't balk at doing it twice.

He barks an order, and the soldiers form a perimeter around the horse that carries Zander and Annika. Another barked order sets them in motion. We move forward in unison, racing along the dirt road, Boaz's metal-clad arms serving as an effective cage, the hooves pounding against the ground. My bones rattle but I barely notice, too focused on what might happen next.

We round a bend and head toward a vast gate that opens upon our approach. Dark figures stand sentry along the top of the wall, their arrows nocked.

We pass through, and I get my first glimpse of what's beyond the labyrinth of cedar hedge.

Fire and chaos.

My eyes widen as I try to process the strange spectacle. I've stepped back in time. The open space past the gate tapers off toward a narrow cobblestone street ahead, lined with two- and three-story brick-and-stone buildings, their roofs pitched at various angles, their windows small and mismatched. Lanterns cling to posts and walls, the flames shimmering within providing the only light beyond that from the moons above. There isn't a car in sight, or even a street sign.

In the air, the stench of smoke hangs thick, and the wails of despair ring frequent.

I gape in horror as we begin the steady march forward in single file, the horses' hooves clacking, past armed soldiers whose faces are smeared with ash, dirt, and blood. To my right, slain bodies lie heaped on a wagon, the draft horses chomping on a bale of hay while they await orders to pull. More bodies are added to the pile.

I've seen dead people before—frozen in bus shelters, overdosed behind a dumpster, stabbed inside a cardboard box—but never so many at once.

Up ahead, a group of people huddle together, some with soot-covered cheeks, others with terror in their eyes as they watch a nearby building smolder, the flames dancing in defiance as people toss buckets of water at them.

A child crouches next to the body of a man, sobbing as she grips his hand. My chest constricts at the sight.

"What happened here?" I hear myself ask out loud.

Boaz snorts. "The Ybarisans happened. *You* happened." He releases the reins and a moment later, a heavy blanket drops over my head, blocking my view. "It's best they don't see that we've brought you back into the city walls. Emotions are running high tonight. We wouldn't want anyone taking away the satisfaction of exacting retribution from His Highness. I wonder what punishment will befit the woman who poisoned a king and queen and plotted to murder an entire royal bloodline? Sending you back to Ybaris in pieces for your treacherous father to ponder would certainly deliver a message. Though, I imagine the king would wish to keep your head. We wouldn't want you somehow returning from the dead *again*."

I focus on my breathing, inhaling the mixture of leather, pine shavings, and hay in the blanket's wool as my stomach threatens to expel its contents. The asshole's trying to scare me. That's all this is.

"Make way for the king!" a soldier shouts.

The horses move forward at a steady trot, and I listen to the cries of anguish as we pass, my own hot tears streaking down my cheeks.

CHAPTER SEVEN

I stumble blindly up the endless set of stairs, Boaz's viselike grip on my arm the only thing keeping me on my bare feet. Only when we reach a landing does he remove the blanket from my head. He shoves me forward.

I falter several steps before tripping over the hem of my dress and falling, smashing my knee against the stone floor. I bite back my howl.

"You *will* explain yourself." He tosses the blanket onto the ground beside me.

Gritting my teeth through the pain, I drag myself to the farthest corner from him like the wounded animal I am, and quickly survey my new surroundings. He's brought me to a semi-circular room with nothing but a small pile of furs over hay on one side and a bucket on the other. A small opening in the wall reveals the night sky.

Boaz fills the doorway, his helm removed and tucked under his arm. He's older than I expected for a man with such strength, a dusting of light gray touching his cropped, mouse-brown hair and frown lines zagging across his forehead. A streak of blood paints his golden cheek. More streaks coat his breastplate. "How did you do it?"

"Do what?"

"Do not toy with me," he growls. "I put that arrow through your heart. I *saw* you fall in the rose garden. You were dead."

An arrow in the rose garden …

I recall the blood-soaked weapon I picked up. Is he saying that was *my* blood? That *he* shot me with that? I peer down at the dark stain in the bodice where the material appears torn. The throb in my chest is not nearly as sharp as it was when I awoke, but it still hurts. But I came to in the cedar maze. How did I get there? I must have crawled. But he didn't shoot me …

"*How* are you alive!" Boaz's deep voice ricochets off the stone, severing my wandering thoughts. He charges forward, his armor clanging with each step.

"I don't know, but I'm not who you think I am!" I curl into a ball, wrapping my arms around my head, bracing for an assault. When it doesn't come, I hazard a glance upward.

He studies me through narrowed eyes. "I do not know what new deception you are concocting. Perhaps you think you can buy time until you are rescued by your accomplices? It will not work. Muirn is dead. The insurgents have either been killed, caught, or have fled the city. *No one* is coming to free you." He spins on his heels and marches out, slamming the barred door behind him.

I listen to his footfalls fade down the steps, waiting until they're beyond earshot before I allow myself a sigh of relief. Though there is nothing to be relieved about. I'm in a predicament that I can't begin to figure a way out of. I should have run like that man said. I'd be living with Annika's death, but I'd be alive and not in this cell. Boaz's threats of dismemberment did what he intended. I'm terrified.

And my hand throbs. I cringe as I inspect the sizable, deep gash across my palm. That will take at least ten stitches to close, maybe more, and something tells me they aren't in a rush to fetch a doctor for me. I need to staunch the blood.

The hem of my dress is ripped. Using my teeth and my good

hand, I tear off a strip and wind it around my injury as best I can, trying to ignore the dirt that's begging to climb into my wound. People have lost limbs from basic infections. Sometimes more. A homeless woman who lived down by the Hudson—we called her Sally Rivers—cut her thumb on a tin can and later *died* of sepsis.

I pull myself off the hard stone floor and head to the tiny window to get a better grasp on my surroundings. Boaz has locked me in a tower, I realize with dismay. The top of a tall tower, the ground at least a fifty-foot drop. Even if I could fit through the opening, I'd break every bone in my body jumping. Fitting my head into the small space, I spot a helmet. A soldier guards the entrance.

Boaz marches across an enormous courtyard with purpose, pausing to speak to two men who are busy hauling logs and dumping them in a pile, directing them with a pointed finger and words I can't decipher. Aside from them, I don't see anyone else. It's quiet here—far more so than along the city streets we passed through.

Despite the warm summer air, this cell is cool, and my dress is sopping wet from the river. My teeth chatter as I attempt to ring water from the countless layers of skirts using my uninjured hand. I can't help but chastise myself for it. But death by hypothermia or pneumonia might be preferential to whatever they have planned for me.

When I can't squeeze another drop of water, I gather up the blanket Boaz left, finding an odd comfort in the earthy smell. The pile of hay layered with sheepskin is my bed, I guess? I'll admit, I've slept on worse, but it's still unappealing.

There is nothing to do now but stare at my muddy feet and wait.

A faint scraping sound carries from somewhere within the tower nearby, prickling the hair on the back of my neck. I move cautiously toward the cell door, searching the darkness beyond the bars. Across the landing is another cell.

"Hello?" I hold my breath, listening intently. Might there be someone hiding within the shadows who can fill me in on where the hell I am? "Hello?" I call again, louder.

A rat scurries out between the bars, startling me. It halts abruptly when it sees me standing there and then veers down the stairs. Otherwise, no one answers.

I test my cell door with a push and a shake. It rattles noisily but does not budge, confirming that it is locked.

I'm trapped and utterly alone, save for the rodents.

How did it come to this?

Moonlight reaches in through the window to bathe the makeshift bed in its silver glow. How many others have waited for punishment beneath that light? Wrapping the blanket tighter around myself, I pick through everything Sofie told me in her frantic march to the vault, and the insanity since I woke up in a maze.

Sofie was adamant that these people couldn't find out who I am. *What* I am. If they do, I won't survive. But this version of Romeria they *think* I am? Apparently, she killed a king and queen and started a war in their city. I'm pretty sure they're going to kill me anyway.

I study the ring she slipped onto my finger. I thought the gem dull, but beneath the moonlight, it shimmers. She said this would protect me, and maybe it will. I still don't understand how it lit up like that in the river, but I guess I'll have to add that question to a long list of events that doesn't make sense.

Maybe I'm losing my mind like my father did. Is this what he feels like? To this day, he is adamant that he sees the truth unfolding before him, and yet everyone around him insists on a different version. I mean, soldiers with swords and a medieval city no one knows of? Two moons? I'm seeing it with my eyes, but have I created all of this in my mind? Is this what it feels like to suffer from delusions that are so vivid, you can't possibly accept them as false?

I *remember* Sofie driving that jagged black horn through my chest, and yet Boaz insists he shot me with an arrow. We both remember two versions of a truth that would explain why my chest aches and my gown is stained in blood, and yet neither of those explanations seems plausible.

Is *any* of it true?

With shaky fingers, I shift the blanket away. As absurd as this dress may be with all its layers and pomp and cleavage-baring style, it must have been stunning before it was ruined. Whoever made it spent countless hours stitching swirls and flowers in golden thread.

The bodice is stiff and formfitting, and it takes effort and the removal of a sleeve to peel the material past the swell of my breast so I can better examine the tender spot in the dusky light. I grimace at the mottled, deep-purplish red mark. I was expecting to find a gash, and yet my skin isn't broken. It looks like nothing more than a nasty bruise.

But I *remember* that horn piercing—

"You heal fast for someone who was dead."

I startle at the voice, yanking the blanket up to cover myself, my cheeks flushing. I recognize that chilly, calm tone. It's the king. Zander. How did he sneak in without making a sound? And how long has he been standing in the shadows, watching me?

A key rattles the lock.

My panic swells as the door swings open with a yawning creak. He ducks as he steps through. Gone is the armor, exchanged for a sleek black ensemble, including a jacket that meets the boots at his knees. Without a helm covering most of his face, I see that he's young—older than me, but younger than I'd picture a king to be. Not that I've ever given the age of a king much thought. The rest of his olive-skinned features are as hard and angular as his jaw, framed by a mane of golden-brown hair that sweeps backward off his face in waves, reaching his nape.

Cold eyes bore into me as he approaches, his hands hanging at his side, next to the scabbard that holds his sword. The jeweled dagger is also within reach, strapped to his thigh.

The thief in me wonders if I could relieve him of the smaller weapon without his notice. But the reason I succeed at depriving people of their belongings is because they don't suspect me. Zander was a split second away from driving that dagger through my chest earlier because he suspects me of a great deal worse than theft. He thinks I murdered his parents.

That I'm still alive is a miracle.

"Stand," he commands, stopping a mere foot away, his hands flexing.

I oblige, not wanting to give him an excuse to kill me on the spot.

He seemed a titan earlier in all that armor. Now, he looms over me, tall and broad-shouldered, but not inhumanly so. He's no less daunting, though. And he is to be king. Even if this place and these people mean nothing to me, I sense the aura of power radiating from him. An arrogance.

His piercing gaze has settled on me. I struggle to maintain composure, focusing on the lapel of his jacket as I scramble to find the right words to convince him I'm not the Romeria he thinks I am.

He reaches for a corner of the woolen blanket, and his intentions quickly become clear.

On instinct, I curl my arms tighter against my body, and spear him with a glare of warning.

His eyebrow arches. "So *now* you're modest around me?"

"What is that supposed to mean?"

"Don't pretend you don't know. Show me the wound. *Now*."

I'm nowhere strong enough to fight him off if he forces himself on me, and I'd rather have some control of the situation. Reluctantly, I lower the edge of the blanket, just far enough that he can see my bruised skin and nothing more. Not that he didn't already get a good look, lurking within the shadows.

I tense as he reaches out, grazing his fingertip across where *something* injured me, horn or arrow. Despite his obvious hatred for me, his touch is gentle.

And despite my terror, a shiver courses through my body.

After a long moment, he pulls away. He turns his back to me and begins pacing around my tiny cell.

I take the moment to adjust my dress, wincing from the trouble.

"You've been busy these past weeks, playing the benevolent charmer, seeking peace between our people, all while plotting to wipe out my entire family. Don't bother trying to deny it. We've questioned your servants, the ones who survived. They all confessed. And quickly, I might add."

I have servants?

"You succeeded at killing my parents. Atticus narrowly missed an arrow through his heart, and Annika was certainly dead until you rescued her. I can't figure that one out, but I'm sure you have your reasons. Perhaps a goodwill gesture when you realized you were being pursued? Still, I'm surprised you didn't put up a fight."

Put up a fight—by myself—against fifty soldiers on horses?

His heel scrapes the stone as he pivots to face me. "How was *I* to go? Poison as well? Or perhaps a well-placed blade while I lay next to you, sated and oblivious?"

I want to deny everything and claim my innocence, but I bite my tongue. The more he talks, the more I'll learn. So far, I know his parents are survived by three children, and it sounds like Zander and I might have been a couple. In that case, the snipe about my modesty around him makes sense.

But what exactly were we to each other?

My gaze drifts to his mouth, to a full set of lips. Have I kissed them before?

Have those piercing eyes already seen everything beneath this dress?

Have we woken up, jumbled in each other's limbs?

It's disorienting to stand before a man who I have no familiarity with when he seems overly familiar with me. A man who accuses me of murdering his loved ones, with ample evidence, apparently.

"Did your father know about this scheme when he bargained with mine? Because I see Neilina's name written all over it. Not that it matters. Unfortunately for all of you, your carefully laid plans fell apart when my parents decided to have their repast *before* the ceremony instead of after." His jaw tenses. "Who within these walls conspired with you? I know you had aid, beyond that of Lord Muirn's. Someone who knew our schedules, knew how to get past the guards. I want to know who betrayed my family. Who betrayed Islor?"

I steady my voice. "I didn't conspire to kill—"

"Who helped you!" he roars, his hand flexing toward his dagger.

I shrink back. There's no use. He's already convinced of my guilt, and he won't listen to me if I keep offering him denials. I need to find some other way to give him the truth. "Sofie."

He falters, as if not expecting an answer so quickly, or one at all. "Sofie," he repeats, his brow furrowing. "I do not know any Sofie."

"That's what she told me her name was, but maybe she was lying."

"Who is she? A courtier? A lady-in-waiting? A servant?"

"Definitely not a servant. She has her own castle. She's tall and thin and has long red hair. She's beautiful. Good with a sword."

He shakes his head. The description must not fit anyone he knows. "Where did you meet her?"

"At a charity event in Manhattan."

"Is that in Ybaris?"

He's a king who hasn't heard of Manhattan? "No. It's in New York. We met there and then flew to—"

"*Flew*? Are you telling me a *caster* was behind this?"

I frown. *A what?*

"Is she an elemental?"

"I don't know?"

He mutters something under his breath that sounds like a

curse. "How powerful is she? Is she within our city walls now?" He fires off questions, his voice suddenly urgent.

How powerful? I can't begin to answer that. "She said she couldn't come here."

He paces again. "And what did you promise that misguided fool, Lord Muirn, for his help with the insurgents?" He hums. "Of course ... your hand in marriage. With all of us dead, you would need an Islorian of noble blood to help you secure the throne. Though you would have had little luck swaying the court with that turncoat. You truly know nothing of Islorian ways."

I try again. "I know you don't believe me, but *I* didn't kill your parents. *I* wasn't going to try to kill you."

"You're locked in a tower and facing charges of high treason. You'll say anything, won't you, Romeria?"

"Probably," I admit. My name on his tongue—as if he knows me so well—is jarring. "But that doesn't change the fact that this wasn't me. I'm not who you think I am."

He stalks toward me and I edge away until my back hits the wall, trapping me from evading his towering form. The moonlight illuminates a face I would admire under normal circumstances. Now, though, I see only hard lines and hatred.

His attention drops to where I clutch the blanket close to my chest, settling on my makeshift bandage. "I don't see any need for you to wear such jewelry anymore, do you?" He holds his hand out, palm up.

It's not my bandage but my ring that has grabbed his attention, and his meaning is clear.

You must not remove this ring for any reason.

I don't want to test the truth of Sofie's warning, so I tuck my hand beneath the blanket in response. Summoning all my nerve, I meet Zander's steely gaze, holding it while I find my voice and say, "It's *mine.*"

Time hangs as my heart drums in my chest and the growing tension swirling around us threatens to choke the air from my lungs. He seems to be trying to read my thoughts as surely as I try to read his.

I pray he can see the honesty and innocence in mine when I say slowly, clearly, "I'm *not* who you think I am—"

"Are you not Princess Romeria, future queen of the kingdom of Ybaris, betrothed to be my *wife*?" he says with deadly calm.

My mouth gapes. *Princess? Kingdom? Betrothed?* "No! I mean, yes, my name *is* Romeria, but I'm not—"

"Enough!" His brow furrows as he reaches beneath his jacket for his hip. His hand wraps around the hilt of the dagger. "Is there *any* shred of you that feels remorse for what you've done?"

I stay mute, afraid *any* answer will guarantee that he draws that weapon from its sheath.

"Do you know how much I wish to believe you were not behind this?" he whispers hoarsely, moving closer. His eyes shine with raw pain. "*Please*, convince me you would not do this to me."

I flatten my body against the cool stone wall and hold my breath, the urge to scream clawing at my throat. After all I've been through, *this* is how I am to die? In a medieval tower cell, at the hands of this emotionally wounded king, mistaken for someone else?

He leans in and his lips brush against mine in a featherlight stroke.

I'm frozen in shock by the unexpected move, and the next one, when he kisses me with more intention. His words find purchase within the swirl of my panic. I was to be *his wife*. He *wants* to believe I'm innocent of these terrible crimes.

Maybe there is a way to convince him still.

It's been awhile since I've kissed someone—a guy at a club six months ago, who didn't bother to remove his wedding band when he propositioned me; I divested him of his Blancpain watch that night—and forever since I meant it. With a deep, shaky breath, I coax Zander's mouth with mine. His lips are soft and warm, such a contrast to his cold, hard demeanor, and they part willingly.

I release my grip on my blanket and it slides off my shoulders, falling to my feet. With tentative fingers, I smooth my uninjured hand over the wall of chest before me, silently admiring the expanse of solid muscle beneath my palm as I lean my head back and taunt him, teasing the seam of his lips with the tip of my tongue.

Zander goes still, and I fear whatever momentary spell he's fallen under has waned as quickly as it struck him. But then, with a sharp inhale, he's responding fervently, reaching to grip the back of my head, his fingers knitting through my hair as he deepens the kiss with skilled strokes of his tongue. Firm hips pin me to the wall, his tense body pressed against mine.

I'm momentarily overwhelmed. I've never been kissed like this—with so much desperation. But I remember my purpose quickly. My hand climbs up over the thick column of his throat to graze that carved jawline with a tender touch. My other one—the injured hand—slips from between us, where it's safe from being crushed.

Where it's closer to the dagger.

Zander's lips shift from my mouth to my jaw, and then to my neck, his breaths coming in shallow pants.

In the headiness of this moment, my body begins to respond despite the peril I'm in. I arch my back to give him better access, and his grip on my hair tightens. He tilts my head at an angle, stretching my neck wide. I shudder at the playful scrape of his teeth, the unexpected sharpness of them sending a shiver to my core.

But when his fingers curl around the neckline of my dress and I feel the jerk of fabric, hear the tear of a seam, I realize I'm quickly losing control of the situation—if I ever had any to begin with.

I never allowed anyone to use me like this when I was living on the streets. I am not about to let it happen now, no matter how dire my situation. But I *will* use it to my advantage.

Night air caresses my bare skin, where one side of my dress

has been pulled down precariously low. I feel Zander's gaze on my body as surely as if it were his mouth, but he hasn't made a move. He has stalled, as if contemplating whether to continue or stop. Any moment, he could decide on the latter.

Gritting my teeth against the sting in my palm, I slip my fingers inside his jacket, skating them over his trim waist to get my bearings before I draw his hips tighter against my parted thighs.

He responds with a guttural sound. His fist tightens on my hair once again, and his mouth moves for my neck. I feel another deliciously sharp drag of his teeth and a soft moan escapes my lips, unbidden. But I use the moment's distraction to brush the dagger's hilt with my thumb, testing its fit in the sheath while searching for a light, unnoticeable grasp.

I pinch the top …

Zander peels away from me suddenly and takes several steps back, out of my reach.

My hands remain empty, my plan foiled.

His Adam's apple bobs with his hard swallow. "We could have brought peace. We could have changed Islor and Ybaris together. But you're right. You're not who I thought you were." His jaw clenches as he studies a long, gold hair pin in his palm. "And I will *never* believe another word out of your treacherous mouth."

"I swear to you, Zander—"

"Don't you *ever* say my name again!" he roars. He pauses a few moments to regain his composure, and when he speaks again, his voice has taken on that cold, detached tone. "You will face your punishment at dawn, along with the rest of the traitors. And I promise, yours won't be quick or painless, as my parents' deaths were not." He nods toward my hand. "Let us see if it can keep you from Azo'dem, for surely that's where the fates will deem you deserve to go." He strolls out of my cell without a backward glance, the bars clanging as the door slams shut. His footfalls down the stairs are swift, and they take all my hope along with them.

Tugging my dress back into place, I rush to the window, ready to tell him *everything*—about Sofie, Korsakov, the horn, this mission for Malachi's stone. But he must have gone another way because the only people in the courtyard are the soldier pacing in front of the tower door and the two men arranging a line of wooden structures.

Icy unease prickles my skin as I survey the structures again with more discerning eyes. Piles of timber of varying lengths are stacked purposely beneath, like kindling for a fire.

Those are pyres and this is an execution square.

And by his last words to me, I'm certain I know which method I'm destined for.

My insides sink as I finally grasp the true gravity of my situation.

The king may still love whoever he thinks I am, but he also just sentenced her to death.

CHAPTER EIGHT

My heartbeat is a relentless anvil against its cavity wall. This is all playing out like some terrible nightmare, and yet my every grain is warning me that if I don't get out of this tiny cell before sunrise, there is no waking up from what will happen to me.

Sofie talked of mythical creatures as gods and making flames dance on her fingertips. She alluded to there being other, far more superior beings. Such as what? All I've seen are more humans. *Angry* humans who think I've risen from the dead after murdering their king and queen, and inciting an insurrection in their city.

But *where* is this Cirilea? Where on earth could there be a medieval city like this, with war in the streets and a king who hasn't heard of New York, who executes people and talks of these *casters* and power like it's a magical force?

Could there be magic in the world?

Centuries ago, they burned women by the thousands for witchcraft, on account of superstition, not fact. Or so history books say. But what if there is truth to the magic? And what if Sofie somehow sent me back to that time, to a place that no longer exists on a map? It's either that, or …

You are about to enter a world unlike that which you know.

There are two moons in the sky.

No, it's not possible.

None of this can be happening. This is a delusion. Just like my father has delusions. My worst nightmare—that his sickness is hereditary—is coming to fruition.

And yet, my palm stings from Zander's blade, and my knee aches from where it smashed against the stone floor, and the sound of the cell door slamming shut still chimes in my ear.

And tomorrow morning, when I'm chained to one of those posts and the wood is lit, I know in my gut everyone will hear my screams.

Wherever I am, this is all too real.

I've been in desperate situations before—hell, the last decade of my life has been one big desperate situation—and yet this time feels different.

I pace around my cell, feeling the walls move closer as the minutes pass. I pause long enough to check the sky. I can see only one moon from this angle—the lower, bigger one—and it is still shining bright, but dawn can't be too many hours from arriving.

I fidget with the ring encasing my finger, twirling it around and around, its white stone smooth against my thumb. "Sofie, if you can somehow hear this … get me out of here," I mutter, my voice a whine of despair. The ring helped me when I needed light in the deep, dark waters. Maybe it can somehow pick the lock or …

Pick the lock.

With frantic fingers, I search the damp mess on my head. My hair must have been styled at some point, secured with gold pins like the one the king held in his palm. If only …

My fingertips graze metal. Relief blossoms as I fish it out, pulling strands of hair with it. I'm nearly laughing as I find three more in this rat's nest. Racing to kneel in front of the cell door, I silently thank Tarryn for yet another skill she passed on to me. Though I haven't picked a lock in years, I remember the basics.

It's difficult to see from this angle, but the lock on the cell door looks like a common padlock, though old and cumbersome and made of iron.

It's an awkward reach but my arms are thin, and the pins are long. And softer than I expected. The first one snaps immediately.

I curse and set it aside. With the second one, I approach with more caution, sliding it into the keyhole. It takes gentle finagling, poking this way and that, my arms aching from the strain of the angle. Finally, a click sounds. Overwhelming relief hits me as my cell door swings open, even though I know it's only the first of many flaming hoops I'll have to jump through to escape my predicament.

With a renewed sense of purpose, I rush back to the window to take a more calculated stock of the situation. Still only one guard patrols the square at this late hour. The workers have left, their jobs complete. I spend a few moments searching the shadows for movement, but there is none from what I can see. Either Boaz is feeling confident about his claim that no one will attempt to free me, or he can't spare more soldiers here when they're needed elsewhere in the city on a night of unrest.

Maybe he should have been more worried about his precious king inadvertently showing me the way out.

I settle in to count the lone guard's steps as I've done so many times before—it's the mark of tired staff trying to survive a long shift. Twenty steps to the hay-filled wagon before he retraces his path to the tower, then heads in the opposite direction for thirty steps to the first pyre. Back and forth he marches, and each time, he takes twenty steps to the wagon and thirty to the pyre.

If I can slip out while his back is to me, I *might* have a chance.

I head for the winding stairs, my blood rushing in my ears as I descend. My knee throbs, but still I struggle to take the uneven steps slowly. I'm forced to pause several times and brace myself against the wall to quell the dizziness. The whole time, I'm counting and hoping I don't misjudge the guard's pace. *Twenty steps to the left, twenty steps back. Thirty steps to the right, thirty steps back.*

By the time I see the wooden door, my bare feet ache and I'm on the verge of vomiting from nerves. But it's now or never, and I'd rather be shot with an arrow trying to flee tonight than roasted in the square for a crowd tomorrow.

Six steps hang between me and either death or escape, if I don't balk.

I take a deep breath and ...

The door creaks open and a hooded figure slips in, pushing the door closed behind them. Frozen, I watch with wide, panicked eyes as the person peels back their forest-green hood, revealing a head of plump blond curls.

It's Annika.

Before I can form a coherent reaction—run or pounce—she looks up and sees me standing there. She lets out a tiny yelp but gathers her composure a split second later. "Fates, you are a resourceful one." She searches my empty hands with bright blue eyes. Under the glow of torchlight, I can see she is as beautiful as her brother is handsome, though they look nothing alike—her skin coloring fairer, her face oval-shaped, her lips naturally curving into a pout. "What did you think you were going to do? Stroll out into the courtyard and wave at the guard?"

Why hasn't she screamed yet? And what is she even doing here in the tower? It's the middle of the night.

She thrusts a folded charcoal-gray cloth toward me. "Here, put this on. We haven't much time. I told the guard that Boaz was looking for him. They'll figure out soon enough that it was a lie, and then there will be no way to get you out of here."

I gape at her. Annika is helping me *escape*?

"Quickly! Before I change my mind," she hisses.

I rush down the last steps, accepting the material. A wool cloak, I realize, draping it over my shoulders.

She peeks out the door. "Keep your head down, *do not* speak, and if you try to run, I *will* scream." She spears me with a warning look before she draws her hood over her hair. I follow suit, and then she's leading me into the night. We turn left almost immediately, avoiding the square. Her pace is swift as she weaves along a maze of narrow corridors and paths. I focus on the swirling hemline of her cloak and nothing else, counting my steps and attempting to track the changing direction. It's habit, though I know in this case, I'll never be able to retrace the path.

The whole time, I'm anxious that she's leading me into another trap, but I don't have any other choice. Staying in the tower is a guaranteed death sentence. Trusting her offers me a shred of hope.

Before long, we're darting down steep stairs and through a long passageway, just wide enough for single file, the ceiling inches from my head. She carries a lantern she collected on the way in. It's the only source of light.

"We should be safe down here at this late hour." They're the first words she's spoken since we left the tower.

"Where are we?" I dare ask.

"Beneath the castle." She opens another door and pauses to peek around before passing through. "It's far safer than going *through* it and taking the streets is too dangerous. Every guard in Cirilea is out tonight and on high alert."

"The undercroft," I murmur more to myself, gaping at the mammoth, endless cavern of vaulted ceilings and massive pillars that makes Sofie's castle look like a hovel. Annika's hurried footsteps echo; mine make no sound. One positive of being barefoot, though I wince at the cuts and scrapes accumulating quickly.

"Mother insisted we not take you down here until we were sure we could trust you. She didn't want you knowing the ins and outs of this place, of how to move about unseen. Zander thought she was being unreasonably distrustful, but he complied." Her voice hardens. "It turns out she was right to be cautious, though it didn't make any difference in the end, did it?"

Because *apparently*, I was at the wheel of a murderous uprising.

"Why are you helping me?" I blurt.

"I owe you a life, do I not?"

"But … you think I killed your parents. *I* didn't, by the way."

"Zander mentioned your continued and adamant refusal on that matter. Though we have sufficient evidence to prove otherwise." She sounds so detached, only hours after her parents were poisoned. At least Zander is passionate over their loss. But maybe she's still in shock. It doesn't seem like her day has gone much better than mine. "A great many things do not make sense right now, beginning with why you would save me from the river when it is quite clear you wanted us all dead. The truth is, I'm not doing this for *you*. I *despise* you. I'm doing this for Islor, and for Zander." She worries her pouty bottom lip. "He ended up caring for you *far* more than he ever expected to when the marriage was arranged."

My marriage to Zander was *arranged*?

"You fooled him. You fooled *all* of us, even though I never cared much for you to begin with. But my brother is not thinking clearly, and I fear having you condemned to death will hurt him more than he realizes. Even if you deserve it." She shakes her head. "I cannot explain this overwhelming sense of foreboding, but I am choosing to listen to it."

The corridor splits off in two directions; she heads to the right. "This way. We must hurry. Boaz will be sounding the alarm at any moment."

"Aren't you going to get in a ton of trouble for helping me?" What is the punishment for breaking out a woman sentenced to die for murdering a king and queen?

"I am the princess of Islor. Boaz cannot punish me," she scoffs.

"And what about Zander?"

"I know how to deal with my brother." The worried look on her face betrays her bluster. Whatever she'll earn for this, it won't be pleasant.

I follow her up a narrow staircase. She draws her cloak over her lantern and then eases open the door. We're back outside, this time in the shadows, surrounded by branches. The smell of cedar fills my nostrils.

"Are we in—"

She covers my mouth with her palm. We stay frozen like that, listening as a clink of metal sounds to my left. Must be a guard nearby. Elsewhere, shouts are rising. I assume Boaz knows I've escaped by now and is anxious to put another arrow through my heart. Still preferential to what they have planned for me.

Annika uncovers my mouth. Together, we creep forward through the covert cedar tunnel as soundlessly as possible, every snap of a twig and rustle of a branch stealing breaths from my lungs. We must be in the same garden I found myself in earlier, though nothing is visible from within these cedar walls.

We reach the end, and Annika uncovers her lantern. She guides me down a set of steps and then along another passageway made of stone, this one smelling of earth and mildew. It's so narrow, I doubt most soldiers could maneuver through, at least not wearing their armor. It was likely built for civilians needing to flee. In some spots, I have to stoop to pass.

"Are we still under the castle?" I ask.

"No. We're passing beneath the curtain wall. I cannot get you out of the city tonight, so I'm taking you to the sanctum where you will seek protection until I can reason with my brother. It's the only safe place for you within Cirilea. Perhaps in all of Islor."

"You think you can do that? Reason with him?" Maybe I can slip out on my own once I have my bearings. This wouldn't be the first city I've slinked around, though it's certainly the first where I'd be hunted by an army.

"It's worth trying. My brother is now king, and there are a great many things expected of him. Hopefully he can learn to make decisions based on his head and not his heart."

Because apparently, *I* broke the latter.

Just recalling the pained look in his eyes brings a swell of pity to my chest.

Annika's shoes scuff along the stone floor with her rushed steps. "How did you break me free of the merth? It was in its raw form, and your hands were bare."

I remember her using that same word down by the river. She must be talking about the silver rope. "It fell apart."

"Raw merth feels like a thousand razor blades slicing across your skin while it subdues you, rendering you utterly immobile. It does *not* simply *fall apart* beneath your touch." Under her breath, she adds, "That does not make *any* sense."

"The story of my life at the moment." People don't wake up in a strange, primitive country with an army chasing them after a crazed woman drives a sharp object through their chest, and yet *here I am*.

"You are different from before. The way you speak, the odd things you say ..."

"I've been trying to tell you guys." Maybe if they start picking up on how poorly I fit into this medieval cosplay, they'll stop insisting on killing me.

We meet yet another set of stairs, but it leads to nothing. "I suppose you *would* seem different, though. This is the *real* Romeria, is it not? The version we saw before was the farce, the one to win us over."

"That's not ..." *What I meant.* I sigh. How am I supposed to explain myself when they don't trust a word that comes out of my mouth? Then again, if I'm to believe Sofie, then knowing who I really am is just as dangerous.

"Take this." She hands me the lantern, and with both hands, yanks on a lever. The ceiling above us shifts to one side with a grating sound—like stone scraping against stone. It opens wide enough to climb through.

Annika collects the lantern and leads me up.

"That's *so* cool," I murmur, taking a moment to appreciate the mahogany pew that shifted over to reveal the secret passage.

"*Cool,*" she echoes as if testing the word. "Ybarisans are strange."

I quickly scan our surroundings. Their sanctum is a church, and it appears we're in the far back corner of it.

"Come, we will find the high priestess. She must be consulted if you are to receive shelter here."

It's the middle of the night. "Won't she be at home, sleeping?"

She scoffs. "On a night like this?"

I pursue Annika as she zigzags along aisles and cross sections of the nave, past stately columns and rows of pews and open areas. Above us, a mosaic of gold shimmers even in the night, but it's far too dark to make out the illustrations and patterns. The air smells of sweet pine and roses.

She cuts across a midsection to take the main aisle, still lit with open-flame torches.

I gape at the floral arrangements lining the path to the altar, of blush-colored flowers the size of dinner plates, their fragrance as potent as walking into a florist shop. There must be thousands of blooms along this center aisle.

"It would have been a beautiful wedding." Annika's gaze drags first over the bouquets and then over my dress, her voice reluctant when she adds, "You would have made a stunning bride, I will give you that."

Her meaning dawns on me, a numbing realization. "I was supposed to marry him *today*." I look down at my dress. Even torn and bloodied and otherwise ruined, it is still remarkable. It must have been my wedding gown. And all these flowers must have been for our ceremony.

But on the day I was to marry Zander, I had his parents killed instead.

Who is this other awful version of me?

"Yes. And you would be in the nymphaeum doing things with my brother that I don't want to imagine." Her button nose scrunches. "And who knows? With the blood moon, the fates may have blessed you with offspring on this night."

The blood moon. Sofie said something about it moments before she stabbed me.

"You might have brought peace to so many lives, if only you could move past your hatred for us." A sheen coats Annika's eyes as she picks up the pace toward the altar. "I will secure your asylum and convince my brother to either hold you prisoner or escort you across the rift to your kingdom. I would prefer the second option, so I nor my brothers must look upon your conniving face again. I doubt the war council will support such a plan, but if they should? You shall return to Ybaris, praise Islor for its mercy, and make sure your people know we are not the monsters you paint us to be. We simply do what we must to survive."

I'm trying to process her rush of words, but my first up close glimpse of the altar distracts all other thoughts.

Or more specifically, the four majestic sculptures that stand at the altar's corners, carved from stone and buffed until gleaming.

My eyes instantly lock on the one with horns coiling high toward the ceiling. His chest is broad and powerful, as is the rest of his sculpted, unclothed form. He stands as a human would, but on hooved feet. There is no mistaking him. He is the carved creature in Sofie's vault, the one she named Malachi. She called him a fate. In the corner opposite him is the tall, lithe woman with petite breasts and a broad crown of antlers jutting from her head. *Aoife.*

Two more statues bank the other corners. I hadn't noticed such creatures in Sofie's crypt, though I was suitably distracted. One is a female with generous hourglass curves and butterfly wings protruding from her back; the other is a stocky man with two shorter curved bull-like horns.

These are Sofie's four fates—four gods—the ones who are responsible for all life, according to her. They must also be the gods of these people of Islor, if they are looming over the altar. I have never heard of anyone worshipping such idols as these.

As we get closer, Annika's expression turns to one of panic. "Margrethe?" She darts up the five marble steps of the dais. I spot the pair of feet poking out of folds of white cloth a second before Annika rounds the altar. Her blue eyes widen and her down-turned mouth opens, and then she lets out an ear-splitting scream that ricochets through the grand space.

I run up the steps, dread seizing my insides as I brace myself for another dead body. What I see is far worse. Half the woman's neck has been ripped out, and holes stare back at me where eyes have been gouged. She's in a pool of blood that soaks into her pristine white garb, torn open across her abdomen by deep claw marks to expose her mutilated womb. There's *so much* blood. "Who would have done this to her?" I whisper.

Annika stumbles over her feet as she scrambles to back away from the body. "We need to return to the castle. *Now*."

"But you said this was the only place I'd be safe from execution?"

"It's clearly not safe *now*! Not with a *daaknar* loose inside our city walls!" She throws a hand toward the maimed body. "Not when it has killed the *only* person in Cirilea who can send it back to where it came from!"

"A *what*?"

"We don't have time for whatever game it is you are playing, Romeria. There hasn't been one of these in Islor in two *thousand* years." She rushes down the center aisle, but then stops and spins around to glare at me. "Of course ... This was you, wasn't it! Did your caster beckon it?"

She must mean Sofie. Did Zander tell her *everything*?

"Is this Ybaris's grand finale, to let one of these beasts ravage our people, on a day that you've already caused so much harm?"

"No!" At least, I hope not. How could anyone be a part of releasing something that would do *that*?

She continues backward down the aisle. "Stay here if you wish. It's your beast, maybe *you* can tame it. But you will not get sanctuary here, not from a corpse."

Movement stirs to my left.

"*I* need to get to my brother before it surprises him—"

"Annika." A cold wash of fear prickles every inch of my skin as I watch a shadowy form rise from between the pews, climbing to a height far greater than any human. "*Stop*."

Either she sees the terror in my face or hears it in my voice, but she follows my gaze and turns to face the figure as it edges forward with slow, stealthy movements along the narrow pew. Firelight from the torches illuminates a creature scarier than anything I've ever seen in any horror film. But maybe that's because this monster is real.

The folded wings of a bat jut out from its hunched back, hanging tattered, as if something with claws had shredded them. Its skin looks charred, like that of blackened chicken, and yellow fluid oozes between the cracks. But it is the two horns that my petrified attention is most riveted to—twisty black horns protruding from a bulbous forehead.

My mouth has gone bone-dry. This can only be the daaknar, the beast that mauled the high priestess. And now it's sizing up its next prey.

"By the fates ..." With stiff movements, Annika steps backward, away from it.

It releases a guttural noise and hops up onto the back of the pew with ease, showing off sinewy hind legs that look powerful enough to launch it into the air, even if its wings fail it. Its head tips back to sniff the air, but its eyes never leave Annika as it sits perched like a gargoyle, waiting, allowing her to put some distance between them.

It's waiting for its target to run so it can give chase before it kills her, as it killed the high priestess.

As it, or one of its kind, must have killed that woman in a factory parking lot.

My father has been telling the truth about what he saw all along.

Now is not the time to reexamine his delusions, though.

Annika is about to be torn apart by this thing because she was helping me escape. Her death will be on my hands, another strike against me in the king's eyes. While I might not deserve to take the blame for what happened before I woke up, letting this happen now will weigh like fault on my shoulders.

If Annika can get to the passage, the daaknar will not be able to follow her through that narrow space. She can get back to the castle and warn Zander.

Adrenaline thrums in my veins as I grab a gold-plated chalice from the altar. "Hey!" I throw it as hard as I can at the daaknar's head. It catches the top of its horn, and the beast roars in response, swinging its glowing red eyes in my direction.

I ignore the shudder that courses through my body beneath that predatory gaze and reach for the next closest thing—a stone bowl that will be harder to throw but more painful if it hits its mark.

I whip it at the creature. This time, it lands squarely against its chest.

With another roar, this one laced with fury, the daaknar abandons its original target, leaping from pew to pew toward the dais, tearing chunks of wood with its razor-sharp claws.

I throw another chalice at it to keep its attention focused on me as I hiss, "Run!" I might be able to buy Annika enough time.

"You're making it angry!" she hisses back.

"Isn't this how you tame one of these things?" I mock, my fear numbing my legs.

"It's going to *kill* you!"

"*Still* better than being burned alive." *I hope*. I fumble for another object, anything I can throw at it. My fist closes over the hilt of a curved dagger, vaguely aware that it's slick with blood. The weapon is not much, but it'll have to do.

The floor beneath me quakes as the daaknar lands on the dais. I dismiss Annika from all thought, my focus now on how I might survive this thing. The way it looks at me as it ascends the steps, its lips unfurled to show a row of translucent yellowed teeth …

There is no taming something like this, even if I was the one who let it loose.

It stalks forward with heavy, snuffling breaths, slowing as if to decide which way around the altar it should take—right, past the carcass of its last kill, or left, around the front. This close, I can see the jagged barbs on the ends of its talons, useful to keep its prey in place.

I struggle to ignore the stench of its rotting flesh, curling my fist around the dagger's hilt as I back away. If I can injure it enough to slow it down, maybe I can get to the passage, if Annika hasn't already closed it. Otherwise, I'll escape through the doors and give Boaz and his men something far more threatening than me to chase.

I give the candelabra a swift kick to send it sailing.

The daaknar swats it away as if it were nothing more than a fly. With a deep snarl, it lunges.

"Go!" I shout, stabbing upward with all my strength, driving the blade into its gut. Its answering roar rattles my eardrums. Not wasting a second, I turn and run.

I make it all of six feet before those barbed claws pierce my shoulder, carving through my flesh and bone. I howl in agony as it hauls me back, the pain excruciating. With its talons acting as hooks to anchor me in place, limiting my ability to squirm, it takes its time, brushing away the loose strands of hair from my neck with its other paw. The gesture is oddly gentle—almost human—and yet the tip of its claw scrapes across my cheek like a razor slicing skin, remind me that it is far from human.

Whatever crazed bravery drove me to challenge this thing has vanished, leaving me trembling in terror.

It leans in and inhales deeply, as if savoring the scent of a fragrant meal it's about to devour. I'm vaguely aware of Sofie's ring hot against my skin, but my thoughts don't settle there long, too busy grappling with the reality that the figment of my father's imagination is about to kill me.

The daaknar opens its maw and needlelike fangs extend from

its upper jaw. A bloodcurdling scream rises to my throat as they sink into my neck. The burn is unbearable at first, but the pain fades quickly, as does any fight I have left.

Somewhere, far in the distance, my mind registers a shrill cry of agony before the darkness swallows me whole.

CHAPTER NINE

Sofie struggled to lift her limp body off the ground. She had never channeled that much power before—she doubted anyone had—and it left her near the point of oblivion. But now was not the time to surrender to weakness.

Something had happened.

She used every ounce of strength and the stone coffin to haul herself up to where the two bodies lay.

Malachi's gift, embedded deep within Romeria's chest and glowing with radiant flame, was quickly fizzling. As was the glimmer of light from the gold in her ring.

Sofie's insides churned with nerves as she watched the tokens extinguish. Her task was complete. Now, there was nothing she could do but wait.

Wait—and pray the girl did not fail her.

She retrieved her engagement ring. The spells she had affixed to it were bound to Romeria's new form now. There was no need to adorn a corpse.

A scraping sound pulled her attention behind her. She knew before turning that Malachi had returned, unbidden. She was on the verge of collapse, but she bowed as she did every time, dropping to her knees, her forehead touching the stone.

"Rise."

The Fate of Fire stood before her with his horn fully restored. He had roared in agony when he severed it, but had promised it would return. "It is complete. She is now tied to Islor for as long as she lives." His piercing gaze rolled over Sofie's shape.

She knew what he had come for this time. Was this a requirement of all his elementals, or was she special in this way?

Shedding her clothes, she climbed onto the altar.

CHAPTER TEN

I wake to the toll of church bells and the memory of fetid flesh lingering in my nostrils.

I'd like to convince myself that it was all a terrible nightmare, that I'm back in my studio apartment in Chelsea with only Korsakov's ire to worry about, but I'm lying in a bed that isn't my own, and my body aches like never before.

I remember ...

Annika leading me along secret passageways and steep stairs to the sanctum.

The grisly remains of the high priestess's mutilated body behind the altar.

That monster with its red eyes and charred flesh, sinking its claws and teeth into my helpless body.

And yet here I am, staring up at a soothing canopy of silks in taupe and robin's-egg blue.

"How am I not dead?" I croak, asking no one in particular.

"Send word that she is awake," an unfamiliar voice whispers.

I try shifting my head toward the speaker. A sharp pain radiates through my neck, drawing a hiss from my lips.

"Be careful. You are still healing." A woman in a white robe trimmed in gold appears by my bedside, concern etched into her forehead. Her outfit reminds me of a nun's habit, though the gold veil is translucent and airy, her corn silk hair visible beneath.

"How long has it been?" My voice is hoarse.

"Three days." She offers a weary smile—the first genuine one I've seen in what feels like forever. "You must be thirsty. Allow me." Settling onto the edge of my bed, she slides a gentle hand against my nape and elevates my head. "Drink, but slowly."

I manage a few sips of water from the silver mug she holds to my lips, my gaze searching her features. Gray touches her temples and weaves through her hair, crow's-feet crinkle at the corners of her eyes, laugh lines frame her mouth. She's in her fifties if I had to guess.

Swallowing hurts.

"Thanks," I say as she slips her hand free. I don't have the energy to pull myself up. "What happened?"

"You do not remember?" Round, steel-blue eyes search my face.

"That depends. Was the big, scary demon with giant horns real?"

"The daaknar. Yes, it most certainly was real."

I sigh. *Thank God.* I thought I'd lost my mind. Though I'm not sure I wouldn't prefer that to the other reality—that my father's been right all along, and demons exist. "It killed that woman."

Deep sorrow carves into her expression. "High Priestess Margrethe succumbed to her injuries, yes."

She knew her. Well, I suspect. Given her robes, I'm guessing she's somehow affiliated with the church. A church that idolizes gods with horns protruding from their heads. What fresh hell has Sofie dropped me into?

"I'm sorry for your loss."

The woman bows her head in acknowledgment.

Sleep tugs at my feeble body, but I have too many questions. "What happened after that thing attacked me?" How did I not suffer the same fate as the high priestess?

"It died. You killed it."

"*What*? No ... that's not possible." I search my foggy memory. It had me in its jaws. I was defenseless against it. "It bit me."

"Yes, we have not been able to explain it either. To my knowledge, no one has *ever* survived an attack like that." Her voice is doubtful, as if she's still grappling with that truth. "We believe the daaknar tried to feed off you, but your blood harmed it."

"It *fed* off me?" My face twists with horror.

"Not for long. It cast you aside and released that *horrific* shrill scream that could be heard across all Cirilea"—she winces as if recalling the sound—"and then it burst into flames. We assume it returned to Azo'dem."

Azo'dem. Zander said that name when he was condemning me to death. Given he thinks I am a murderer, it must be their version of hell.

"Only an elemental caster has ever been able to banish a daaknar." She studies me closely.

There it is again, this talk of casters. Zander mentioned it in the tower, and then Annika did so in the sanctum.

Annika.

"Did she get away? The king's sister was there that night—"

"My sister is well," a deep voice cuts in.

The woman tending to me scuttles off the bed and bends in a deep curtsy. "Your Highness. I didn't expect you so soon."

I swallow against the flare of nervousness and fear, and listen to the steady approach of footfalls, dreading that I've survived a demon's mauling only to land myself back on a bonfire. That wouldn't make sense, treating my injuries only so he could watch me die. But people sometimes choose irrational paths in search of reprieve from heartache. My mother taught me that.

Zander appears at my bedside. He is wearing all black again, though the jacket he wore to the tower cell has been replaced with one more regal, made of a velvety material. The embroidery along the lapels reminds me of waves crashing against rocks, the ochre thread accenting the deep gold highlights in his hair. His sword and dagger remain at his side.

And that stony, unreadable mask is firmly in place.

I find myself unable to look away from this man—this king—whom I was supposed to marry, who now wishes me dead. The daylight offers me a glimpse of his face that the moonlight did not, one that reveals a perfect balance between the hard edges and symmetrical, softer features—a square jaw that surrounds full lips, sharp cheekbones that frame large, deep-set eyes, a long, slender-tipped nose that meets a shapely brow.

Though I know it's probably not wise, that it could be seen as a challenge, I hold his steady, dissecting gaze. His eyes are a light hazel. They would be pretty if they weren't so full of hate.

"How are her wounds?" he asks after a moment.

"Healing well, Your Highness."

"Show me."

His words are an echo of those he spoke in the tower when he demanded to see the injury to my chest. The memory of his gentle touch against my bruised skin sends an unexpected shiver through my body.

The woman's fingertips are cool as she peels back the bandages, exposing my neck.

Zander's expression reveals nothing.

"How bad is it?" Am I missing a chunk of my body like Margrethe was? Will I have use of my right arm after that thing tore through my shoulder?

"Not as bad as one might expect." She tacks on a quieter "Your Highness" at the end, and I realize she's talking to me.

I'm not anyone's Highness, I want to say. I'm just Romeria, or Romy for short. But I remember who I'm *supposed* to be, who *everyone* believes me to be.

"Why don't you show her, Wendeline," Zander suggests.

The woman—Wendeline—nods and rushes to somewhere nearby, returning a moment later.

The entire time, Zander's unwavering eyes remain locked on mine. It's like he's waiting for a twitch or clue, an unspoken answer to his thoughts. It's unnerving, and I can't help but divert my gaze.

She holds up a hand mirror bordered with elaborate gilded curves in front of me.

My face reflects within the frame.

My face. The one I've known all my life, back when my life was ordinary in East Orange, Jersey, and then when my life became anything *but* ordinary. The same blue eyes of Alton's Adriatic Sea, the same hair, as black as a starless night. The same dusting of freckles across the bridge of my nose, almost too light to notice.

How can I be the Romeria that I've known all my life *and* this other Romeria, this princess of a kingdom in a strange place?

One who journeys to a foreign land.

Sofie said so little in our short time together, her words vague and random at the time, and yet the connections keep snapping into place.

"It will take time for me to repair them, but I have no experience with healing injuries from a daaknar. I fear there will be scars," Wendeline offers, reminding me that I have an audience watching me closely.

I pull my attention from this face that is mine and yet also a stranger's, and inspect the two puncture wounds over my jugular. They're no more than small dots, so contradictory to the lethal fangs that sank into me. What did Wendeline mean when she said she healed them? Even as I ask myself this question, the answer is there, lingering at the recesses of my mind. Is she talking about ... magic?

"What about her arm?" Zander asks.

Wendeline nods and shifts her focus to my shoulder, pushing aside the loose cotton material. It's then I realize someone has changed me out of my sullied and torn wedding dress. It's an unpleasant feeling knowing I was undressed while I was unconscious, but I push it from my thoughts because it's in the past and something else worries me more.

Sofie's ring.

Relief washes over me when I feel the band against the soft pad of my thumb. They didn't remove it. Could it have been the ring that somehow protected me against the beast? Is that what Sofie meant by protection? Did she know I would be attacked?

Zander watches where my fingers fidget, missing nothing. His brow pinches with confusion before smoothing over once again. It's a fleeting tell, and it reminds me that he tried to take this ring from me.

Wendeline peels away the gauzy bandages from my shoulder and holds up the mirror. "It was *much* worse to begin with."

Four grisly streaks—each at least six inches long and an inch wide—mar my skin where the beast's claws sank into my body. Oddly, there are no stitches. I would've expected dozens, and yet my flesh appears to have knitted together without the help of needle and thread. The scars will be ghastly, but it could have been much worse. I still have my eyes.

"Leave us," Zander commands softly. It reminds me of how Korsakov's voice used to go soft when he'd send people away. It meant he was going to exact revenge and didn't want any witnesses.

"Your Highness." Wendeline curtsies and darts out, her cloak swooshing with her hurried steps. Is that a sign of respect—are people expected to jump and run at his every word?—or is it that she's afraid of him?

He's a king, but what kind of man is he? All that power, people bowing and rushing around to do his bidding. Even as scary as Korsakov was, you'd never catch Tony or any of the other guys calling him anything remotely close to *Highness*.

Zander shifts closer to tower over my feeble body. "Feel free to speak your mind."

And say what? This man condemned me to death. *After* he kissed me.

I meet his examining gaze. "I'm good."

The corner of his mouth twitches as he watches me curiously. "Annika said you were *different* from before. I can't say I didn't notice it. I had the priestess search for signs of whatever elemental magic courses through your limbs. There is no other explanation for you surviving that which should have killed you *twice* now."

"You think I'm using *elemental magic*."

"I do not know, but I will get the truth out of you." His cool fingers slip around my forearm, lifting it into the air. "In case you get any ideas, these will keep you in check."

I frown at the cuff around my wrist. It's plain and black and fitted as if molded especially for me. It reminds me vaguely of the black obsidian horn Sofie impaled me with. I can't find a fastener or even a seam. A matching one graces my other wrist. "How?"

His responding smile doesn't reach his eyes. "Islor has a few secrets of its own, still." He releases his grip of my forearm and wanders from my bedside.

My hand. The one he sliced with his dagger.

I study my palm. There is only the faintest line where the sizable gash existed. I open and close my fist several times, testing it. It's as if it didn't happen at all. "You cut me," I hear myself say. He did, didn't he?

"You did far worse to me." He sighs. "What am I to do with you, Romeria?"

Now that I know half my neck isn't missing, I grit through the sting and turn my head to follow. The bedroom they've put me in is a vast improvement to the tower cell. Here, patterned paper and painted portraits adorn the walls and furniture fills the corners. The ceilings arch twenty feet over my head and daylight streams in through three grand windows. A set of glass doors are propped open.

Zander stops in front of them. "Annika tells me the daaknar was intent on her until you drew its attention to you. Why did you do that?"

"Because it would have killed her." I don't have an explanation beyond that. I didn't think; I acted.

"And you knew it would die if it attacked you?"

"I didn't even know that thing *existed* before that night. So, no. I guess I figured my time was up."

He peers over his shoulder to shoot me with a flat look. "You expect me to believe you didn't know daaknars exist."

"It doesn't matter what *I* believe, because you're not going to trust *anything* I say."

His lips twist. "Finally, something out of your mouth I know to be genuine."

I could speak all kinds of truths right now—that demons are hallucinations of my mad father, that magic only exists in the world of my mother's cult—only I'm no longer sure they'd be truths. Everything I thought I knew has been flipped upside down by a red-haired woman with flames dancing along her fingertips and a desperate need to resurrect her dead husband.

My father believes in demons. He's railed against those who told him they didn't exist, and look where that has gotten him? He's been cast aside, an unfortunate case left in society's gutter. Now here I am, in a place where *everyone* seems to believe demons and magic exist. I'm wearing scars to prove the former. Am I to hold fast to my denial and become an inverse reflection of my father?

The only certainty I see before me is that there are too many things I can't explain with what I thought I knew. But Sofie warned me of that too.

The rules of the world to which you are accustomed are about to change.

And in the world that I'm currently trapped in, there are kingdoms to kill for, beasts who feed off people, and magic I'm sure I can't fathom.

God only knows what else there is.

Zander's attention veers back to his view outside. "How did you destroy it?"

"Honestly, I *don't know*. I don't understand what's happening to me." Sofie was adamant that these people not discover my true identity, but what does that mean? That I'm *not* Princess Romeria of Ybaris but a doppelganger she has somehow planted at the worst possible time? That I'm not from Islor or Ybaris and had never heard of either place until a few days ago? Where even *is* the real princess? What did Sofie do with her body?

Is *this* somehow her body?

A shiver of panic courses through my limbs.

Regardless, I can't imagine how knowing who I really am could be more dangerous to me, but I have to believe Sofie was speaking the truth. She thinks my success will bring Elijah back to her, and she wouldn't risk that.

Still, how am I to survive in this place as the woman who murdered a king and queen?

With a version of my reality, I guess.

I take a deep breath, not sure how this will be received, other than—likely—not well. "I don't remember *anything* before waking up in the garden, the night I pulled Annika from the river."

Zander's chuckle carries through my room. "Innocence by oblivion. How convenient. Has anyone used that defense to explain away murder in my court yet?" He pauses with dramatic effect. "No, I do not believe so. You are the first. Congratulations." His tone drips with sarcasm.

I roll my eyes at his back. "It's the truth, whether you believe it or not. I don't remember my life in Ybaris. I don't remember coming here. I don't remember meeting you, or *anything* that might have happened between us." My cheeks heat at the implication.

The silence stretches on and I hold my breath, studying his form while I wait for his response. Broad shoulders lead into a tapered waist. Beneath the cover of that jacket, I acutely recall powerful thighs pressed against my hips and hard curves against my fingertips. Under other—vastly different—circumstances, I would be looking for ways to gain his attention. Now, I wish I could disappear from his bitter thoughts forever.

Finally, he turns and leans against the frame to face me, folding his arms across his chest. It's a casual stance, but nothing about his harsh expression reads as casual. "You're losing your talents. I've already caught you in your lie."

"What do you mean—"

"Sofie. The name of your coconspirator?"

Shit. He's right. How could I remember her if I don't remember anything before that night? "That was a lie," I blurt before my alarm gives away too much.

His eyebrow arches, but he says nothing. He's waiting for me to elaborate.

I don't dare to look away for fear of appearing guilty. "I was terrified, and you were demanding a name, so I made one up."

"You are telling me that no such caster exists."

"Yes. That's what I'm saying," I lie, while convincing myself it could be the truth. Is Sofie her real name? Do I know for certain she is one of these casters?

He seems to consider this. "But you *did* have help from someone in Islor. Either someone within the court or the household."

"If I did, I don't remember. I don't remember who I am." Not *this* version of Romeria, anyway.

"And yet you remember your name." He turns back to peer out the window.

The mental energy it's taking to navigate a conversation with Zander while avoiding pitfalls is wearing on my fatigued body. As the silence drags, I allow myself to shut my eyes. I'm moments from drifting off when his voice drags me back.

"Annika claims you were as surprised by the daaknar's presence as she was."

"Like I said …" Up until now, they've only existed in my father's cracked mind.

"Yes, well, you've proven that we can't take *anything* you say or do at face value."

Right. Of course.

He sighs reluctantly. "But whatever your intentions were, you saved my sister from a grim death. For that I am grateful."

I replay his words, unsure I heard them correctly. Was that a thank-you from the king? How grateful is he? Enough to cancel my death sentence? I'm almost afraid to ask. "So, what happens now?"

His focus is transfixed on something far in the distance. "The guards and servants who accompanied you from Ybaris have already been punished for their treason. You didn't miss much. It was swift and, dare I say, merciful."

Zander went through with the execution? He ordered it? Did he watch?

I cringe with the gruesome image that stirs, the wood assembled in piles waiting for a match or flint or whatever they use around here. The smell of burning flesh in the air.

"You seem upset for people you don't remember."

I look up to find him watching me. My horror must be splayed on my face. "How is being burned alive merciful?" The screams carry on far longer than can be considered humane.

"They were barely alive by that point." His jaw clenches. "And it is far more so than being poisoned."

I didn't poison your parents! I want to scream, but it's no use. How did Princess Romeria do it? What did she use? Ricin? Cyanide? Anthrax? Do those even exist here? Did she slip it into their drinks? Their food? Did they choke over their dinner plates? Was Zander there when it happened? Much of what he said to me in the tower cell about my supposed duplicity remains murky. The bits I remember don't offer any coherent clues. But I don't dare ask for specifics now. Making him relive the details can only raise his ire with me, if that's possible. And it doesn't matter, anyway. All that matters is he believes *I* killed them.

"Tomorrow, the king and queen will be laid to rest as befitting their status"—he swallows, the only sign that speaking of his parents' deaths is difficult—"and then Islor will move forward, and we will *never* again entertain an alliance with your kind."

My kind. He means these Ybarisans.

My thoughts veer to a blue-eyed woman with envious blond curls. "What about Annika?"

"Your continued concern for my sister baffles me." He shakes his head. "She betrayed me and yet, had she not, there would be a daaknar running loose in my city. The harm would have been catastrophic. I have not determined how to punish her."

I force myself to ask, "And what about me?"

"What about you ..." He reaches up to smooth the tassels on the window curtain. "Somehow you managed to tear apart *and* save Cirilea in a single night, and you claim to not know how you did any of it." He sighs heavily. "The people believe you to be dead. I do not feel the need to correct them yet. And holding the future queen of Ybaris prisoner could prove far more beneficial to me than executing her."

So, prisoner it will be. Not Annika's preference for an escort and a release, but far better than the alternative.

I allow myself the faintest sigh of relief.

The corner of his mouth curls, as if he caught it. "I do not care to lay eyes on you ever again after today, or give you another moment's thought."

Likewise.

"You will remain in these rooms, *alone*, now that all your servants are gone. I will grant you a kindness by allowing the priestess to tend to your wounds so they don't fester, though her talents would be far better used elsewhere. Don't expect any more from me, though. You will spend your days here with no friends, no allies, no one to count on."

Alone and with no one to count on, I can do. I've been doing it for years. "For how long?"

"For as long as I deem it so. Certainly, until you give up playing victim to this convenient fog you claim to be stuck in, not knowing who you are or what you've done." He pulls away from the door to face me, that hard mask firmly in place. "Or until you do something foolish, and I decide it is no longer worth the effort of keeping you. The tower square isn't going anywhere."

The threat hangs in the air. A pyre will be there, waiting for me, and he will dangle it as an option.

He continues in that cold, harsh tone. "You will cause no trouble. You will not plot against Islor. And if you ever harm another hair on any Islorian's head, I will kill you myself. And I promise you, I will ensure you never return." His eyes glide over my neck and my shoulder before drifting around the bedroom. "I do hope you enjoy your accommodations. You'll be spending *a lot* of time in them."

I watch his back as he strides out, drawing long breaths to calm my racing heart.

An open-ended prison sentence. Will that mean weeks? Months? Something Sofie said triggers in my mind, and I feel the burden of her words settle. He could hold me here for *years* as his captive. At least it doesn't sound like he's sending me back to that horrid tower room, though.

As precarious as my situation still is, it's far better than the one I found myself in three nights ago. The king may despise me, he might still wish me dead, but it sounds like he won't execute me unless I give him reason.

That's progress.

CHAPTER ELEVEN

The bells have just finished tolling to announce the noon hour when the door to my sitting room creaks open and a familiar shuffle of feet approaches.

"Will you take your meal in your bedchamber or in the sitting room?"

Eat in my bedchamber or my sitting room. Those are the only choices I'm presented with on any given day. I guess I could *really* mix it up and force food down my gullet while perched in the copper bathtub.

I abandon my bored gaze out the window to greet Corrin. The uppity servant stands in the doorway with a tray of food. I know without looking that it holds a cup of diluted wine, a bowl of meatless stew, a slice of crusty bread, and either an apple or pear. Every meal is the same, varying only in the ratio of mushy vegetables and blend of herbs.

"In here. Thank you."

Corrin strolls in to set my lunch on a small desk in the corner, her navy-blue skirt rustling with her rushed steps. Aside from short daily visits from Wendeline to tend to my wounds, the petite servant has been my sole companion. If one can call a woman who delivers food and fresh clothes and glares at me with naked animosity a companion.

She was assigned to me because of "the king's kindness" she announced when she arrived on her first day to drop off a meal and collect soiled towels, her face pinched as if smelling something foul. She then went on to list all the things she would *not* be doing for me—helping me dress, groom, bathe. All things I don't expect or want help with, even with my injuries, but she wore a smug look as she listed them out loud, as if reading from a petty *Fuck you to the fallen princess, Signed, the staff* letter.

I wonder what she did to earn this unpleasant duty.

My contentment with simply being alive has faded over the past three weeks. These walls may be adorned in pretty paper and molding, but it doesn't mask the truth of what they are—my prison. I have a bedroom for sleeping and changing, a "sitting room" where I pace, and a small room with a bath I can't figure out how to operate. The primitive-looking toilet, miraculously, flushes waste with a swirl of water when I pull a chain. I suppose I should be thankful that I'm not stuck with a chamber pot in a place that lives at the mercy of lantern light.

My door is locked from the outside and guarded at all hours. I know this because I've laid on the floor in front of it, watching through the gap as boots pace. The daytime guard takes eight steps each way and drags the ball of his left foot. The nighttime guard takes ten, with a slight spring in his step. They're the same guards every day.

In the early days, when I was still mostly bedbound from the daaknar attack, I spent my time imagining all the places where a secret corridor out of my rooms might be hiding. But I've searched every panel of wall, every floorboard, beneath every rug, and either they've hidden it well or, more than likely, they've locked me in a room without any escape.

I am a prisoner who has no idea where she is being kept, and no way of gathering information, per the king's declaration that *no one* entertain my amnesia farce by answering questions, on threat of harsh punishment. Wendeline informed me of that when I asked her about the cuffs around my wrists.

And so, I remain completely ignorant to my surroundings, mentally reviewing over and over the few bits that I *have* learned so I don't lose track. If there is any silver lining, it's that these weeks have allowed me to come to terms with the idea that demons and magic exist. Except now I'm that much more impatient to learn what else is out there in this strange world. A world I suspect is not my own in the most profound ways.

"I'll be back this evening to draw your bath and bring a freshly laundered dress." Corrin gives a pointed look at my nightgown, her eyes heavy with judgment. I've taken to not changing out of it as of late. The loose gauzy cotton is far lighter and more comfortable than the heavy layered silks and brocades, and what does it matter what I wear? I have nowhere to go. "Will there be anything else?"

I can tell she's holding her breath. She always asks me if there will be anything else and she *always* holds her breath, as if praying there isn't.

Do I even bother? "Can I please have a window opened? Just one? It gets hot in here in the afternoons, and some fresh air would be appreciated." If I'm not pacing, I'm staring through the panes at the expansive vista of treetops and, in the far distance, hints of forests and rolling hills. The glass doors leading to the balcony are locked, and the small panels on the grand windows that appear capable of opening have been secured, though I can't figure out how or why. My rooms must be several stories up—too high to climb down from. My ears catch hints of life below—the sounds of laughter, the clash of metal that I've figured out are sword blades—but I can't see the sources.

"I will share your request, *Your Highness*." That's been her standard response every time I've asked for something—a book, paper and pencil to draw with, access to the balcony, a different meal. And yet no book or paper has arrived, the balcony door remains locked, and I'm choking down another bowl of bland vegetable stew.

Corrin makes to leave.

"Could you also see if Annika can visit me?" I have nothing to lose by asking, and I'm desperate to speak with her again. Even if she despises me, she seems the most likely to go against the king's order and enlighten me.

Corrin's scowl is unmistakable. "The princess has been sequestered in her wing while she serves out her penance for helping *you*."

So, Zander has punished his sister after all. How long will she remain locked up? Not nearly as long as I will be, I'm sure.

The door to my suite swings open then and Wendeline passes through, carrying a jar of salve. An arm donning the black and gold of Cirilea's colors pulls the door shut behind her. I've never seen either of my guards' faces. The only reason I know they're men is by the sound of their voices. One carries a pleasant accent.

"If that is all, *Your Highness.*" Corrin spins on her heels and marches out before I can utter another word, barely offering Wendeline a curtsy in her rush to get away.

"Somehow she makes those two words sound like a spit in my face."

The priestess's eyebrows arch in question. "And what has offended her on this day, Your Highness?"

"I *dared* ask to open a window for some fresh air."

She hums her understanding. "Try not to take her disposition personally. It's simply safer for her if she keeps you at arm's length."

Because the king deems it so. Little human interaction. No fresh air. No books. No information about this world I'm trapped in. No television, no internet, no phone, because those things don't seem to exist here. Zander doesn't realize how effective his punishment is. I didn't fear being alone. I've been alone for years. But trapped like this, without being able to step outside, is suffocating. Lately, I feel like throwing my head back and shrieking at the top of my lungs.

"I think she genuinely *hates* me. Don't be surprised if she poisons my stew one of these days."

Wendeline's lips press together, and I can almost hear the words on the tip of her tongue: that it would be a poetic end, given what *I*'m accused of.

Despite the short stay and the lack of conversation, I've grown fond of the caster who tends to my injuries. She has a calm and nurturing presence that puts me at ease. Most important, if she wishes me dead, she hides it well. I look forward to her daily visits.

So many questions threaten to spill out, as they do every time I see her. Was she born with her power or is magic taught? How does it work? Who else has it? What can she do? But I hold my tongue firmly between my teeth. The king's order won't allow her to answer, but I fear my overwhelming curiosity and my ignorance will somehow reveal that I am an imposter in this world.

"How are your wounds today?" she asks.

"The same. I think." Raw and red and sore. Though they have healed greatly, there hasn't been any noticeable improvement since last week. Ignoring my food tray, though my stomach grumbles, I wander over to sit in my customary chair. It's positioned by the glass doors where Wendeline insists the light is best.

"It *is* warm in here," she murmurs, setting her jar on a nearby table.

"If only doors and windows were designed to open." My voice drips with sarcasm as I unfasten the tie at the front of my nightgown and push one side off, my modesty around her long gone.

A small smile of amusement touches her lips. "Perhaps your request will be accommodated."

"She's not even going to ask."

"The king requires that we report any requests you make, and Corrin is not foolish enough to withhold things from him out of spite."

"He wants to know what I *ask* for? Why?" So he can get satisfaction from *not* giving it to me?

"He is the king. He does not explain himself to anyone. But you and whatever plans you've made to steal his throne remain especially important to him."

So much for him not affording me any more thought. "But I've already failed at that, haven't I?"

Wendeline pushes my hair to one side and checks the two faint silver dots across my jugular. "Perhaps he worries that you will somehow send messages to your supporters who remain in hiding if, for example, you were to request for paper and graphite."

"I *did* ask for those, but it was to draw." I could entertain myself for hours if I could sketch faces and landscapes. It would make these monotonous days go by faster.

Her prodding touch is as gentle as always. "His Highness is in a precarious position. Someone in his household helped you plot against his family. His own sister released you. He does not fully trust *anyone* at the moment."

"He trusts you."

Her eyes flash to mine. "Enough to heal you, and no more."

And Corrin, enough to not lace my food with arsenic or whatever they use around here to poison people. And the night guard, to not slit my throat while I sleep. "So, you would tell him if I asked for anything?"

"I've sworn fealty to him. I have no wish to earn his wrath." Her mouth curls with a frown of satisfaction. "Your neck has mended well. The scars are almost invisible. One more session and they should be gone."

That, at least, is good news, but my thoughts are still hung up on Zander. He said he wanted nothing more to do with me—didn't want to see me or think about me—that day he came to inform me personally of my punishment, and yet he's getting daily updates? I'll bet he's hoping to catch me in a lie. Though, if that were the case, it'd be smarter to let me build relationships.

Nothing loosens lips faster than a sense of comfort. "What have you told him about me so far?"

"The truth. That the wounds on your shoulder are tricky to heal and that you've given no indication that you remember who you are or what you've done." She studies the claw marks. "I'm going to try something different. It might help with these. If not ... I'm not sure what more I can do." She takes a seat in a chair next to me, and opening the jar, she sets to smearing the paste over the unsightly gashes.

I inhale, expecting the mild, floral fragrance of the usual salve. Instead, my nostrils fill with a putrid stink. "Oh my ... what *is* that?" I turn away and gag. The only thing worse smelling would be the daaknar itself.

The corners of her eyes crinkle with her chuckle. "A great many things you would rather not know about, but most important is the *haldi*. A shipment of it arrived at the port the other day. I was able to secure this salve from the apothecary before it was gone, which was no small miracle."

I focus on breathing through my mouth while her fingertips stroke gently over my wounds. The only hint that the stench affects her is a slight flare of her nostrils. All the while my mind gathers her words. She said port, which means ships. Ships from where? Regardless, it means there's a way out of Islor, *if* I ever manage to escape.

Wendeline is far chattier today than she ever has been before. I press my luck. "Do you think he'll ever let me out of these rooms?"

It's a moment before she answers, and she is choosing her words carefully. "As of this moment, few people know for certain that you are still alive. There are whispers, of course. Questions of where your body may be and how you died. Plenty of rumors and speculation. The king has not officially confirmed or denied any of them, leaving both Islor and Ybaris in turmoil regarding the fate of Princess Romeria."

"Why hasn't he told them?"

"He has his motives," she answers cryptically. "There would need to be a purpose for allowing you to leave these rooms, and a reason why the kingdom would be better served with the knowledge that you are alive rather than dead. It *could* happen. With time, he *may* grant you freedom to roam the castle, with an escort."

"And outside?"

"I imagine so. The royal grounds, anyway."

"Not the sacred garden?"

Her eyes dart to me.

"Annika mentioned it," I lie, hoping no one ever calls my bluff.

"You mean the nymphaeum."

My heart skips a beat. *Nymphaeum.* Is that what they call it? Regardless, it's *exactly* where I need to go if I am to find this stone for Malachi. Malachi, who is one of their gods. I'm stealing an artifact from a sacred place. It's counterintuitive. Not that it matters. I'll do whatever is necessary to get back to my life—one where I'm no longer imprisoned or indebted to anyone. "What's so sacred about it?"

"That's where—" She halts abruptly, as if catching herself.

"That's where what?" I probe in as innocent a voice as I can muster. I don't want to get Wendeline in trouble with Zander, but I need to start collecting information should I ever hope to be free of these papered walls.

"It's a place where the people of Islor go for Hudem."

"*Hudem*?" I echo, letting the word dangle like bait on a hook.

She caps the jar of salve. "The night of the blood moon."

Both Sofie and Annika have mentioned this blood moon. It must be important. "What happens on that night?"

"Are you trying to get me flogged by the king?"

I wince, thinking of Korsakov whipping the skin off that lecher's back. "No. I was just curious." I hope I don't sound too eager. "And dying from boredom."

With a heavy sigh of resignation, she wipes the residual salve from her fingers on a cloth. I've often admired her fingernails—neatly sculpted, the beds long. "Those wishing to be blessed with a child go to the nymphaeum."

Annika said something about Zander and Princess Romeria "being blessed" with offspring. "The blood moon was the night of the attack."

"Yes. A royal wedding on Hudem. It was to be quite the affair." Her knowing eyes flicker to me.

I assume that means they would have gone into the nymphaeum after the ceremony. But instead, she had his parents murdered and inspired a war in the city streets.

It's impossible to feel guilty for something I haven't done, and yet *somehow* that uncomfortable twinge stirs in my gut. "When is the next blood moon?"

"It arrives every third lunar cycle of the common moon, to usher in the change of seasons with its brilliant light."

The common moon. That must be the second moon that sat high in the sky. But what is a lunar cycle here? Is it the same as the one at home? And will I still be trapped in these rooms for the next one? I look up to the ceilings. God help me if I am.

As if able to read my thoughts, Wendeline says, "Should the king grant you freedom from this room, do not do something as foolish as attempt to flee. I promise you won't get far, and I'll have wasted all my efforts on you."

"Because he'll string me up on that pyre he's saving for me. I remember." Under my breath, "monster" slips out.

"Many would say the same of you, whether you remember what you've done or not."

What does Wendeline think of me? The idea that she might feel the same pricks me more than I expect. She is my only ally here, and she likely reports my every word to Zander. What does Wendeline think of this young king who hates my guts? Is she loyal to him because she has to be or because she chooses to be?

I wish I could voice all the questions that have been swirling in my mind for the past three weeks. I'm used to relying on myself and trusting nobody, and yet here, trapped within these walls, I'm desperate for just one person to lean on, one person who can fill in all the blanks.

"Hold still for me. And do not talk." She places her hand over my shoulder, closes her eyes, and bows her head.

That god-awful smelling salve is new, but this part of her process is familiar, and no less fascinating now than the first day I witnessed it. At the time, I assumed she was praying, and that the faint tingling was the salve absorbing into my skin. But then she held up the mirror to show me that the lacerations were markedly smaller and less angry when she finished, and I realized she had to be healing me with her magic. Actual *magic*.

Now, I watch her furrowed forehead as she concentrates, enthralled. I can never tell how much time passes—there are no clocks, and bells only toll at the hour—but when her eyelids finally crack open, that familiar red tinge looms.

"Does it hurt you to do that?"

She shakes her head. "It tires me. I am nowhere near as powerful as Margrethe was. She was a healer too. She might have been able to do more for you." Her gaze settles on my shoulder and she smiles. "Yes, I think that is better." She eases out of her chair and slowly shuffles—another result of her healing—to the vanity to collect the handheld mirror.

Margrethe was the high priestess. I'm assuming that's a rank position. "Have they replaced her yet?"

"No. That is ... not an option."

"How many of you are there in Islor? Casters, I mean."

"Few remain now. It is quite the journey to get here, and most are not interested in taking the risk."

"Why not?"

"Because." I sense her shutting the door on that conversation. She lifts the mirror in front of me.

I check my reflection. The marks haven't shrunk much, but the raw redness of the knitted skin has faded noticeably.

"I'm sorry I couldn't do more. If we are lucky, the scars will turn silver. They may be almost invisible under certain light."

I highly doubt that. I'll never be able to wear a tank top or bathing suit—if I ever get out of this hellhole—without attracting notice, but it's a far cry better than what it was. I stretch my arm above my head. It's a bit stiff, but the ache is gone.

Wendeline caps the jar as I pull my nightgown back into place. "The salve will keep working through the night. I know it will be tempting, but do not wash it off when you bathe tonight. Whatever healing you have left will happen while you sleep. You can remove it in the morning." She nods to herself as she collects her things, as if satisfied. "Very well, then. Take care, Your Highness."

"Romy," I push, as I often do when she calls me that. Something about her farewell this time feels different, though. She doesn't normally curtsy that deeply. "I'll see you tomorrow?"

The doubtful look on her face answers me before her words do. "If the king deems it beneficial, but I've healed you as much as I can. I don't know that my skills will make any more difference."

If Wendeline doesn't come back, I'll be left with no one but Corrin and the footsteps of two guards. Dread tugs at my insides. "What about my mental health? Does the king *deem* to know when I lose my damn mind locked up in here?" I can't keep the bite from my tone. I hope the question reaches his ears. Maybe it'll satisfy him to know his punishment is working, enough that he'll relent.

Her attention veers toward the sealed windows, her brow furrowed deeply. "He is not the *monster* you think him to be."

Says the woman not being held prisoner by him. "He executes people. *Burns* them." From previous experience, those people are *all* monsters.

"And you would not?"

"No. I'm not my—" I cut my words off. *My mother.* Except we are no longer talking about Romeria from New York.

"His Highness did what *any* king or queen would do, given the situation. Your parents have executed traitors for far less." Her eyebrows arch as if daring me to challenge something she knows is the case. "As a queen, you would, as well."

Her early words spark something Annika said in the sanctum. So far, I've pieced together that Princess Romeria's marriage to Zander was arranged by her father, the king of Ybaris, under the guise of an effort for peace between the two kingdoms, though in reality, she was conspiring with an Islorian named Lord Muirn to raise an insurgent army and take the throne. Someone else—someone intricately connected to the royal family—helped her. And, on the day she was to marry Zander, when everyone was focused on a wedding and enemies easily flooded through the gates, her scheme unfolded. But obviously, all didn't go as planned.

What I still don't understand is, why Princess Romeria felt she needed to murder them in the first place.

I choose my words carefully. "Why would I do the horrible things I'm being accused of?"

"Why else does one kingdom fall but for another to rise?"

"I plotted to wipe out the king and his entire family, so I could have Islor's throne?" Which Princess Romeria was already destined for, as Zander's queen. Maybe she didn't want to share? But if Zander is right and she promised marriage to this Lord Muirn, then she would have had to share, anyway. It doesn't add up.

Setting the salve on the table again, Wendeline returns to my side. "You were taught from a young age that Islorians are your enemy. I know what that is like, to be raised with hatred for something you do not understand, for I was taught the same in Mordain. It can be hard to accept that you were wrong all this time about an entire people. But the Islorians are no different from you or me. We all want to sleep soundly in our beds and protect our loved ones."

She ties the strings of my gown, her fingers working unhurriedly. "I'll admit, *I* was afraid when I left my home to come here. I've found a life now, among them. But Ybaris has never tried to understand or accept them, not in all the centuries since the Great Rift. They're a people born of the same elven blood that courses through your veins, and yet you have labeled them demons and cast them from your lands."

My skin tingles. Did I hear that right? Did she say elven?

As in *elves*?

Is she saying I'm surrounded *not* by humans but by *elves*?

That Princess Romeria was *not* human?

Wendeline doesn't seem to notice the waves of shock slamming into me. "When I saw you and the king, how close you two were, I had hoped ..." Her words fade with her sigh.

She had hoped that we were truly in love, that our marriage would bring an end to whatever strife exists between the two kingdoms and people, just as Annika hoped.

Elves.

"The mortals of Islor have learned to coexist with the immortals, and while there is still friction, the crown has made many strides." She bites her bottom lip in thought. "If you would open your heart and your mind, you would see they are not the barbaric fiends we were taught to see them as. In fact, you may find a kinship with them."

Elven.

Immortals.

I force myself to keep engaging, though my thoughts spiral with all this new information. "A kinship from my prison cell, with the constant threat of death?"

She hesitates, then lowers her voice to say, "Somehow, you killed a daaknar. At the moment, you're the only one in *all* of Islor who can do that."

People tend to keep those of value alive longer. Sofie's words echo in my head. "I'm more useful to the king alive than dead."

Wendeline confirms it with a knowing look. "Take whatever comfort you can in that." She collects her things again.

"Thank you. For everything. You've been kind to me."

She purses her lips. "I believe you shall see some freedoms

soon, now that you are mostly healed. But when that happens, do not expect you will find *any* allies within these walls."

"Right." A not-so-subtle warning to not trust anyone. Perhaps not even her.

"And Romeria?" She pauses at the threshold to my sitting room. It's the first time she's used my name. "Assume the king is always one step ahead of you and listening closely." With one last hard look, she departs.

That night, I toss and turn in a fitful sleep. The stench of Wendeline's salve fills my nostrils, and its burn toils away inside my wounds while elves and demons torment my dreams.

But it is the tall, regal figure I sense looming over me that wakes me with a gasp. I search the dark corners of my room, only to find them empty.

And yet long after I close my eyes, I feel the lingering shadow of a king.

I wake to a knock on my bedroom door. A second later, Corrin barges in. "Are you ill?" There isn't a hint of concern in her tone.

"I didn't sleep well," I say groggily. I watch Corrin as she sets a tray of food on the small desk in the corner. What is she? I assume not a caster like Wendeline. She looks human, but so does everyone else I've encountered, and now I know some of them are elven.

Barbaric fiends, whatever that means. Corrin's personality is brackish, but I wouldn't call her barbaric.

I've read countless stories and watched many films about fantastical creatures, enough that the term triggered a myriad of ideas to dwell on late into last night—everything from sharp physical features and unnaturally long lives, to arrogance and wicked manipulation, to supernatural speed and powers tied to nature. I'm having a hard time applying fable to fact, though. Wendeline called them immortal, but they also assumed Princess Romeria dead, so immortal does not mean unkillable. I have yet to see any odd-looking appendages. Everyone appears human.

Everyone including *me*.

Am I not supposed to be elven too?

Except I'm not, I'm human. These limbs, this face, my thoughts … they're human limbs, a human face, and human thoughts. They're all that I know. So how am I to tell the difference between everyone else?

And how has Wendeline *not* discovered what I am yet? She's been healing this body for weeks. Certainly her magic would notice a difference in *species*?

Unless … the fleeting thought that this somehow isn't *my* body that I'm in but Princess Romeria's, resurrected, skitters through my thoughts yet again. It is the only viable explanation.

"The king has requested an audience with you." Corrin sets a mug of drinking water on my nightstand, pausing to sniff the air. She grimaces. "Did you *not* bathe last night?"

"Wendeline told me to not wash off the salve," I explain, distracted. *Zander wants an audience?* He was adamant he never wanted to see me again. *Why now?*

"Come, we must hurry. You cannot present yourself in your nightgown, smelling like a fermented fish." She draws back the lengthy curtains, and I blink against the blinding sunlight that streams in. It's the first time I haven't been awake and pacing before sunrise since my imprisonment.

One by one, she pries the window panels open. Laughter that was once muffled now carries to my ears, raucous and clear. Somewhere nearby, birds sing.

A quick twist of her wrists releases the balcony doors, and she throws them open, too.

I gape for a moment. "How did you do that?"

"I turned the knob, *Your Highness*."

I've rattled those doorknobs a hundred times, *at least*, and they haven't budged. I roll my eyes at her back, even as a victorious warmth swells in my chest. Zander must have approved my request.

"I will draw a fresh bath. When you have finished *properly* washing, don the blue dress that I leave out for you. It should suitably cover those scars so no one sees them during your escort."

While I know my injuries are far from appealing to look at, her words are a sharp prick to my confidence.

"Put your nightgown in the hamper and I'll have it laundered." Under her breath, I hear her mutter, "If there's any salvaging it." As quickly as she stormed in, she departs.

I clamber out of bed to dart for the door. The sun is high in the sky and blazing, its heat roasting the balcony's stone, but I barely notice the burn against my bare feet, too busy gaping at the splendor before me.

I arrived in Cirilea in the cover of night, and my brief travels within the city have been beneath hoods and blankets and through underground tunnels and dark stairwells. I had yet to even glimpse this castle I've been incarcerated in, beyond a cold tower and my papered walls.

It's like nothing I could ever have imagined.

Stone the color of pale sand shapes walls that are sculpted into countless pointed arches. Multiple towers reach into the sky, and the spires—I count a dozen from where I stand, though there are surely more—are capped in rich burgundy pinnacles and adorned with a contrasting black detailing. The windows are massive, copious, and ornate, with geometric patterns crafted by an artist's hand.

If I'm reading the sun's position correctly, I'm on the third and top floor of the east side, though it feels so much higher given the height of the ceilings. A mirror of this wing stretches from the other side of a center section. Only the top floors have these circular balconies, all supported by a complex construction of pillars and stonework beneath. There must be *hundreds* of rooms within this place.

Peeling my stunned gaze from the castle for a moment, I shift my focus to the grounds below. It looks more like a botanical park, the manicured space stretching far, most of it obscured from my view by foliage. Intricately laid stone paths meander around leafy trees, beneath vine-clad trellises, along ponds, over decorative bridges. I hazard a person could get lost in that expanse, even without the cedar labyrinth.

The wall I escaped through that first night surrounds the entire vast grounds and on the other side of it, below the ridge, are lush, green rolling hills and dense forest as far as the eye can see. The city of Cirilea must be located on the other side of the castle.

And somewhere within this space has to be the nymphaeum.

I inhale. There is a faint, familiar scent in the air, though I can't place it.

A shout calls out, followed by a clash of metal. I seek out the source. Nimble bodies are sparring with swords in a courtyard to my right. Many are men, though I spot the feminine curves of several women. Back and forth, they parry in pairs, an intricate, skilled dance, their blades gleaming in the sunlight, proving they are not mere wooden props.

I smile as I admire their proficiency and fearlessness. That takes so much more talent than pointing a gun and pulling a trigger, and can be just as deadly, if Sofie proved anything in the warehouse that night. While I don't envy her talents as a cold-blooded murderess, learning how to throw a dagger to stop a threat is a skill I wouldn't mind acquiring.

These people must practice often. Are they the royal guard? Or maybe nobility? Do they live within these grand walls? Someone other than Zander and his two siblings—and unfortunate prisoners such as I—*must* occupy these rooms. Just one of these wings could house multiple families.

My gaze sweeps across the castle again. There, on the palatial balcony overlooking the sparring courtyard, a man with hair that gleams gold in the sunlight, dressed in all black, leans against the railing.

Even from this distance, I know it's Zander, and while it appears he's watching the action below, my gut tells me his attention is not on them.

Wendeline said there would need to be a reason to let me out of my rooms, to let people know I'm still alive. I'm being escorted somewhere, which means people will see me. What does he have planned for me?

The brief excitement over my window victory fades. I skulk inside to prepare for what is to come.

My fingers are occupied with the tiny, embroidered flowers on my skirts as the guard leads me down flights of stairs and along the seemingly infinite corridors of the castle. I struggle to remain composed as I take in the opulence. Floors of marble in tones from a rich charcoal to a bottomless black gleam beneath the candlelight of enormous candelabras, lit to counter the moody darkness inside, a stark contrast to the gushing sunlight outside the windows. Gilded pillars reach to the domed ceilings, where a vast and endless mural begs for attention.

Footfalls and voices echo, and everywhere we pass, people stare and whispers follow. At least the servants are more discreet. The nobility—I assume, based on their richly colored silk clothing and gleaming jewels on their sword hilts—openly gawk.

I guess I've earned that notoriety, given who they think I am and what they think I've done. Or, more likely, it's because they thought I was dead. I'm suddenly thankful to Corrin for ensuring the dress she brought did an adequate job of hiding my scars. The foul-smelling salve did wonders, slogging away through the night as Wendeline promised, but the dragging claw marks on my shoulder are far from invisible, and it will take time for my confidence to come to terms with them. I don't like this attention, but I can't avoid it, so I hold my chin high and return the favor of staring.

What are they?

Human?

Caster?

Elven?

How am I to know? They all look *just like me.*

And what is it about the Islorians—elven by blood—that would make the Ybarisans hate them? What would make Ybaris cast them from their lands? Does it have something to do with their church and the gods they bow to? It's far from unheard of, for a belief system to cause friction and war. A *Great Rift,* as Wendeline called it.

Some of the servants bow as I pass. I note that they all wear the same jewelry Corrin wears—an inner conch piercing that loops around the cartilage of the right ear in a gold cuff an inch wide. The metal is engraved with a symbol, but she has never come close enough for me to decipher it.

It isn't just the servants who wear them, I note. Several young women and men in fine clothing also have their ear pierced in the same manner.

The guard accompanying me—a tall, slim man with dark curls and tawny brown skin—reminds me of a volunteer at one of the soup kitchens. Becks was a bank manager who doled out food to the needy the first Sunday of every month. He always had a broad smile and a second helping for me.

This guy hasn't smiled once, though, and keeps his hand on the hilt of his sword at all times, watching my every move from the corner of his eye, as if expecting me to bolt or attack.

Is he human or elven?

His rich brown eyes flash to me, and I realize I'm staring at him.

"How much farther is it?" Half of me could walk forever without reaching our destination. The other half would prefer to get this *audience* over with.

"About thirty paces, Your Highness," he answers civilly, his voice hinting of his accent. Maybe not everyone despises me as Corrin does. I decide to test that out. "How did you get so lucky?"

He frowns. "I do not understand the question."

"You're at my door every night, for at least twelve hours. You normally change your shift at the sevens, except you're still here, escorting me. That's a long day. Does the king not believe in sleep?"

His steady march falters. "How did you know it was me?"

"You have a slight spring in your step, and you're better at polishing your boots than the day guard."

Another beat passes and then the corners of his mouth curl. Is he picturing me with my face pressed against the floor? It's the only way anyone could pick up on something as minute as foot-fall pattern and basic cleanliness while locked inside that room. He dips his head. "Not to worry. I will have my rest soon, Your Highness."

We stop where two grim-faced guards secure a hall. The one on the right spins and leads us down. At the end is a set of double doors, and loud angry voices behind it.

My blood pounds in my ears as the guard pushes open the door.

"—someone give me a name!" Zander roars. "How are we not capable of even that much!"

I find myself standing in a tall, circular, windowless room, surrounded by hostile faces.

"We will have it soon, Your Highness." Boaz bows his head, his voice apologetic even as his words make promises.

The king of Islor is hunched over a round table, his palms splayed on either side of an enormous map, his golden-brown locks falling in disarray, his jaw tense with fury and frustration. When he lifts and affixes that probing gaze on me, I struggle not to squirm. It's been weeks since I've faced him, and the swirl of fear, confusion, and anxiety that instantly rises threatens to stall my lungs.

My guard bows once and ducks out, leaving me to face two people I've never seen before and two I wished I didn't have to see again.

I force my shoulders straight under their hard eyes. This must be his war council, as Annika called it. There are three others present in addition to Zander, and all are dressed in various versions of a black-and-gold, save for the woman who wears head-to-toe russet-brown leather. Hair the color of ripe wheat is pulled into three thick braids that reach to her hips. A long, thin scar follows her hairline, from the center of her forehead down to her right earlobe.

A man with a brawny frame and cropped golden-blond hair that hints of curls stands to her left. He looks young, only a few years older than I am.

None of them appear pleased to see me.

"Princess Romeria, how nice of you to grace us with your presence." Zander pulls himself up to his full height. He's at least a head taller than everyone in the room, save for Boaz. "I trust your *accommodations* are to your satisfaction." The corner of his mouth twitches.

If Wendeline repeated my plea that she continue visiting me, then he must suspect I'm pacing my "accommodations" like a feral animal in captivity. He's toying with me for his amusement. That makes him an ass. He *did* have the locks on the windows and balcony released, though.

And he can have them put back in place.

I quell my natural urge to respond with anything but courtesy. I'm not dealing with Tony or any of Korsakov's other brutes. "They're fine. Thanks."

"You will address the king with respect!" Boaz snaps, his face turning red with anger. I haven't seen him since he threw me into the tower. I would have happily avoided him for eternity.

Zander waves a dismissive hand. "At ease, Captain. She has forgotten proper decorum, what with her recent bout of total memory loss. Rumor has it she's taken to wandering around her balcony in her nightdress."

Derisive chuckles carry through the room, and I feel my cheeks flush. He's mocking me, making me look the fool.

"And the servant I selected for you, I hope she's meeting your needs? She's one of our finest."

He handpicked the saltiest woman in the castle and probably gave her carte blanche to treat me like a pariah. "She's an utter delight, *Your Highness*." I don't mean the address to come out sounding hostile, but I realize how satisfying it is. No wonder Corrin is always doing it to me.

Something dark flashes in Zander's eyes, and I instantly regret my cheekiness.

Boaz charges forward.

"Leave it." Zander's sharp tone slices through the air, stopping him dead. "We have more pressing matters."

The captain stops abruptly, but with a withering glare and clenched fists. I'll bet he's imagining putting another arrow through me. He despises me. The feeling is mutual.

Zander collects a tiny roll of paper from the table and stretches it out between two fingers. Unfurled, it's much longer than it first appears. "'King Barris is dead,'" he reads out loud.

They're all staring, waiting for my response. Clearly, it's supposed to mean something to me. "That's … unfortunate?" I offer.

Zander's head cocks, his expression turning curious. "I tell you that your father is dead, and your answer is 'that's unfortunate'?"

King Barris is Princess Romeria's father. The king of Ybaris. That makes sense.

"Heartless," Boaz mutters.

My father is likely curled up on a grungy street in New York, warning everyone about demons, I want to say, but I bite my tongue and wait, hoping to glean more information from whatever they're about to accuse me of. That's how our conversations always unfold.

"I guess the rumors of your dislike for him were true, despite what you once told me." The king tosses the paper to join a collection of others of varying sizes. "Aren't you the least bit curious to know *when* he died? *How* he died? Or should I assume that's old news for you?"

"No. I mean, yes, please tell me." Any snippet could be useful in figuring out where I am and how to get out of here. I can practically hear Boaz's molars grinding, so I cap my request with a delayed "Your Highness," more conciliatory this time.

"He died the same day of the attack on Cirilea. A fatal blade to the heart. Much faster than being poisoned with deliquesced merth."

That silver rope that was bound to Annika. That's what she called it: merth. I take it that's how the princess killed Zander's parents. Did they eat it? Drink it? Was it a tainted dagger tip that did them in? I guess it doesn't matter. Any one of those versions is terrible.

"This news, of course, sheds new light on the situation." His footfalls echo through the chamber as he paces around the table. "The fact that King Barris, who forged this alliance between Ybaris and Islor, died in such a tragic and intentional manner on the same day as the king and queen of Islor, and yet Queen Neilina remains unscathed, suggests that your father had intentions of honoring the arrangement. Your mother, however, had other plans." My nose catches a sweet woodsy scent as he approaches, stopping just before me. "Did you scheme together, or were you simply carrying out her mission?"

The wall of chest, much too close for my liking, forces my eyes upward. I meet his frosty gaze.

"What was the plan, for her to rule Ybaris, and you, Islor? Or would she insist on ruling both, being the power-starved tyrant that she is?"

Behind him, Boaz shifts his weight, his hand on his sword, as if he might need to spring forward and protect his king at any moment against me, the unarmed woman in the pale blue dress.

I swallow against the growing tension in the room. "I can't—"

"Yes, yes. You can't recall. That part, *I* remember," Zander cuts me off, his tone bored, dismissive. He pivots and continues his pacing. "Of course, your mother has claimed that Islor are the perpetrators behind their beloved King Barris's death, that we *somehow* crossed the Great Rift into Ybaris and assassinated him as a means of ending an alliance we did not want. She's claimed *we've* murdered *you*." He snorts. "Ironic, no? And according to rumor, we have refused to deliver your body for proper burial, as would be civilized. But of course, Islorians are so brutal and uncultured, we've done unspeakable and savage things to your body. She's using her vast network of spies and messengers to spread these falsities through Ybaris like a virulent plague, flaring a fresh wave of hatred for everyone and everything south of the rift. No doubt her army will be double before long."

What he's alluding to finally clicks. "You think the queen had the king killed."

"Neilina has been described as cold and cunning. Dare I say that's a tree whose fruit hasn't fallen far." He shoots a dirty look my way. "It would certainly explain why the commander of her royal army is now warming her bed, barely a fortnight after her husband's death."

My eyes widen at that salacious morsel. Dear queen mother was having an affair with her war leader behind her husband the king's back? "Please tell me he's not her twin brother," I murmur under my breath.

Zander's eyebrows arch. "Pardon?"

I clear my throat. "Nothing."

He opens his mouth but then clamps it shut, his fingers aimlessly flittering through the unfurled papers as thoughts seem to occupy his mind. They're messages, I realize. Some are folded, with broken wax seals of various colors. Official correspondence to the king. Others are tiny scrolls of paper likely sent by spies that could be hidden in sleeves and pockets or shoes. Or maybe tied to carrier pigeons? I've always been intrigued by the idea that birds could be trained to deliver secret messages.

"Who are your soldiers working with in Islor?" the woman asks, her tone harsh. She's the smallest of the group but looks no less threatening, her limbs muscular, her leather vest marred with stitches from various tears.

I pick through my memories. "I thought it was Lord Muirn?" Wasn't that the man I was accused of conspiring with?

"And yet our ears tell us that *someone* is still rallying Islorians against the king," Boaz says. "They may be working with the Ybarisans. The ones who managed to flee Cirilea that night."

My thoughts veer to the man who tried to drown Annika. Is he Ybarisan or Islorian? Human or elven? He was strong. He threw Annika and the boulder over the rail with inhuman ease, so ... elven? And how many more of *my* people are out there?

This is what Zander was raging about when I entered the room. Someone is still threatening his throne. I guess that's par for the course—there's always someone who wants to be king.

I shake my head. "I have no idea."

The woman's lips curl in a vicious smile. "Perhaps we will *find* an idea beneath your skin when I peel it from your body."

"Enough with the idle threats," Zander cuts her off with a heavy sigh, though nothing in that woman's cold stare suggests her threat is idle. "Elisaf!" he barks.

The door creaks open, and a moment later, my nighttime guard is standing at attention beside me.

"Her Highness has offered me all the insight she is able or willing. Please escort her back to her prison cell." Zander turns his attention back to his map, his brow furrowed deeply.

He's clearly concerned about this threat and he was hoping I would be able to provide insight where others could not. Though, he could have come to my rooms to ask. There was no need to parade me through the castle, in effect revealing that Princess Romeria is still alive, a card Wendeline alluded to him only playing when it made sense. So, was there another reason to bring me here?

Elisaf bows and gives me the subtlest nod, beckoning for me to follow. Far more civilized than being manhandled by the likes of Boaz.

But my memory is caught on something. I hesitate, torn between getting out of here as fast as possible and providing information that *might* earn me some goodwill. "Is there a place called … Lindor? Or something like that?" The name reminded me of chocolates.

Zander's joyless gaze is back on me. "Lyn*del*?"

"That might have been it."

His eyes narrow. "What about it?"

"That night the man tried to drown Annika—"

"The sapling?"

"Sure." I need to figure out what that means. "Anyway, he knew me, and he mentioned that place."

"Why?"

I shrug. "He told me to go to Lyndel and then he dumped your sister over the rail and ran."

Zander looks to Boaz. "I struggle to believe that Lord Telor would betray the crown like that. He has always been supportive."

"As do I." The brooding captain's mouth curves in a thoughtful frown. "But *someone* is helping the Ybarisans. *Someone* is swaying loyalty. We've already scoured Lord Muirn's lands. Our spies have heard nothing in Kettling. Now we must look at those we least expect. Lyndel is close enough to the mountain range. They could be harboring dozens of them in that stronghold for all we know. And his men are formidable. If we don't have their full support at the rift, it is best we know now." His eyes cut to me. "It could also be a trap, though the princess would be a daft fool to spring such a thing, given she is imprisoned here."

"I'm telling you what I remember." I clear the shake from my voice. "It could be nothing, or it could be something."

"I will take my men there to investigate," the man with the short golden curls says. He's been silent up until now, his hateful blue eyes locked on me, watching my every twitch.

"Telor will be wary of the commander of *the king*'s army arriving at his doorstep," Boaz counters. "Besides, you are needed elsewhere, Atticus."

Atticus. That name rings a bell. Zander mentioned him in the tower. That's his brother, the one who was shot with an arrow the night of the attack. I study the man again. A prince, I suppose. He looks nothing like Zander, but he bears a remarkable similarity to his sister from what I remember of her. He is strikingly handsome with high cheekbones and full lips, though I would dare say not so attractive as the king.

Zander grips his chin in thought, his gaze on the map. "What do you recommend, Captain?"

I note how Atticus's jaw tenses.

Boaz nods toward the woman who threatened to skin me. "Send Abarrane and a handful of her soldiers there with a summons. Have Atticus split our forces. Prepare half to march on Lyndel if needed and keep the other half fanned out along here"—Boaz drags a finger across the map—"to catch any contingents moving for Cirilea. Any who reach these walls, I will manage with the royal guard."

Atticus opens his mouth to speak, but Zander lifts a hand, stalling his brother's words.

His lips press into a thin line. He seems to be weighing his captain's opinion over his brother's, also in a high-ranked position. Boaz looks maybe two decades older than Zander, who I doubt has reached thirty, but there is a wisdom in his eyes only earned with experience. He is clearly one of the few people Zander trusts after what happened to his parents.

What must it be like to be thrust into the position of king so suddenly, and so young?

Then again, they're not human. How old are any of them, really?

This constant questioning of *everything* I know … it's enough to drive a person insane.

"Very well." Zander nods toward the woman—Abarrane, I gather. "I will provide you with a summons letter. Seek shelter at Lord Telor's stronghold before escorting him here, under the pretext of important courtly matters. Search for any evidence of Ybarisans, but not openly. I do not wish to cause discord with one of our strongest supporters, especially considering our source."

"Your Highness." She bows deeply and then, spinning on leather boots, storms out, slowing long enough to spare me a contemptuous glare.

I avert my eyes, letting them fall on the expansive canvas stretched across the table, on the oddly shaped land mass that looks to be hand drawn in ink and surrounded by water. It's too far from me to read any of the script.

"That will be all," Zander says.

I take that as my signal, and I turn to follow Elisaf out.

"Not you."

My back stiffens. Somehow, I know without looking that he's talking to me.

Atticus's cold, calculating gaze is on me as he passes. He slows long enough to whisper, "How unfortunate it is that you didn't choose someone more skilled with a bow." His hand curls around the hilt of his sword, as if to make a point. Surely, he'd use it on me, if his brother would allow it.

I'm sure I've had people curse the thief who made off with their jewels, but I've never had so many people wish me dead to my face.

Everyone files out, and I'm left alone, standing across the table from the man who decides whether those wishes are fulfilled.

The moments drag without a single sound as I wait impatiently and try not to stare at him, my curiosity about his elven kind competing with the anxiety I feel, knowing he would much rather have me dead. He *needs* me, though, should another daaknar show up. A reality that must burn his insides. Is that the only reason I'm still alive?

What would he do if one did suddenly appear? Throw me to it like chum to a shark so it can sink its fangs into me?

Princess Romeria chose to murder a king and queen and lead an insurrection rather than marry this man. Is it as Wendeline says? Was that choice about power and deep-seated hatred? Or is there something more?

Still, he says nothing. Is he waiting for me to grovel at his feet for my release? I haven't reached that point of desperation—yet. But I'm not here to win a battle of wills. That would be stupid. I clear my voice. "Thank you, for taking the locks off the balcony."

He doesn't acknowledge my appreciation, instead gesturing toward the map. "Go ahead."

I hesitate.

"You seem extremely interested in it, and I would prefer you interrogate me rather than my caster on matters of our kingdoms. Besides, there's nothing here you haven't seen before."

I highly doubt that.

What has Wendeline repeated of our conversations? I'm beginning to assume *everything*. Did she tell him that I called him a monster? Would he care?

I approach the table cautiously, struggling to ignore the feel of his gaze on me, like cool fingertips against my skin. I tilt my head to better read, feeling a slight pull where the daaknar bit my neck, even though the marks are now invisible.

The map is drawn in ink and intricately detailed, on paper or canvas much thicker than anything I've ever seen. I don't have anything to judge scale, but the various mountain ranges would suggest a vast expanse of land. Off the southwest corner of Islor is Seacadore, separated by Fortune's Channel. In the southeast, Islor connects with Kier. In the north, Ybaris borders a large country named Skatrana. To the northeast is an island called Mordain.

"Something perplexes you," Zander murmurs.

More like something is becoming shockingly clear. "Is this the only map you have?" I struggle to keep my voice calm.

"No, but it's the most extensive one of the lands." He folds his arms over his chest. "Why? Do you believe something to be missing?"

The Americas, Europe, Africa, Australia ... I may not be a geography expert, but I know enough to recognize that this is not any of those continents, in any time frame.

It is far from here.

I calm my breathing. "What other places are there? Like, on the *other* side of this Endless Sea?"

"Espador and Udral, but we don't concern ourselves with them. They are too far for benefits of regular trade."

There's no way people in North America or the other continents would *not* know of this place. It's too big to be missed.

I slide into the empty chair to hide the fact that my legs are wobbling.

"Please, make yourself comfortable," Zander mocks, but he's watching me closely. After a moment, he offers, "You are suddenly rather pale, and I would prefer you not collapse on my table. I have work to do." His eyes flicker to my shoulder where my scars are concealed. "Should I call for Wendeline?"

What could the caster tell me about sending people to other worlds with magic? Perhaps *everything*. And perhaps admitting that I'm not from this world is precisely what will make Zander decide I am, in fact, *not* more valuable to him alive than dead, daaknar or not.

I shake my head. I'll gather that information some other way. For now, I should learn as much as I can from this map while Zander seems willing to share information. "Have you been here?" I point to Seacadore.

"Yes. Islor can produce most everything it needs on our lands, but there are things we enjoy. Their latest ruler, Empress Roshmira, is an especially keen partner in commerce."

Commerce like the ingredients for Wendeline's salve, I imagine. I tap Mordain. "And Wendeline's from here, right?"

He stares at me without answering for so long that I begin to fear I've earned the priestess a flogging for admitting even that much about herself.

"Yes, she is," he finally confirms, his tone calm, conversational. "As are *all* casters."

"They're *all* from this island?"

"No, but they are sent there at an early age to receive their training. Afterward, they are required to serve Ybaris."

"But not Islor?" Like Wendeline and Margrethe?

His lips twist. "Ybaris does not allow them passage through the rift to come here."

"Why not?" My questions are tumbling from my mouth without touching a scale first to decide if my curiosity might be dangerous.

"Because Ybaris does not want Islor having access to *any* of the casters' power."

The "why" is on the tip of my tongue, but I sense Zander's irritation growing, so I hold it and refocus on the map, tracing the path from the island, through Ybaris, to where the cartographer illustrated a long, jagged canyon across the mountains. Great Rift is written across it. Wendeline wasn't talking about a great rift as some sort of schism in their relationship. Or at least, not entirely.

This Great Rift is a literal split between the two kingdoms.

The only viable passage across on land is through an ominous sounding Valley of Bones, but he's saying they're not permitted to go through there. "So Wendeline got here by ship, then?" I follow the map south from Mordain, through the Grave Deep.

"Not that way. In two thousand years, no one has ever survived that sailing route. They traveled across Ybaris, into Skatrana, boarded a ship from Westport"—his long index finger traces the path to a port city in the far west—"to Seacadore, and then crossed the water to our port."

I see now that Cirilea is on the southwest side. A channel cuts into the land, leading ships directly to it. "That's a long way to travel to get here." Wendeline did say as much.

"And I appreciate her for it."

"Enough to flog her just for talking to me?" It slips out before I can stop myself.

"You forget yourself," he warns through gritted teeth.

I bite my tongue and study the smaller details on the map—the towns and castles. Lyndel, where that man told me to run, is north, past the dense forest, protected on the north and west by the mountain ridge, in the south by hills. To the east is a great expanse of land where the towns are numerous. "What is this? The Plains of Aminadav," I read out loud.

That question earns me an eyebrow twitch—of surprise or amusement, I'm unsure. "That is the reason your father wanted this union in the first place."

"He wanted *land*?" My arranged marriage to this guy is over *property*?

"We would never *give* him any part of Islor, not even for you. But he wanted what the plains produces, for your people." Zander lifts a leg and settles on the side of the table. It's an oddly casual pose and different from what I pictured—him sitting stiffly on his throne. "The plains have the most fertile soil in both our realms. The crops harvested there are plentiful, year after year. It easily sustains all of Islor. Ybaris, on the other hand, has boglands and dead woods. It's overcrowded and has been plagued with blights and disease for centuries. Your kingdom cannot sustain itself for much longer, no matter how much of the casters' magic you wield to try to fix it."

"So, you and I were supposed to get married and then Ybaris would have access to these farmlands?"

"To a percentage of its harvest, yes. As well as resources from our mines."

Princess Romeria was a bargaining chip. The only one? "And what would Islor get in return? Besides my delightful company."

His jaw tenses, and I quietly chastise myself. Angering him

won't get me more information. "Ybaris would send us casters and twenty thousand mortals to work the lands. They would ensure safe passage through the rift, and we would help them reestablish in Islor. Give them homes and jobs. Your father knew some would take issue with this proposal, with the idea of trading so many mortal Ybarisans to Islor and giving us access to caster magic, but he hoped they'd see the benefit in time, once their bellies were full of the food it produced, and their strongest were not sent to slaughter in battle."

I eye the map again where the two countries share a border. *The Valley of Bones.* "I take it there are a lot of bodies down there?"

"There is far worse than that down there," he murmurs, more to himself. He shakes his head. "Your father wanted to help his people, and his own family killed him for it. I cannot imagine what his dying thoughts would have been." His eyes flicker to me, as if testing my reaction.

He won't get one. I'm too curious to feel empathy for a stranger at the moment. "Why wouldn't the queen … my mother"—I test that out—"want that too?"

"Neilina?" he scoffs. "Because she is hungry for power and wants our land for herself, and she would gladly watch every last one of us burn. She has been the serpent whispering of war and conquer in your father's ear for centuries. Her in one ear, and Caedmon in the other. I don't know how he resisted it."

Centuries.

He's saying Princess Romeria's parents were king and queen for hundreds of years.

I clear the shock from my voice. "How old are you?"

A slow, vicious smile touches his lips. "Oh, come now. And to think the idea of someone much older than you was *so* appealing before. What was it you said to me …" He bites his bottom lip, but something tells me it's all an act. I doubt he has to search his thoughts for anything. "You were happy to marry someone so much more *experienced.*" His gaze drops to my mouth. "Actually, happy was not it. *Eager to learn* were the words you used."

"I did *not* say that."

"Do you want to know what other things you whispered in my ear—"

"*No.*" I feel my face burn.

His expression smooths over. "Good, because I'd much rather scrub those memories from my mind forever."

What must Zander have been like when he didn't despise me? A flash of the night in the tower hits me, of those few brief moments when his anger gave way to pain and desperation. I remember the look in his eyes. He wasn't hateful. He was vulnerable, hurt. He was still in love.

He hasn't answered my question. I try a different tactic. "How old am *I*?"

"Just a baby." He pauses, as if deciding how much more to reveal. "You just passed your twenty-fifth year."

Princess Romeria was twenty-five. *Is* twenty-five? Is she dead, or am I? Regardless, she is four years older than I am. Another piece of the puzzle to stew over.

"Why are you willing to tell me all this now?" What does he *really* want with me?

"Because if there is any shred of truth to this story of yours, perhaps filling in some blanks will help jog your memory. And then, *perhaps*, you will be inclined to share what you know. Now, if you have no other questions about the map, I have important letters to dispatch. We'll see if that scant detail you provided is of any use at all." He doesn't wait for my response, sliding off the table and moving for a chair on the opposite side. "Elisaf!"

My guard steps in again.

"Please escort Her Highness out of my sight."

"Yes, Your Highness." Another deep bow. Do they get tired of the same stuffy salutations all the time?

I rise, hoping my legs don't betray me. This audience wasn't as dreadful as I'd anticipated. At least Zander has given me plenty to digest while I'm back in my rooms. Or out on the balcony. "Thank you for allowing me some fresh air."

"You already said that," he mutters, annoyed.

"I know. I just ... I'm grateful." *Everything* I have, I have by the grace of this man who hates me.

His expression is stony, unreadable. "I heard your rooms were in need of airing out."

My nose scrunches at the memory of the salve. Corrin dumped so much lavender and jasmine in my bathwater, I was plucking petals off my skin even after I'd dried myself. I returned to my bedchamber with incense burning in a corner and my bed stripped.

How does he know, though? I answer my own question with my next thought. Wendeline must have told him. Maybe she urged him to accommodate my request, if anyone besides Boaz dares urge the king.

His attention is on the lengthy white feather he dips into an inkwell when he says, "They may remain open, but they can just as easily be shut. Do not get any ideas of escape. A guard will put an arrow through you before you reach the ground, and if you come back from the dead *again*, you'll find yourself in the tower cell for good and a caster will not be there to heal your wounds."

Noted.

I hesitate. "It would be great if Wendeline could keep checking in on me."

The corner of his mouth pulls. "So, *that*'s what you're after. She has informed me that you have healed sufficiently." Again, his eyes dart to my shoulder. Would he consider my scars as grotesque as Corrin makes them out to be?

"I am. I'm just ..." I'm lonely. I haven't felt it so acutely in so long. That's what he wants, though. No friends, no family, no allies. "I appreciate her company."

"What you appreciate is of no concern to me. Priestess Wendeline is terribly busy with duties far more essential than entertaining a prisoner. You may *go now*." He adjusts his sheet of paper and sets to writing, his jaw tense.

"Thank you, *Your Highness.*" It doesn't sound nearly as contrite as I mean it to.

Zander's eyes break from his page to snap to me.

I duck out quickly behind Elisaf. Tony was right. My smart mouth will get me into trouble one day.

One by the statue.

One circling the gazebo.

At least two pacing the lengths of the exterior wall, disappearing into the cedar abyss.

Are the royal castle grounds always so guarded at night? Or is it because of the recent attack?

Or maybe it's because I'm out here.

I wrap my bedsheet tighter around my shoulders as I play spot the guard in the tranquil garden below. The air has a slight bite to it now that the sun has been replaced by a moon—the common moon, I'm guessing—that is three-quarters full and offering a mere fraction of the light that the blood moon did. I don't mind the darkness, though. I've been outside all afternoon since returning to my rooms, so long that my cheeks feel tight from the sun.

Can elves get sunburns?

I have so many questions still, but I hesitate asking. I would think that under normal circumstances, it wouldn't make sense for me to be struck with amnesia and suddenly forget what it means to be human, to believe myself to be a cat or a bird, so why would I forget what it means to be elven?

They all think I'm elven, so elven I need to be. I will get my answers somehow.

My attention wanders to the main section of the sprawling castle, to the balcony where Zander stood earlier today. Is he there, somewhere within the shadows? More than likely he's below, beyond those doors where people filter in and out and the sounds of laughter and violin notes carry.

He handed me several clues to a grand, confusing riddle, and by his own admission, he did it because he's finally entertaining the idea that I'm not lying about my memory loss. That's another tiny step of progress.

At this rate, maybe my feet will touch grass again by next year.

One tucked under the trunk of that leggy oak.

That guard is watching me intently. Is the bow in his grip, arrow nocked, simply to send a message? Or does he think I'm about to swan dive off the balcony?

His undivided attention taints my enjoyment of the night air. I head back inside, leaving my doors wide open for fear they'll somehow lock if I shut them. I'm far from tired, though there is little else to do besides go to bed.

I tread lightly over and take up my usual spot, in front of the door, my cheek pressed against the cool floor.

Ten steps, with that slight hop.

Elisaf is working again tonight. Knowing his name brings me comfort, some tiny thread to grab onto. Does Zander address all his guards by their first name, or just this one? That he might treat his staff as people rather than nondescript pawns would make the hateful prick *slightly* more endearing.

Suddenly the footfall pattern breaks with a twirl and a two-footed slide, as if its owner broke into a dance.

It's so unexpected, I can't contain the snort of laughter that escapes me. "How did you know I was here?" I call into the silence.

It's a long moment before Elisaf answers. "You breathe as loudly as a daaknar, Your Highness." There is a teasing lilt in his voice.

"I doubt it. Have you heard one of those things breathe?" The memory of its grunts and snuffles stirs a shudder through my body.

"If I had ever been that close, I wouldn't be guarding your door tonight."

"That's what they tell me," I murmur, more to myself. "Did you grow up in Islor?"

"No. I am from the far southwest of Seacadore originally. But I have been here so long, I now consider this my home."

I hesitate. "Didn't the king tell you not to speak to me?"

"The king told me to guard you with my life and ensure you do not escape. He didn't expressly forbid me from speaking to you." There's a long pause. "Rest well, Your Highness."

I smile. It's a dismissal, but a pleasant one. "Good night, Elisaf."

CHAPTER TWELVE

The man tending the rosebush yanks his hand back with a yelp. Tugging his glove off, he sticks his thumb in his mouth to quell the sting.

I guess fist-size roses come with dagger-size thorns.

Probably human.

After a week of watching the daily happenings of the royal garden from my balcony, I'm beginning to suspect that most if not *all* the staff at the castle are human. There's nothing definitive, no box to check. It's a gut feeling, and my gut doesn't usually lead me astray. The nobility who stroll the pathways have a certain natural arrogance about them, the same natural arrogance that people raised with money and privilege exude at the high-society events I've robbed. But there is something more to them—an eerie calm, as though they do not ruffle easily, and a grace in the way they move. It could simply be a matter of breeding.

Or it could be that they're not human.

The gardeners work tirelessly from dawn until dusk every day, perfecting cedar hedges and plucking errant grass that sprouts between the intricately laid stonework, pausing long enough to bow to the garden's patrons. It's mostly women who frequent the royal gardens during the day—in elaborate silk and chiffon gowns. Some hold parasols to shelter them from the hot sun as they spend their afternoons admiring the blooms. Sometimes, if they're close enough, I catch drifts of conversations. Not enough to understand, but enough to know they're gossiping about court members. Few have noticed me up here, but those who have watch cautiously as they pass.

The atmosphere in the garden shifts once the evening settles in, when lively instrumental music carries through open windows and three women dressed in garb identical to Wendeline's sweep through, the lanterns igniting as they pass. The first night I watched them do it, my mouth gaped, allowing a bug an opportunity to fly in and choke me.

Men in formal coats and women in flowing dresses venture out, and couples of every combination disappear into the park for so long, one might worry they're lost. But I hear the odd sound—a laugh, a cry, a moan—and they always reappear eventually, often checking their buttons and adjusting their skirts.

These frisky revelers have provided the bulk of my nightly entertainment since Zander ordered my balcony door unlocked—and each night there are more of them than the last. But during the day, I'm equally enthralled with watching blades clash in the distant sparring court, the speed and footwork jaw-dropping. I find myself holding my breath as their boots pivot on the compacted dirt, especially after the other morning when a sword sliced through a man's thigh. No one panicked as he hobbled off, so I assume it wasn't serious, or it happens often. Either way, there was a lot of blood, and I heard Wendeline's name being called.

"You've caused quite the stir in the court."

I startle at the familiar voice and spin around to find Annika standing in the doorway to my bedchamber. The last time I saw the king's sister, I was launching anything I could find at a hellish beast to distract it from tearing her apart. I haven't seen so much as a hint of her since. That she is here now … unexpected delight stirs in my chest. "You're out."

"Of my prison. Yes, for a few weeks now. Though my brother is still 'extremely disappointed in my betrayal.'" She mimics a deep voice before rolling her eyes. She steps out onto the balcony, the skirts of her sapphire-blue dress swishing around her ankles. Her blond curls reach her waist in a cascade of plump corkscrews that seem impossibly springy under such weight. "Wendeline said she healed you as best she could?" Her voice is measured, reserved.

"Can barely tell," I joke.

Blue eyes the color of hyacinths dart to my shoulder, where my dress's collar doesn't cover the marks. "It's not *too* bad. The way he described it … it sounded much worse."

I'm assuming *he* is Zander. They've been talking about me. I should expect as much. But what has been said? How much does he confide in his sister? "It *was* a lot worse."

"Yes. I recall. The beast nearly tore you in two." Her forehead furrows deeply as though plagued by a bad memory.

"You stayed?" I wondered if she had run when I told her to.

"I was halfway to the passage when I heard you scream. I looked back and …" She averts her gaze, but not before I catch the flinch. "But then it threw you across the dais as if you had burned it, and it let out that awful screech. I hear it sometimes, in the still of the night." She shudders. "Then it burst into flames. The guards stormed into the sanctum as I reached you. I was certain you were dead. Your injuries were …" Her words fade. Quietly, she adds, "And yet, *here you still are*."

Like a cockroach that won't die, I hear in that tone.

I don't expect a hug from Annika, but does she still despise me, after I saved her not once but twice in one night?

An awkwardly long moment hangs between us.

Annika takes a deep breath and pulls her shoulders back. "The king has deemed that I shall accompany you for a walk of the royal grounds, if you are so inclined." Her words are formal, her voice flat, her reluctance painted across her face.

Normally, I wouldn't jump at spending time with someone

who looked like she'd rather eat broken glass than stand in the same room with me. Now, though, the chance to find this nymphaeum far outweighs my pride. "Yes!"

She sighs. "Corrin has a shawl for you."

From my balcony, the royal grounds appeared immense.

As Annika and I walk side by side along the stone path and I revel in this false sense of freedom, they seem infinite. Everywhere I look are sculpted hedges and shrubs bursting with blooms and mammoth trees that cocoon seating areas in shade and privacy beneath their weeping branches. We've crossed three elaborate stone bridges and passed a network of streams and ponds, the carrot-orange scales of the koi gleaming in the afternoon sun.

"Has anyone ever gotten lost in here?"

"Not for more than a few hours."

I peer over my shoulder. The colossal castle is entirely shielded from view within the dense depths of the foliage. I'm not surprised I didn't see it that first night, despite the dazzling moon. That I ever found my way to the opening in the wall is no small miracle.

Elisaf trails close behind us. Another day shift to follow the one he spent patrolling my door, but he looks no worse for wear from the lack of sleep. I feel him watching my every move intently, but at least his hand isn't resting on his hilt as if primed to cut me down.

Elven, surely.

My eyes widen at the couple sitting on a bench beneath a tree with pink floral blooms—the man's face buried in the woman's neck, his hand snaked under her skirt. They're tucked away but not *that* hidden.

"You still wear his ring. Why?"

"Huh?" Annika's question catches me off guard.

"The betrothal ring my brother gave you. You're *still* wearing it."

I peer down at my hands, as if there might be jewelry there that I hadn't noticed before. But aside from the cuffs on my wrists, there is still only one ring—the one Sofie slipped on my finger and warned me never to take off.

And apparently, also my engagement ring from Zander.

Is this the same ring? It *looks* the same, but the design is basic, and easily mimicked. Just as Princess Romeria and I *look* the same. Though, I hazard, that design is more complicated.

Annika is waiting for my response. What do I tell her? "The king told you that I don't remember *anything* before the night the captain shot me with the arrow, right?" There isn't even the faintest mark across my chest to hint at the wound.

"He did."

I hesitate. "Do you believe me?"

"It would certainly explain many peculiarities."

That's not an answer.

We cross paths with a group of three women who quickly shift out of the way, curtsying deeply, their murmurs of "Your Highness" like a song's chorus. I don't know if it's on my account or Annika's, or both. Whatever the pecking order in this family, I suspect the king's sister ranks high.

As with every courtier we've met on our walk, I sense their wide-eyed gapes at my back after we pass, and I instinctively pull the knit shawl closer to my body.

"Wendeline believes you," she says when they are out of earshot.

A hopeful flutter stirs in my chest. "She does?"

"She shared a theory with us that would make sense. If *anything* does."

I wait a long moment before I push. "What's the theory?"

Annika's pouty lips twist with a smirk. "There's only one way you could come back from the dead after taking a merth-forged arrow to the heart, and that is if a caster summoned the fates for you."

I don't understand what she just said, save for one thing. "Wendeline thinks a caster did this?" That has to be Sofie. Does she have ties to this world? Did she know Princess Romeria? She must have. Except … Sofie never said anything about taking over the throne of Islor. I have one task here—to get Malachi's stone so Sofie can save her husband from wherever he's trapped.

"Not just *any* caster. Margrethe."

"The high priestess who was killed by the daaknar?" The woman who was supposed to grant me sanctuary.

"Yes." She watches me a moment, as if searching for a reaction to that suggestion, beyond my shock.

"Why would she do that?"

"That is an entirely different question. But it is the only explanation for the daaknar in Cirilea that night. We haven't seen one in these lands in almost two thousand years, and the night you come back from the dead, one of Malachi's henchmen from Azo'dem appears. It is far too coincidental to mean anything other than that Margrethe summoned him."

Malachi. The one with the twisty black horns. A god with demons at his disposal? "So, casters can bring people back from the dead?"

She studies me through shrewd eyes. "What do you remember about elemental power?"

What the hell is elemental power? I want to say. I'll never figure out anything in this world if I hold all my cards too close to my chest. Wendeline has handed me a precious gift: a viable excuse for my lack of knowledge. I need to use it—and Annika—to my advantage. "All I know is Wendeline healed me, but I don't understand *how* she did it. I don't understand these fates. I don't know why Ybaris and Islor have been at war. I don't know who I am."

"You *really* don't remember *anything*." Her plump lips are parted in thought, her bright eyes worlds away as she seems to process that.

"*Nothing*. And it's infuriating."

"Yes, I can see how that would be," she says absently. "Where to even begin … my foolish brother. This is Wendeline's area of expertise, not mine." She sighs, as if preparing to settle into a long explanation. "All casters are born with an innate connection to one of the elements. Those are the forces that ensure our existence. Water, air, earth, fire. They draw their power from that element and can weave spells. The stronger they are, the more complex the spells they can weave. Some casters are weak, able to do little more than spark candles with a flame. Others can whip clouds into storms and control what you see and hear, or *don't* see and hear. Though, those powers are far more effective on humans than on our kind. Their minds are simple, pliable."

I study the stone path, afraid she'll somehow read my simple *human* thoughts in this elven body I've occupied.

"And sometimes, a caster is born with a connection to two elements. Even three. Those casters are called elementals. They are rare but extremely powerful. Margrethe was an elemental. She had a connection to both air and fire."

"They're strong enough to kill daaknars."

"As long as they don't allow it to get too close, yes. Margrethe must have been surprised by it." Annika's brow tightens, the only sign that the high priestess's grisly death bothers her. "But also, elementals have enough power to summon the fates and make requests that only they have the ability to grant. No one can alter the fabric of life, save for the fates themselves."

Realization washes over me in a wave. "Like bringing a person back from the dead." Is that what Sofie is? An elemental who talks to the gods?

"The elementals can ask for virtually *anything*. For resurrection, immortality, a child from a dead womb. But when the fates grant an appeal from an elemental, it always carries risk. A woman pleads to be blessed with a child, and she may birth a fiend. A king demands unnatural strength in a coming battle, and he may wake as a lion. A princess begs for everlasting life for her lover, and he may be turned into a creature. It's rarely without consequences, and some of those consequences change everything we know."

Her thoughts veer somewhere for a moment. "Kings and queens of the past caused such catastrophes with their requests that summoning the fates has been forbidden for centuries. It is far too dangerous a power for anyone to wield, especially for their own gain."

"But you think Margrethe broke the rules and summoned the fates to bring me back to life?"

"And to keep you alive, if the daaknar attack says anything. Except when you came back, you did so not remembering who you are."

Or I came back as someone else entirely. "You're saying that's a consequence of her summons."

"Yes, that is the theory at the moment, though many questions remain." Annika goes quiet as we encounter two more courtiers out for a stroll.

The one on the left, a woman with sleek inky hair that contrasts with her ivory complexion, offers a shallow curtsy as compared to her companion—almost as if she deems herself above stooping to anyone. But then her coal-black eyes swing to me, and I see the hostility in that dark gaze and pinched mouth. She is not happy to see proof that the rumors of Princess Romeria's demise were false.

The moment is fleeting and then we are continuing along the path.

"We haven't had an elemental here for almost two centuries, and now Margrethe is dead. I fear we will see no elementals for many more years, all while your mother collects them like precious dolls on a shelf," Annika says, jumping back into our conversation.

And because Neilina doesn't want her enemies having access

to such dangerous power. Maybe she has good reason. "Where do these casters come from?" I ask, desperate to piece together this fascinating world of magic.

"They are born to Ybarisan mortals. It is said that for every thousand humans born, one will be gifted. They're all tested at birth, and any gifted baby identified is sent to the isle where the caster magic is most potent, to be trained by the guild. They are assigned roles within Ybaris when they come of age. All elementals are required to serve the queen in Argon. I heard she keeps them collared and in a special tower within the castle. Not an unpleasant one, but a prison all the same. They serve her every whim and wish."

"Mordain allows that?"

"They are not given a choice. Mordain bows to Ybaris's rule, and Queen Neilina bows to no one."

This woman—this *queen*—sounds tyrannical. What did she raise her daughter to become? By all accounts, equal to her in hatred and deviousness. "How many elementals does she have? Do you know their names?" Does one have hair the color of copper?

"If what you told us before is accurate, there are never more than twenty at any given time, but I do not know of them. Our spies have not been able to infiltrate the queen's private household yet. And besides, the elementals take ill frequently and change often. They're never with her for more than fifteen years, two decades at most."

We pass through a tunnel where a thick bramble has been trained to climb hooped iron trellises, the prickly vines coiling around the metalwork. I flinch as something bites into the back of my hand. An errant tendril somehow missed by the gardeners' judicious pruning. The cut is just deep enough to draw blood. Another mar to add to my collection. "How powerful is Wendeline?"

Annika watches me swipe at the wound with my thumb. "She is not an elemental, if that's what you're asking. But she has the strongest affinity to an element of the seven we have left, and is ranked highest. She is the only one of our casters who can heal. We value her skills greatly in Islor."

"And what happens to the gifted babies that are born in Islor? The ones born to humans here."

"Oh, you truly are so clueless." Her perfectly shaped eyebrows curve with amusement. "There *are* no gifted babies born in Islor."

My annoyance flickers. "Why not?"

"Because the fates have deemed it so," she answers vaguely, leading us to the left, around the bend in the cedar hedge, her fingertips skating across the trimmed branches.

Another piece to add to my collection of information that I hope will make sense one day. I open my mouth to press her with more questions when I realize we've ventured into the rose garden. Three burly men in shabby brown pants and jackets far too heavy for the warm temperatures haul the last of the stone rubble onto a wagon. Beads of sweat drip from their faces and the pungent odor from their bodies carries all the way to my nose. Draft horses graze on strewn hay while they wait for their task.

Humans, certainly.

The men pause in their labors long enough to offer us deep bows before continuing their work, groaning and huffing.

"This is where he shot me," I murmur, more to myself.

Annika's eyebrows spike. "You remember something?"

"No. But I remember being here that night. I found an arrow right over here." I wander to the spot. "Or over there." The landscape all looks the same: rose bushes and cedar hedges, veering off in numerous directions.

"Yes, I believe it was this side. You were running from the guards. Boaz shot you down on the south side, right around *here*." She waves a dismissive hand at a spot on the stone. "He fired true. He always does. It was utter chaos. They left your body there while they chased down the rest of the insurgents, with plans to retrieve you later. They assumed you wouldn't get up and run away." Annika reaches out to touch a bud on a rosebush. It unfurls beneath her fingertip, opening into a magnificent yellow bloom, the petals countless.

It takes everything in me to keep my jaw from hanging. "How did you … are you a caster?"

"No. I'm elven," she responds evenly, adding, "as much as Ybaris refuses to accept that we are the same."

Elven have affinities to the elements too? Does that mean—

"Yours is to water." She taps the smooth black cuff around my left wrist. "You can't feel it because of these."

I eye the matching brackets with a new, albeit bewildered, understanding. Zander said they would keep me "in check" if I got any ideas. I didn't understand what that meant, but Annika is saying they quell my ability to use my affinity.

But I wasn't wearing them that first night, and I didn't feel any different. Then again, I was in a state of shock. Would I know what to do?

"My mother wanted to cuff you when you arrived, but my father insisted it would be a show of bad faith." Annika's lips purse. "I don't know that it would have made a difference to the outcome of the night, but at least you wouldn't have been able to turn a water fountain into a weapon." She looks pointedly at the center of the garden where the pile of rubble has been cleared.

"*I* did that?"

"You maimed a dozen guards doing *that*." Her blue eyes cut to me before reaching for another bloom. The yellow rose that unfurls beneath her touch is larger than the first.

Yes, I get it. Princess Romeria was evil. Annika wants to make sure I receive a full and thorough list of my crimes, seeing as I can't recall them.

"To think you could have harnessed that river for your escape, and yet you did not. Instead, you saved me, allowing yourself to be captured."

"Should I have left you down there to die?"

She sniffs. "It would have made far more sense."

Boaz warned Zander about the water that night, and then

Zander sliced open my hand with the dagger. Is this affinity what he was talking about? I study the pale line running the length of my palm. "What can I do?"

"Besides make water fountains explode? I'm not permitted to tell you that."

I sigh heavily, my frustration swelling. I nod to the roses. "Fine. What can *you* do then?"

"Very little. Our affinities aren't as strong as those of our Ybarisan cousins. Cheap parlor tricks, mostly. Coax flowers into blooming and hedges into growing." Her blue eyes flash to a climbing rose vine. I watch with fascination as a tendril uncoils from the lattice and lashes out like a whip, cutting through the air, its thorns searching for a victim.

My narrowed gaze flips to her to find a small smile curling her lips. Suddenly the cut on my hand from the leafy archway doesn't seem like an accident. What was it? A test to see if I would suspect her?

"Compared to what *you* can do, it is nothing," she says, adding abruptly, "I think I've filled your head with enough for one day."

"Already?" But I still have so many questions—about these casters, about the fates, and the nymphaeum. Where even is it?

She must see the crestfallen look on my face, with the knowledge that I'm going back to my prison. "The king has informed me that I will be responsible for taking you on escorts around the grounds going forward. So, perhaps I can provide you more information on another day."

My heart skips a beat. I know there is likely some ulterior motive to all these considerations as of late—some way that I am being used that I am unaware of—but I will happily accept any benefits. "Tomorrow?"

She sighs heavily. "We'll see what Zander wants."

It's nearly midnight when I settle onto the floor beside the door, my legs crossed at my ankles, the bowl of fruit in my lap that Corrin delivered with my regular meal this evening. I'm still riding the high from today's stroll through the grounds with Annika, and the hope that the long days of being locked within these walls might soon come to an end.

"What kind of grapes are these?" I call out, knowing Elisaf is on the other side, pacing. I hold my breath, hoping for an answer.

"The kind that grow on vines, Your Highness," comes the composed response with the telltale lilt of humor.

I grin. "I've never had anything like them." The entire bunch fits in the palm of my hand. The fruits are a deep bluish black, no bigger than jumbo blueberries, and sugary sweet. I have yet to find a seed on my tongue. If they'd served these at those high-society charity events and not slimy fish eggs, maybe I would have been more eager to sample the food.

"That you can recall."

A flash of panic stirs in my gut. "Right. None that I can recall." I need to guard my words better before I inadvertently talk of a life I'm not supposed to remember.

"They are a treat from Seacadore and highly sought after. We don't often have them, as they spoil quickly once pulled from the vine. A shipment must have arrived at the port in the last day or so."

"I'm surprised Corrin gave me any," I say more to myself, studying my spoon. I spent the past hour with it wedged between my wrist and the cuff in my attempt to pry this magical shackle off and discover this affinity to water I'm said to have. But the cuff remains intact, my wrist is sore, and I imagine Corrin will have a lot to say about the utensil's bent handle.

I work on straightening it while I listen to Elisaf's hollow footsteps, deciding which angle to coax a conversation from him. "Hey, were you my guard before the attack?"

"No, you had your own escort, Your Highness."

"Honestly, Elisaf, you can drop the formality. It's just us."

There's a long pause and then, "As you wish."

"What was I like?" I ask around a mouthful of grapes.

"I didn't spend much time in your immediate presence."

"But you must have heard something? Or *seen* something? I know you're *always* watching. I can practically feel your eyes boring through the door."

His chuckle is soft, relaxed. It's a moment before he answers my other question. "You smiled a lot. *All* the time when Zander was near. You made him smile, as well."

"*That's* definitely changed." I think the man's face would crack if he strained his stony expression.

"Your hands were never far from each other when you were in the same room. You would take long walks through the gardens at night, and you'd cling to his arm and flirt the entire time. You did not care who saw you. You appeared truly smitten with Zander."

I think of the long walks I've seen the courtesans take and of the couple on the bench beneath the floral tree today, and my cheeks burn. "I'm having a hard time picturing that." Then again, all I have to do is recall that moment in the tower to remember there is another side to Zander. I note the ring of familiarity in the way Elisaf said his name. "You're friends with him. The king."

"We've known each other for many years. Yes."

"How many?"

"Too many." Elisaf's voice is closer. He must be crouching. "And I suggest you save questions about the king *for* the king so that I am not flogged."

"Does he do that a lot? Hand out punishments every time someone does something he doesn't like?"

"You'll have to ask him."

Right. I'm sure that would go over well. "So, what else can you tell me about the other version of me? You know ... *evil* Romeria."

Another soft chuckle carries from the other side of the door. It's been so long since anyone I've spoken to has laughed in a genuine manner. "She was highly agreeable. She went out of her way to show herself to be a supportive queen when the time came for King Eachann and Queen Esma to pass the kingdom on after the union, and she deferred to Zander's opinion in all matters of the court."

"Such as?"

I hear a soft thud against the door, Elisaf's head leaning back, probably. "Such as matters relating to the laws that govern both mortals and immortals, and changes the mortals are desperate for."

Mortals. "You mean humans?"

"Yes, Your Hi—" He catches himself. "Yes. And the few casters we have, of course. But mainly the humans."

"And what changes are they asking for?"

"The most provocative would be the opportunity to live and work freely, as the immortals do. To not serve."

I frown as his words take meaning. "Humans don't live freely right now?" It's obvious there is a social order within these walls, as I suppose is to be expected when you're dealing with royalty. But is he saying it's *outside* of these walls too?

"Cirilea is more progressive, but many lords across Islor would prefer to keep mortals in servitude."

A wave of surprise washes over me with that word. "Are you saying humans in Islor are *slaves*?"

"That is not a word Islorians favor, but yes, in general, humans serve the immortals."

"*All* humans?"

"You will find few households without at least one mortal in servitude. It is a requirement," he says softly. Perhaps with a hint of shame? "There are degrees and ways they are in service. If you pay attention, you will see the marker in their ears that bears the house name of their keeper."

"That's what those are? Tags for *ownership*?" It's like tagging cattle. I grimace. Under different circumstances, *I* would be "in servitude" here. Sofie called humans the lowest of creation. She said far greater beings walked among us. Is that what humans are to these elven? Lesser than, that they can dominate?

"In exchange for their service and loyalty, the mortals are guaranteed accommodations and protection for themselves and their offspring."

"Protection from what?"

"Those who would abuse them if given the opportunity. Anyone who wears an ear cuff is considered property, and anyone who harms another's property will be punished accordingly."

A bitter tang fills my mouth. "And is that a big problem in Islor? The immortals abusing the humans if they don't have owners?"

"We call them keepers, and we have strict laws against the abuse of the mortals, but some regions enforce those laws more readily than others. In Cirilea, it is considered a great honor to hold a position within the castle and the court."

Is that true or is that what the slavers tell themselves? Do those gardeners who toil away in the hot sun from dawn until dusk feel *blessed*? Does Corrin feel fortunate to cater to the Ybarisan prisoner?

Korsakov owned me, and though my freedoms were many and my lifestyle was a far cry better than what I faced while on the streets, I felt trapped. Even with his name in my pocket to use as a shield if needed, I didn't feel safe.

A thought strikes me. "Does Ybaris enslave humans too?"

"They do, though it is not the same as in Islor. Mainly with the nobility."

The nobility, which would include Princess Romeria. I pluck the last of the grapes off the vine, hoping Corrin might deliver more tomorrow. "Did I bring any of them with me, here?"

"I believe there were three mortal lady maids with you. One died in the attack and the other two were punished accordingly."

"And they were probably just doing what they were ordered to do," I mutter.

"That is a safe assumption."

I have so many more questions about the humans of Islor, but I'm desperate to glean more about my predecessor. "What else do you remember about evil Romeria?"

"The humans adored you. They thought you beautiful."

I roll my eyes, even as the stroke to my vanity causes warmth to swell in my chest.

"There were whispers among the court, though—"

"Let me guess, the court are *all* immortals?"

"Yes. There were doubts about your acumen for politics. Some thought you simpleminded, better equipped for donning pretty dresses and warming Zander's bed than ruling."

My eyebrows lift. "You mean they thought I was an *idiot*?" It's not even *me* they were whispering insults about, and yet I burn with indignation.

"They questioned whether King Barris may have been quick to make the arrangement so that his son Tyree could rule Ybaris in your stead. They say he is his mother's likeness in both looks and disposition."

"Princess Romeria has a brother?" Growing up, I always wanted a sibling.

"Yes. An older one. But as is custom in Ybaris, female offspring are considered first in line to the throne."

"And do you think that's true? Getting rid of me so my brother could take over?"

"I do not deem to have an opinion on Ybarisan matters. But King Barris first reached out to King Eachann when you were merely a babe, so your political shrewdness would not have been in question at that time. Besides, I believe you proved that you were well versed in scheming, and not at all the fool, even if your plans were foiled by a change in schedule."

Right. "How exactly did I poison them?"

"I am not permitted to give you details of your failed coup."

"Because I'm going to try it again? From *here*?" I shake my head. "Why didn't King Barris and Queen Neilina come to Islor, anyway? Don't parents attend their children's weddings?"

"They did not feel it was wise to leave their kingdom unattended." I note the slight hesitation in Elisaf's voice. "But Prince Tyree traveled with you."

"And where is he now?"

"His body was not found among the dead, so it is assumed he fled the city as soon as the alarms sounded."

"And left his sister here to die." It is interesting, though. He must have been involved in the plan. "So, basically you're telling me the peasants thought Princess Romeria 'pretty,' and the court thought her a fool." Not exactly a glowing reputation I inherited, even without the murder worked in.

"I believe the exact term was 'witless fool.'" I hear the smile in his voice. "For your part, you fed into that notion well. But some saw through the act, believing you were putting on a show to please the crown and the future king, but that you had ulterior motives."

"Hope they dropped some coin on those odds. They could have made serious bank," I mutter dryly.

"I've never met a Ybarisan before, outside of battle. Do they say such odd things as you do?"

I wince. I need to watch my words more carefully. "The queen didn't like me, though, did she?"

"The queen did not trust you. Princess Annika was not an enthusiast either."

"She still isn't." And yet she went to all that trouble to help me the night of the attack. There's only one explanation—she must love her brother.

"You got along well enough with Atticus. He and a contingent of the king's army escorted you and your entourage on the journey from the rift. Though, he could make pleasantries with his worst enemies."

"I'd say that friendship is over." I set the stone bowl down on the floor beside me. "And what are people saying about me now?"

"At the moment, most of Islor still believes you dead. There are a great number of rumors drifting through the villages and cities, causing confusion and fear."

"Such as ...," I push.

"Many are calling you the Royal Slayer. Some believe the king should have made a spectacle of executing you with the rest of the Ybarisans for your treason."

The urge to deny my supposed misdeeds blisters my tongue for what feels like the hundredth time. This is what innocent people accused of heinous crimes must feel like. Though, in my case, my inculpability is only half-true. "I guess I can't blame them." Zander *would* have executed me had the sun rose with me still in the tower. I have both Annika *and* a demon to thank for escaping that fate.

"But there are some who mourn you, who are certain you didn't have any knowledge of your mother's hand, that you were duped as surely as the rest of us."

A spark of hope unfurls in my chest. "Is that possible?" Could I have been framed for all this?

"Your first lady was found with the vial of poison hidden in the seam of her dress, and your guards sang like songsters upon questioning, their stories about your duplicity all the same. So, no, I would say it's highly unlikely."

I swallow. "And the king? I mean, Zander. Was he ever suspicious of me before that night?"

"He was." There's a lengthy pause. "But he fell for your act harder than anyone."

"That's what he likes? A mindless woman who wears pretty dresses while smiling incessantly, and who will warm his bed?"

There's no response, and I suspect that's all I'll get about Zander. I smooth my fingers over the cuffs on my wrist. "What's your elemental connection, Elisaf?"

"I do not have one."

I frown. "Why not?"

Voices carry somewhere in the hall. "Sleep well, Your Highness."

"Wait!" I know that's his polite way of telling me he's done answering questions, and I appreciate the details he's offered, but I have one more question that burns for an answer. "What about the king? Does he have one?"

"He does."

"To what?"

There is a long pause, and I assume I'm not going to get a reply.

"Fire." Elisaf moves away from my door.

CHAPTER THIRTEEN

Corrin sets the food tray on the desk with a clatter. "You cannot wear *that*," she scoffs at my gown.

"What's wrong with it?" It's pleasantly simple in style, the pale yellow reminding me of duckling's feathers before it molts. It will be perfect for a walk through the grounds with Annika, which I'm desperately hoping will happen today, after three days of waiting. "This is the one *you* left me to wear. *And* it's the only dress I have." It's either this or my nightgown.

"Yes, well, that was before you were summoned by the king." Corrin disappears into the sitting room.

"*Again*?" It's been ten days since I saw him. What does he want now? Is there news from Lyndel? Am I about to be accused of lying to him? My anxiety flares.

Corrin returns a moment later, her arms loaded with a flowing sage-green gown, its chiffon skirts puffy around a cinched bodice. "This will be more suitable for your day."

"Which includes what? A royal ball? Where do you keep finding these dresses, anyway?"

"That is not your concern. All you should be concerned with is that it fits," she retorts.

I note the sleeves and collar. The material is sheer and embroidered with delicate gold flowers that will mask my scars. "Where am I going?"

"Wherever His Highness says you are going. And eat quickly." She gives the tray a small push. "We haven't much time, and the king has insisted we not make him wait again."

I groan, wandering over to the table. Everything with Corrin is always rush, rush, rush. She's grown bolder as the days have passed, chastising me every chance she gets. In return, I've grown surlier, not bothering to hide my irritation. "Fine. But is it going to be as difficult to put on as this one was? It took me *forever* to figure it out."

Corrin huffs. "Eat. And turn around." She sets to unfastening the back of my dress as I pick at the apple slices and watch her in the reflection of my dressing mirror. The gold ear piercing is the first thing I notice every day, now that I know what it means. Does it bother her that she is tagged like a stockyard animal?

"You were going out like this? Three of your buttons are still undone!" she ridicules.

"I don't have rubber arms and eyes in the back of my head. And no, I was going to ask Elisaf to help me." I'm only half kidding. Elisaf already finished his shift by the time I was dressing. The foot-dragging guard is back on duty.

The appall on Corrin's face in the mirror makes a bubble of laughter climb out of my throat. I choke on the fruit in my mouth, and it takes a few coughs to clear it. "What? Isn't this why you chose this dress for me in the first place? To torture me? Because it's *impossible* for a person to do up on her own." I cursed her name a half dozen times this morning, picturing her smug smile as she hung it on the dressing hook.

She scowls but says no more, her nimble fingers flying over the buttons.

My day guard, the foot dragger—a stone-faced man with bland chestnut-brown hair and small, squinty eyes who told me his name was Guard when I attempted conversation—walks behind me and barks orders of "left" and "right" as he escorts me through the castle's vast halls.

I note the statues and vases on pedestals as we pass, marking them as I mentally map out the castle while trying to ignore the countless stares from every direction. I can't tell if the attention is because I've risen from the dead—more literally than they probably realize—or if it has to do with my extravagant appearance. After Corrin practically chased me into this dress, which fits as if tailored for my body (I can only assume it is part of Princess Romeria's wardrobe that Corrin is hoarding somewhere), she pushed me into the vanity chair, muttering about my unkempt mane. Her fingers moved quickly, winding and twirling and pinning until the bulk of my hair was fastened in an intricately braided weave. I caught the fleeting appreciation on her face, but when she saw I was observing her, her expression morphed into that of haughty disdain.

After a lengthy walk, we step through a set of doors and enter a courtyard. A dozen horses clad in the royal black and gold wait next to their respective soldiers. Behind them, more horses loiter in stalls, chomping on fresh hay that the stable boys are delivering with pitchforks.

My nose curls at the stench of fresh droppings on the stone nearby, but I try to ignore it, and the wary looks from the soldiers. "Where are we going?" I ask Guard, hoping he'll at least answer that much.

"For a ride through Cirilea." Zander strolls past me without a glance my way, looking as tall and fearsome as usual, his golden-brown hair swept back, his tailored, knee-length jacket a rich forest green today. He slides a polished leather boot into a stirrup and pulls himself onto his horse with grace.

The soldiers take that as their sign and rush to mount. A stable hand—a boy of maybe fourteen with a gold cuff in his left ear—

carries a wooden step stool over and places it beside Zander's sleek black stallion.

Zander turns to stare at me.

I finally clue in. "You want me to ride *with you*?"

"I'm certainly not giving you a horse of your own to barrel through the city streets on."

I eye him cautiously, perched in the saddle, his thighs that look lean but muscular in black pants waiting to bracket mine.

He gestures to the piebald ahead of him where Boaz waits, glowering. "Unless you'd prefer to ride with the captain—"

I march straight for the step stool, gathering the layers of my dress so as not to trip on them. I ease up the two steps, cursing Corrin in my head the entire way. Who rides a horse in a fucking ball gown? She couldn't have found me suitable *pants*? The yellow dress would have been more appropriate for this.

With a sigh of reluctance, Zander holds out his hand.

As much as I'd like to rebuff his offer of help, the chances of me humiliating myself without it are high. After a moment's hesitation, I rest my small hand in his much larger one, feeling his smooth skin beneath my palm. How many times has he held this hand? How many times have his hands—those strong, long fingers—touched this body I inhabit? How intimately?

Zander's gaze settles on my ring. His jaw tenses as his grip tightens, supporting me while I swing my leg over the saddle and settle down in front of him. The layers of chiffon bunch around me like the walls of a deep nest. I do my best to smooth down the fluffy material, only to graze Zander's inner thigh. The muscles in his leg visibly flex in response.

"Sorry," I murmur. I lean forward, my back ramrod straight as I try to put distance between us, praying this is a short ride. The dress does offer one positive: it's an effective barrier between us.

Zander reaches around to collect the reins, effectively caging me in, that sweet woodsy scent that I'm coming to recognize as him tickling my senses.

I curl my arms closer to myself in response.

Boaz gives a command, and the horses shift into formation—two lines, save for the additional soldier flanking us on our right. It's Elisaf.

I smile at the sight of him, relieved for a friendly face.

The head dip he offers in return is barely noticeable, but I catch it all the same.

We move through the castle courtyard, hooves clacking against the downward slope of stone in a steady clatter, the soldiers, save for Elisaf, giving the king a wide berth. My body jolts continuously.

"Elisaf, have you ever seen anyone look so awkward on a horse?" Zander asks, his tone taunting.

"No, Your Highness. Can't say that I have."

"Have the fates taken your ability to ride as well?"

I had never been on a horse until I came here, I want to say, my cheeks flushing. "I'm trying not to crowd you." *Your Highness.* I hold back the acknowledgment, mainly to see if he'll remark on its absence.

"You're going to be in great discomfort by the time we reach the lower streets."

"I'll be fine."

"You *can* relax. I won't bite." Zander adds with a touch of grim humor. "We all know what happens to the wretched creatures who dare." When I don't respond, he urges, this time more commanding and annoyed, "Sit back."

I realize I'm holding my breath. I release it and loosen my muscles a touch, but not enough to make physical contact with my co-rider.

We move toward the stone wall and a set of heavy iron gates flanked by guards. None of this side of the castle property is familiar to me, but I wore a blanket on my head the night they brought me here, and then I used tunnels to escape with Annika. To my right, a tower stands alone. It must be the one Boaz threw me in. Somewhere below it is the square where they executed Princess Romeria's servants and guards while I lay unconscious in a bed. Were they truly deserving of such doom, or were they simply following their princess's orders? Was the execution a big event? A celebration? What even earns a person an execution in Islor? Is it only the most treasonous of crimes or is it anything that annoys the king?

"Go ahead, speak freely," Zander prompts. "Say what you want to say."

"Why? So you have an excuse to *flog* me?" It slips out before I can stop myself.

"You are fixated with being flogged."

"I'm not." More like terrified, but I push down my fear.

"I wouldn't have to search for an excuse. I'm the king, and your list of infractions is long." There's an edge to his tone. "Are your thoughts worthy of punishment too?"

I clamp my mouth shut.

"Come now. You spent weeks guarding your tongue and saying all the right things. Believe me when I say I'd much prefer you speak your mind and say all the wrong things. Especially now that you have not a hope of earning my trust or my gaze again, no matter how much effort you put into it."

"You think I'm ..." My words fade. *Effort?* What effort? I look down at the layers of chiffon and realize he means my appearance. "I didn't choose this *absurd* dress. My *charming* attendant that you handpicked forced it on me."

"The dress *is* absurd. At least, for horseback," he mutters, gathering the reins in one hand to fuss with something behind me. "I'm sure Corrin meant well."

I dare glance over my shoulder to see him swatting at the sage-green material that puffs halfway up his chest between us. I press my lips to stifle the laugh, and it escapes in a snort.

But then I make the mistake of looking up, and the fleeting humor dies in my throat. From this proximity, it's easy to pick out the deep flecks of gold woven into his hazel irises and measure the length of his thick fringe of lashes.

His eyes probe mine, searching for something.

I shift back to face forward. "You wanted to *execute* me. Trust me, I'm not trying to earn your trust *or* your gaze. You're a stranger to me."

"And yet you still wear my ring."

I look down at the smooth, white stone. It must seem odd to him that I do. "I can't explain why, but it feels important to me." As vague and as close to the truth as I can get.

To that, he says nothing.

We've passed the looming inner wall. Beyond it is a narrow street banked with steeply gabled houses, much like I remember from that first night. Only now there are no buildings smoldering, no wagons full of bodies, no children crying over fallen parents. The azure sky is smeared with wispy white clouds, and a warm breeze disturbs the stray hairs around my face.

The procession swerves right where the street splits off to another, and suddenly the vista opens to the broad expanse of water beyond the city's limits below. On the far horizon, a faint line hints of more land. I try to recall the map in Zander's circular room. Is that more of Islor? Seacadore? I committed all the names to memory as soon as I returned, and yet I know nothing of them.

I inhale the slight waft of brine from the sea. It's calming.

"You don't feel *any* pull from the water?" Zander asks, and there is genuine curiosity in his voice.

He knows Annika told me. Of course. Wendeline warned me that all my conversations would reach his ears. "I'm not supposed to, am I?" I hold up my arms to show the cuffs. "What could I do if I weren't wearing them?"

"Besides wreak havoc on my city again?"

"How would I do that?" Other than exploding water fountains, what can this elven body I've inhabited do?

"You think I'm going to give you detailed instructions?"

"As if they'd be of any use to me." I have no interest in attacking Cirilea. I just want to better understand how it all works. "What about you?"

"What about me?" A pause. "Oh, that's right, I heard you've been interrogating anyone who might listen," he says dryly.

I steal a glance Elisaf's way and find his focus ahead. Do they *all* repeat *everything* I say to Zander?

I change the subject. "Where are we going?"

Zander gives the rein a tug to guide the horse to the right, the move causing his biceps to brush against mine. "To parade the princess of Ybaris around Cirilea. It's time everyone knows you are alive and well, and the best way to do that quickly is by allowing the people to see you."

"And why do you want them to know? Why do you care if people think I'm dead?" What use does Zander have of me?

"Because I want people to see that you are still here, within the royal court, and close to me." I'm acutely aware of him leaning in, his voice dropping an octave. "Few know what happened, and of your memory *affliction*. Only those I trust with the truth. We've heard that Queen Neilina has been frantically searching for proof of your survival, so perhaps your dear mother does love you after all. We are assuming she is ignorant to the fact that you no longer remember who you are."

"You believe me?"

"I believe Wendeline."

And she's mostly right, I feel the urge to say but bite my tongue. She doesn't have all the details. "And what happens after word spreads that I'm alive?"

"I am expecting those who helped you before will believe you've convinced me that you are innocent of any wrongdoing, that you were merely a scapegoat for Queen Neilina."

It clicks. "You want to draw them out."

"Eventually, they will find a way to contact you again. When they do, we will punish them accordingly."

A thought strikes me. "Did your soldiers find anything at Lyndel?"

"Yes. Lord Telor's army, ready to defend us against Ybaris."

I feel my shoulders slump.

"Were you hoping for another outcome? Perhaps to find one of my strongest allies had turned on me?" he asks. He senses my disappointment, but he has misread it.

"No, it's good. I just ... with everything I've heard about what happened that night, and what Princess Romeria did to you—"

"What *you* did to me," he corrects.

"Right." Leading him on, making him think she was in love with him. "I was hoping that what I remembered might have been helpful. For *you*." Which, in turn, might be helpful for me.

He's quiet for a long moment. "There are mountains north of the stronghold that the Ybarisans could be using without Lord Telor's knowledge."

"So, you might still find them there?"

"If we looked. We *could* expend efforts trying to ferret them out, but we are otherwise occupied with protecting the border from an invasion from Ybaris in retaliation for killing their princess and their king."

Even though I'm alive, and Queen Neilina killed her own husband. "Do you think they'll invade?"

"I think your mother is desperate for our land, but if she can find a way that doesn't guarantee mass casualties in battle, she will be searching for it. Our best plan is to wait for your kinfolk trapped within Islor to make their next move. They cannot get back across the rift, and with no more than two hundred of them left, they cannot win against my army on their own."

He sounds so confident, but is it an act?

Ahead of us, the street we're traversing meets another livelier one where the buzz of voices carries and pedestrians mill about, their arms laden with breads and flowers.

"What is that?"

"The market. Those within the city and neighboring towns gather here to buy and sell produce from their gardens and wares from their forges and such."

I smile as I think of hot summer days walking along the crowded, narrow aisles of the Saturday market back home. It feels like an eternity ago that I left. I'm sure my potted plants on the windowsill have all shriveled from lack of water. Rent is long past due. Has my landlord been by to collect? He must realize I'm missing by now. Would he have reported it? Does anyone care that I'm gone?

"I have a proposition for you, Romeria," Zander says, cutting into my thoughts. "Or rather, you have a choice to make. At the end of this ride, you can go back to your confinement, continue being a prisoner of Islor, waiting with bated breath day after day for an escorted stroll through the grounds, hoping I don't lock your windows and take away your bird's-eye view of the happenings of the Islorian court. *Or* you can help me safeguard the strength of Islor and gain some semblance of freedom in the process."

Prisoner or freedom—whatever that means in this world. But he must know it's an especially delectable candy to dangle. He's been spoon-feeding me tiny mouthfuls of a life outside my walls, and already I'm pacing each morning like a well-trained dog, impatient for more. How long has Zander been scheming about this "choice" he would give me? Is it only recently, or has it all been part of a carefully orchestrated plan since the day he condemned me to my rooms?

I grit my teeth against the bubble of resentment that flares. What is it with these people offering me lopsided choices? First Korsakov, then Sofie, now Zander.

But Sofie's words echo in my head, a reminder: *You will have to earn your way in, which will take time.* Did she know the kind of dilemma she would be dropping me into? Is this what she meant? That I somehow would have to win over a king who I have deeply betrayed in the most unforgivable of ways?

"Do you need time to consider?" Zander asks, annoyance in his tone.

"No, I'll help you." Yet again, I don't see myself as having any choice. At least this time, there is more honor in what is being asked of me than stealing trinkets from the rich. I feel no allegiance to any of these people. I have one task, and no one has so much as hinted that they suspect it. So, let Zander think I'm focusing only on helping him while I help myself by finding a way into that nymphaeum. "What do I need to do?"

"To begin, remove that stick against your spine and make it look like you wouldn't rather be dwelling at the bottom of the sea than sharing a horse with me."

I process his words with a frown. If we are to pretend that I was an innocent victim in Queen Neilina's schemes, then it would mean ... My skin tingles. "You want people to think we're still *together*?" That the king is still interested in Princess Romeria. I peer down at my hand, at the gold in my ring that glints in the sun. Not just *interested*.

Still engaged to be married.

Is this why he never took away my ring?

"You think that'll work? That people will buy it?" I ask doubtfully.

"The alternative is implausible."

That he would embrace a woman who murdered his parents and nearly toppled his kingdom. "Right. I guess."

"I would argue this is *far* more difficult for me to digest. To you, I'm a stranger."

"Who wanted to execute me."

"Can you blame me?"

Fair enough. But can I play this role?

"You are a serpent who said and did *many* things to win my affection." He sighs heavily. "But if I focus on the reality that you are only her in physical form, then perhaps I can begin to see you as a stranger, as well. That would be to both our advantages."

But to him, I still look like a snake, and few find those creatures appealing. I guess the one superficial positive is that, on appearance alone, Zander is not repulsive. This would be far more difficult if I had to play kiss the king with Korsakov or Tony. Just the thought of that threatens a shudder.

But will I have to *kiss* him?

I have a hundred more questions—mainly, how us together will help strengthen Islor and what *exactly* does selling this story to the people entail—but we've almost come upon the market street. Taking a deep breath, I let my body relax until I feel the solid wall of his chest against my back.

"Take the reins," he commands softly.

I do as told, seizing the thick leather cord within my hands. It allows him room to slip his arms beneath mine, his forearms resting in a more relaxed, intimate pose in front of me as he resumes control of the horse again.

My ears catch his deep, steadying exhale, but it is his breath skating across my neck that sends a shiver through me.

"See? Not completely insufferable," he murmurs.

"No. I guess not."

"I was speaking to myself."

Up ahead, a trumpet sounds and the throng disperses, people moving out of the way as the procession of horses turns right.

Hundreds of people crowd the street, shouting. Some don drab clothing and the telltale metal ear cuff marking them as humans and slaves, while others wear finer leathers and scabbards at their hips.

I spot many shocks of surprise when they set eyes upon me, but also some deep furrows and scowls.

So many eyes on me, sitting atop my equine pedestal.

The Royal Slayer.

My chest tightens. Even flanked by a horse on either side, I feel exposed. "Some of these people think I'm to blame for what happened."

"That's because you *are* to blame for what happened." Zander's voice is so much closer now, and it rings with a hint of bitter amusement.

"Aren't you *at all* worried what they might do? I mean, is a crowd *this big* safe?"

"Even if they wish to harm you, no one will dare risk catching me in the crosshairs."

"I'm glad *you're* confident about that." I hope not foolishly so. But it makes sense now, why Zander insisted I ride with him. Alone on a horse, I would be an easier target.

He curls an arm around my waist and pulls me the last inch backward until our bodies are flush, and I feel the warmth of his thighs against my hips even through the layers of chiffon.

I force myself to relax against him.

"Many in Islor want a union between us. Seeing you with me like this will quickly sow doubt in what they fear to be true, and soon they will think what we want them to. Besides, even if one of them does attack, what are you worried about? Won't you come back from the dead again?"

I snort at his poor attempt at humor. "I'd rather *not* test that theory." Because the truth is, I'm not sure if that's accurate. Sofie was adamant that if the Islorians discovered my true identity, they would kill me, so it seems my death *is* possible.

The horse canters forward, and I'm acutely aware of the feel of Zander's body with every bump and jostle, but I do my best to focus on the action ahead. We cut a straight path in the street at a steady clip, people giving the animals a wide berth.

Between the shouts and claps, the mingling scents of freshly baked bread, fish, leathers, and sour bodies, my senses are overwhelmed, and I find myself unintentionally pressing into Zander's frame for protection. People wave hats in the air and call out for their king and for the strength of Islor from every direction, and every so often, my ears catch my name, sometimes with a "queen" attached to it. I remember what Elisaf said about the princess's incessant smiling, and I plaster one on now, though it feels contrived.

As the street meanders and approaches an area closer to the water, the surroundings change, as does the mood. The buildings nearest the market were two to three stories high and adorned with shutters and fancy grillwork on the windows, but here the houses that line the left side by the water are plain and battered one-story shanties, offering little to admire beyond their view of the ocean. To the right is a tall stone wall—a divide between this side and the nicer buildings. The demographic has shifted to a much older crowd, the people's clothing shabby, their weathered faces and wiry bodies showing signs of hardship. The air smells foul, of raw sewage and filth.

I don't need my extensive experience with poverty to recognize this is the poor area of Cirilea.

"Here." Zander reaches down near our legs, searching beneath the layers of my skirts. He fetches a velvet satchel that was tied to the saddle and sets it in front of me, the contents clinking with a recognizable sound. He deftly unfastens the tie with one hand. "Toss them out."

I reach into the bag and collect a handful of gold coins, marveling at the weight and size of the currency. "*Toss* them?"

"To the people."

I look to a rickety porch ahead. An elderly couple stands in the doorway of their hovel, the man hunched over a wooden cane, the woman shielding her eyes from the bright sun with liver-spotted hands. "Shouldn't we stop?" How are these people to collect when they can barely stand?

"Not long ago you were fearful of an attempted assassination, and now you want to stroll through the rookery on foot with a bag of coin?" Zander mocks.

"Why? Is it dangerous here?" It can't be worse than some of the shelters I found myself in, back in the early days, before I made friends and learned how to navigate the city's system. Some of those places were more hazardous than sleeping on a park bench.

"Not with me beside you."

The elderly man's desperate gaze is on the velvet bag within my grasp as they wait patiently for a handout. Nearby, a younger, more nimble man eyes the situation closely. An opportunist. I know his kind—he'll swoop in to collect whatever the elderly couple isn't fast enough to gather.

"Then *be* beside me. They're people, not a flock of geese. I'm not throwing coins at them like bread crumbs. Help me off this horse." I turn, softening my voice to add a "please."

Zander's piercing eyes bore into me for a long moment before he calls out, "Hold!"

The horses come to a standstill.

"Elisaf, take the reins." Zander slides out of the saddle to land on the stone path with poise. "Well?"

With considerably less grace, I grip the bag of coin and the horse's robust neck while easing my leg over. Strong hands seize my hips and guide me to the ground as if I weigh nothing. Zander does not release me immediately, leaning in from behind to whisper, "If this is a ploy to escape ..."

"Yes, yes ... off with her head." Though I'm not sure the guillotine is part of the square's repertoire.

He inhales sharply, his grasp of my body tightening, though not painfully so. "You enjoy testing me."

Maybe I do, which means my fear of him is waning. I don't know if that's good or bad. "I'm sorry, you told me to speak freely. Would you rather I bite my tongue and smile like a mindless fool?"

"In front of others, that would be ideal."

I peer over my shoulder and up at his handsome though hard face, and flash him the widest, fakest grin I can muster. "Better?"

With a strangled sound, he releases me, only to set a hand on the small of my back. I coax myself into relaxing against his touch and together we walk forward.

Boaz's expression is pinched. "Your Highness, would it not be better if a guard—"

"As you are," Zander cuts him off as we pass.

Apprehension laces the aging couple's face as we approach, the stench of unwashed skin filling my nostrils. The man's shoes are torn, his toes hanging out. "Your Highness. Your Highness," come the murmured echoes. The woman curtsies deeply before us. The old man attempts to bow, but it's clear his hip won't allow it.

"Please do not trouble yourself, sir," Zander says with kindness in his voice that surprises me.

Up close, the woman reminds me of Inwood Park Ina, a woman who lost everything to medical bills and crippling depression after her husband passed away. When she wasn't doing daily safety checks of her fellow homeless friends, she could be found down by the river, building *inukshuks* on boulders. I heard she died last year, alone by the water.

I reach into the bag and drop a handful of coins into this woman's waiting hand.

Her eyes widen. With a sputtered whisper of "Fates bless you, Your Highness!" she glances around furtively before tucking them into her pocket for safekeeping.

Zander guides me along to the next shanty. "Maybe one per person going forward? My generosity is not bottomless."

"And yet you live in a castle painted with gold," I mutter.

He snorts. "That is rich, given what you have come from."

A three-hundred-square-foot studio apartment with a noisy toilet, I want to say, but I know he isn't talking about me.

We work our way down the street, the horses moseying alongside us, their riders ready to leap at the first sign of trouble. These people are not looking for anything but help. They're visibly nervous as we greet them—varying degrees of fear and confusion in their exhausted eyes. Some have rattling coughs, the kind that never goes away. They remind me of the destitute I knew in New York, a community who guard their meager belongings while looking out for their neighbors, who move slowly, with limps in their step, and hunches in their shoulders, whether from physical pain or simply too many years of bearing the weight of a heavy life. Many of these people are missing limbs.

This rookery is full of people who were once slaves to the immortals. I see the scars in their ears, holes that will never close after so many years filled by metal tags. On some, the cartilage is damaged as if the cuff was too tight and cut into their flesh. A few are missing entire chunks of ear where the marker must have been torn out. Those people duck away, attempting to hide their secret with scarves and hats, as if afraid of being apprehended.

I merely smile and slip two coins into their hands instead of one, because their situation must have been especially grim for them to maim themselves. But that begs the question—what did they run from? What have these people endured?

By the time we reach the end of the road and the end of the velvet bag, my chest is both light and heavy, the bleakness of these people's lives climbing under my skin.

Zander helps me into the saddle and remounts behind me. "You enjoyed that," he says with bewilderment. It's not a question.

"I don't think *enjoyed* is the right word." It was depressing. Back home, I can't pass a homeless person on the street without digging through my purse for some loose change, a few dollar bills. It's never enough. "Can we do that again?"

He takes the reins from Elisaf and the horses begin again at a steady canter, Boaz's command laced with his eagerness to get away from these people. "We're not emptying the royal coffers for the rookery, if that's what you're asking."

How many of those bags of coin does he have, anyway? Perhaps with my newfound freedom, I'll be able to find my way to these coffers. I would love to divest *His Highness* of some of his riches before I escape this place. "What is the rookery?" Besides crammed with old and sick ex-slaves who look like they're waiting to die.

"It's where many mortals go once they are of little value to Islor."

"Of little value," I echo, taking a moment to absorb those words and for my disgust to root.

"The crown gave them these quarters by the water, and the people pay us a small fee in rent for the privilege of living within the city walls."

"The *privilege*."

"Must you repeat everything I say?"

"I'm trying to understand *this*." It's basically a subsidized housing program for elderly human slaves Islor has discarded, only it's little better than an alleyway of cardboard-box homes.

Is he *proud* of it?

"You do not approve that we should do this for them?" He pauses. "Some in my court would not be bothered. They say they are a drain on our resources. They'd rather put them out of their misery."

"Maybe some in your court belong in your death square," I throw back, my anger flaring. My father would fall under the "of little value" umbrella in this world. These Islorians treat humans little better than lame horses or dairy cows that stop producing milk.

From the corner of my eye, I catch Elisaf's eyebrows climb halfway up his forehead. I can only imagine the look on Zander's face, if it isn't stony.

"Why do you care what happens to the mortals?"

Because I am one. Though I know I should stay quiet, I find myself unable. I've lived in poverty. I've seen the many ways that systems built to help people have failed them when they're at their lowest. This is the first time I've sat next to someone who has the power to do something about it. "They spent their entire lives serving you, and now that they're old and broken, you corral them into this squalor and pat yourself on the back for your benevolence? No, I don't approve of this. I think you should do more. They're *people,* even if *you* can't find a use for them anymore. They're not inferior to *your kind*." My feelings tumble out, unrestrained and unmeasured.

He is quiet for a moment. "Did you know that the crime for ending the life of any mortal Islorian, regardless of age or capability, is death? It's a law my father decreed and that I will uphold without compromise."

"A person can plead for a dog's life while still locking them in a cage."

"And what more would you have me do for these people?"

"How about you don't enslave them?"

"Yes, of course, I'll just snap my fingers and change *all* of Islor. How *everyone* thinks and lives." There's a curious edge to his voice.

"Aren't you the king?" I quip, but even I know it isn't that simple. "I don't know. Why don't you start by melting down one of your *thousand* gold pillars and build these people something nicer? Outside the city, in the countryside?" I know it exists. I can see the rolling hills in the distance from my balcony.

"Again with the gold, from a princess raised in a palace of jewels."

"I don't remember any such place."

"How convenient," he mutters. "Besides, it's far safer for these people within the protection of our walls than it is out there."

"It sounds like they need protection from some of your court."

To that, he says nothing.

The procession veers right, away from the rookery and uphill, and I sense we're making our way back to the castle. The moment we turn onto a quiet street, away from the spectators, Zander releases my waist and puts space between us.

The return ride is silent, save for the plod of horse hooves, and I'm relieved for it. When we reach the courtyard by the stables, the boy from earlier rushes up with the step stool. Zander is the first one to dismount, offering me a stiff hand while I descend.

I expect him to release me the moment my shoes land on the ground, but he pulls me in toward him. The move is so unexpected, I stumble a few steps and fall against him, my palm landing on his chest. He easily secures my balance with a hand on my waist, keeping me in place, our bodies pressed together.

He leans forward and I inhale sharply, bracing myself for our sham to lead to a kiss I have not yet mentally prepared for. His mouth moves to my ear instead. "Do not think for a moment that you are fooling me," he whispers, his bottom lip grazing my lobe. "This lapse in memory may be genuine, but I know you are hiding something."

Despite the tension between us—or maybe because of it—his proximity makes my pulse race. But his accusation stirs my panic because it's true. I *am* hiding something. I'm not entirely sure what, though.

I've already learned simple denials don't work with Zander, especially not when he has already decided on an answer. "You're one to talk," I say instead. He's been guarding every morsel of information I receive, feeding me in small increments as he deems sufficient.

"I've hidden *many* things from you," he admits, releasing my hand to slide his fingers over the small of my back. To anyone watching, we must look like a couple about to make up after a fight—our expressions somber but our touches intimate. "Some, for good reason."

I gather my courage and tip my head back. "Maybe we *all* have secrets for good reasons."

"Perhaps. But I *will* uncover yours, eventually." His eyes drop to my mouth, and I hold my breath, an odd, conflicting mix of dread and anticipation stirring within.

Abruptly, he releases me and storms away, as if suddenly desperate to have me out of his sight.

CHAPTER FOURTEEN

"Where are you taking me? This isn't the way to my rooms." The color scheme and moldings are similar, but we've climbed another flight of stairs and I don't recognize any of the busts that sit on the plinths.

"To your new rooms, Your Highness," comes the wooden response. Guard pushes open a set of double doors. "The queen's quarters."

I gape at the suite I walk into. "*Seriously?*"

He spares me no more than a strange frown before pulling the door shut behind me.

But ... the queen is dead, I think to myself as I wander through the luxurious sitting room, decorated in rich shades of eggplant, gold, and blush. It's a ballroom, easily three times the size of my previous cell block, its ceilings soaring and windows allowing daylight to stream in. A magnificent candelabra dangles in the center. Gilded furniture upholstered in silk and damask fabrics form an area for entertaining by a grand marble fireplace. Arrangements of fresh ivory and blush blooms in urns embellish throughout.

A cupboard door slams shut somewhere within the suite. I

follow the noise to an adjoining room—the bedchamber. It's no less exquisite, the rich plum-colored walls adorned with opulent moldings. An enormous bed sits at one end, dressed in ivory and gold, its stately, velvet-clad headboard reaching halfway to the ceiling. Another fireplace and smaller seating area occupies the other end.

Corrin bustles around in her usual flurry. When she notices me standing at the threshold, she makes a point of slapping the pillows she's fluffing extra hard. "You've certainly been busy this morning, *Your Highness*." Her clipped tone suggests that's meant to be a slight.

"Yes, handing out coin to the poor. *How dare I*?"

Her mouth hangs a beat, as if caught off guard, but she regains her composure quickly. "Can't say I've ever seen a fox invited back into the henhouse after the slaughter."

She doesn't trust me. Is it because she's human and she doesn't buy into Wendeline's theory, or is there some other reason for her contempt? "I didn't ask for this. It's what the king wants, so why don't you question him about his choices? I'm sure he'd *love* to explain himself to you." How much does Corrin know about Zander's scheming? Obviously enough to know that I'm no less guilty in his eyes now than I was this morning, otherwise she wouldn't dare give me such attitude.

She harrumphs but says nothing more.

The clang of metal against metal draws my attention to the open doors. I wander out onto a deeply set terrace, adorned by bursts of red geraniums and sun ferns in planters. While navigating the halls inside left me lost, from outside, I'm quickly able to find my bearings again. The vast royal grounds are still within view, only from a different angle.

I'm in the center portion of the castle. From here, a long, narrow walkway along the exterior wall connects to another sizable terrace. I'm almost positive it's the one Zander was standing on that day.

The king's chamber.

He has moved me next to him.

Smart, given we're to keep up appearances of a relationship. Whoever in the royal household helped Princess Romeria is likely still within these walls, watching. If Zander has decided I am innocent of any wrongdoing, it wouldn't make sense to keep me locked up in another wing.

It's a strange concept that the king and queen would have their own bedrooms. Whether they would use them as such is another matter, I guess. But given our situation, it's ideal. I'm sure Zander would rather sleep in a pit of vipers. I can't say I feel much differently.

And yet, the memory of his arm around my waist and his thighs against my hips lingers.

"You fight with Malachi's wrath fueling you today," a man says through ragged breaths. "What bothers you?"

Directly below me is the sparring square. I immediately recognize Elisaf's curls. He has removed his royal uniform jacket and dons a leather vest that shows off sinewy arms and tawny brown skin. He's facing off against a man with golden-brown hair whose every step oozes grace and confidence.

"Do you yield?" comes Zander's measured response, the sword blade dangling within his grasp. His green jacket lays folded on the nearby grass, leaving him in black pants and a loose white tunic. He must have headed straight here after the ride through the city, in search of something to stab.

Even from this vantage point, I can see the sweat glistening across their brows.

"Have I ever?" There's that teasing lilt in Elisaf's tone. It's coupled with a swagger that does not exist when they are king and guard. In this square, they are friends.

Elisaf lunges, and they fall into a well-timed dance, twirling and deflecting, their moves and countermoves fluid and practiced.

I've witnessed knife fights before—clumsy jabs and shuffling feet as one opponent swings their pocketknife at the other in hopes of connecting with flesh.

This? This is art, their footwork impeccable, each turn swift, each strike precise.

But where Elisaf's breathing has turned ragged, Zander looks like he could fight in his sleep. *Fueled by Malachi's wrath,* Elisaf had said. The black-horned god who enjoys releasing demons upon the land.

The threat to Zander's throne must be significant for him to stomach this scheme with me.

Zander blocks a thrust and then with lightning-quick reflexes, pivots and swings. His blade slices across Elisaf's biceps. I gape in horror as my night guard drops his sword with a clatter and grasps at his arm, his grimace laced with pain. Blood pours between his fingers in rivulets, splattering the dirt below.

"Fates, are you trying to send me to Za'Hala before dark?" Elisaf says between gritted teeth, his face turning ashen.

"If only." Zander seems unperturbed, but he hollers to someone unseen. "Fetch Wendeline!" To Elisaf, he says, "Here. Staunch the blood with this," and peels his shirt up over his head, tossing it to his friend.

I cringe at the gaping wound revealed in the split second it takes Elisaf to grab the cloth and wind it around his arm.

"I apologize. My head is not focused on the right things," Zander says somberly.

Neither is mine. While I'm still fretting over Elisaf, I find myself quietly admiring the smooth olive skin and cut planes of Zander's back. He's built but not brawny, his muscles evenly distributed. I'd sensed the strength in his arms while bracketed between them earlier today, but now I can see they are perfectly honed, his shoulders sculpted with strength, likely from countless hours of swordplay.

"Your Highness! The seamstress is here to take your measurements!" Corrin announces loudly from the threshold, drawing both men's eyes up to where I lurk above. A shirtless Zander turns, giving me an eyeful of a torso thickly padded with muscle.

I rush inside, my cheeks burning.

Where Corrin is a sopping towel thrown over a lit hearth, Dagny is the party guest who radiates warmth the moment she steps into the room.

"Oh, Your Highness! This one was surely spun with you in mind!" The short, stout seamstress holds up a gauzy, bluish-gray fabric against my cheek. "The merchant said it was the color of a dove in the evening light, and he would be right!" She was sent here to take my measurements so she can craft me a new gown, and she hasn't stopped prattling on since she laid eyes on me. There's not a hint of animosity to be found in her flamboyant personality or her thick, lilting accent. If I had to put her in any camp, it would be in the "dear, sweet Princess Romeria could never have done such appalling things!" category. It's a nice change from Corrin's surliness.

"Look at that color against your skin. What a lovely hue." Dagny's brow furrows as she tilts her head and studies the material from that angle. She wears the telltale gold band on her ear and the engraving—a symbol I can't read—matches the one on Corrin's. I assume it's a brand for their servitude to Zander and the royal family. Her hair is coarse and feathered with gray, the strands fraying in all directions from her bun like loose wires. Compared to everyone else I've seen in the castle so far, she's an unkempt anomaly. It's refreshing. "Don't ya agree, Corrin? Isn't that the ideal color?"

"I think any time you'd like to stop flattering and take measurements so Her Highness doesn't have to attend gatherings in her nightgown would be ideal," Corrin says crisply.

I spear my attendant with a flat look. "Don't you have somewhere else to be?" Someone else's mood to sour? The woman never lingers in my rooms. This is new. Then again, everything today is new, and changing rapidly.

Corrin folds her arms over her small bosom. "I am *exactly* where I need to be." To Dagny, she says, her tone a touch more conciliatory, "Her Highness has much on her schedule. Please do make haste."

I have a schedule now? I glance at Corrin, but she doesn't elaborate as she helps me out of my dress.

Dagny gasps at the sight of my shoulder, visible in my shift. "Goodness, Your Highness!"

"Yes, yes. They are dreadful," Corrin dismisses. "The king would like them covered."

Her words are a sharp prick to my ego.

"Are the stories true, then? About the daaknar?" Dagny whispers, as if afraid to utter the words out loud.

"Of course not!" Corrin snaps, glaring at the seamstress like she's an idiot for even suggesting it. "If a daaknar did *that* to Her Highness, she would be *dead*."

"That's what I understood, but the stories …" Dagny blusters, her cheeks flushing.

I feel bad for her. Her kind heart is no match for Corrin's brusque nature.

"Her Highness was attacked by one of her own when she tried to stop the insurgents. They used *caco claws* on her." Corrin shoots a sharp glare my way, as if warning me against countering her lie.

"Oh, those wicked people." Dagny's head shakes furiously. "Such wicked people, what they've done to their own princess. Oh yes, I have just the design in mind for you, Your Highness."

"So, you're going to *make* me a dress."

She chortles, as if my words are hilarious. "Well, yes, I am Her Highness's seamstress. I will make *all* your gowns. New and proper ones that will hide what needs to be hidden." She sets to measuring my body, as if suddenly frantic to get to work.

"Would you mind not making it so … poofy?"

Dagny's eyebrows squish together. "*Poofy*, Your Highness?"

"Poofy." I gesture to my hips, holding my arms out wide, and then point to the dress I wore today. "I'd like something a little more formfitting, and not so heavy." I think back to the one I was wearing the night I met Sofie. I've seen nothing remotely similar in style so far.

"But *that* is the style for women of the court!" Corrin blurts, as if my request has personally offended her, adding crisply, *"Your Highness."*

Maybe it's time for a new style, I want to say, but I'm supposed to be blending in, not shining a light on the fact that I'm an interloper. At least I can be thankful these outfits don't come with hoops and bum rolls. "The king was annoyed by it while riding through town." *And God forbid we annoy him.*

Whatever rebuttal Corrin was lining up dies on her pursed lips.

"Formfitting." Dagny scratches her chin. "I don't suppose I know what ya mean by that?"

"May I?" I hold out my hand toward the rudimentary pencil in her grasp.

She obliges with a curious frown.

I pause for a moment to marvel at the pencil's design—the graphite wrapped in stiff string to keep markings off fingers—before quickly sketching a silhouette on the sheet of paper on the coffee table, the long strokes of my hand a comforting routine from my old life. If only I had paper and pencil to occupy my time. "Something like that?"

Dagny's head cocks as she studies it. "I've never seen anything like it before. Do they have gowns like this in Ybaris?"

I have no idea, and in any case, Princess Romeria wouldn't remember, but it's clear Dagny isn't within the trusted circle. "Just an idea I had," I say instead. A dress that "fell off the truck" with the help of Korsakov's men. I adored it but passed it over for fear it was too opulent and flashy to wear in a place where I needed to go unnoticed. But it would fit well with the dress styles I've seen here so far, and this gauzy material Dagny brought would be perfect for its design.

"May I take this with me?" Dagny holds the sketch as if it's a prized possession.

"Yes, of course."

"I'll see what I can do. And I promise, the king won't see those ghastly marks."

I don't care what the king cares to see or not see, but I bite my tongue and watch with fascination as Dagny measures and fills a page with scribbled numbers, all while prattling on about her husband Albe and her son Dagnar—I assume, named after her. When she's done, she curtsies four times, gathers her bolt of fabric, and rushes out, all while humming to herself.

The room feels uncomfortably quiet once she's gone.

"What are caco claws?" I ask.

Corrin collects the dress I wore today, smoothing the skirt with a forceful hand. "A weapon they use in Seacadore, made to look like a beast's talons."

How appropriate. "Did the king say he didn't want to see my scars?" I can't be the only one in Cirilea to have them. Abarrane wore hers proudly. I assume she earned it in battle. Well, so did I, in a way.

Her eyes flash to me. "It isn't about vanity, if that's what you're asking. Both Wendeline and the king feel that the fewer people who know you survived a daaknar attack, the better. Information is a commodity, and anyone with too much can become a danger. Besides, you'll garner more sympathies painted a victim of your own mother than you will as an immortal who has defied certain death *twice*."

Corrin knows far more than she has previously let on. Who is this human to Zander that he would trust her so? Clearly someone who knows the inner workings of the court and how to survive.

She marches into a small room off my bedchamber while still talking. "Dagny is a rare talent as a seamstress, but she's also an insatiable gossip. It works to our benefit on this day. She will spread that version of the story through the castle faster than a family of rats finding their way to a barrel of grain. Of course, no one with half a brain in their head will believe those scars were caused by caco claws, even ones forged from merth. But we will cover them as best we can to hide the fact that you were injured by something far worse. Soon, the gossip will focus on more important things. Like your nuptials."

She emerges with a black dress. "I had your full closet transferred here. Most of it isn't sufficient, but Dagny will make a few capelets for you. This should work for today."

"Wait—he doesn't actually expect me to *marry* him, does he?" This is supposed to be an act to lure my accomplices.

"Why don't you question him? The king would *love* to explain himself to *you*," Corrin parrots my earlier snipe nearly word for word, capping it off with a triumphant smirk. "Come. I will draw you a bath and then you will begin to learn how to behave less like a peasant and more like a future queen."

A firm knock sounds on the door to the sitting room moments after the bell gongs five times.

I frown from my spot on the settee. My only visitors since I've been imprisoned have been Corrin, Wendeline, and Annika, and they've never knocked before entering.

"Come in!" I holler.

The door creaks open and Zander strolls through. "Your manners are impeccable," he says dryly.

A flutter of nerves stirs in my stomach at the sight of him. I stand and take a deep breath, reminding myself that we're now temperate allies.

He looks fresh and clean in a black-on-black embroidered jacket. How many of those does he have? I'm sure at least as many as there are gowns in my dressing room. Princess Romeria traveled here with a wagon full of luxurious outfits for her role as queen.

The heels of his boots click against the marble as he approaches, his attention on adjusting the cuffs of his jacket and not on me. "Where is Corrin?"

"She said she had things to do in the kitchen." I add under my breath, "Thank God." She made me stand before the mirror in my bedchamber and practice my curtsy for a half hour straight, calling me everything from lout to heathen until she was satisfied I could pass for regal.

"Is her help not appreciated?"

"I guess, but so is privacy." I practically had to chase her out of my bathing chamber—a windowless, marbled room with an elegant tub in the center. Sculpted especially for the queen, Corrin made sure to inform me, an opulence for the royal household, as are the flushing toilets. "I thought she was going to climb into the bath with me at one point."

"Princess Romeria's staff did *everything* for her."

"Well, I'm not her. I've told you that." And there is far more truth to that than he will ever realize.

"And I told you that you will need to learn how to be her." Finally, he lifts his gaze to meet mine before it shifts to my dress. Corrin was right in that the design suitably covers my scars, the gold embroidery cinching around my neck in a fitted decorative collar, the three-quarter-length sleeves opaque. But the plunging keyhole neckline coupled with a snug bodice that pushes everything up does little to hide much else.

Whatever Princess Romeria was, she wasn't modest. And while I've worn my share of risqué outfits, having Zander's attention on me now makes my heart race. The same questions as always cycle through my mind. How many private memories of this body I inhabit does he have? How many private moments with *his* body have I had that I am entirely unaware of?

I'm beginning to think complete ignorance will be my saving grace in all this. "How is Elisaf?"

His hazel eyes flip back to mine, his expression unreadable. "Wendeline is tending to him. It was a superficial wound."

"You're kidding me, right? I saw his bone."

He sighs, as if searching for patience with a petulant child. "I meant, it was made with a basic steel blade. Not one like this." He pulls his jeweled dagger from the scabbard at his hip. "Remember this one?"

"How could I forget." I flex my hand where the faint line remains.

"I had no choice. I had to ensure you wouldn't use the river to attack us."

"And maiming me would stop that?"

"Pain would, yes. You cannot channel your affinity through it." He approaches, holding the dagger for me to get a closer look. The silver gleams like nothing I've ever seen before. "The blade is forged with merth, meaning it takes much longer for your wounds to heal and scars are inevitable. Though, apparently, minor on you." The corner of his mouth tugs. "*And* if you had been successful at distracting me and lifted this weapon from my scabbard as you were intent upon doing, and then stabbed me with it, the wound would've been much more difficult to treat. Depending on where you hit me, possibly fatal."

So Zander *was* aware that I tried to steal it. "Aren't you afraid I'll try again?"

"I think you're smart enough not to."

True. Now that I've seen firsthand how talented he is with a weapon, I can appreciate how foolish my attempt was. Are all elven as skilled as he is?

He slides his dagger back into its place at his hip. "Do your injuries still hurt?"

"Not really. Tight more than anything."

"Perhaps Wendeline should take another look."

"I thought her talents would be far better used elsewhere."

"Do you plan on throwing back every word that's ever escaped my mouth?"

"I don't know. I guess we'll see what I remember."

"Which is quite a lot, ironically." He smirks. "Are you wondering why I've moved you here?"

"No. I understand."

"I'm glad you haven't lost your keen skills for deception." His interest drifts over the mantel, the flowers, the furniture. Everything but me.

"So what's the plan?"

"As I expected, the rumors are running rampant in the court. You will meet me in the throne room shortly to receive your formal absolution for all crimes. Tomorrow, Wendeline will begin helping you fill in holes in your memory, so you can at least appear to have some knowledge of who you are. You will smile and listen and not speak."

"At all?" A princess who defers to her betrothed on all matters of the court.

"As little as possible," he amends. "Should someone attempt to make contact, you will tell me."

"Of course." I have no reason not to.

He wanders, his fingers absently grazing a bloom in an urn. "Word that you are alive will reach your mother quickly, which is precisely what we want. She will not try to cross the rift with an army if she thinks you are still manipulating me. She would much rather claim this throne through duplicitous schemes than bloodshed. She will also likely attempt to contact you through her network of spies."

"She has spies here, in Cirilea?"

"Surely, just as we have ears in Ybaris. They are not the most reliable or connected, but they are better than nothing."

I frown. "How do you have contacts over there?"

"That is not your concern."

I sigh. Another secret to add to the list.

"You will not be permitted to move about freely. Elisaf will be your escort any time you leave this suite."

I expected as much. *I* wouldn't let me roam freely either, and

Zander is strategic, not stupid. I don't mind having Elisaf as a permanent sidekick. "Sounds simple enough." Not a necklace or ring to be lifted.

"Fooling some of the Islorian lords and ladies will be *anything* but simple. Though you did it once already." His jaw clenches. Is he thinking what I'm thinking? That Princess Romeria fooled him too? "While in public, we will appear as if all is forgiven, and we are still very much enamored with each other. I assume that won't be a problem for you. If the tower is any indication, you are more than capable of pretending, even without your memory intact."

He's not going to let that go anytime soon. "And what does being enamored entail *exactly*?"

"Take my arm when we walk, hold my hand occasionally. Pretend we enjoy each other's company. We used to spend time walking the grounds in the evenings. I suppose we should begin doing that again. Though, for both our sakes, we can make sure your performance is far more *respectable* this time around."

My cheeks grow hot, given what I suspect those cedar hedges and leafy corners are privy to once the sun slips beyond the horizon.

I'm not the only one, I'm relieved to note, as a slight blush mottles Zander's cheek.

"Holding hands. Got it." *And nothing more.* "Corrin mentioned a wedding. It's just talk, right?"

"The king is expected to have a queen by his side to rule, and we have to give people something to look forward to. But we will push it to Hudem, under pretenses of proper mourning for the late king and queen. That will give us time to ferret out anyone within the castle who was working with you and buy time with your mother."

That's the night of the next blood moon. "And what happens if this traitor doesn't come forward by then?"

"They will. They *must*."

"But *if* they don't ...?" I press.

His gaze skitters over my dress again. "Then I suppose Islor will have its Ybarisan queen. At least, in appearance."

I feel my eyes widening in shock. He's saying I'll have to marry him?

"Unless you'd prefer to go back to your confine—"

"No. It's fine."

His brow is furrowed tightly. "Let us hope it doesn't come to that." He looks no more thrilled by the idea of marriage than I am.

But my opportunistic mind works quickly. "Would we be going into the nymphaeum too?"

His eyebrows pop with surprise.

"Wendeline mentioned it," I add.

"Then she would have also mentioned that there is only one reason for us to go there."

Two reasons, one of which you know nothing about. "I know."

His teeth grit. "I would never force that upon you, if that's what you're asking. I'm not a monster, despite what you think."

Is there nothing Wendeline didn't repeat?

Marrying him is bad enough, but somehow convincing Zander that I *want* him to take me there might be my best chance for snatching that stone. Malachi could whisk me away with his godly powers before I'm required to consummate anything, and I can put all of this—including my marriage to a king—behind me.

But I am a snake to him. He still doesn't trust me, even if he believes Wendeline's version that the old Romeria is gone. He would never fall for that a second time.

Still, if there is some way the new Romeria can win him over ... it might be my only opportunity.

His lips are pressed flat as he regards me a moment. "If there's nothing else, I will see you in the throne room. Try to act like the future queen and not some boorish laborer imbibing at the tavern." He strolls stiffly toward my door, pausing when he reaches it, his back to me. "Corrin was the queen's lady maid and confidante—a rare position for a mortal. She feels responsible for what happened to them because she did not see it coming until it was too late. My mother trusted her implicitly, which is why I also trust her. That she was willing to take on your care despite her anguish is a testament to her love for my family, and for Islor. Perhaps you can keep that in mind when you show such casual disregard for her services."

He leaves without a second glance, quietly pulling the door shut behind him.

CHAPTER FIFTEEN

Elisaf stands next to a coat of arms, dressed in his formal uniform, gripping the hilt of his sword with the arm that Zander nearly hacked off earlier.

I can't help but beam as we approach him, my relief temporarily overwhelming the nerves churning in my stomach.

He bows and announces, "I will escort Her Highness from here per the king's orders."

Guard—I still haven't learned his name—doesn't need to be told twice. He offers a curt "Your Highness," and marches away.

"I don't think he likes his current assignment," I mock whisper.

"I think you may be correct." Elisaf falls into step beside me. "But Her Highness seems delighted."

"I'm happy to see you're not dead. I was worried about you."

He offers a bashful smile. "No need to worry yourself. The priestess is more than capable of managing a mild wound." He lifts his arm as if testing it and winces a touch.

"Right. *Mild.* And would Wendeline have been able to reattach your arm?"

"I do believe that would have been more problematic."

I shake my head at his glibness. "And you're not the least bit annoyed at your *friend* for maiming you?"

"My *friend*'s thoughts are weighed down by many challenges presently, one of which I'm leading into his throne room. I do not begrudge him for his miscalculation. Besides, I knew his head wasn't clear. I should have stopped it."

We turn down a grand hall, empty save for the royal guards that bank the sides every third gold pillar, standing sentry. At the end of it is a tall set of double doors that I assume is my destination. The rash of nerves that have accompanied me since leaving my suite come back with a vengeance. "What exactly does 'receiving my formal absolution for all crimes' mean?"

"His Highness did not explain?"

"I think he was more concerned with getting away from me as quickly as possible."

Elisaf mutters under his breath. "Permission to speak freely, Your Highness?"

I groan. "You don't have to ask me that." I'm about to scream with all these formalities.

With a slight head dip, he lowers his voice. "Most of Islor's immortal population despises Ybaris. Some of the more powerful lords and ladies openly challenged this union to begin with."

"They don't want peace between the two countries?"

"Peace is not so simply secured through a marriage. Our history is fraught with hatred that is deeply ingrained. It took great effort by King Eachann to convince the court this arrangement would be beneficial to Islor, but after what happened here and what Neilina did to her own husband, those lords and ladies will not be swayed again. Others want to believe but are wary. And now there is no benefit unless you and Zander can negotiate with Neilina." He hesitates. "The Islorians have grown accustomed to living a certain way, and they fear change. They want the power of the casters returned to Islor, but they deem a union between you two is a trick for Neilina to seize our land, and the most recent assault only confirms that."

"But he's the king. Does it matter what they want or say?"

"He *is* the king," Elisaf echoes. "No, he does not need their permission, but he also cannot rule a realm as vast as Islor on his own. The lords and ladies are the stewards of this land and its people. They ensure crops are sown and harvested, taxes are collected, and the king's laws are upheld. Their soldiers may be bound to the king, but first and foremost, they are loyal to those they know. If the nobility does not respect the monarchy, ruling over Islor becomes more difficult for Zander. His laws are not upheld without challenge, uprisings and rebellions stir, allegiances with enemies prevail."

"Like with Lord Muirn."

"And whoever else feels they can do a better job of ruling in his place."

"Are there others?"

"Always."

"And could they? Rule better, I mean." It's a provocative question.

Elisaf's firm "no" followed by a resolute head shake and a stern expression tells me he believes it wholeheartedly. That, or he would never want to be caught saying otherwise.

"Zander must make a formal declaration in front of them all, as king, that you are innocent, and that you will be queen of Islor."

"And then they'll accept it?"

"No. But it is a first step and one he feels he must take to travel down this path he sees himself heading." Worry blinks in Elisaf's brown eyes.

We're approaching the doors, and I feel ill-prepared. Elisaf slows, bowing toward me to ensure only I can hear what he has to say next. "Walk in there with your head held high as your *evil* Romeria would. Do not speak more than necessary and do not forget proper salutations. The last thing the king needs is Boaz losing his temper and barking at you like some feral dog in front of the court."

"I think that guy would *kill* me in front of the court if allowed." *Again*.

"Likely. Though, he is not so bad."

I can't keep the soft snort from escaping.

Elisaf's lips purse. "A plot unraveled beneath his nose that killed the king and queen he is charged to protect and ravaged a city his men are trained to keep safe. The burden he shoulders is heavy."

I've been too busy despising Boaz for his cruel treatment of me, I never considered that. "He feels responsible." As Corrin feels responsible, being a part of the queen's staff whose duty it was to care for her. "Well, if it's any consolation, he did kill me with that arrow." I just didn't stay dead.

Elisaf gives me a look. "He begged Zander to take his life as punishment for his failure."

"That's messed up." But I suppose it speaks to Boaz's honor and sense of duty. I've been so focused on *my* situation and how to be free of it, I haven't thought about others within these walls who are in their own dreadful situations, still mourning losses. While *I* may not be guilty, Princess Romeria is, and that's the only person they see when they look at me. I'm a conniving murderess within their midst, who they're now forced to guard and feed and serve for the sake of Islor. Whether some invocation has wiped my memory or not means nothing to them. How would I react in their place, other than with anger and hate?

I swallow against that sobering thought. "What did Zander do? I mean, besides not killing him, seeing as Boaz is still around."

"Zander has few people he trusts. Boaz is one of them. He served King Eachann for the entirety of his reign, as well as his predecessor, never taking a wife, never fathering a child. That is a loyalty to the crown that you cannot buy for all the gold in the kingdom."

"For how many years?"

Elisaf smiles. "I think you mean to ask for how many centuries?"

The set of doors parts then, distracting me from giving his shocking words the attention they deserve. Guards dressed in full livery push either side open, the strain visible in their faces and arms suggesting it requires strength. Beyond them, a grand ballroom and a crowd of well-dressed people stands between me and Zander, who sits in his throne upon a dais at the far end, his expression stony. He gestures at me with a slight wave of his hand. *You may enter*, he's saying.

The muscles in my legs tighten, the urge to run overwhelming.

"I'll be behind you the entire time," Elisaf whispers. "Stop before the first step. Remember what I said."

"That they all hate me," I whisper back. "Got it."

His barely concealed snort gives me a second's respite from the tension coursing through my limbs. Taking a deep breath, I tilt my head and begin my trek forward, reminding myself that this is no different from slinking into a hotel ballroom full of strangers and pretending I'm someone else. Except I'm the center of attention, strolling down a makeshift aisle banked by a hundred people, all eyes on me.

If this were a job for Korsakov, I'd be quietly casing the situation and doing my best to blend in, not appear guilty. I do that now, trying to ignore the judging stares and buzz of hushed whispers, shifting my focus to my surroundings without looking enthralled. It's difficult not to be. The room itself is magnificent, several stories tall and constructed in limestone and gleaming marble of every shade from ivory to ebony, the floor decorated in a swirling pattern. Busts of former kings and queens on pedestals fill the space between gold pillars.

At the opposite end, fifteen steps lead to a dais and two thrones, their forms cast in entwined ebony horns like the ones on Malachi's head. Behind, a canvas of decorative windows reaches from dais floor to vaulted ceilings, allowing daylight to stream in.

To my right, at floor level, are two stately chairs. Annika and

Atticus occupy them, their faces reserved and revealing nothing. Now that they sit side by side, I see how similar in appearance they are.

I spare them one more second of attention before shifting my focus to where it should be—on the king.

Zander's expression is even as he watches me approach, his posture oddly casual, his elbow resting on one armrest, his chin braced by his palm. He's not wearing a crown, I note. Perhaps his throne is enough.

I stop at the bottom of the stairs as Elisaf instructed and curtsy as Corrin taught me, keeping my back stiff and dipping my head only slightly. *You are the future queen, not his wench!* she had barked. I steal a glance to my left to where Boaz stands, his hand on the hilt of his sword, his face steely. I'm trying to picture the glowering captain on his knees, begging to be executed, and I can't. At least he appears satisfied by my efforts, so far.

A hush falls over the room as everyone waits for the king to speak.

Zander allows that deathly silence to stretch, until every cleared throat cuts like the whir of a chainsaw in a still morning, every whisper like a howling wind passing through a cracked window.

I fight the urge to squirm. Has he changed his mind about this scheme? Decided he can't go through with it? Maybe I am to be sentenced to death instead.

"There have been many rumors traveling through Islor as of late that I would like to lay to rest once and for all." His voice is deep and commanding, carrying through the hollows of this massive room. It doesn't waver from nerves or a heavy heart. "I have summoned you all here on this day to bear witness to the truth. Princess Romeria of Ybaris is as much a victim to Queen Neilina's duplicitous scheming as I am. She traveled here to fulfill the agreement made between King Barris and King Eachann for our union, and she did it with honor. At no time did she conspire against Islor."

Zander pauses, barely concealing the foul taste of those words. This must curl his insides to say out loud. "While the obligation to Ybaris is now forfeit, Her Highness wishes to remain in Islor, at my side, in hopes that our union will bring future peace between our realms. I am amenable to that arrangement."

A mix of gasps and soft murmurs flares behind me.

Zander raises his hand, cutting off the sound instantly. "Queen Neilina is at the root of all evil. Through her sycophants, she persuaded the High Priestess Margrethe to summon Malachi for the purpose of unleashing chaos on us. Neilina assassinated her own husband and now she tries to amass an army based on a web of lies, including one that claims Islor murdered the heir to their throne." He smirks as he gestures toward me. "As you can all see, we did no such thing."

I steal another glance at Boaz.

His eyebrow twitches, the only response to that lie. But it is not the only falsehood Zander just told his court, not if what Annika said about Margrethe summoning Malachi to bring me back to life is true.

I suppose this is all one big, bloated lie, though.

"Her Highness is alive and well, despite being attacked while trying to stop the insurgents. She has chosen Islor, and we will make sure that news reaches the farthest corners of Ybaris. It will make a compelling declaration against her mother's treachery, and should we face our foes again in battle, we will make sure they question their own allegiances." His gaze roams the faces in the standing-room crowd, as if daring any of them to challenge him.

No one utters a word.

Would they ever speak out against the king? How would Zander react? Would his carefully crafted composure break? Would he roar his displeasure? I've felt that rage before, directed at me. But it was fueled by emotion, by heartache and agony.

Here, he leads with a commanding calm. I can't decide which is scarier.

Shifting his attention back to me, Zander dips his head once, ever so slightly. It's followed by Elisaf's barely audible throat clear. A signal that this political display is—thankfully—over already.

I stifle the urge to sigh with relief, offering Zander another tempered curtsy and a murmur of "Your Highness" without any bite in my tone, counting to three in my head so I don't appear as though I'm bolting out of here.

But then Zander does something that catches me off guard. He smiles. A lip-parting, eye-twinkling, dimple-popping smile that promises mischief, transforming his handsome, albeit severe, face to one of boyish charm. It appears so genuine that even *I'm* having a hard time reminding myself of the loathing behind it.

We have a secret, the king and I—and a few trusted others.

I feel my own face transform with a smile that is for once not forced but relieved and maybe even a touch giddy. For a moment —a split second—the throne room, the audience, our sordid history ... it all vanishes from my mind. How did Princess Romeria meet that smile time and time again while plotting his murder and *not* waver in her plans?

Surprise flashes in his eyes. I swear, sometimes I think he can read my thoughts. But if he could, he would know my secret.

"Your Highness," Elisaf whispers behind me, and I realize I've been gaping openly at Zander for far too long.

We're playing a part, I remind myself, my cheeks burning. And by the heady buzz of titters and whispers growing behind me, we're doing it well. They all think me dim-witted, so I suppose this works.

I keep my head up as I turn and stroll past Elisaf, who waits to follow me out. I feel oddly lighter than when I came in, despite that spectacle. Or perhaps it's the vibe in the room that is lighter, the faces staring back at me reflecting more curiosity than animosity.

Not all faces. I spot the woman from the royal grounds, the one with coal-black eyes and a visible hatred. Even now, her jaw is set firmly as she watches me pass, her attention shifting downward to my ring or my cuffs, I can't be sure. I need to figure out who she is.

The moment the doors seal shut behind me, I release my heavy sigh. "Bloody hell, I'm so glad that's over."

Elisaf frowns strangely at me. "I fear it is only beginning, Your Highness."

CHAPTER SIXTEEN

"Is there anything else tonight?" Corrin asks from the threshold of my terrace, the usual bite in her tone absent.

I pause in my nightly ritual of spying on courtesans to spare her a look. Her eyes wear the dark circles of a woman who has been on her feet all day, preparing my accommodation, making sure I have everything I could possibly need in addition to whatever other responsibilities she has in the castle. Me, the woman who caused the death of her beloved queen.

I once joked to Wendeline that Corrin would one day poison my meal. Now that I know more about the lady maid, I can't believe she hasn't. "No, I'm good." I hesitate. "Thank you. For *everything* you've done for me so far."

Her mouth falls open a moment, as if taken aback. "I only do what is required of me."

I highly doubt Zander required her to go down to the port and fetch those prized grapes, and even if he did, it wouldn't have been for his prisoner. But I also suspect Corrin will never admit to that unnecessary benevolence. She likely considers it a betrayal to the memory of Zander's mother to show me *any* kindness. I know *I* would wrestle with that guilt, if I were in her shoes. "Regardless, thank you. I know this can't be easy for you."

"Yes, well ..." She presses her lips together. "I suppose it's not effortless for you either, not remembering who you are."

"And yet the more I learn about that person, the more I despise her."

Corrin grunts. "Her Highness said your tongue was forked like a serpent and silvered like a siren's song. She was concerned her son could not think as a king should when you were around. He was too busy chasing your skirts." Her eyes flicker over the rose-colored robe and nightgown set I found in my closet. The robe's hem sweeps the floor, the lace trim at the edges a delicate accent that balances out the sheer tulle sleeves and oversize sash ties at the center. The silky nightgown beneath is subtle but provocative—more in line with what I might choose for myself if I were shopping back home in New York.

I brace for her mocking remark—something about me strolling around in my underwear, no doubt—but she only says, "Do not spend all night out here. You are to meet the priestess in the sanctum early."

I groan.

"It's important that you understand their ways if you are to survive around these—" Her lips press into a thin line. "With the court."

I detect a hint of animosity, but it's Corrin. Animosity laces most of her words. "I know. I just don't have fond memories of that place."

Her face softens a touch, her gaze flickering to my shoulder. "I will wake you in the morning, if you are not already up. Your Highness." She curtsies and turns to leave.

"I don't think I looked like a peasant in the throne room today."

"I heard your performance was exemplary and sufficiently to task. You're welcome," she calls over her shoulder as she marches away.

I smile as I turn back to take in my view. The same one, and yet from a different angle than what I woke to this morning. I'm still technically an inmate, unable to come and go as I please, but it's a much more comfortable disguise. My eyes drift over to the darkened wing where my prison walls remain. What will they do with those rooms now that I've vacated them? Do they accommodate guests there as readily as prisoners?

A flicker of light draws my attention to Zander's terrace. Someone has lit a candle inside his rooms. Is he in his suite for the night, or is a servant preparing it for him? I returned here after that public spectacle in the throne room and had a quiet dinner while the court gathered and reveled somewhere beneath. I was happy for the solitude after such a long day. I need time to learn all that I can before I tackle this role of Princess Romeria.

But I've found myself glancing at my door, listening for footsteps, for a firm knock, for Zander to stroll into my sitting room once again. I'm anxious to hear what he thought of today's declaration.

But if I'm being honest, I'm also interested in catching another one of those smiles he produced as part of this ruse.

Without considering it too much, I take the narrow path between our terraces, my bare feet soundless as they pad against the cool, gritty stone floor. I pause, my heart racing. This might be a foolish decision. Though, if he were worried about me trying to kill him, he wouldn't have moved me where he did. Still, I'm creeping over to his room as if I'd be a welcomed visitor—in my robe, no less.

I take a deep, calming breath and then poke my head around the corner.

A woman with long, blond hair the color of corn silk and skin so pale I might doubt it's ever been touched by the sun sits on the edge of the bed. She's wearing a burgundy cloak over a white gown. A candelabra on the nightstand casts a healthy glow over her high cheekbones and smooth, youthful complexion. Her hands are folded in her lap, her fingers toying with each other.

"You've got to be kidding me," I mutter, cold realization sinking my stomach. It's not a surprise she attracted his attention. She's stunning, in an innocent, wholesome way. But on the same day Zander announces to the court that we're back together and moves me into the suite beside him, he brings *another woman* into his bed? Is he a fool or a bastard? Or is this simply the way of a king?

Regardless, how can these optics not work against us?

Zander walks into view from another room, and a sharp intake of breath sails through my lips. He has removed his jacket and loosened his tunic, the light, white linen unlaced at the top to hint at a chest padded with muscle. He walks with a casual swagger I've never seen from him before, and the smile he offers the woman is genuine and soft.

She looks up fleetingly, long enough to smile demurely before her focus drops to her lap again, as if afraid to meet his eyes.

Who is she? Another courtesan who strolls the grounds during the day? There's something different about her, though. She's far less poised than those I've seen. Did he have a few glasses of wine and decide to work out his frustrations here rather than in the sparring court? Does he even drink? I know *nothing* about Zander.

But I *hate* this tight feeling in my chest as I watch this exchange. I can't pinpoint what is causing it. It can't be hurt, because this is all a charade. It can't be jealousy, because aside from that devastating look he laid on me this afternoon and a few desperate moments in the tower that first night while he was threatening my life, he's never been anything but the king who holds me captive.

He pauses in thought, a strange look skipping across his face. I ready to jump back the second he turns toward the terrace, even if there is no way he can find me within the shadows.

He says something to her. She nods and reaches up to unfasten the clasp on her cloak. The material slides off to pool on the stark white bedding, revealing a simple dress much like the nightgown I used to wear, except this one has a plunging neckline and wide collar, the linen fabric settling off her shoulders. It's seductive in design, exposing plenty of skin and the swell of the woman's full breasts. She may be playing demure, but she is not prim.

How he likes his women, based on what I've heard.

And now that her hair has fallen back, I see the thick gold band on her ear. She's a royal servant. A human.

The king is bedding a slave?

He says something else, and she nods again, and her throat bobs with a hard swallow. She's a servant who's nervous to lie with the king. I don't blame her. Zander is intimidating in regular conversation. Sitting on his bed with him looming over you like that?

Did Princess Romeria ever sit on his bed like that, waiting for him? A strange feeling stirs deep within me at the thought. Corrin said he was busy chasing her skirts. Did she let him under there? Or did she play her game like a pro, giving only so much that he wanted more while she ensnared him in her web?

Zander reaches out and slides a finger along the servant's cheek, shifting a wayward strand of hair off her face. It's a tender gesture, and one that is about to lead to more as he kneels on the bed beside her and grips her chin, pushing her head back to expose her long, slender neck.

I should turn around and head back to my rooms—

He parts his lips and, with a slight wince, two white, needle-thin fangs descend from his upper jaw.

I blink several times.

This can't be right. I *must* be hallucinating.

My hands muzzle the scream that threatens to escape my mouth as I watch Zander lean forward and sink his teeth into the woman's jugular, while easing her back on his bed. She doesn't fight, flinch, or recoil.

He's *feeding* off her.

Just as the daaknar tried to feed off me.

My head spins as I struggle to absorb what I'm seeing, my mind unable to form a coherent thought. The woman's chest heaves with deep breaths; her hips curl toward Zander's body. She reaches up to smooth her hand over his shoulder and along his back, the gentle stroke one of affection. Though I can't hear anything through the closed doors, I can imagine any sounds she's making are of pleasure.

She's *enjoying* what Zander's doing to her. *How* is she enjoying this? Even now, the excruciating burn of the daaknar's teeth where it bit into my flesh is still fresh in my mind.

Zander suddenly pulls away from the woman's neck, and his head reels toward the terrace. His heavy-lidded eyes meet mine as surely as if he can see me in the darkness.

As if he knew I was there all along, watching this horror unfold.

I jump out of view and rush back to my side, my feet slapping on the stone, my heart pounding in my chest. I dart through my bedchamber and keep going, running through the vacuous sitting room, pitch-black save for the light of a lone lantern, all the way to the door, my robe a billowing mass around me. I test the handle with a frantic jiggle. As usual, it's locked from the outside.

"Elisaf?" My voice is hoarse and brimming with panic. "Elisaf!"

Silence answers.

I lean my forehead against the wood with a soft thud. I've spent five weeks confined and yet I haven't felt this trapped since the night of the tower. "*Please*, I know you're out there." I don't, and the door is flush with the floor, offering me no glimpse of anyone beyond, but he's *always* out there. I hold my breath and listen. A boot scuffs against the marble. "I don't understand what's happening."

But I think I do. *This* is what Wendeline was talking about when she said she was afraid to come to Islor. She was afraid because Islorians are … what are they?

Vampires?

A version of elven who drink blood?

It dawns on me. *This* is the difference between two people who once shared the same ancestry. At some point, Islorians began *feeding* off humans like bloodsucking vampires.

And King Barris shuttled his own daughter off to marry one of them. Princess Romeria didn't want to marry Zander because of *this*. It's all beginning to make sense, finally.

Wendeline, Elisaf, Corrin ... all of them know.

It is a requirement. That's what Elisaf said about the human slaves, how almost all households have them. He said so many things that I now see through an entirely different lens.

"Elisaf?" Still no answer. Is he truly not there, or is he ignoring me? I hesitate. "Are you one of them?" He said he was from Seacadore, which means he isn't fully Islorian. So maybe he—

"He feeds off mortal blood, if that is what you're asking. We all do," comes Zander's chilly voice behind me.

I let out a yelp as I spin around, pressing my back against the door.

Zander approaches from the vast darkness like a wraith in the night, his footfalls making no sound. He stops inches from me. "It is safe to assume you haven't been lying about your memory loss."

My body is rigid with terror. "What are you?"

His lips twist in a toothy smile that doesn't reach his eyes, no hint of fangs to be seen. "I'm like you."

"No." I shake my head. "I don't do *that*." Do I? My tongue smooths over my incisors, searching for evidence to say otherwise.

His gaze tracks the move, as if he knows what I'm checking for. "I was shocked when I realized you did not remember the profound difference between your people and mine. That Malachi would deprive you of that knowledge was ... interesting. I can't figure out why he would."

Because I'd be horrified?

His eyes drop to my disheveled robe. "That night in the tower, I was *so* close ..." His fingertips push the collar open to expose where the daaknar left its mark. "What would have happened to me?"

I flinch at the feel of his index finger tracing the scar closest to my collarbone. What would have happened had he bitten me, he means. I remember the moment—he tore at the seam of my dress and lingered over my skin. He wasn't deciding whether to fuck the woman who broke his heart and betrayed his kingdom; he was deciding whether to sink his teeth into her.

And if he had, he might have died as the daaknar did.

"You can't feed off me," I say out loud as I process this.

"I certainly wouldn't try." He collects my chin. His eyes are no longer sleepy. They're full of heat and anger and something else entirely. "Now you know why your kind finds ours so repulsive. Perhaps you'll remember that the next time you look at me the way you did in the throne room."

I struggle to push down the paralyzing fear gripping my body. Is that what this demonstration is about? "And what way was that?"

His eyes search my face as if there might be a truth hiding within my features. "As if there could ever be something real between us. There cannot." He releases his grip of me and strolls away, disappearing into the shadows, back the way he came, to his room and his willing victim.

And I stay pressed against the door for many long moments after he is gone, my limbs shaky, my thoughts scattered.

Elisaf, Annika, the soldiers, the nobility …

All these Islorian immortals *feed* off humans. And Ybarisans, apparently, though they can't feed off me.

And I've agreed to play smitten queen-to-be to their blood-sucking king. I clutch my hands against my chest, feeling the pound of my heartbeat. I need to find the nymphaeum and get out of this hellish place as fast as possible.

I cradle the stone mug within my palms, savoring the hints of orange and licorice in the herbal tea Corrin delivered. Below me, the lone swordsman twirls around the empty sparring court beneath the touch of dawn's light. He swings his blade with smooth, practiced strokes as if from memory, a choreographed dance that he has run through a thousand times.

I didn't realize it was Boaz at first, and when I did, I couldn't believe it. The gruff, ill-tempered man moves like an armed ballerina. It's impossible not to admire his talent, even if I don't care for him.

Even if I now know what he is.

In theory, anyway.

Last night, under the glow of a lantern, I scoured my room for a secret passage, an escape. But my desperate search failed, leaving me little choice but to curl up in my stately bed and dwell on a hundred new questions and fears about this world I find myself trapped in. The hours faded, and while I can't say what time I drifted off from exhaustion, it couldn't have been long before Corrin marched into my room with a tray of breakfast. She took one look at my face, nodded solemnly, and stepped out. She knows I am finally privy to the true nature of the immortals of Islor.

What must it be like to be her, serving people who might order your vein as easily as a pot of tea? Do the immortal Islorians drink or eat as we do? How often do they sink their fangs into necks? I've been so isolated up until now, I haven't had the opportunity to notice anything *off* about them. That must have been Zander's goal all along.

Do these creatures exist in *my* world? They must. How else would vampire fables exist? Except they're not like the nightmarish tales of my world. They don't hide in the shadow of night and sleep in coffins and attack unsuspecting humans, stealing their mortality. They stroll down sunny paths and sleep in beds and toss gold coins to the poor.

A slight scuff against stone is the only warning I have that I'm no longer alone on my terrace. A fresh wave of tension slides along my spine as Zander leans against the railing beside me, his hands casually folded.

I pull my robe tighter around my chest. If Corrin returns while he's here, she's going to scold me for being indecent. I don't see why decorum matters. I'm surrounded by people who drink blood.

"He is something to behold, is he not?" Zander says softly, as if afraid his voice will carry and disturb the captain. "He practices like this every morning. Always has, for as long as I can remember."

I can't help but stare. It's as if last night's horror never happened. Zander's handsome face is serene, his shoulders relaxed. Is his oddly light and cheerful mood because he feels sated by that woman's blood? Or is it about what they did *after* he left me alone in my room, terrified? I'd be an idiot to believe he didn't get his pleasure from her. Zander may be a king, but he's a male who brought a willing female to his bed, and I saw how she responded to him.

But to let me find out this monstrous secret the way he did, and then stroll out here this morning as if all is well in the world ... my anger flares at his callousness, and it helps drown out my fear of him.

"You don't have to guard your tongue, Romeria. As I've already told you, I would rather have your candor than your false fealty." There's amusement in his tone. "Speak freely. It's just us here."

"Is it, though?" I make a point of shifting my gaze toward his terrace.

"I assume you're referring to my guest last night? The one you saw while skulking outside my bedchamber?"

"I was *not skulking*." My cheeks redden. "And bringing a woman to your bed the night you announce we're together was not a wise move." Regardless of his sinister reasons. "I thought you were smarter than that."

Zander's eyebrows arch.

Maybe I *should* guard my tongue a touch, but now that he's committed himself to this scheme, I feel less risk of punishment with speaking my mind. If he wanted me dead, he could have killed me a thousand times over. "I hope you were at least discreet about your *needs*."

"I'm *always* discreet," he counters smoothly.

"Is it normal that the king would openly screw other women when his future queen is in the room beside him, or is that only our arrangement?" How often will he be bringing women to his room?

"*Screw*?"

"Bed. Hump. *Fuck*."

His eyes flash. *That*, he understands. "Not as normal as it would be for the queen to join him."

My mouth gapes.

"Should I expect this foul mood in the mornings going forward?"

"I don't know. Do you have any more life-altering surprises to share with me?"

He mock frowns. "Not that I can foresee."

I shake my head. He's far too glib about it, especially for a man who last night used his disturbing nature as a warning against developing feelings for him. As if I ever would.

He sighs heavily, and when he speaks again, there is a hint more somberness in his voice. "Honestly, I don't know what would be normal, given a Ybarisan and Islorian have not married for two thousand years, and your needs are not the same as mine. The need for mortal blood, I mean." He surveys where my hand grips the front of my robe. "The other one is quite universal."

I tighten my hold, swallowing against the unwelcome physical reaction the attention stirs.

Something flashes in his eyes. "The tributary left immediately after, so *those* needs were not met, in case you were wondering."

"I *wasn't*," I snap.

The corners of his mouth twitch. "At least you are not so terrified of me today."

I set my chin. "It was … shocking, is all." But I've learned to bury my fear to survive. "Tributary? What is that?"

"A human servant who makes themselves available to us specifically for feeding."

And fucking, apparently, if he's in the mood. How do those deadly looking incisors slide out? I never felt so much as a hint of them when we kissed that night.

"You cannot see them unless I make a point of showing them to you."

I realize I'm staring at Zander's mouth, searching for evidence. I refocus on my mug of tea. But his words are not lost on me—he intentionally revealed them last night. He wanted me to know the truth about him.

I hesitate. "Are you a daaknar?"

"They are repulsive beasts with decaying flesh and tattered wings. Is that what you think of me now?" he says, a sharp edge in his tone.

I shake my head. Opposite of that, despite the fangs, which were not nearly as long or horrid as that of the demon's. It's obvious I've hit a nerve. "There is one rather glaring similarity."

"Daaknars are said to come from Azo'dem, where evil resides. It has been suggested they once walked the living realm but upon death were morphed by sin and cruelty and turned into creatures like the one you saw."

Azo'dem is their version of hell, I'm certain now, so the daaknar are demons. I remember the way it lingered over me, stroking the strands of hair away. It seemed oddly human—or elven—in that moment.

"How did it start?" What made them drink human blood? Wendeline made it sound like the Islorian immortals weren't always this way.

"The priestess will explain all of that to you. I have neither the time nor the inclination for that history lesson." Zander watches

Boaz collect his sword and jacket and quietly leave the court. No one is out, except for a few guards. "I find myself oddly relieved that you now know about our nature. Though I cannot explain why I would care," he mutters, more to himself. "But will you be able to put this revelation past you and play your part when the time comes?"

"Do I have any other choice?" I must, if I want to buy myself enough freedom to find the nymphaeum and get out of this place. "Yes, but can you at least warn me next time, so I don't stumble on *that* again?"

He dips his head in agreement. "I won't need it again for some time."

"Can you live without it?" Is what I witnessed happening in Zander's room more about pleasure or need?

Zander remains quiet for a long moment. I have *so* many questions, but he is not eager to fill in the blanks. "Not indefinitely," he finally admits. "The longer we go without mortal blood, the weaker we get." He pauses. "What were you doing on my terrace in the middle of the night, anyway? In your nightgown, no less. Did *you* have a need you wanted me to help with?"

My face bursts with heat. "No!" I scoff. *Arrogant prick.*

He smirks. "Then perhaps coming to try for my dagger again?"

"I came to see how things went with your court after I left."

"They went exactly as I expected them to," he says dismissively, studying the hills in the distance. "Many questions about where you've been and why I've been hiding you all this time, why you didn't join me last night. Others danced around their displeasure in our union while trying not to offend me for fear of earning my wrath."

"Your Highness," Corrin calls from the doorway, curtsying deeply to Zander. Her shrewd eyes turn to me, and there is no missing the rebuke in them even before she speaks. "Your gown is laid out for you, *Your Highness.*" She looks pointedly at my robe.

"Thanks, Corrin. I'll be there in a sec."

She opens her mouth, but a quick glance at Zander has her scurrying back inside.

"Corrin isn't one of these tributaries, is she?"

"She was for a short time when she was young, as are all humans of a certain age. She was miserable in the role, and not particularly good at it. But my mother saw intelligence and loyalty in her, so she ordered her services as a lady maid, freeing her from other servitude." He smiles, a genuine smile that makes his eyes crinkle. "She said Corrin was too sour to be a tributary. Her blood would poison people as surely as merth."

Amazing. Bad vampiric humor. I bite my tongue against the urge to say as much.

A grave expression passes over his face, and I sense his mood darkening. "That is how my father and mother died. You learned of their tributaries and had your lady maid taint their beverages with deliquesced merth. We had no idea it was even possible to create a poison like that. My parents always took their repast at night, but they decided to call for their tributary *before* our wedding ceremony on that day." His jaw tenses. "The poison tore them apart from the inside. It took about fifteen minutes. I made it in time to see the end."

So that's how Princess Romeria did it—by targeting the humans who were supplying the blood.

While I struggle with how I feel about these Islorians feeding off humans, I don't revel in stories of their suffering. Annika described touching merth as having a thousand razor blades slicing across your skin. What would that feel like from the inside? I cringe against the gruesome thought. "What did the merth do to the humans? The tributaries?"

"Nothing. It's tasteless, odorless. They genuinely had no idea what had happened when they offered themselves. They were devastated."

Devastated by the death of the king and queen feeding from them?

"You will never understand the bond that immortals can form with their tributaries," he says, as if reading my thoughts.

Because this body I inhabit is immortal, and Islorians feed off human blood. Something strikes me as odd. "What were you going to do to me in the tower that night, then? I'm not mortal." At least, this body isn't. What need would he have for biting me?

His eyes trace my neck. "We can still feed off elven, though we don't gain any sustenance from it. There are other, more intoxicating reasons to do it. But I planned to help you become that which you despise most. One of us. Let you live in our skin for a few hours, until you met your end in the square." His gaze ventures off toward the rising sun, a somber look across his face. "Let you know what it's like to be at the mercy of that craving."

I feel my eyebrows arch. "You were going to turn me?" My God, they *are* like vampires.

"You are certainly safe from that now." With a smirk, Zander moves for his terrace, calling over his shoulder, "Enjoy your lesson with Wendeline."

I watch him vanish, an odd mix of fear and curiosity swirling inside me.

CHAPTER SEVENTEEN

My wary eyes drift over the sanctum's interior. The mahogany pews are smooth, the marble tile floor on the dais gleams white, and a waft of sage incense permeates my nose. All signs of the daaknar attack have been erased, as though it never happened.

Yet, if I inhale deeply, I smell its foul stench. If I listen intently, I hear its claws scraping against the wood. And in the darkness of my mind's eye, I see the pool of blood and maimed body behind the altar.

Outside, the sanctum is a jaw-dropping Gothic splendor of countless angles and spires, a cathedral made of obsidian, but trimmed in so much gold, silver, and bronze that it glimmers like a beacon under the sun.

Soft footfalls sound. I turn to find Wendeline approaching, her translucent gold veil shimmering in the streams of daylight that shines through windows high above. Warmth instantly blooms in my chest at the sight of her friendly face.

"Your Highness." She curtsies deeply. Her voice is a soothing song. "It's good to see you again. Things have changed considerably since we last spoke."

I smile through the sting of resentment I feel toward her and Elisaf for dancing around the Islorian's dark truth, even if Zander gave them no other choice. "More than I expected."

Her vivid blue eyes venture to my shoulder, hidden beneath the maroon brocade. "Are you feeling well?"

"I'm fine. *Hot.*" I tug at the collar that reaches to my chin. The dress Corrin insisted I wear today is heavy and better suited to cool temperatures, and I'm already sweating from the short walk here.

She smiles. "Then I suppose not *everything* has changed."

I chuckle despite my bitter mood. "No, I guess not."

"His Highness has requested that I tutor you in all things divine." She holds out her arms, palms up, gesturing to the towering figures surrounding the altar.

"*And* some things that aren't." Would anyone call what these Islorian immortals are *divine*?

She dips her head in acknowledgment. "His Highness has finally revealed himself to you."

"That's one word for it." I glare at Elisaf. Between the sheepish look he greeted me with this morning and my bubbling antipathy for him after standing outside my door last night, listening to my terror and saying *nothing*, our walk over was silent and tense.

Elisaf has the decency to avert his gaze. "Do you need me here, Priestess?"

"I do not anticipate another daaknar attack. Thank you."

They share a lingering look before Elisaf bows to me. "I'll be outside if you require my assistance, Your Highness."

I required it last night, I want to say. My eyes trail after the guard as he marches down the center aisle, wondering how often he feeds off humans, and who he feeds off, and whether I wish I'd never found out. No ... I'm glad Zander let me in on his secret. Maybe things will begin to make more sense now.

Wendeline studies me intently.

"It's so bare in here without all the flowers."

"It sounds like they may be back again soon enough?" There's a teasing lilt in her tone, though I'm not sure Wendeline is capable of taunting. And my situation is far from amusing. The flat look I give her says as much.

She gestures toward the first pew, guiding me to take a seat. "We can speak openly. There is no one else here."

The wood creaks as it accepts my weight. "How much do you know?"

"His Highness honors me by seeking my counsel," she admits, settling onto the bench.

It dawns on me. "You knew of his plan, that last day you came to visit." She hinted at my release.

"I knew he was considering it, yes," she confirms with a solemn nod.

"He trusts you. You're the reason he believes I'm not lying about not remembering who I am." If not for her, I'd still be locked up in that room. "When did you figure out Margrethe summoned Malachi to bring me back to life?" It feels odd to talk about something as if I understand it when I don't have the first clue.

"I suspected it after the daaknar attack and then was quite certain once the king described your conversation to me. But he wanted to be sure it was not another scheme. You needed time to heal, and the king needed time to decide his next move."

"He already knew I was telling the truth that day he brought me to his war room," I say more to myself. The day I saw the map. But he kept the pretense of doubt and suspicion going. I'm not the only one who knows how to pretend.

"We have much to discuss, and while I've secured time for us to speak freely, we do not have the sanctum too long. There are other casters needing to attend to their duties." She claps her hands together. "Where should we begin?"

"How about the king's fangs?"

She dips her head. "To understand how the Islorians came to be, first you must understand our creators."

"Fine." I turn to the four looming figures before me.

"Vin'nyla, Fate of Air. Aminadav, Fate of Earth." I shift from the statue with silver wings affixed to her back to the one with bronze bison's horns, reciting the names Wendeline gave me. Those are the two Sofie hadn't mentioned, and I imagine I'll need to repeat their names a dozen times before they're firmly set in my mind.

Wendeline nods once, prompting me to continue.

I move on to the one with a broad crown of antlers branching wide like that of a mature deer. "She is Aoife, Fate of Water."

Find the gilded doe.

I shove aside my father's voice and settle on the last one, the statue with grand twisty obsidian horns. "Malachi, the Fate of Fire." The fate who has sent me here to complete a task. The four statues stand at the corners of the dais surrounding the altar, equal in size and stature. The gods of creation, the elements that make up all of nature, that gave life. They're anatomically similar to humans, except with hooves and horns, and wings in the case of the Fate of Air. Both males are well-endowed. Surely, those two created themselves.

Obsidian, gold, silver, and bronze. This entire sanctum is clad in those metals. Though I note with curiosity as I study Malachi, its outer walls seem an ode to him.

"Are any of them more powerful than the others?"

"That depends on who you ask. The appropriate answer would be that they are equal in power and equally worthy of our fealty."

"But ..." I sense it behind her words.

She takes a deep breath, her eyes flashing to the statues as if worried we've caught their attention. "It is said that the Fates of Fire and Water are not easily countered, and that they are often at odds with each other. It isn't a surprise. Malachi is known to be courageous and passionate, but he's weakened by envy and obsessiveness. He is the spark for all the lust and wrath in the world. Meanwhile, Aoife graces us with our forgiveness and humility. She promotes healing, peace, and trust. Yet she can be erratic, showing indifference in the face of agony. Both anger easily, especially when they're not shown the respect they feel they deserve.

"Elementals are all born with affinities to at least two of the fates, and for whatever reason, one of those affinities is *always* either to fire or water. For an elemental to summon Malachi, they must have an affinity to him. To summon Aoife, they must have an affinity to her, and so on. Long ago, when it was permissible to summon the fates, elementals most often bound themselves to either of these two over Aminadav and Vin'nyla, for it was the lust for power or the desire for mercy that often inspired the elemental or the king and queen in power."

Sofie said she serves Malachi. This must be what she meant. "But the elementals are forbidden from summoning the fates now."

"That is correct. The fates only meddle in our world when they are given the opportunity, and it became clear that it is *never* a good idea to give it to them. They thrive on conflict, with each other, and within their subjects. Answering a summons has less to do with the caster's requests and more to do with what the fate wants. There are always consequences. Sometimes they are not felt immediately."

Malachi allowed Sofie to pull me, a human doppelganger for Princess Romeria, from my world and drop me into her immortal body, which he resurrected and made lethal to a daaknar's bite. He can't be doing all this just to free Sofie's husband for her, especially not when he's the one holding the man hostage. So what is he after? "What kinds of things do the fates want?" I ask.

"Besides adoration? That is a question that I nor anyone else can answer with any degree of certainty. Some claim it is the unwavering devotion of the elementals, while others believe it has nothing to do with the elemental and everything to do with a bigger plan that we are not privy to." She smirks. "The more cynical among us assume we are but pawns on a game board to amuse the fates in what is an otherwise tiresome eternal existence of creating and watching. But that would mean the fates feel the same passage of time as we do, and I suspect that is not the case." She waves a hand dismissively. "That is a complex idea for a different day. Suffice it to say, it was agreed by both Ybaris and Mordain that the world is better off when the fates are not given an occasion to meddle."

And Islor only had one elemental capable of breaking that rule. "Why did Margrethe summon Malachi to bring me back to life? Is it true, what Zander said to the court?"

Her jaw tenses, the only hint of anger I've ever seen in the priestess. "There was no hiding the fact that a daaknar had been released into Cirilea that night. Its distinctive shrill scream has haunted children's tales for centuries. Too many recognized it for what it was. The king had no choice but to lay blame at Margrethe's feet in the way he did, to quell rumors and questions."

Is that how she truly feels, or is that the official answer? I study her. "But she didn't ask Malachi to send it here to tear apart the city, did she?"

"Margrethe would *never* have summoned Malachi for the purpose of chaos." Wendeline's answer is quick and uncharacteristically sharp. "Islor was her home. She summoned him to bring *you* back to life, to protect her home." Wendeline's frown deepens as she reaches into the folds of her robe to produce a paper that reminds me of parchment in its crinkly texture. "I found this in her desk. Obviously, she had her secrets." She adds more quietly, "As we *all* do."

I smooth my thumb over the swirling M of the broken wax seal before unfolding the letter.

The Princess of Ybaris must survive at all costs, by Malachi's will. – G

By Malachi's will. Is that a call to summons? "Who is G?"

She shakes her head. "Someone deeply knowledgeable. That is an official seal of Mordain's scribes. I'm not entirely sure how they learned of Margrethe. But nothing stays hidden forever, I suppose. Not even on this side of the rift."

"I thought Mordain is *against* summoning?"

"The guild is, officially, and they would demand Margrethe's execution, but we are far from their jurisdiction. Exiles, as far as they're concerned. But there are *always* those who oppose the ruling power, and who believe a different way of life would be better. Mordain has a long and complicated relationship with Ybaris. That is *also* a history lesson for another day. But whoever sent this to Margrethe"—she taps on the letter—"must have discovered something in the recorded prophecies that they feel is of great import as it relates to you."

I assume prophecy means the same thing here as it does in my world.

"Mordain has an endless library filled with *thousands* of years of visions from the seers. Things they've prophesied to come. Many have lost faith in the foretellings, seeing them as nothing but ramblings. The library has become a dusty museum during Neilina's rule, the visions' worth diminishing to nothing more than fodder for delusions. But there are still those in Mordain who find great value in the old texts, and who continue to scribe and study and search for the path forward."

My focus wanders to the altar to where I met this delinquent elemental. What could these seers foretell? And what might they have told the high priestess? "How well did you know Margrethe?"

"Well, and not at all, it would seem." Her gaze follows mine. "In Ybaris, casters are assigned various roles. Healers, light bringers, horticulturists, alchemists. My role was as a tester. I would attend births in the villages and assess the babies for caster abilities. I remember the day Margrethe was born well." She smiles fondly. "She had enormous brown eyes, far too big and alert for a newborn. I knew before I tested her that she was an elemental. To my dismay, she held affinities to both fire and air. The affinity to Malachi meant she would be put to death. I will explain that," she adds quickly, seeing the shock on my face.

"Her mother handed her off to me, not wanting anything to do with a caster child. She could not remain in Ybaris as she was, and if I brought her to Mordain, they would kill her. So I ran and brought her here where I could heal rather than harm, and taught her what I could of caster magic."

I listen to Wendeline rationalize kidnapping a child with a gloss coating her eyes, and the image of the mutilated body behind the altar hits me with greater meaning.

She takes a deep breath and then releases it slowly, as if calming herself. Does it anger her that the girl she raised as her own had secrets? "But we are not here to discuss prophecy, or Mordain and all its political motivations. You are here to learn of Islor." Wendeline's gaze slides over the grand forms surrounding the altar. "There may be questions about equality of power among the fates, but there is no question that they are uniformly arrogant in their need for reverence, and spiteful when they are not shown it. Summoning them has been expressly forbidden for almost two thousand years, but even when it wasn't, it was known that to beseech the aid of one fate would be to choose them over the others, and once an elemental did that, they were bound to serve that fate for life."

That means Margrethe would be bound to the Fate of Fire. "But it was Malachi's own demon that killed Margrethe."

"Yes. The fates have been known to be callous with their elementals. I suspect once she brought you back to life, Malachi had more use of the daaknar than he did of her." She flinches. "The fates are creators, but sometimes what they create also has the ability to destroy. And *that* is what we are here to discuss today."

I bite my tongue from interrupting more, sensing Wendeline's reluctance to speak of the high priestess any longer.

"Two thousand years ago, this land was all the kingdom of

Ybaris and ruled by King Faolan and Queen Rhean, elven who resided in Argon, the capital city where you were raised. Their eldest daughter, Princess Isla, was in line to assume the throne of Argon. In the meantime, she was ruling in Cirilea, considered the most important city within a southern land heavily dominated by humans. She was doing so admirably, according to history texts. But then Mordain sent her the elemental Ailill to serve, and she did what she should not. She fell in love with him.

"The king and queen did not approve of the union, but they did not fret because they assumed Ailill would not survive long, being an elemental and a mortal, and Isla would find an elven male to marry. It was a foolish assumption to make, and in hindsight, anyone could guess what would happen. Princess Isla was determined to reign as queen of Ybaris with Ailill at her side. And Ailill, of course, was eager to live as an immortal king. He bound himself to Malachi and implored the fate's passionate side to grant him the immortality of the elven so Ailill and Isla could spend eternity together. The Fate of Fire answered him."

I peer up at the figure with the black horns. "And he granted Ailill immortality?"

"He did, but not in the way Ailill hoped. Not in the way that Isla was immortal." Her brow furrows. "He granted him the long life of an elven, making him stronger and faster to move and to heal, and more difficult to defeat in battle than the elven, but he cursed him with an eternal bloodlust for human mortals that was challenging to control. It was like an infection in that it could spread to others if the impulse wasn't managed. Of course, Ailill did not understand what he had become, only that he had instincts he could not restrain. He bit Isla, infecting her as well. She in turn infected her lady maids. The disease quickly ran rampant through Cirilea and then beyond, into villages and towns, changing both human and elven into these new creatures. Elven lost their affinities when they changed. Casters who were bitten died."

"Why would Malachi do that?"

"Some believe it was in retaliation of something the other fates did that he did not like. Others believe he wanted to create a superior being. This bloodlust, while hard to manage, gave his creatures power and dominance. Both views may be correct.

"When the other fates learned of Malachi's handiwork that was quickly ravaging Ybaris and their creations, they were angry. They did not like seeing their creation corrupted in such a way, and so they unleashed a wrath like never seen before. Aminadav's fury cracked the land in two, creating a deep fissure through the mountains that, save for a small passage between, is perilous to cross. That is the Great Rift. Aoife, in her rage, stirred the western waters south of Mordain with a current so violent, no ship has ever survived sailing through since. That is the Grave Deep. Vin'nyla was the gentlest in her retribution, churning the wind into a funnel that tore through Cirilea, toppling buildings and killing thousands."

My eyebrows pop. "*That's* gentle?"

"Short-lived, at least, and possible to repair. But it was King Faolan and Queen Rhean who were perhaps the harshest with their punishment. They banished their daughter to remain south of the Great Rift, to never return upon penalty of death. They knew of the infection sweeping through the southern lands, and the terror it brought. Instead of sending their army into battle for their people, they used their elementals to build an impassable wall to keep the infected from crossing the rift into Ybaris. They abandoned their people to protect Argon.

"Isla and Ailill established themselves as the new king and queen, and the land became Islor, named after Queen Isla. They were the original Islorians, the first of their kind, which Ybaris to this day call Malachi's demons." She peers up at the Fate of Fire's ominous form. "Many struggled with accepting what they had become, including Ailill and Isla. Some tried feeding from animals to stave off the blood hunger. Others abstained altogether, continuing with their usual diet, and they grew weaker by the day. They realized that not feeding off the mortals wasn't an option, not if they wanted to survive. Given the lifespan of an immortal—"

"Which is what?" I cut in. Lifespan suggests they don't live forever.

She frowns curiously. "It varies greatly, but I would say anywhere from eight to ten centuries. Some, much longer."

I bite my tongue against the expletive that threatens to slip out.

"And with that many years, they feared soon there would be no mortals left. And then what? How would the Islorians survive? Through Malachi, Ailill learned that the blood curse is spread through a venom that the Islorians release through their bite, and that they could control the urge to release this venom and not infect the mortals. They educated the immortal Islorians and established the tributary system, where humans were protected and the immortals were fed. It took years, but it worked. It is still in use today."

"Except that humans are now enslaved and used as blood bags." I can't keep the horror from my voice. "They're not given a choice, are they?"

"It is the only way for *all* to survive," she says with a wince. "With hunger comes desperation. The humans will bleed regardless, but without a system in place, it will be under far worse conditions. At least this brought law and order. A civilized framework to an uncivilized situation."

And what about all the humans who are deemed cooks and laborers? Who lug blocks of crumbled stone from gardens with sweat pouring from their faces as courtesans stroll by, twirling their parasols? Is that *also* for the survival of the Islorian immortals? I don't bother asking; I already know the answer to that.

"The result of the fates' anger was far more reaching than originally thought. Mordain is like the pulse of caster magic. Aminadav's rift in the land was said to be so deep, it severed Islor from that source. There were no more gifted babies born to humans in Islor, and the casters who lived south of the rift were dying off. It was assumed that this was Aminadav's intention—to cut off Malachi's demons from all elemental magic so they could no longer beseech the fates. Soon, Ailill became the only elemental power in all Islor. He was fearsome, his elemental powers to fire and water impressive."

"To Malachi and Aoife."

"Yes. And he *chose* Malachi." She gives me a knowing look.

That would have angered Aoife.

"But the gifted babies were not the only ones missing in Islor. Malachi had created these immortals in a way that would not allow them to bear offspring. This was an especially tragic circumstance for Queen Isla, who was desperate for children of her own to pass on the throne of Islor. So desperate, they were willing to risk the consequences of summoning Malachi again. He was kind to them this time, though. He taught them how to tap into the nymphaeum's power."

"How?" I blurt. A spark of eagerness hits me. *Finally*, an opportunity to get more information about the sacred garden without appearing obvious.

"The nymphaeum is also a source of magic, much like Mordain. It is an ancient power, grounded in nature and creation, but older than that of the casters. It was here long before our time. We do not understand exactly how it works, but it is said to be most potent on the night of the blood moon. Malachi taught King Ailill and Queen Isla how to utilize the magic of the nymphaeum on those nights to create a child. They did as told and were blessed with a son they named Rhionn. They had many more children after that, and since then, every blood moon, hundreds of immortals beseech the king for access to the nymphaeum in hopes of being granted a child by the nymphs. That is who lives within the nymphaeum."

The nymphs. "As in faeries?"

"Old texts speak of their kind inhabiting our lands *many* thousands of years ago. They're said to be diabolic creatures with a wicked bone that inspired so much chaos that the fates decided it was best they be confined. They are locked behind a door, unable to leave their sacred garden."

Another creature to add to my collection of fables come alive. "Where is this nymphaeum?"

"In the royal grounds."

"But *where*?" How big is this garden within a garden, the one that confines these devilish creatures?

"Near the lake."

I'm about to press for more details, but she waves me away. "Back to the crux of this conversation, which is Malachi's pet, King Ailill."

I struggle to temper my frustration.

"He should have been content, but he had not learned his lesson. Or perhaps the gift of Hudem had fooled him into thinking that summoning Malachi wouldn't have consequences. Things were complicated with a newly forged kingdom. There were skirmishes and struggles for power, as immortal lords and ladies looked for an opportunity to establish themselves as rulers. There were still elven within Islor's lands who had avoided the plague and held on to their elemental affinities. Some of them were powerful and were attempting to usurp the throne. Through the nymphaeum's blessing on Hudem, immortal babies were born with elemental affinities much like their Ybarisan cousins, though not nearly as potent.

"Ailill wanted more strength. Again, he went to Malachi and implored him to make him stronger so he could defeat the threat to the throne, once and for all. What Ailill was asking for was impossible. The fates created the world together, and it is their combined power *within* this world that generates the affinities for those who live within it. Affinities cannot be acquired. Ailill knew this already, but he challenged Malachi to find a way.

"In return, Malachi quested him with obtaining a key caster. That is an elemental with affinities to all four elements. They are *extremely* rare and *extremely* powerful. They are the closest thing to the fates themselves walking this earth. And one had just been born—a girl named Farren. She was in Mordain, where her power could be reined in by the guild. Malachi promised Ailill that if he brought Farren to the nymphaeum, Malachi would show him how to wield her power for himself.

"King Ailill said it was impossible. Mordain would never give up a key caster willingly, and to capture one would mean contending with their power, and *that* is not as simple as muting an elven's affinity with a blade's strike. So, Malachi gave Ailill a rare gift to help. A piece of himself, of his corporeal horn, to cage the key caster's power." Wendeline taps the cuff around my wrist. "That's what these are made of. They have been hidden away in the royal vault for nearly two thousand years. Most in Islor don't realize what they are."

I skate my fingers over the smooth, obsidian jewelry with new understanding. "That's how they work."

"These in particular, yes. They work on both caster and elven affinities. Tokens from the fates can do all sorts of things. They can be used to restrain, control, mask, or amplify affinities. They can create illusions."

Or you can stab an unsuspecting woman in the chest and transport her to another realm to inhabit someone else's body, apparently.

"King Ailill could not sail through the Grave Deep to Mordain, and he could not invade Ybaris with his army when he needed them at home to protect his hold of Cirilea, so he sent his eldest son, Rhionn, in a Seacadorian ship along the western coast and through Skatrana to Mordain in secret. It took years of careful planning, but Rhionn found a way in, captured the key caster Farren, and returned with her. He brought her to the nymphaeum on Hudem as instructed by Malachi. It could not have come at a better time, according to King Ailill, whose opposition was gaining momentum within Islor.

"But Ailill soon discovered that wielding Farren's power himself was impossible and that Malachi's primary focus was not to help him, but to open the door in the nymphaeum. He thought combining Farren's immense caster power with the ancient power of the nymphs on Hudem would allow that to happen."

Blood rushes to my ears. I assume this is the door *I'm* supposed to gain entry to. "Did it?"

"Not only did it *not* open that door, but combining all that power tore a seam in the fold between our world and another, a dark place called the Nulling where otherworldly beasts are often banished by the fates themselves. An army of fierce creatures that made the daaknar seem a kitten by comparison came up through the Great Rift. They could not be controlled, and they wreaked havoc on Islor and Ybaris for decades. It took both immortals and men to kill them and the power of every caster in Ybaris to seal the tear. To this day, some of these creatures still linger, making a home deep within the rift, in the mountains, and in the sea."

Zander said there were things worse than bones down there. "Why did Malachi want that nymphaeum door open?" I ask, though *I* already know the answer. To get this stone. But why?

"He did not explain himself, but ancient texts from the seers foretell of the fates using the power of the nymphs to walk among us in flesh and blood, and to rule over the people. Regardless, the door remained shut, as it still does today."

But it sounds like Malachi hasn't given up. Why would he think *I* can open it if one of these insanely powerful key casters can't? "What happened to King Ailill?"

"He had tempted the fates and plagued the lands once again. He could not be trusted with the power he held. His own son Rhionn killed him and claimed his throne, citing all the harm his father caused so many people on both sides of the rift. No one argued that Ailill deserved it, not even Queen Isla. But some say Rhionn had other reasons for killing his father. He had fallen in love with Farren during their long journey home, and they had made plans to beseech the fates to give her an immortal life. But using her power in the nymphaeum destroyed her and left him heartbroken.

"As king, Rhionn attempted to heal the relationship with

Ybaris, but it was to no avail. They were bitter and wanted nothing to do with the Islorian blood curse. They had not fared well after the Great Rift cut the realm in two. Their lands were far less substantial than that which Islor assumed, riddled with mountainous regions and boglands and nothing comparable to the rich soils in the Plains of Aminadav. Trade with other realms had become difficult. Their relationship with Skatrana had been lukewarm to begin with, but after the rift, Skatrana wanted nothing to do with any magic wielders or those kings and queens who used them. The Grave Deep plagued the eastern waters, and ships in the west faced fierce sea sirens. As far as Ybaris was concerned, Islor was and forever would be an enemy, and Malachi a villainous fate."

"But Rhionn was King Faolan and Queen Rhean's grandson."

"And a demon king as far as any Ybarisan was concerned. It did not matter that Ailill was dead. His legacy lived on in the most terrible of ways. Their only consolation was that Islor no longer had the ability to summon the fates for anything, and Ybaris vowed they would never again allow the fates the opportunity to meddle in our lands. They condemned to death all elementals with an affinity to Malachi. When Neilina came into power, she demanded added measures, so the guild used gifted tokens to create collars that would mute the ability to summon the fates. All elementals are required to wear them, and any who refuse are put to death."

"I'm surprised she wouldn't use these elementals for her own gain."

"That would require her relinquishing control to an elemental, and effectively to Mordain. She is no fool to risk losing what she rules. Her clutch over Ybaris and the casters is fierce, and her own affinity to Vin'nyla is said to be unparalleled. I've heard she can steal the air from a person's lungs with a thought ..." Her voice drifts off as three women slip into the sanctum from an unseen door, garbed in the same white-and-gold gowns as Wendeline, their shoulders hunched with age, their hair various shades of gray and white. They nod to Wendeline before moving for the altar. "I'm afraid we have run out of time for today, but I think I've given you plenty to digest."

Plenty to digest, and plenty to try to unravel. Namely, what part does a human jewel thief from New York play in all this?

CHAPTER EIGHTEEN

"You have been unusually quiet on the walk back, Your Highness." Elisaf pauses as we move through a set of open doors into the castle. The air is stifling, the sun bright, and yet candles flicker nearby.

"Just thinking." I feel the curious stares following me and catch the bows and curtsies as I pass. From guards, from nobility, from servants. The servants are the only ones I feel truly safe around, now that I know everyone else has fangs that they'd sink into my neck if permitted.

Sofie said the Islorians could not find out what I am, but I still don't understand why, and Wendeline's history lesson didn't shed much light on that. All it succeeded in doing was to make me wary of this nymphaeum and the seemingly straightforward task I must accomplish if I want to get out of here. If what Wendeline said about Malachi is true, then sending me here to steal this stone is likely tied to something else. Possibly something horrible, with dire consequences.

"I do miss our conversations."

Elisaf's voice pulls me from my thoughts. "Huh?"

"I would have liked to have had one last night, if I were

permitted." He smiles sheepishly. He is trying to apologize for abandoning me when I was on the verge of tears.

It doesn't help to be angry with him anymore. Besides, he's one of the few friends I have here. Alienating him would not be wise. "You said you were from Seacadore. Was that the truth?" His faint accent surely marks him as a foreigner.

"I have *never* lied to you, Your Highness. I simply omitted some details." Earnest eyes meet mine, his voice low so as not to carry. "I *was* from Seacadore, in another life. I was a ship hand, and I often traveled across Fortune's Channel to Islor and Kier."

"You *wanted* to come here?" Knowing what these Islorian immortals are?

He grins. "I was young and naive. It was fascinating to me, this land that the fates had plagued, both mortal and immortal living together as they did. I would leave the port to enjoy Cirilea's nightlife, which can be lively at times. If you ever have the opportunity, I recommend it."

I snort. "Something tells me I won't be allowed out to enjoy the city's nightlife."

"Perhaps you are right." He dips his head. "The night I was attacked, I had spent the evening at the Goat's Knoll in a jug of mead, and I was on my way to my room. The immortal grabbed me in an alleyway outside the tavern. I had no servant's cuff, so I was fair game as far as he was concerned. Things were different back then. I tried fighting him off, but he was too strong and I too inebriated.

"Zander came upon us. He was in the city that night, prowling in the shadows amidst the commoners as he sometimes used to do. He stopped my attacker, but it was already too late. The man had infected me."

I file away that tidbit on Zander. "Why?"

Elisaf shrugs. "I did not ask him."

"What happened?"

"My attacker suffered a public and vicious execution. It was meant to be a peace offering to the Seacadorians. Islor's relationship with them is important, and their people need to feel safe. I was no longer allowed to return home. Seacadore may enjoy trade with us, but they certainly don't want us on their lands. Zander took pity on me. He helped me through the adjustment period, and I became a soldier for the royal guard."

"So he *can* be caring."

"He can. Though, dare I say, you knew that already, did you not?"

With Corrin, with his mercy for Boaz, with his kindness toward the hobbled old man in the rookery. "He's using me," I remind Elisaf, as if to sway the pendulum back in a more comfortable direction, where Zander has no appealing qualities. It dawns on me. "This is why you don't have an affinity."

"Because I was born by infection, not by the nymphaeum's power," he confirms.

I hesitate. "Do you prefer this? Being what you are?"

"Sometimes. Sometimes not. I do not care for the way mortals are treated here." His brow furrows deeply. "I remember my life in Seacadore, sitting across from my parents and sisters at the dinner table, discussing what paths we might choose. They seemed endless. The mortals here do not sit around the table, having those same discussions. Outside of fantasy, of course."

"Maybe you should talk to your friend *the king* about that." He *is* part of the problem and *could* be the solution.

"Do not assume Zander does not take issue with the system currently in place."

"Right. He's appalled by it. I could tell last night." Though that slave didn't look miserable about her predicament.

"It is complicated."

"It isn't, really. The immortals were taught that they can take what they need, and two thousand years later, the humans kneel, or they die, but either way, they bleed."

"I suppose when you put it like that, it does sound rather simple." He sighs. "There have been uprisings. Mortals have fought for the end of the tributary system. The last time ended poorly for them. The immortals are too strong."

"But with the king's support, they could win. If he truly has an issue with it, why doesn't he do something?"

"You believe he wields a magic wand with that title." Elisaf's brown eyes search our surroundings, as if to ensure ears aren't following our conversation. "For years, Zander has spoken of an Islor where the mortals are given a choice, and their blood serves as their own commodity rather than that of a keeper's. The mortals support him wholeheartedly. Some immortals do, in *theory*. Others vehemently oppose. He tried convincing his father to bring about change. King Eachann thought him radical. He went as far as to tell Zander that he agreed with him, but it would never happen in Islor, and trying to make it so would spell ruin for their reign.

"Now Zander is king, and the court knows where he stands. Tension is growing with those who oppose him. They fear giving the humans too much sovereignty will threaten Islor's well-being. Others are not keen on the idea of parting with their coin to entice their household to stay."

"And they can't find a way where everyone gets what they want?"

Elisaf's smile is patient. "Unfortunately, many of our kind have not been blessed with such an altruistic nature. But when it is a matter of survival, selflessness is harder to come by, and justifications are much easier. That is true of our kind, but also of any other."

Indignation pricks me. I know a thing or two about survival and justification. I'd spent years justifying every wallet, dollar, and jewel I plucked from the unsuspecting. It was easier than attempting a different way of life. It doesn't mean I didn't know that what I was doing was wrong.

At least all I was stealing was material things.

These immortals are stealing people's lives.

But Elisaf's explanation helps me understand more about the

dynamic of this place. "Is this why Zander thinks someone is rallying Islorians against him?"

"They fear his plans for Islor." He nods. "Tensions in the realm were already high when Eachann tendered the queen's throne to a Ybarisan who has no idea what it's like to be one of us. Couple that with a king who would prefer to forget what he is, and you have adversaries bold enough to begin making moves."

Elisaf's words settle uncomfortably on my shoulders, especially when they're paired with Zander's.

Let you live in our skin for a few hours.

Let you know what it's like to be at the mercy of that craving.

The elusiveness.

The discretion.

The way he bristled at being compared to a daaknar.

Zander may radiate arrogance, but he takes no pride in what he is, a realization that stirs my pity.

"Are you feeling well, Your Highness? Your cheeks are flushed."

"I'm fine." I wave off his concern. "It's a hundred degrees in this dress. I need to get it off before I pass out." I tug at the collar to emphasize my discomfort. "I'm going to strangle Corrin."

Elisaf chuckles. "I will take you to your rooms for your midday meal and so that you may change and *not* assault your lady maid. Annika has offered to escort you through the grounds afterward. The king thought you might like that."

I would have, before I learned what she is. Now? I guess I still might. There is something decidedly real about Annika that I appreciate, even if she loathes me. Besides, she can't hurt me. I'm toxic to her. To *all* of them. There's solace in that.

But right now, I need a moment alone to process the truths about this world that have been dumped in my lap. "Maybe after I've changed and rested. I didn't sleep well last night." Did I sleep at all?

His brow pinches with concern. "Very well, Your Highness."

I'm collecting my skirts so I can manage the stairs without tripping when a man yells, "Halt!"

Elisaf and I turn to see three soldiers marching toward us at a rushed pace.

My wariness stirs. "What's going on?"

"I do not know." Elisaf steps forward. "What is this, soldier?"

All three bend at the waist before the one in front announces, "The king has requested Princess Romeria's presence before the court."

"*Again*?" I blurt. I was there yesterday.

"When?" Elisaf asks cordially.

"Now. We were sent to fetch her urgently. Please, come with us." With another bow and murmur of "Your Highness," all three spin on their heels, the expectation to follow obvious.

I share a look with Elisaf as we trail them down the hall, my anxiety swelling. That Zander didn't warn me about this when we spoke this morning sparks my annoyance *and* my worry. He said himself that he wants to keep me away from the court until I'm better prepared. What has changed? Thoughts of the night Korsakov insisted on seeing me at the warehouse come flooding back, as does the horrifying bloodbath I walked into.

Am I walking into a trap? Has he figured out who or what I am?

Not likely. I school my tone to keep the shake from it, reminding myself that I am playing a role. "What is happening in the throne room today, soldier?" I ask, addressing him as Elisaf did.

"Ybarisans were captured near Eldred Wood, Your Highness. They've been taken prisoner and brought before the king for questioning."

Ybarisan soldiers. That means Princess Romeria's men. But why does Zander want me there? It's not like I'll recognize any of them.

"And *the king* insisted Princess Romeria attend the session?" Elisaf must have the same thoughts.

"Yes, sir."

I give Elisaf another questioning look.

My dutiful guard shrugs but then offers me an assured smile, as if to tell me it will be fine.

By the time we reach the long hall to the throne room, my cheeks are burning, my tongue is parched, and sweat builds around my collar and down the center of my back. The grand doors sit open, and a heady buzz of voices carries where before there was pregnant silence. Perhaps the court is normally like that, or perhaps it's the excitement of their enemy capture.

"Remember who you are," Elisaf whispers.

"The problem is I remember who *they* are." Or rather, *what* they are. I'm walking into a room full of vampires. Courage from my "you are toxic" mantra isn't kicking in. Right now, all I want to do is hide.

"They can't hurt you."

"*They* don't know that."

"Come on ... You've already battled a daaknar and won. Where's that reckless courage Annika boasted about?" Elisaf goads. "You're the future queen."

"I don't want to be the queen," I hiss, but I lift my chin and steady my breathing, as if I were strolling into a high-society event where I belong. A noticeable hush falls over the crowd as my escort leads me up the center aisle toward the dais without any preamble or announcement.

Zander sits on his throne. Atticus leans into him, whispering something in his ear. That mane of thick, golden-brown hair tumbles back in a wave to frame his riveting face. My pulse skips as it always seems to when I first lay eyes on Zander. It's annoying that those nerves haven't settled any. In fact, now that he's no longer threatening to execute me, I'm quickly losing my fear of him, despite last night's reveal.

Zander notices me approaching and waves a dismissive hand to his brother before standing. He takes the fifteen steps down with slow, casual ease to meet me at the bottom. Deathly silence falls over the room, as everyone waits for our exchange. I feel like we're two savage beasts being introduced at a zoo exhibit before an eager audience. The question hangs in the air: Will they attack each other with claws and fangs, or will they mate?

Certainly not the latter.

"Romeria," Zander murmurs, dipping his head in what I assume is the king's version of a bow.

We're doing first names now. "Zander," I respond with a slight curtsy.

He displays that intoxicating smile that ensnared me the first time, and then holds out his hand, palm up.

You agreed to this. My heart races as I slip my sweaty fingers next to his cool, smooth ones. Would I have, had I known what he was?

Of course, I would have, the same way I agreed to be Korsakov's chameleon, and how I followed Sofie out of that slaughterhouse and onto a plane. I would have, because it is a means to an end, and I am a survivor.

I remind myself of this as he leads me back up the steps and whispers, "Take your place." I don't ask questions. I settle into the smaller throne.

A flurry of murmurs erupts.

Zander sits next to me, and resting his elbow on his throne's arm between us again holds out his hand, palm up.

I slip my fingers between his. It feels awkward and forced, and yet his touch isn't unpleasant. I steal a glance his way to find his face smooth and unreadable as he watches me.

I smile, because that is what Princess Romeria would do. We're acting. This is all an act, albeit a strange and complex one. But the most foreign part of it all may be that I am not on my own, as I have grown accustomed to being for so long. Now, I have a partner in crime.

While the buzz continues in the court, Zander leans over to whisper in my ear, "How was your history lesson this morning?" It's a decidedly intimate move, his breath grazing my skin.

I know it's for the sake of a show in front of these people, and yet my pulse stirs at the low timbre of his voice and his proximity. The danger of having him so close to me. I'm safe, though. I am a drink box full of cyanide to him. To *everyone* here. "Educational, though I have many more questions."

"Why am I not surprised?" he says dryly, seemingly unaware of my inner turmoil. Then again, I've always been good at hiding it.

"How was *your* morning? Any more guests?"

His lips twitch. "I told you there wouldn't be for some time."

I silently chastise myself. I didn't mean to bring that up again, but my thoughts are scattered, and it was the first one I grasped onto. "What am I doing here? I'm not the queen."

"No, you are not." His shrewd gaze rolls over the court's attendants, still whispering as they watch and wait. "But having you seated on the throne while the Ybarisans are presented to me for questioning and punishment may help our cause."

"Will they be executed when you're done?"

"Eventually. Yes."

An image of pyres flashes in my mind, and my stomach clenches.

He smirks. "I forgot. A queen who doesn't believe in punishing criminals."

"Punishing is one thing. *Executing* is … I don't know how you can do it."

"*I* don't. I have henchmen for that."

"Still, you give the command." Even with Sofie as my own henchwoman, her blade against Tony's neck, I couldn't give the order. I'd make a terrible queen in this world.

"We will see what information we can pry out of them first. Find out what they've been doing in my lands. Who knows, they might not even survive questioning to make it to an execution."

"That brings me *great* comfort," I say with sarcasm. "I don't need to do or say anything, right?"

His breath skates across my cheek as he leans in close and

whispers, "Besides look especially hateful and not let on that you have no idea who they are? No. It's best you remain silent."

"I can handle that."

"Your mood hasn't improved much since this morning."

I sigh, hoping it releases some of this building tension.

"That is quite the choice of attire." His eyes flicker downward at my dress. "Were you planning on traveling to the mountains of Skatrana today?" There's a teasing lilt to his tone that is a reprieve to talk of execution.

"Is it cold there?"

"Bitterly so, I've heard."

"Then, yes. Please. Take me there. Actually, I was on my way to my room to set fire to this thing when the guards called for me, so thank *you* for ruining my plans."

His chuckle is dark. "I will gladly burn it for you."

"With me still in it?" I throw back. How does his affinity to Malachi's element work? Could he do that? Set fire to someone's clothes with a thought?

"Don't be silly. You'd remove it for me first." His eyes flash to mine, his words painting an intimate image that makes me blush. "They're watching our *every* move," he whispers in my ear, his thumb stroking across knuckle in a slow drag, followed by another. "You need to relax."

"I'm trying. It's just ... a lot." And this is all part of the performance. He's intentionally flirting with me, saying things to make my cheeks redden and stir my blood, because that's how people who are enamored with each other might act. That's how Princess Romeria and Zander acted, by all accounts—foolishly in love. I shouldn't be shocked by it, and yet my pulse is racing.

Zander is dangerously good at this game.

I take a calming breath as I glance around. I focus on Atticus, exchanging words with Boaz. "Your brother looks so much like Annika."

"Not surprised. He was born a few minutes before her."

My eyebrows jump with surprise. "They're twins?"

"Yes, though Annika tries to forget. The first of their kind to be blessed by the nymphaeum."

"Do they not get along?"

"Some days more than others."

Atticus's gaze flips to us where it lingers a moment. "And what does your brother think of this plan of yours?" Obviously, Atticus is in Zander's trusted inner circle. He has as much reason to hate Princess Romeria as his siblings do, and if that display in the war room is any indication, he does hate me.

"Careful." Zander leans in close to my ear again. "Some in the court are proficient at reading lips, after so many years of scheming for power and wealth. I wouldn't want them to read yours." His mouth accidentally grazes my skin, and gooseflesh skitters along the nape of my neck in response. Thankfully, he shifts away a touch. "He does not agree with it."

I stall, suddenly wary of my words. "Why not?"

"He thinks it a waste of time, and that we should deal with our problems with our army. But he is young and still thinks *every* battle can be won by the stronger force."

"Ybaris didn't need an army to do what they did."

"Exactly. Just a few well-placed and especially convincing enemies, though we were fortunate that he had the sense to camp a battalion outside the gate. It made seizing the Ybarisans and Lord Muirn's men easier." He pauses. "Atticus believes I should marry Saoirse, Lord Adley's daughter. That solidifying a union of Cirilea and Kettling would be enough to quell any uprisings."

Kettling. "On the southeast side." I remember seeing that name on the map.

"Yes. A large port city, and an important one. They are second only to Cirilea. They do significant trade with Kier, and they have a substantial population. Before our fathers arranged our union, it was expected I would marry Saoirse. Even *I* assumed I would, though I wasn't in any rush. Lord Adley, of course, believes his daughter is the most suitable choice to be the next queen of Islor and is not pleased that a Ybarisan sits up here, especially when we will not be getting any humans or casters out of this arrangement as King Barris promised."

"Maybe he's right."

"Maybe you shouldn't be in such a hurry to become inconsequential to me." Again, his lips skate across my ear, and I no longer think it is accidental. He's trying to get a reaction from me. That, or he's testing me. He pulls away to meet my eyes before shifting his focus to his subjects.

That he casually threatened me again makes my anger flare.

Zander can play this game, but so can I.

Steeling my nerve, I lean in close, pressing myself against his arm and taking a second to inhale the sweet woodsy scent of him. "And yet it seems like I'm becoming more important to you by the minute," I whisper. "Ferreting out traitors, keeping Neilina's army away, *and* avoiding an unsavory marriage?" The truth is, the more I learn about the politics and tension of Islor, the more I sense I am a multipurpose tool.

His chest rises with a deep inhale. "It is true that the situation with Kettling is another reason why this current arrangement between us is beneficial."

I smile with satisfaction as I pull away and scan the unfamiliar faces below us. There are so many. Is the person who Zander is so certain conspired with Princess Romeria in this room right now? Are they watching me, wondering how I convinced Zander that I was innocent?

Hawkish black eyes grab my attention. It's the tall, thin woman with the black hair. She's standing next to a man with matching dark hair and pale skin. Her lips move with quick—likely unfriendly—words. I wish I could read them. When she realizes she has my interest, she lifts her chin and offers a haughty look that couldn't be mistaken for anything but a challenge.

"Saoirse wouldn't happen to be in the front row, would she?"

Zander's mouth curls at the corners. "However did you guess?"

"She is *definitely* unhappy to see me alive." And is no happier to see me up here, by the sour look on her face. That explains the weak effort of curtsying that day along the path. This Saoirse has already placed herself above both Annika and Princess Romeria.

"I imagine not. A Ybarisan has stolen her throne, one who, according to many whispers, doesn't have the sense to rule in Islor."

"I've heard. I was too busy pretending to fall over myself for the future king."

His lips twist as if he's bitten into something curdled. I've struck a nerve. Zander was falling over himself for Princess Romeria, too, and it wasn't an act. "Saoirse will be looking for any reason to find you unfit to be Islor's queen, so she and her father can turn the court in favor of a union with Kettling."

"I take it they don't support your views on mortal freedom?"

He falters, his eyes flittering to Elisaf. "No, they do not."

"And can they do that? Dictate who you marry?" It's odd to be whispering of conspiracy and treason with an audience, and yet Zander doesn't seem the least bit wary of doing so. He is the king, though. He does what he wants.

"No. And they will certainly earn my ire for trying, but given the pressure from Neilina in the north and growing strife within Islor, they might see it worthy of the gamble. I need Kettling's force behind me, not against me. They know that, and they will use it to their advantage. There is no mistaking that Lord Adley wishes to rule Islor. It would be easier to do so with his daughter as queen, but I wouldn't put it past them to attempt to remove me altogether."

"Could they be working with the Ybarisans in hiding?"

Zander shakes his head. "He despises your kind. He would *never* form an alliance with them, but we do believe he is behind this call to arms against me. Covertly, of course. Within the court, he'll try to sway other lords and ladies to his concerns without being obvious about it, so he may steer their support his way."

"So, you have more than one enemy to contend with at the moment—is that what you're saying?"

He smirks. "I'm a king. For every enemy I face, there are ten I cannot name, but they are always there, waiting for an opening."

"Which one do you focus on?"

"The one that is most dangerous at that given moment."

I steal another glance Saoirse's way. Does she know we're talking about her? She may want me dead, but I'll bet she knows how to behave as a queen. I could stand to take a few lessons from her. That's how I've always survived—by watching, learning, adapting to my surroundings, blending in. Korsakov was not wrong when he gave me my pet name. "You still can, you know. Marry her. Once you've found your traitor and *this* little charade is over." I waggle my finger between us, sounding more confident than I feel.

"First you reprimand me for who I bring to my chamber, and now you are choosing a wife for me? This grows more amusing by the moment."

"Just trying to help out. At least she's beautiful." Like a jagged, snow-topped mountain range primed for an avalanche is beautiful. But more important, she'll be here long after I've found my way out of Islor.

"Saoirse is spiteful, manipulative, and narcissistic. And beauty ..." His eyes drift over my features. "Look where that nearly got me before."

My heart stutters at the compliment, even though I doubt he meant it as such.

Surprise flickers in his expression before he smooths it over. "I wouldn't be shocked if she's making plans to have you vacate this throne before your place becomes permanent. I would avoid her at all costs." His eyes drop to my mouth, and it seems as if he's going to kiss me, right here in front of everyone.

I inhale sharply.

With the tiniest of smirks, he turns back to the crowd.

It's all a game to him, and I feel like I'm losing. I lean in again, this time letting my bottom lip graze the skin below Zander's earlobe. "Who else do I need to know?"

Zander clears his throat. It's a moment before he ducks his head and responds. "I will go through the entire court with you, but we do not have time for that now. I can point out a few. That man in all black, to your far left? That is Lord Telor."

I follow his direction and spot a tall, regal man in a ranked soldier's uniform, his lengthy white hair pulled into a ponytail. He's talking with a man next to him. "From Lyndel." I recall that name.

"Correct. You have never met him. He continues to be loyal to my family, and to our cause. He leads the ongoing rift border control."

"If he's here, who's leading his men?"

"His son, Braylon. It would be wise to ensure your smiles to him are as genuine as you can fake. The couple in matching green, standing near him, are Lord and Lady Quill. I awarded them with Innswick after stripping the lands and title from Muirn's surviving family."

I eye the youthful-looking pair who beam at me. "I take it they approve of us too?"

"Perhaps. Perhaps not. But they will never voice a word otherwise, not with the windfall I granted them. Beside them are Lords Sallow and Edevane of Bythesea and Wingsby, respectively. Also considered loyal to me and to my vision of Islor. The man next to Saoirse is her father, Lord Adley. I've told you of his motives, so you should not be surprised by anything but the charm he wields. He could talk the robes off a priestess with his slippery tongue, but always assume he has a purpose that suits him. Of them all, he is the most likely to speak out of turn, but he does it with such elegance, it is difficult to chastise him without earning the disapproval of the court."

"And that matters? Their approval?" I haven't seen any signs of a democracy, but I haven't seen much of *anything*, aside from the pleasant daily social lives of the aristocrats within these walls and the glaringly harsh situation for those lingering in the rookery, waiting to expire. There must be something in between. "Why don't you strip his lands from him and give them to someone else?"

Zander laughs, a mirthless sound. "That is certainly something Neilina would do. But I don't have cause. Only in those cases where unsurmountable proof of treason is presented is it considered appropriate, and Adley is too smart to get caught. He would raise a daunting army of sympathizers against me just for trying."

From our spot on the dais, we can see clearly down the long hall beyond the throne room. A small procession of soldiers marches along it now, the clatter of their approaching boots and armor giving the lords and ladies something else to gawk at besides me, many turning to watch. In the center of the horde are five dirt-covered faces. The woman in leather from that day in the war room walks with them, smeared with blood and mud.

"Who is she?"

"Abarrane? She leads Islor's Legion. They are our elite, our deadliest soldiers."

"And she *knows*?" I give him a pointed look. We're sitting so close, I find myself admiring his long lashes.

"She does. Her subordinates do not," he answers coolly, seemingly unfazed by our proximity.

I take a deep breath and try to mimic his composure. "So that threat she made to skin me alive was an act?"

"Not in the least. I've seen her do it before. Don't take offense, though. She doesn't like anyone. She barely tolerates me."

I shudder. "Has she threatened to cause *you* bodily harm?"

His eyes flicker to my mouth. "She has suggested doing a few things to my body, but I doubt any of them would cause me harm."

My words get caught on my tongue. I don't know what's more surprising—that Zander so casually said it or that one of his war chiefs would have the gall to proposition him.

Zander's eyes sparkle with amusement as he watches me search for a suitable retort. He enjoys flustering me.

"And does she know she's not your type?"

"And what is my type, pray tell?"

This is not the time or place to be having such a conversation, and yet I find myself leaning in to whisper, "Smiley, agreeable, *meek*. Isn't that what worked for me last time?"

Zander's stern attention shifts to the approaching procession. "You're certainly none of those things anymore."

The soldiers stop a few feet from the dais and part, leaving the scruffy men with shackled wrists alone in a line.

"Come forward," Zander commands, all hints of his relaxed, playful tone disappearing.

The prisoners are shoved. They stumble, two of them falling to their knees.

The rough treatment trips a memory of Boaz pushing me into the tower and my knee smashing against the stone. I wince before I can stop myself.

Zander's hand squeezes mine, and I sense the warning in the simple move. *Everyone* is watching for my reaction. I can't show sympathy for these Ybarisans, regardless of my reason.

Only one man manages to stay on his feet, and when he looks up and sees me sitting on the throne, his blue eyes widen with shock.

"You believed your beloved princess dead, did you not?" Zander taunts. "Unfortunately, you failed to kill her as you failed to kill me. Fear not, the union between Ybaris and Islor will still take place, and Ybaris will receive nothing in return. I cannot wait to see what sort of offspring she will produce with Malachi's demon." Zander's goading him. He enjoys doing that. He's done it to me.

"I demand a parley," the man says in a deep, authoritative tone that makes me think he is more than simply a lackey soldier.

He's quickly brought to his knees with a swift kick from Abarrane. "You will not speak unless given permission, prisoner," she hisses. "And you will not demand anything of the king."

"But I am—" His words cut off with a grimace, the point of Abarrane's sword digging into his nape.

"Not another word, or I will slice your voice box with my blade."

The man presses his lips tightly. He lifts his gaze, not to meet Zander's but to meet mine. In those eyes is a deep recognition as he silently pleads with me.

Princess Romeria must have known him well.

I assume he is the leader of this lot. They look ragged and weak, their wrists bound, their clothing tattered, their faces bruised and bloodied and scowling with pain. Each of them has a gaping wound across their forearm, as if someone methodically slashed them.

I check Abarrane's sword. It's been cleaned of gore and gleams like Zander's dagger, which was forged with merth. And if these prisoners are all Ybarisans, then it is safe to assume they have affinities to an element. She must have slashed them all to keep them from using those links as weapons, as Zander did to me.

"How many of you are left in our lands?" Zander asks.

Silence answers.

"Where are you hiding?"

More silence.

Abarrane presses the tip of her blade into the brunet's neck. "You will answer. Now!"

"I will answer when you grant me a parley, and not before," the man says through a seething grimace.

"The time for diplomacy ended when Queen Neilina had my parents murdered. We will get the answers out of you, one way or another." The smile Zander levels the prisoners is menacing. It quickly sours. "And then you will face execution for your crimes against our people. Get them out of my sight—"

"Your Highness, if I may." Lord Adley steps forward and offers a shallow bow that hints to how highly he considers himself.

I dislike him already.

"What is it, Lord Adley?"

"I think I speak for all in the court when I say we would like to hear what the princess of Ybaris has to say. After all, these are her subjects." Coal-black eyes that match his daughter's flicker to me.

Look hateful, stay quiet. Those things, I can do. Speaking to all these people was not part of the plan.

"Her Highness has not yet been crowned and is not required to speak on matters of the court," Zander says coolly, but his body radiates tension, his fingers within mine clenching.

"But you have obviously placed such value in Her Highness's opinion, given you have her seated on the throne before her coronation, or even an exchange of vows. A bold move, its first in Islor's history, I dare say. Surely the court, as your humble servants, could all benefit in hearing from such an esteemed voice in your ear." He glances around the room, as if searching for support. Numerous heads bob.

Zander was right. Adley is a beguiling snake. Shrewd too. He's made it difficult for Zander to deny him without discrediting my opinion, which then begs the question—why am I on this throne today? Besides to look pretty and whisper and hold hands, which is exactly what I've been doing.

A queen without gumption. Too delicate to rule. I wouldn't be surprised if it was Adley or Saoirse who started those whispers, especially given Saoirse now stands behind her father wearing a smug smile.

My anger flares. They mean to make me look the idiot in front of all these people.

Beside me, Zander's teeth grind. "As I've already—"

"What is it you would like to hear, Lord Adley?" My voice sounds foreign as it carries through the massive hall. Zander squeezes my hand in warning. I squeeze back, my heart hammering. As much as I'd prefer to shrink into the shadows, I haven't survived this long by playing the lamb when a wolf is needed. "That my mother betrayed me? That she has committed atrocities? That she is consumed with her own agenda and will stop at nothing to get what she wants, including sacrificing her daughter?" All things that are true of my mother, and probably also of

Queen Neilina. "My mother is dead to me. Is that what you wish to hear?"

"It is ... uh ... reassuring, yes." Lord Adley falters a moment. He nods to the line of prisoners. "And what of these men?"

"What of them?" I throw back, allowing irritation to seep into my tone, even as my hand trembles within Zander's. Thankfully, we're too far and high up for anyone to see. "They've conspired to commit murders in their queen's name, and they deserve to be punished for it. *Your king* has already deemed it so. What more value could I possibly add to that?"

Adley's brow pulls together, his surprise apparent.

"I'm sorry, were you expecting a different response? Or a different queen? Perhaps a witless fool too flimsy for a throne?"

Lord Adley's eyes flash wide. "Your Highness. I would *never* suggest such a thing—"

"I should hope not." I'm waiting for Zander to squeeze my hand in warning again, to tell me to shut my mouth, but he remains motionless. Still, I'm probably not doing a convincing job of playing the old Romeria. "I apologize if I don't sound like myself to those who know me, but I suppose being so deeply betrayed by my people has hardened my heart. I do not feel any love or loyalty for Ybaris nor for *anyone* who schemes to harm us."

I steal a pointed glance at Saoirse, who looks like she's sucking on an especially bitter pill. "But I do appreciate that you value my opinion so highly, Lord Adley, that you would urge me to speak today, even though I am not yet officially queen. We thank Kettling for their support of this union."

Beside me, Zander makes a sound.

"Yes, Your Highness." He pauses. "And perhaps you would deem a royal repast at the coming Cirilean fair to celebrate delivering justice to our enemies. And, of course, this coming union." He gestures toward us.

Repast. Zander had used that word before. I don't know what it means, but I understand the words *fair* and *celebrate*. I don't dare look to Zander for approval. "Yes, I believe that would be in order."

A buzz erupts in the crowd with conflicting expressions of everything from glee to dismay. It stirs my unease. What have I just agreed to?

"Very well." He offers a much deeper bow this time.

"The Legion will guard and interrogate the prisoners," Zander says coolly.

Abarrane's lips peel back in a sinister smile that makes me struggle not to cringe.

"Your Highness, if I may suggest ..." Apparently Adley isn't finished, his attention back to Zander. "I'm sure I speak for many *again* when I say the court would appreciate a public interrogation of the Ybarisans. I believe it would alleviate any concerns that might linger—"

"The Legion will guard and interrogate," Zander repeats, his tone sharp as he cuts off Adley. "And *anyone* who interferes with their work in *any* way will land themselves in the square by dawn for treason, without a trial. That will be all." Zander stands and guides me to my feet and down the steep steps by our joined hands to the sound of murmurs.

At the bottom, we veer left, away from the crowd and toward a small door at a quick pace. The guard opens it for us, and we take the long hallway in silence. Zander does not pull away immediately as he usually does, not until we pass through a second door and enter the round, windowless room with the map. It's empty, save for us.

The moment the door clicks shut, he spins me around. "Who are you?" he demands.

CHAPTER NINETEEN

"I don't know what you mean." Blood rushes into my ears.

Zander releases my hand, shifting to loom over me. "You don't remember who you are, and yet you seem eager to play the role of queen." His tone is thick with accusation.

"You're the one who put me up there! I was only doing what you asked me to."

"I asked you not to say a word. That back there?" He points to the door we just passed through. "That was more than a few words."

"What else was I supposed to do? Smile and nod like a fool? Which would make *you* look like a fool, too, in case you didn't realize."

He shakes his head and mutters something under his breath that I don't catch. "You have been off since you arrived in the throne room."

"Maybe because I wasn't prepared for this ambush."

"No," he says resolutely. "It's the way your pulse races. You are worried about something." He searches my face. "What was it about your conversation with Wendeline today that unsettled you?"

"Nothing. I don't ... I'm not ... I just ..." I fumble for an answer, all while I try to process his words. "What do you mean, the way my pulse races?" Is that a figure of speech? "You can read my pulse?"

His head falls back with a humorless chuckle, showing off a long, columnar neck and pristinely white, straight teeth. "You are so naive. Sometimes it is delightful to watch."

"I'm not naive," I snap. "What are you talking about?"

His eyes are alight with dark mischief when they meet mine again. "I was never able to read you before. You veiled your emotions so well. But since you were brought back from the dead, your ability to do that is slipping, and quickly. Today, on that throne, your heart was a steady, hard thrum that flared every so often." He drags a fingertip along my jugular, sending shivers through my body. "See? Just like that. You can't hide that from me. So, I'll ask you again, Romeria, what are you concealing?" The calm in his voice prickles the hairs on the back of my neck.

He may be able to read my pulse, but at least he can't read my thoughts. If he could, I assume he would have the answer to that. "Nothing." It comes out hoarse. *Everything.*

He steps forward, forcing me backward until I hit the wall. This feels like the prison tower all over again as he leans down, his mouth inches from mine, our stares locked. "Do you know what *else* I can sense, besides the way your heart beats when I am this close to you?" he whispers, his breath skating over my lips.

I shake my head, not trusting my voice.

"The way it beats when you're lying," he hisses. Resentment flares in his eyes as he stares down at me.

"The happy couple," a male voice cuts in from somewhere behind the wall of Zander.

Zander peels away and moves for the table, revealing a smug-faced Atticus standing in the doorway.

One ... two ... three ... I take deep breaths as I count, regaining my composure. Meanwhile, Zander has seized the back of the chair in a white-knuckled grip, as if trying to choke the life out of it. Whatever semblance of trust I've been gaining with him—however small—I sense it slipping away.

If only I'd had time to myself to sort out my thoughts and worries before being thrown into this circus.

"It's foolish to let the Ybarisans live. If I were king, I would make a point of executing them where they stand."

"But you are not king," Zander retorts through gritted teeth. "We will do this *my way*."

Brushing off his brother's brusque response, Atticus makes a grand display of bowing for me. "I suppose formal reintroductions are in order? It's a pleasure to meet you *again*, Your Highness. I'm Atticus, Zander's much younger brother. Certainly *not* the king, as I've just been reminded." They have the same deep timbre in their voices, though Atticus has a youthful charisma, and that edge of disdain that laces Zander's every word is missing.

I struggle to force away the panic Zander stirred. "I remember you from that day in this room." When he looked ready to cut me down with his sword.

"Yes, I apologize if I wasn't myself. I was having a difficult time accepting this theory the priestess concocted."

"But you do now?"

"Let us just say that version back there?" He points behind him, toward the throne room. "I have never met *her*."

Does he wish that version dead too? Elisaf said Atticus is hard to read. I see what he means. His steely gaze is so contrary to his light mood.

"Neither have I," Zander mutters. "Who knew she had such reckless pride."

"Lord Adley annoyed me."

"Clearly." Atticus folds his arms over his broad chest, a playful grin on his lips, even as his eyes drift to my neck where the daaknar's teeth marks are no longer visible. "I liked this phony version of you, though. Has more *bite* than the other phony version. And it was effective with Adley. He's been known to drone on forever.

I don't know that I've ever seen him retreat so quickly. You were convincing."

"Maybe too convincing," Zander says. "I doubt anyone conspiring against me will be in a rush to approach you anytime soon after that spectacle. I hope you are ready for a marriage neither of us wants."

"You can always marry Saoirse instead."

Atticus snorts.

Zander's responding glare is lethal.

"And nothing I said out there will deter anyone. Whoever helped me must know it's all an act, because they were part of it," I counter. "They *know* I'm guilty. But no one with half a brain would come forward right now, anyway, and this person isn't stupid or they would have already been caught. They're going to sit back and watch for as long as possible. Figure out how I tricked you into buying my victim story."

"Listen to the little conspirator. She's right." Atticus strolls over to his brother to give his shoulder a squeeze. Standing next to each other, I see they're the same height, though Atticus has a wider build. He drags a chair out to settle into it, his powerful legs splayed. "You've given this until Hudem to play out. Now you must be patient, brother. I know that's not one of your strong suits."

Zander pinches the bridge of his nose. "This isn't effortless for me."

Atticus's blue eyes skitter over my frame. "No. But I could think of a far worse situation."

Atticus doesn't agree with his brother's plan to use me to draw out the traitors in their midst and hold back Queen Neilina's advance. Would he enjoy watching it all fall apart so he has an excuse to go to war? He seems the type—arrogant, and with enough clout to be dangerous.

Zander frowns deeply. "Until then, you had better hope Abarrane manages to kill them in her interrogation. Otherwise you'll get the pleasure of a royal repast."

"What is it, anyway?"

"It's where the prisoners are paraded through the square before being chained up, and anyone who feels obliged has the opportunity to take their vein. The court first, of course. And it's not often done gently, as we might with a tributary. I imagine you will get to watch it all with Adley standing beside you. It is a lengthy process, aided by the power of the priestesses when we are fortunate to have one. They can help slow the flow of the prisoners' blood for *hours*. And when it's time, what's left of them is sent to their afterlife by fire."

My face blanches. "I thought you lived off *mortal* blood."

"It's not about survival. It's about control, dominance, and humiliation." And by the bitter twinge in Zander's voice, he doesn't approve or enjoy it. That is some small comfort.

"It used to be a common practice in Islor, with prisoners of war. It hasn't been done in centuries, much to the dissatisfaction of some," Atticus adds soberly.

"We had Ybarisan prisoners after the last attack. The court pushed for a royal repast then, but I refused, executing them swiftly instead. Mercifully. But I will not be able to avoid it again, thanks to my darling betrothed. It will be quite the event, given it is to happen during the city fair, when half of Islor has journeyed to Cirilea. And I do not see a way for you to avoid it, not without making yourself look weak, and the fates know how much you do not want that."

My gut churns with dread. I should have kept my mouth shut. Adley took advantage of my ignorance without realizing it. "What was that guy demanding? A parley?"

"A meeting to discuss our *dispute*. It is intended to find diplomacy in the threat of war. But I'd say we are long past mediation." Zander snorts. "Besides, anything he says will no doubt be a lie."

Atticus cocks his head at Zander. "You didn't tell her who Abarrane captured, did you?"

"I thought her ignorance would be more effective. Otherwise, she might give him too much attention."

I frown. "Who is he?"

"Prince Tyree of Argon." Atticus smiles. "Your brother."

My mouth drops. No wonder the man looked at me the way he did. "He knows things."

Atticus's head tips back, and he bursts with laughter. "Dare I say, he knows *everything*."

"*I mean,* Princess Romeria's brother would know who within the castle helped her."

"I like how she talks about herself in third person. It's as if they're two different people and she takes *no* responsibility for what she's done," Atticus muses.

"Welcome to my world." The muscle in Zander's jaw ticks. "And Abarrane could pull Tyree's arms off and he wouldn't tell us anything."

I grimace at that gruesome image. "What if *I* talk to him? He might be willing to tell me things, thinking I'm his sister. I could make it look like I'm sneaking down there—"

"No."

"That's not a bad idea," Atticus says. "Why don't I take her down?"

"*No.*" Zander glares at his brother.

"But he doesn't know that I don't remember who I am—"

"You are *not* going *anywhere* near him or any other Ybarisan!"

I steal a look at Atticus, who shrugs nonchalantly. If he's bothered by Zander's stubbornness, he doesn't let on. "We have both of Queen Neilina's heirs. What do you suppose she'll do when she discovers that?"

But Zander isn't sharing in his brother's amusement, his jaw rigid as he weighs me beneath a calculating gaze. "By the time she hears of it, one of them will already be dead. I'll be sure to send along his remains for her this time. Elisaf!"

My guard pokes his head in almost immediately. "Your Highness."

"Romeria wishes to return to her rooms for the rest of the day. I believe she has some garments to burn."

I guess that means no afternoon walk with Annika. That's fine. I think I've had enough of this place and these people for the day.

"Lovely, Your Highness." Dagny's words are muffled around brass pins held between her pursed lips.

I had barely sat down to my bowl of potato and parsnip stew when the seamstress arrived for a fitting, her arms laden with silk and chiffon, already cut to size in a gown. I didn't mind the interruption, though. The woman's jaunty personality is a welcome reprieve from boredom.

Corrin was right, I admit, as I peer in the full-length mirror and take in the tangible version of my sketch. Dagny is a marvel, and she works quickly, her nimble fingers adjusting the seams to better fit me. The cinched waist, the sleek, delicate sleeves that reach to the marble floor, blending in with the skirts in a cape-like fashion. The material covers all my scars without mummifying me, and the color—a pale bluish-gray shade I never would've chosen for myself—flatters my eyes and skin and contrasts well with my hair.

"Just how you wanted it, yes?" Dagny's muted green eyes are dazzling with excitement as she steps back.

"It's incredible." I shift my leg, watching the material part on my thigh.

"It might be my greatest piece yet. No one has seen anything like it, you can be sure of that."

No one *here* has seen anything like it.

"You will be the talk of the court, Your Highness."

"I'm *already* the talk of the court." I smooth a finger over the seam at the waist.

"Oh, don't worry. That will flatten out when I stitch it properly." Dagny waves my hand away. "Well?" She turns to Corrin, who has been oddly quiet. "Don't you think Her Highness looks radiant?"

"If attention is what she wishes, she will certainly succeed. You'll be showing off your undergarments."

She's referring to the high slit, no doubt. "I won't wear them." It wouldn't be the first time I avoided seams by leaving my panties at home.

Corrin's mouth gapes and she mutters something I—happily—don't catch.

"Oh, one more here." Dagny reaches for another pin, tucked into a small tin that sits on a side table. "Yes. That's better." She nods with satisfaction. "I'll have this finished up in time for the royal repast."

"Can't wait," I mutter. A new dress for a torture celebration.

"I suppose those Ybarisan monsters will get what's deserved." Dagny flinches. "Begging your pardon, Your Highness."

"No, it's okay. They *are* monsters." May as well play the part convincingly. Though I don't know if being chained up and fed from is what *anyone* deserves.

"I hear those brutes killed one of Lady and Lord Rengard's tributaries. Slit her throat from ear to ear." She tsks. "Just terrible."

"Those men killed a mortal?" Nobody mentioned that.

"You be careful removing that gown. It's full of pins. You're liable to bleed all over that light material and ruin it before you get to strut around without your underthings," Corrin answers curtly, steering the conversation away from talk of murder and gossip.

"Oh yes." Dagny's head bobs. "We wouldn't want Her Highness poking herself needlessly."

I shimmy out of the gown and into a sleeveless peach dress from my closet, returning as Dagny is gathering the last of her things.

She scowls at the scars on my shoulder, as if they somehow harmed her personally.

Ignoring her pity, I slide on the capelet she brought with her—a creamy gossamer material trimmed with gold embroidery and scalloped to look strangely like wings, though not at all silly. It ties with gold ribbon in the front and covers the scars on my shoulder impeccably. "Thank you for this."

"If Her Highness finds it pleasing, I will surely make a dozen more, in every color imaginable."

"Please, Dagny." It would make something as simple as getting dressed in the morning far less difficult. "If I ever have to wear another dress like the one I wore yesterday, I might die."

Corrin rolls her eyes.

"Oh goodness, Your Highness, don't say such things." Dagny curtsies and then bows, and then curtsies again, as if she can't decide which is more appropriate. "Before I forget, I brought ya some things to draw with." She nods toward the graphite pencil and sheets of paper sitting on the table and then lowers her voice conspiratorially. "I was thinking, if Her Highness has any ideas for more gowns she may wish me to sew, I would be delighted."

I steal a wary glance at Corrin, expecting her to bluster about my jam-packed schedule not allowing for frivolous things such as art, but she doesn't seem at all concerned by Dagny's kindness.

"I might have a few. Thank you, Dagny. That was thoughtful of you."

Her eyes twinkle. "'Specially one for next Hudem. Something the king might fancy. We should get started on that soon. Those gowns always require *much* labor. All the stitchwork and the detail."

She means a wedding dress for my marriage to Zander. I feel a flicker of guilt that this woman might slog over something I'll never wear. "I guess a replica of my last one would be in poor taste?"

She titters, though her nervous gaze flips to Corrin. "It would be too revealing, surely, Your Highness."

"Right." I sigh. The scars.

"There's a ship comin' in from Seacadore any day now, in time for the fair. It promises bolts of the finest fabrics we've ever seen. I've demanded the port master inform me the moment it arrives, so that I may secure the nicest of the lot. No one should be privy to them before they are offered to the future queen. Until then …" She holds up the dress, beaming. "I'll get finished with this one straightaway, Your Highness."

When she leaves, Corrin taps the paper. "I've already counted. There are five sheets of equal shape and size." She gives me a look.

"So, no secret messages to my accomplices who I can't remember? Is that what you're saying?"

"Not unless you'd like to earn the king's mistrust," she retorts, ignoring my sarcasm.

"I have that." And I'm guessing it's worse after yesterday. I haven't seen him since. I shake my head. "Who am I going to send messages to? Honestly, Corrin, *you* could have been conspiring with me, and I'd have no idea."

A startled—and horrified—look flashes across her face. "Enjoy your afternoon, *Your Highness*." She spins and marches out.

I sigh. I need to learn to keep my mouth shut.

If someone had told me that listening to deadly blades clashing would be soothing, I would have thought them crazy. And yet here I am as the sun wanes and the air cools, settled in my makeshift patio furniture—a chair and table I dragged from my bedroom—discomforted by the silence that blooms below me after hours of melees and shouted instruction.

I set the dulled graphite pencil down and stand to stretch my legs. An array of people have occupied the square all afternoon—noblemen and a few women, royal guards, their skills varying greatly, and soldiers dressed like Abarrane who fight with incomparable speed and grace.

Now a group of ten children line up in the square, gripping wooden staffs in two hands, waiting eagerly as their instructor approaches. They can't be more than seven years old.

Abarrane is rigid and purposeful as she strolls toward the

weapons rack to collect her staff. She has bathed since I saw her in the throne room and swapped her brown leather outfit for a similar one in all black. Her blond hair is freshly plaited in three thick braids.

She looks no less fierce standing before these children. Are they her elite soldiers of tomorrow? Her future Legion, here for their training?

"Stance!" she barks, and her pupils jump, repositioning their feet and their grips, holding their staves in the air before them.

"One!" she commands, jabbing with a measured thrust, the muscle in her arms honed to perfection, her form taut.

The children mimic her, though less gracefully.

"Two!" She spins and stabs the air. "Three!" She continues counting and working through thrusts and spins and pivots by rote, and the students follow, some clumsily, others with surprising skill for ones so young, all with potent enthusiasm.

They're immortal children, I'm assuming, if Abarrane is training them to fight. Born courtesy of the magic in the nymphaeum. I still know little of these elven and even less about the Islorian version, but I'm piecing bits together. Zander said this body just passed its twenty-fifth birthday, so I assume these children will develop as humans do up to a certain age. In as little as ten years, these kids could be full-grown soldiers.

But do they feed off humans? Do they have the same bloodlust that Zander and the others do?

"You're slow today, Abarrane!" a familiar voice teases.

My smile falters as Zander comes into view, but it's quickly followed by a heart skip that I can't explain. I *should* despise him. I *should* be repulsed by what he is. And yet I'm not.

"I would like to see how fast His Highness moves after three days without rest." Abarrane pauses her instruction to bow—no curtsy from this warrior—and the children rush to do the same, tripping over their feet, two dropping their staves.

"You may be surprised to learn I'm ahead of you in that regard." He shucks his jacket and shifts into the square, rolling up the sleeves of his black tunic to reveal sinewy forearms. "Continue."

With a secretive smile, Abarrane executes the routine again, her voice sharp and commanding, even as she moves with the grace of a dancer. The children follow suit with more zeal and with frequent glances at the hovering king, their eyes wide. They want to impress him.

Zander walks quietly between them, sliding in to adjust a stance and point out form weaknesses and errors, guiding them on ways to improve. The children listen, punctuating their moves with eager nods.

Again and again, they practice, each time their strikes smoother, their form more fluid, their strength steadier.

Zander's usually hard face is soft, his words of encouragement sincere. It is an entirely different side of him from what I'm used to. It doesn't seem possible that he is the same man who stood across from me that first night, wishing me death. Not that I could blame him. And perhaps that's why I don't hate him. Even though Princess Romeria would deserve everything he's threatened to deliver, he hasn't made good on any of it.

A shimmer of gold catches my eye. Wendeline glides along the path toward the square, pausing long enough to curtsy to Lord Quill, who is arm in arm with … I frown. That young brunette is not his wife. And she's clinging too tightly to him to be a friend or sister. I watch with suspicious eyes as she reaches up to stroke the hair off his forehead. He collects her hand in his, bringing it to his lips.

Not a sister and surely not a platonic friend.

Is he that brazen to cheat on Lady Quill so openly?

Childlike laughter below pulls my attention back to the sparring court, and I chuckle at the scene unfolding, a boy and girl attacking Zander from either side, trying to best their king as he spins and ducks from their staves with ease, his arms blocking their attempts. He moves fast, as fast as Sofie moved the night she embedded daggers into Tony's and Pidge's wrists. This is how Malachi designed King Ailill and his descendants to be: stronger, faster, harder to kill. Rivals to the Ybarisans. Malachi's demons.

Abarrane's hand is on her hip, the other propping up her staff, her expression bleeding annoyance. "Is the king here to assist or to pester?"

"Why not both?" He sweeps a little girl off her feet with one arm, earning her squeal and kick before he sets her down, his soft, musical laughter missing its usual derisive tone. I haven't heard that sound from him before, and it catches me off guard.

"Perhaps you'd like to help me demonstrate proper technique to our young fighters, then." She gestures at the rack.

His hands are out to his sides in challenge. "I thought you'd never ask."

"I would take any opportunity to knock His Highness on his back." Her responding grin is downright savage. Given what Zander told me earlier of her bodily threats, I can't help but think there's a hidden message in those words.

He chuckles. It's the kind of laugh that would pair well with a gentle finger stroke against a cheek or a whisper against an ear. A completely foreign sound, but I already know he's capable of that tenderness. I saw it the other night with that woman, just before he revealed his unsettling secret to me.

"Alas, I must decline for the moment. I believe I have a visitor." He strolls toward the edge of the sparring square where Wendeline stands, wringing her hands.

"Your Highness." She curtsies deeply. "You summoned me." Her voice carries a hint of tremor that she always has when he is near. I used to think it was fear, but I'm beginning to see it as the nervousness that comes with her reverence toward him.

"Yes. Priestess. Please." He motions toward a path.

Below me, Abarrane's barked orders fade into the background as I watch Zander and Wendeline stroll away, their pace slow, Zander's arms folded across his chest as he listens. He's probably demanding that she regurgitate every word shared between us in the sanctum, trying to figure out what had me rattled when I arrived in the throne room.

Her gaze drifts up to my terrace; his follows.

Yes, they're talking about me, and now they know I'm spying on them.

Whatever she's saying to him, he's shaking his head firmly. He doesn't agree. She's imploring him, going so far as to reach for his arm. He doesn't shuck the contact, but he appears bothered by what she's telling him, his free hand pushing through his hair, sending it into disarray.

My graphite-tinged thumbnail finds its way between my teeth as a fresh wave of anxiety washes over me and my urge to flee kicks in. I always have a way out, a getaway route at the ready. Finding it is part of my planning in the weeks leading up to whatever I'm slinking into—a way to slink back out. Yet here, I am trapped. It's unsettling, compounded by the reality that there's still too much I don't know—about why I'm here and why Malachi might want that stone.

I need to find the queen's secret passage.

I'm mentally checking off all the spots in the bedchamber I've investigated so far to consider what I've missed when, from somewhere deep inside the cultivated grounds, a woman's bloodcurdling scream pierces the tranquil evening.

CHAPTER TWENTY

"What in fates' name ..." Corrin's arms are laden with the meal tray as she steps out onto my terrace, staring with bewilderment at the furniture I dragged out. "Why is half your bedchamber outside?"

I ignore her melodramatic question—there are only two pieces —and point to the flock of sentries who circle Boaz, awaiting his instruction. "What's going on down there? What happened?" Zander took off running toward the screaming woman at a speed that dropped my jaw. Abarrane dismissed her pupils, collected a sword, and chased after him.

When they reemerged, it was at a brisk, purposeful walk toward the doors that lead into the main hall, Zander's shoulders rigid with tension. Since then, the patrons who were wandering the grounds have rushed away, and the guards are out in full force.

Desperate for information, I ran to my door in hopes that Elisaf was there, but it was the unfriendly day guard, and he gave nothing more than a grunt of "no idea."

Corrin sets my meal on the side table, her expression somber. "Lord Quill has been murdered."

"What?" My eyes widen. "But I saw him walking into the garden not ten minutes before that woman screamed."

"And he will not be walking out. He was poisoned the same way King Eachann and Queen Esma were dispatched." She gives me a pointed look.

I hold my hands in the air in surrender. "You can't blame *me* for this. I've been locked in here all afternoon."

"Certainly, I am not suggesting that you somehow snuck out and poisoned anyone," she says crisply.

I think back to the couple in matching green from the throne room earlier, smiling, oblivious to what was in store for one of them. Well, at least Lord Quill was oblivious. "The woman he was with wasn't his wife."

"No. It was his tributary."

"Someone tainted her blood." They were going out there so he could feed off her. "I'm … shocked."

"Indeed."

"Is it normal to be *affectionate* with your tributary when you're married?"

"I am here to ensure you are fed and bathed, not to provide you with idle gossip." Corrin's fingers graze the stiff paper as she studies the dresses I sketched. "You illustrated these?"

I'm not going to get anywhere with her. "Yes." One is based on a tulle ball gown that a guest at a charity event wore and I admired from afar, with embroidered flowers and a seductive V-neckline. What is the point of having my own royal seamstress if I don't have her ripping off couture? Another design is my own, layers of sheer fabric that offer full coverage while allowing provocative glimpses of a female silhouette with high slits along the thighs. I'm curious to see what Dagny might do with these.

Corrin spreads the sheets out, the paper crinkling under her touch. "How do you know such styles?"

I study my graphite-soiled fingers. "I don't know. I just do," I lie.

"You are talented."

I mock gasp. "Is that a compliment?" I know I have skill. On my first day of art class, the instructor took one look at my sketch of the quintessential but tedious fruit-in-bowl model and informed me that I had signed up for the wrong session, that I should be in her advanced level. She asked where I learned my technique. I shrugged. How did I explain that I'd spent years sitting in parks, quietly sketching strangers with stolen art supplies?

Corrin rolls her eyes and taps the tray she set down. "This is red lentil and potato. Don't wait until it cools, or you won't enjoy it as much."

"Does nobody eat meat around here?"

"Of course, they do. But Ybarisans live off a strict diet of vegetables, fruits, and grains, so that is what I've brought you."

"Yes, *every* day for *weeks* and *weeks*," I drawl.

"Is this suddenly not to your satisfaction, *Your Highness*?"

Corrin bristles so easily. "No, it's not that." It's strange, what a person can become accustomed to and how quickly they forget past struggles. There was a point in my life when I would've been overjoyed to have someone deliver food—*any* food—to me on a platter several times a day. I spent years eating whatever filled my stomach, whether it be stolen off a cart or scrounged from a dumpster behind a restaurant. Once I was able to support myself, I became more finicky, choosing the organic apples and ensuring at least one meal a day was green.

But right now, I would kill for a greasy burger on a brioche bun from the pub three blocks from my apartment. That, or one of Alton's sauerkraut-laden hotdogs.

She frowns strangely at me. "Are you saying you suddenly crave animal flesh?"

I cringe. "Not when you call it *that*."

"But you would eat it? After a lifetime of *not* …" Her words fade, her frown growing deeper.

"I was just curious." I quietly chastise myself. I'm beginning to feel like every question, every idle curiosity might out me as an imposter. "What do the Islorians eat? You know, besides …" I give her a knowing look.

It's a moment before she abandons whatever thoughts are cycling through her mind. "I assume you're referring to the immortals. Fruit, breads, meats, cheeses. They have an appetite as the mortals do, in *all* manners, though it does not fully sustain them. As far as the tributaries go, some indulge more than others. Some, nightly. Not all are like His Highness in that regard."

"And how often does he have them come to his room?"

"Only when required," she answers vaguely, peering over the rail at the horde of soldiers milling about.

I hesitate. "How does the tributary system work, anyway?"

"Dreadfully."

I sigh with exasperation. "Corrin. Come on … help me out here. *How* do people become tributaries?"

"By being mortal." Her lips purse with reluctance. "The first Hudem of every year is called Presenting Day. Young women and men are lined up in town squares and bid upon by immortals. It is a *requirement* that every human serve as tributary once they reach a certain age. Of course, the more desirable ones fetch higher coin and land in noble homes, sometimes even here within the castle if they're *blessed*." She sneers at that last word. "The less appealing are purchased by the commoners. The tradesmen and farmers and the sort. *All* are taken from their families. They serve as tributaries until they reach their midtwenties, when they are required to marry and breed. They may remain on as tributaries for some years still, or if their keeper prefers a *change*, they might offer them another position of servitude. If not, they are sold to another keeper who can utilize them."

She tells me this matter-of-factly, but I hear the bitterness in her voice. She may be loyal to Cirilea and to the king, but this isn't a life she wants to see for her kind. "If they're fortunate, they'll have a keeper who ensures they and their families are properly cared for."

"And if they're not?"

Her lips twist with contempt. "Then they're worked to the bone while they starve and their keepers flourish."

And then, at some point, they find themselves in the rookery, feeble and broken and struggling, but free. "And what if they don't want to get married and have children?"

"As if they have a choice in the matter," she scoffs. "Besides, no woman wants to find herself unwed and end up with a keeper who has a penchant for the business of breeding."

"What do you mean by 'breeding'?"

"Do not try to tell me the fates have stripped your knowledge of procreation," she mutters. "It means *exactly* what you think it means."

I cringe. Wendeline called this a civilized system where everyone survives. I don't see anything civilized about it. "But Zander wants to change all this." He sees the problem with it.

"It is a far-fetched notion that will never work, but a noble one." She peers up at the dimming sky, now a murky blue. A line of clouds rolling in from the east are faintly visible, and the air has cooled from this morning. "The priestesses have predicted rainfall tonight. This furniture needs to be returned before you retire." She lifts the table.

"I'll move it back later." It's been so nice sitting out here, even with the sour turn for Lord Quill.

"But the rain will ruin—"

"I'll move it in before it rains. I *promise*." I feel less like the queen-to-be and more like a misbehaved child who used her mother's best linens to build a fort.

With a huff, she sets the table down. She scowls at my pencil's stubby end.

"It needs sharpening."

"I see that." She slips it into her pocket. "Perhaps Dorkus can help."

My eyebrows pop. "I'm sorry. *Who*?"

"Your other guard."

"His name is *Dorkus*?" I struggle to hold my immature giggle. Maybe *that's* why he wouldn't share it.

She frowns curiously at me but then dismisses her thoughts with a wave of her finger around the terrace on her way out. "Before the rain!"

Nobody ventures along the winding paths of the royal grounds tonight, other than Boaz's guards. Two hours ago, the same burly men who lugged stone from the shattered water fountain the other day hauled Lord Quinn's lifeless body out of the garden on a stretcher. Darkness has descended since, and the priestesses have passed through to light the lanterns with their caster magic.

But no one comes. There is no sound of music or laughter carrying through the cracks in the doors either. Nothing but subdued voices. Everyone seems anxious, as they should be. Someone in the court was murdered today.

"Who is this woman?"

I startle at Zander's voice suddenly behind me and spin around. "Can you please *not* sneak up on me like that?" I haven't seen him in hours, since he disappeared into the main building with Abarrane and Atticus. A dim light glows from his bedchamber windows, and the door sits propped open. He has shed his jacket and sword, and his tunic is untucked, the front unlaced, as if he began undressing and decided to come out here partway through. Does he have a servant who helps him as Corrin begrudgingly helps me? I've never seen a hint of one.

"It is not my fault Ybarisans lack stealth." He smirks, but his rapt attention is still on the paper in his hand. "Who is she?"

Sofie's face stares back at us beneath the lantern light—delivered by Corrin when she returned with a freshly sharpened pencil, courtesy of dear Dorkus. Faces have always etched their way into my mind, and yet I'm surprised by how precisely I remember the cunning woman's upturned eyes and jagged cheekbones, having spent not even twenty-four hours with her. Just long enough for her to alter my life irrevocably.

"I'm not sure." It's a lie but also a truth. Who is Sofie? An elemental, surely. Brokenhearted and desperate over her husband's dire situation, also true. But beyond that, I don't know anything about her.

I watch Zander closely, searching for any hint that he can read my lie in my pulse as he did earlier. But he's studying the sketch with a creased forehead.

"Why? Does she look familiar to you?" Has Sofie been to Islor before?

He shakes his head. "I thought so, but no." He breaks his gaze of my illustration to peer at me. His eyes drop to where the daaknar's claws sunk into my flesh, visible in my peach gown. His jaw tenses. With revulsion or pity, I can't tell.

I fight the urge to shrink away, feeling self-conscious despite my resolve to not care what he thinks.

His attention shifts back to Sofie's face, but he offers, "I imagine that must have hurt."

Not as bad as being poisoned with something that burns you from the inside out, I'll wager. I'm about to ask him about Lord Quill when a large raindrop splatters onto the paper. It's followed by a second and a third in quick succession.

I curse as I dive for the table. "Corrin is going to *murder* me if this furniture gets damaged!"

"She does pride herself on immaculate upholstery," Zander says wryly. "Here." He gives me the sketch, freeing his hands to collect the sizable wing chair and side table with ease.

I grab the lantern and together we rush inside as the deluge hits. I quietly trail Zander through my bedchamber toward the fireplace. Around us, the room glows with the various candelabras and candlesticks that Corrin lit on her way out. Coupled with the old-timey grace of the room, it creates an ambience that one might find romantic, under different circumstances. "I heard what happened."

"I believe *everyone* in the castle heard what happened."

"Do you have any idea who did it?"

"Not precisely, no." He sets my furniture down, taking a moment to arrange it properly.

"The woman who was with Lord Quill, his tributary, was hanging off him. Do you think maybe his wife got jealous and—"

"Lady Quill did not murder her husband. She knew where he was and who he was with. *And* what they were doing."

"And she didn't care that her husband was getting more than his fill of blood? Because there is no way that wasn't happening, and don't even try to tell me differently."

Zander brushes absently at wet spots on his shirt. "How they choose to conduct their relationship is none of our business."

"Right. Of course. I forgot that's how it works around here." Just like it's none of anyone else's business that Zander brings his feeder stock to his bed when his supposed bride-to-be is right next door.

Zander's eyebrow raises in question.

"Never mind," I mutter. Can he read the irritation? I hope so. There is no way I would tolerate him bringing women to his bed for *any* reason if this thing between us were real. "Fine. Maybe this tributary felt differently, though. Maybe she was in love with Quill and wanted him to leave his wife and turn her, and when he wouldn't, she got angry and poisoned him."

"I think I liked it better when you knew nothing of our ways." Zander flops into the chair he set down, as if the weight of the day has overwhelmed him. "Highly doubtful. It is forbidden to turn a human, even if that human is willing. Doing so would be an immediate death sentence for both parties. Besides, I was there shortly after Lord Quill fell. Humans are embarrassingly easy to read, and there was nothing but agonizing heartbreak in her."

"So, you're saying she *did* care for him."

"Yes, and that is not surprising. Many of them bond with their keepers. But that does not change reality. Humans are taught from an early age that to be a tributary is an important role, but a service and nothing more."

"Such an important service that the more attractive, the better, I've heard." My voice is full of scorn.

"It certainly makes the necessity more pleasant," he retorts with a challenge in his stare.

How many of his tributaries has Zander slept with? Would he have climbed on top of that last one had I not been there to catch him in the act? A mental image of what that might look like skitters through my thoughts unbidden, and I feel my pulse quicken.

Heat flashes in Zander's eyes, and the corners of his mouth curl as if he has a secret. "Please, continue whatever line of thought you are on. I *much* prefer your reaction to that than the swirl of fear and guilt that consumed you earlier."

My cheeks flame. "How can you do that?"

He shrugs casually. "I just can. And for whatever reason, it's becoming easier to do so with you."

Is it because my mind is human? Or is it because I don't know how to use this elven body and its abilities?

"Unfortunate for you, isn't it? Especially when your thoughts veer in *that* direction."

I set my jaw, wanting to steer this conversation *far* away from any direction that gives him the upper hand. "Someone else targeted Quill. Why? What enemies has he made?"

"We all have our enemies, but I doubt he made any so profound that he would be wary. He was an easy target. Also, my supporter. That's another strike against him."

"But why kill him now?"

"I retract my earlier comment. You still know nothing." He rubs the bridge of his nose. "To stir a new wave of suspicion now that you have risen from the dead and your brother is sitting in the dungeon, awaiting execution."

"So, this has to do with me after all."

"Doesn't everything lately?" he mutters, more to himself.

"Who would want to ..." My voice drifts. "Lord Adley."

"Or one of his staunch supporters. You are finally catching on."

I glare at him.

"What? You barely knew your own name a month ago."

I knew my name well. It's everything else that was a mystery. "Are you saying this is retaliation for yesterday?"

"For humiliating him in front of the entire court?" He smirks. "That was something to behold, even if it was not according to our plan. I will admit I enjoyed it."

"Really? Because I remember your reaction being different afterward."

"It was just ... unexpected, is all. In any case, it was probably happenstance, given poisoning Quill required planning. Adley would benefit from chaos and division within the court, people forming backdoor alliances and pacts, and naturally, everyone is now speculating how many more will suffer the same fate with *you* sitting on our throne."

"But *I'm* not poisoning them."

"Technically, that's not true. The raw merth vine only grows in the Terren mountains, which means the poison was brought here when *you* and your people crossed the rift. While we may be playing a game of your innocence, we both know you were fully aware of what you were shuttling in your pocket."

"Fine, but none of *them* know that." I ease into the formal settee across from him, tucking my legs beneath me for warmth. Outside, the rain pelts mercilessly against the windows. "Maybe Atticus is right. You could avoid this if you married Saoirse. Adley wouldn't have any reason to kill anyone."

"You do not know of what you speak." His jaw tenses. "The duplicity would be tenfold. People like Adley and his ilk have no place ruling Islor."

"But *they* think they do, and you're only antagonizing them by dangling me over the throne like a threat."

The corner of his mouth curls. "Perhaps."

Realization strikes me. "That's what you want. You want to

force Adley to make a move so you have an excuse to charge him with treason and punish him."

"Something reckless and ill-planned would be preferred." His grin is both evil and playful. "Welcome to the throne. Threats come from every direction, and they do not wait in line for their turn."

I shake my head. "No thanks." I'd rather lurk in obscurity.

He smooths a finger over the carved detail in the chair's wooden arm. "I cannot rule Islor with someone like Saoirse, but it doesn't matter who I share the throne with—you or Adley's daughter. He does not want me sitting here, period." His full lips twist as if considering his next words, whether to say them at all. "You are aware of my vision for how I'd like to see the kingdom of Islor progress in the future. For the mortals."

"Where the humans are not forced into this tributary system. Yes. Elisaf told me." A future where they are free to sit at their dinner tables with their family and dream of destinies that don't involve servitude.

"I realize it is likely an unsurmountable feat, and yet I know in my heart it is the right course." His forehead creases. "I do not feel that the mortals are inferior. I have never felt that way."

An unexpected wave of respect washes over me as I regard this Islorian king, his words echoing my accusation from the day in the rookery.

"We have rules in place to try to protect them. Laws against turning mortals, and against children entering the tributary system. Punishment for harming them without cause. But there are whispers coming from the east of mortals being bred like cattle and sold in an underground market. It has always existed, but it is quickly becoming more prevalent. Children are being ripped from their parents' arms and fed upon. The younger they are, the sweeter their blood."

My eyes widen in horror.

"I, of course, would not know that firsthand," he adds quickly. "But many cities in the east have become cesspools of indecency, and that indecency is now spreading across Islor like a plague as virulent as the blood curse itself. These immortals mock the laws we have in place to protect mortals and threatens to return us to dark days from our past. It is the opposite of what I want for Islor's future, and I fear that is part of the reason for the increase. It is a bold declaration of opposition."

Kettling is in the east. "Adley doesn't care about how these mortals are being sold in his city?"

"Who do you think is at the helm?" he says evenly. "On the surface, Adley professes his undying devotion to Cirilea and the throne of Islor, but Kettling has always been an adversary, even as far back as the days of Ailill. He does not want a society where mortals are equal to us. He would put them *all* in chains and cages if allowed. My father knew of this. He knew what Kettling was doing, but he turned a blind eye in favor of keeping the peace. That's what he wanted to be known as—a peacemaker. That is why he forged this union with King Barris, who was said to be a progressive man, not so entwined in the religion of fates and caster power. The same cannot be said for his wife."

There's a twinge of bitterness in Zander's tone. "But my father was far from perfect, and he made many mistakes. One of those was believing Adley is an anomaly. The truth is, there are many who share his beliefs that mortals exist solely for our survival. My father gave Adley too much time and leeway to make Islorians wealthy and therefore loyal to him. They have no interest in sacrificing their affluence for my plans. I am a threat to them. And while there was a time when Adley could have been easily removed from his position and this situation we find ourselves in avoided, that time has passed. He has too many ardent supporters."

I can hear the passion and frustration in Zander's voice—but also the hint of resignation. "Can't you send Atticus and the army there?"

"That was my plan. After we married and my parents abdicated the throne. But now we face pressure from Ybaris. Half the army is camped near the rift with the other half ready to march at the first sign of trouble. To call arms against Kettling now would mean dividing the men even more.

"While those loyal to Cirilea are many, we cannot battle both Ybaris *and* Kettling, especially not if Adley calls on allies from Kier. They are daunting warriors, even for mortals, who fought alongside Kettling long ago, the last time Kettling rose against Cirilea. And every day I receive more messages that men are allying with Adley. If the east joins together under him, they will be formidable against me."

And yet the man stood in the front row of the court yesterday and bowed to his king. I sneer with distaste. "I don't know how you didn't sic Abarrane on him."

"Believe me, it is an urge I struggle with daily."

I shake my head. "Whoever betrayed you in the castle is the least of your worries right now."

"Perhaps." But the dark expression that passes over his face says otherwise.

My thoughts wander in the lingering—and oddly comfortable —silence, back to Lord Quill's unfortunate demise. "Elisaf said they found a vial of the poison in my lady maid's dress."

"One tiny vial, easily hidden in her clothing. From what she told us upon questioning, each tributary only needed to ingest a drop's worth in their drink. There were almost twenty drops in that vial when the priestesses tested it."

"But you took it from her."

"We did, and it is still safe within the royal vault. Untouched."

"That means there's more than one. How many did I bring?"

"We do not know. But Abarrane found another one on your brother when we captured him." And by the troubled look on Zander's face, I'm guessing that's also a concern to him.

"How would Adley get hold of this poison?"

"*Another* fair question that I do not have an answer for. I've received reports of Ybarisans seen in Meadwell in the east and Salt Bay in the south. They are traveling in groups of two to three, slipping in and out of taverns, asking about tributaries of the nobility."

I follow his train of thought. "You think they're carrying more of these vials with them and targeting the humans to get to the lords and ladies."

"It would be smart to assume they are. At the moment, though, much of the court is here for the coming summer fair, and their lands are being governed by stewards."

But they're not safe here, either, if Quill is any indication. "The seamstress, Dagny, said the Ybarisans killed a tributary."

"Lady and Lord Rengard's of Bellcross, on the other side of Eldred Wood," he confirms. "Males matching their description were seen fleeing as the body was found, so it is safe to assume they had a hand in it."

"Why would they kill her?"

"That remains to be seen." Something in his voice makes me suspect he has an idea that he doesn't want to share with me.

"Hey, you know who would know?" I pause for effect. "Tyree."

Zander's attention shifts to the hearth, the logs stacked neatly in the grate. "I've already provided my answer for that suggestion."

"But that was before Quill was poisoned."

"And for all we know, that has nothing to do with Adley, and it was a message to *you* to let you know that you still have allies within the walls."

I hadn't thought of that. "Wouldn't it be good to know that?"

His lips purse. He knows I'm right.

"Next time it could be Annika or Atticus who is poisoned. Or you." What would happen to me if Zander died? Would they simply let me go?

"We are far too careful to allow something like that to happen to us, after our parents' demise." He pauses. "You are quick and persistent with your offers of help. Why do you feign to care what befalls us?"

"Because I have nothing better to do?" My flippant answer rolls off my tongue before I can stop myself.

His eyes narrow. "Or this demonstration of fervent support is an attempt to gain my trust?"

I snort. "We've both agreed that there is *nothing* I can do to gain that." But it is becoming increasingly clear that Zander weighs *every* action and word out of my mouth, looking for duplicity. "Do you think in any way other than in angles?"

"Betrayal rarely approaches from a straight line." He watches me evenly.

"Fair enough. How about this reason"—I lean forward—"because it's worth trying before someone else dies."

A long exhale slips from Zander's lips. "We will see how things progress."

At least that's not a flat-out no. "What happens now?"

He studies his fingernail intently. "Boaz and his men are investigating. I suspect they won't discover anything of import. People will be fraught with tension until they settle their nerves or someone else turns up dead."

"Something to look forward to, then," I mutter, curling my arms around my chest. The rain has brought damp and chilly air with it, and the hairs on my arms stand on end.

"You are cold," Zander says.

"You don't miss much, do you?"

"I do not miss *anything*. It is best you remember that." His gaze is steady on me for a moment before it flips to the hearth and a rush of flames engulfs the logs in the iron grate.

My mouth drops. It's the first time I've seen Zander use his affinity.

He chuckles. It's the same easy, beguiling sound I heard in the sparring square earlier. "You look like the children who watch the priestesses light lanterns for the first time."

"I guess they're as new to it as I am. Or as I feel," I quickly correct. "How did you do that? You can just set things on fire?"

He nods to the sconce on the wall, its flame dancing within the glass as if disturbed by a faint draft. "As long as there is a source, I can manipulate it in whichever way I choose."

"And it's the same for me with water?"

"As fun as it might be to teach my enemy how to use her element the moment her cuffs should come off, I'm afraid I must abstain," he says dryly.

I let my head fall back as I release an obnoxious groan, earning another chuckle from him.

Zander isn't in any rush to leave my bedchamber, his attention on the flames in the hearth, his thoughts seemingly miles away. What must it be like to sit upon that throne and rule all these people? To have the ultimate power and yet be wary of all those plotting to take it for themselves? It would make a person perpetually paranoid. I don't envy him.

"What do you suppose will become of you once this charade"—he copies my gesture from earlier, waggling his finger between us—"is over?"

I'll go home. Not to Ybaris, but to New York. I can't say that. Sofie warned me not to, and until I know more about the nymphaeum, her words are my lifeline. "You mean, if I'm not a prisoner here anymore?"

"I do find it odd that you did not negotiate your release as part of this arrangement. It is almost as if you don't expect to leave."

Because I banked on Malachi getting me out of here when the time came, as Sofie promised. Now I'm wondering if that was foolish. "I guess I assumed you'd do the honorable thing. You know, being the decent person you are."

He smirks.

But his question sparks a thought: What if there is no way back?

If what Wendeline told me of the Fate of Fire is true, he is not averse to using his subjects for his own ambitions. Do I even *want* to retrieve this stone for him? And will I be able to open this door? What makes him think I can, where the powerful key caster Farren could not? And what if Zander's big plan to out Princess

Romeria's accomplice works, and we find them before Hudem? There won't be a wedding—not between us, anyway. Will I be able to find another way into the nymphaeum? I still don't know where it is.

"There it is again … that swirl of worry around you." He cocks his head. "What troubles you so?"

I *hate* that he can do that.

"Those children today, the ones in the sparring court, you were good with them," I say, changing topics.

He takes the bait. "You are surprised?"

"Yes."

His lips curl at the corners, hinting at the dimples that emerge with his rare smiles. "Teaching weaponry has always been enjoyable to me, especially to the young ones. Sometimes I wish I could leave this and play soldier all day long. I envy my brother for that." He reaches over his head to grip the back of the chair in a leisurely stretch.

I try to ignore the pull of material across his chest. "Seeing you with them made me think you aren't awful," I admit. Every day I spend a little more time with him, I remember less of the intimidating king in his suit of armor who was seconds from driving a dagger through my heart. Zander is quickly becoming like any other guy I might know, one who's overwhelmed by his lot in life at the moment.

Except with fangs, I remind myself.

But it's surprisingly easy to forget that, too, especially as we sit across from each other and talk like equals, rather than king and captive.

"Don't worry. There's still time to change your mind back," he murmurs. "You were intrigued by Abarrane's lesson."

"You knew I was watching?" He hadn't looked up once while he was with them.

He smirks. "You're *always* watching. Standing outside as if these walls might suffocate you." His eyes roam the gilded casting along the ceiling, the sharp jut of his throat protruding. "You watch the fighters on the court all day and the lovers in the grounds all night."

"Is that what we're calling them?" The guards down below must be reporting in to him. Does he ask for daily accounts from them too?

"And what would *you* call them?"

"I don't know, but they're feeding and fucking, and they're not exactly discreet about it."

Amusement gleams in his eyes, but I don't miss the flash of heat as well. "Islorians aren't known for our discretion."

You are, I want to say, but bringing up his late-night visitor yet again would definitely send the wrong message. "It's amazing, the way the fighters move in the sparring court. I've never seen—I mean, I *can't remember* watching anyone fight like that. I wish I knew how."

Maybe Tony wouldn't have so easily wrestled my knife from my grip. But then what? Would I have stabbed him? Do I have it in me to stab a person? I've always prided myself on not getting lured down the path of violence and drugs that so many other kids on the street travelled down.

"You were semicapable with a blade before."

"I also knew how to ride a horse, didn't I?" I found an outfit of breeches, a tunic, and leather boots tucked in my closet, suggesting Princess Romeria sometimes donned something other than silk and lace.

"You were proficient at riding." A secretive smile makes me wonder if his thoughts are somewhere far less wholesome. "And now apparently you are an artist." He nods toward Sofie's face. "It's almost like you're a different person."

I take a deep, calming breath, struggling to steady my heart rate as I meet his penetrating stare, my panic threatening. "I *am* a different person than the Romeria you used to know. She's gone." At least for now. What will happen to her when Malachi pulls me out of Islor? Will this body crumble like an empty shell, or will the sadistic, evil version return? I hope not the latter, for everyone's sake.

"Yes, that is becoming more apparent with each day that passes," he says quietly. "But, as talented an artist as you may be, it won't protect you. You should join the children for their staff lesson next time." Humor laces his voice.

"With Abarrane? She's almost scarier than the daaknar."

He chuckles. "Perhaps with a different teacher, then?"

"And who would that be? *You*?"

His gaze touches my bare shoulder before meeting my eyes again. An expression passes across his face that I can't read, but it reminds me that we have a past, full of heated looks and intimate promises that I don't remember but he does, no matter how much he may not want to. The bit I do remember—in the tower, pressed up against the wall—is enough to make my cheeks burn now. Knowing he can sense lustful thoughts makes them flame even brighter.

I swallow. "What did Wendeline want to tell you?"

"That's between the priestess and me."

"But you *were* talking about me."

"Yes." No hesitation in admitting that.

"You seemed bothered by something."

"You and I held hands and whispered in each other's ears in front of a crowd yesterday, and you think you know me deeply now? That you're privy to my thoughts and conversations?"

"You're right. I've changed my mind back already. You're an asshole."

He responds with a deep laugh, unbothered by my insult, and I find myself grinning.

He hauls himself out of the chair and moves toward my terrace.

I feel the unexpected twitch of disappointment that comes with the realization that he's leaving. "When is that royal repast happening?"

"The fair begins day after tomorrow and runs for ten days. We have a tournament of skill within the square during this time. Adley and the others have propositioned ending the day with the royal repast. A grand finale of sorts. I do not see us avoiding it."

"Can't wait. The naive princess will have a new dress for it and everything," I say with mock excitement.

His attention drifts to the flames in the hearth where it lingers a moment, a pensive look on his face. "I am willing to release you once we've uncovered the traitor who aided in killing my parents. You will be free to leave Islor and return to your kind, if that is what you wish. I will even attempt to coordinate a peaceful transfer across the rift for you."

"You'll let me go? Just like that? After what I've done?"

"Now who is thinking in angles?" He smirks. "You have my word. Good night." Zander strolls onto my terrace and disappears into the rain.

I had big plans to scour every corner of my rooms again, but I take a moment to curl up in the settee and watch Zander's flames dance as I pick through the decidedly civil conversation between the king and me.

And that is where sleep claims my body.

"Smells of soot in here!" Corrin marches into my bedchamber with a breakfast tray, waking me from a deep slumber. I groan and struggle to orient myself as she draws the curtains and pushes open the terrace door. Blinding sunlight streams in. It looks like it will be another sunny, warm day.

"What in the fates are you sleeping in?"

I look down at my peach dress, the one I wore yesterday. It takes me a moment to remember—I drifted off in it, on the settee.

And yet now I'm beneath the covers in my bed.

I do not remember getting up in the night.

"Never mind. I'll find you a proper gown," Corrin mutters.

"You are to walk the grounds with Annika today. Make yourself known. Ideally without causing trouble."

"I don't cause trouble."

"You've caused nothing *but* trouble since you arrived." She pulls a roll of paper from beneath her arm and holds it up. "I managed to scrounge up four more sheets to keep you busy. And some fresh graphite."

Warmth spreads through my chest. "Thank you. That was kind of you." And unexpected.

"It's the king's kindness. Thank *him*. I ran around half the castle trying to find it. They've been sending out so many messages lately that our supply is dwindling. Paper takes time to make. It cannot simply be churned out ..."

Corrin prattles on about paper and pigeoneers and spies, and my eyes dart over to the settee where I fell asleep, to the table where I left the sketch of Sofie.

It's no longer there.

CHAPTER TWENTY-ONE

"Must you keep looking at me like that?" Annika says crisply. She twirls the vibrant pink cosmos between her fingertips before tucking it into her curls to join the others. She looks especially radiant today, in a silk gown of deep fuchsia that matches the shade of the petals precisely, her hair flowing loose down her back.

"Like what?" I feign innocence, which earns me a flat glare.

Like she drinks human blood.

My awareness of this fact comes in ripples—a little voice that speaks up now and then, a strange disquiet along my spine that flares every so often. But then I remember I am safe from those hidden fangs, and besides, these Islorians aren't anything like the parasitical creatures of fiction.

We've ventured to a different section of the royal grounds on our walk today, to where paths amble through endless beds of cutting flowers. Workers are clipping spent blooms and yanking thistles that have wormed their way between the dense foliage while servants fill baskets of freshly cut roses and dahlias and a dozen flowers I do not recognize. Some of those will no doubt find their way into my room before tonight.

After a long and uncomfortable silence, Annika says, "I truly relished the look of misery upon Saoirse's face."

"You don't like her either?"

"I dislike her more than I dislike you, if that says anything." Her attention skims over the gauzy cream gown Corrin fished from my closet and paired with the capelet Dagny delivered yesterday. I'm beginning to see that lady maid's insistence on dressing me is a matter of pride rather than chore.

"*Wow.*" I grimace. "That bad, huh?"

Annika's unexpectedly deep, husky laughter carries along the stone path, and I could swear the nearby blooms pivot toward her. "Your act with Lord Adley left my brother more conflicted than I have ever seen him." Her blue eyes twinkle with delight. "He didn't know whether to laugh or scream. I was waiting for smoke to drift from his ears. Right, Elisaf?"

"The vein in his forehead was pulsating, Your Highness."

She cackles again.

That they are finding amusement at Zander's expense is oddly comforting. "I thought he hid it well." Until we were in private.

"Zander is not used to people ignoring his demands. He was born to be king, after all." She shakes her head. "I don't know if his efforts are worth it. Though, if this traitor among us was bold enough to betray us once, there is nothing to stop them from betraying us a second time."

"That's what I told him."

"At least no one else seemed to notice my brother's annoyance. They were all too enthralled by this new, feisty Princess Romeria of Ybaris. That's all I've heard about through the court. Well, that and Lord Quill's unfortunate departure." If she's bothered by the murder, she doesn't show it. Annika could challenge Sofie in the "impossible to read" department.

"Who do they think did it?"

"The court? No one has outwardly accused anyone yet, but there are plenty of murmurs." She shoots a knowing look my way, and I know at least some of the murmurs are directed at me. It's to be expected, I guess.

"What else did you hear?"

"Mostly gossip about you two. That you weren't as *friendly* with each other as you once were."

"We spent the *entire* time attached." Whispering about scheming noblemen and setting fire to things, but they wouldn't know that.

"Yes, but they're used to seeing you cling to him like a second skin."

An odd flutter stirs in my chest at the thought of getting even closer to Zander than I already have. "So, they're not buying his declaration that I'm innocent?"

She shrugs. "Some say you are guilty of every suggested crime against you, but that you've somehow conned Zander. Others think he's forcing you to marry him as punishment. The most prevalent rumor, though, is that he was bewitched by the casters to fall all over himself for you."

My jaw drops. "Do you mean like some sort of love spell?"

"Consumed by your beauty and blind to your treachery."

"Can they do that with caster magic?"

"Not with caster magic. Something like that would require a summons, and Neilina collars her fates to ensure that does not happen."

"Unless *she* had one of their collars removed and demanded they summon the fates on her behalf." As Isla and Ailill once did. "Would she do that?"

"It would go against everything the Ybarisans have stood behind for two thousand years, her most of all. But we don't know Neilina. Not like you do. Or did. So, who knows? Regardless, none of those scenarios reflect well on Zander as a ruler, making sound decisions for his people. And I'm certain Saoirse is behind the one that marks him as under a Ybarisan spell. I do not know what advantage she seeks to achieve in stoking that rumor, other than in hopes of it getting inside Zander's head. She's constantly scheming to get her bony behind seated on the throne and her spindly legs wrapped around my brother. It will never happen. Zander will *never* marry her."

Not based on what Zander has told me of Kettling. But if her father is behind Quill's death, then I can assume she has influential allies in her corner, working to make this happen. "What's her affinity?"

"To Aoife, like yourself, though nowhere near as powerful. Another burn of jealousy, I'm sure."

And yet, with these cuffs on my wrists and my complete ignorance of what this body can do, I'd say Saoirse has the advantage.

Patrons mill the royal grounds today as if the murder never happened. If anything, they seem energized, either by the perceived threat or the swirl of gossip. A couple bow before us, and I note how their reverence is no longer centered on Annika. Their greetings are aimed at me. I want to tell them to stop.

Farther down the path, a sparkle catches my eye, drawing my focus to our left to where the gardens part and the sun shimmers off a small lake. A family of swans float on the water's surface.

"Your Highness?" Elisaf prompts. "Is something the matter?"

I realize I've stopped dead. "Wendeline said the nymphaeum was by the lake." I look around me. "Is this it?" I see nothing but trees and cutting gardens and hedge. There are no statues or stones. Nothing that appears sacred. I don't know what nymphs look like, but I don't see anything that might hint at them.

"Here?" Annika laughs. "No. It's up ahead. Come. I will show you." She beckons with a nod. "This way."

We continue along the cobbled path, and I struggle to contain my exhilaration. It comes with a pinch of trepidation. "Can you read me like Zander does? My pulse, I mean." Can Elisaf?

"He's finally told you about that." She twists a fat corkscrew curl between her fingertips. "Interpreting a Ybarisan immortal's pulse is particularly difficult for our kind, nowhere near as easy as reading a human. I cannot read you. That my brother can, though ... that is something peculiar." She smiles secretly, as if she has thoughts on that but either doesn't want to share or isn't permitted to. "Did you know that my mother arranged a marriage for me as well?"

Her words temporarily distract me from the topic of reading pulses. "I didn't."

"Yes. I fought with her about it, many times. The last conversation I had with her, we argued." Annika's eyebrows gather, the only sign that she is bothered.

"Who are you supposed to marry?"

"A human prince from Skatrana."

"And that's bad?"

She sneers. "Their lands are nothing but an abyss of trees and mountains and frigid temperatures. Their capital city, Shadowhelm, is built within *caves.* Caves! Me, with my affinity to this"—she casts her hands toward the hedges and flowers —"living in a *cave* with those primitive mongrels."

"Have you met any of these Skatranans?" I didn't think there was much travel between the countries.

"Well, *no,* but I've heard about them. Did you ever meet anyone from Skatrana in your sails as a Seacadorian, Elisaf?" She doesn't look back. She assumes he's listening.

"I did sail that way once, yes. We docked in Westport, Your Highness."

"And how would you describe them?"

I glance over my shoulder to find his mouth curved in a thoughtful frown. "Fierce warriors. Adapted to a *humble* lifestyle."

She grunts as if his answer is proof of her claims. "I doubt they've ever even seen a rosebush. They'd probably eat it if they did. Mother was corresponding with the king for years through letters couriered by Seacadorian ships. My betrothed is to come of age next year, and with your union to Zander, she was hoping to secure safe passage for me through Ybaris. Then, all Islor would need is for Atticus to flash his dimples at a Kier princess, and our family would have its fingers touching four thrones."

"Will Zander make you honor the arrangement?"

"Even if he wanted to, they will want nothing to do with me given what happened in Cirilea. Islor is too volatile. Besides, I cannot sail to Skatrana. The sirens do not allow immortals to pass in the waters, and I'd prefer not to spend the rest of eternity at the bottom of the sea."

I file these sea sirens under "more monsters to learn about."

"I guess we've all avoided marriages arranged by our parents."

She purses her lips. "Does my brother not appeal to you *at all*?" There's genuine interest in her tone.

He appeals to me more with each encounter I have with him, but I'm not about to admit that to his sister. "Forgetting Zander's utter hatred for me for a second, since I woke up in the hedge that night, he has sliced open my hand, locked me in a tower and condemned me to death, then imprisoned me indefinitely." I use my fingers to mark the many ways Zander has made my life hell so far. "Oh, and now I'm being forced to play his future queen."

She smiles. "Is that all?"

"Actually, no. There's the whole 'bringing women to his bedroom to feed on them' issue. I'd say we have a few too many hurdles to overcome."

"He does not enjoy it, if that makes any difference to you."

"He sure looked like he did," I mutter before I can stop myself. But I've seen and heard enough to suspect that what she says is true. "Why are you asking, anyway?"

She shrugs. "Most would scheme and kill and trip over themselves to be in your position, even if it's nothing more than a farce."

"I'm not like most around here. I don't have any interest in being a queen. And besides, Zander likes obedient women, remember? I can't even pretend to be that."

"That is *not* the woman for Zander." She shrugs. "For what it's worth, I do not think my brother hates you any longer. Or at least, he's beginning to separate this incarnation from the previous version." She gestures ahead of us. "Here it is. The nymphaeum."

I study the stone pavilion and its unadorned surroundings—a stretch of meticulously groomed lawn banked on three sides by tall cedar hedges but otherwise, there are no shrubs or flower beds. The open structure itself reminds me of something that might belong in a cemetery, the four corners comprised of pillars with carvings of the fates. In the center is a simple rectangular stone block maybe seven feet long by two feet wide and a foot high. The back is closed off with a wall decorated in an intricate swirling design.

"This is it?"

"You sound underwhelmed."

"I just expected something … different." I step onto the base. It's not a sacred garden. It's like an open tomb. And it's small. I doubt it could fit five people. And where are these nymphs that have supposedly been banished here?

Her musical laughter carries. "Most do."

Above the block—an altar, perhaps?—is a circular opening in the roof.

"To allow the blood moon's light to shine in," Annika explains, following my gaze.

To shine onto the stone.

I press my hand against its cool, smooth surface. Is *this* the stone Malachi means? There is no "retrieving" this. It must weigh several tons.

"You would not believe how many offspring have been produced on that spot."

I peel my hand away, earning her tittering laughter. It dawns on me. "When Wendeline said people come to the nymphaeum to be blessed, she meant …"

"They must take the stone and go through the act of conceiving, yes. That *is* how children are produced. Do you require lessons on that? I'm sure my brother would be willing to explain it all to you," she teases.

"Oh, I'm sure." I mock. "But right *here*. Out in the *open*. Taking turns." Wendeline said hundreds of immortals beg to use the nymphaeum every Hudem. I study the long path leading here. Is that where they all line up?

"Their desire for breeding outweighs their need for privacy. And besides, what does it matter? We assume the nymphs are somehow watching it all. They were known to be devilish creatures."

"Islorians are strange," I mutter, circling the sex altar. But Annika's words trickle down my spine like icy water.

She said they must *take* the stone.

I am supposed to take a stone in the nymphaeum.

Is *this* what Sofie meant? Did she mislead me in her choice of words? Does *retrieving* this stone for Malachi mean lying on my back for one of these Islorians in some bizarre ritual? One that would produce a *child*?

No wonder she didn't tell me. A flare of anger sparks as I realize I've likely been duped. And if she was lying about this, what else has she lied about?

"Something troubles you?" Annika asks.

I'm scowling. I smooth my expression, refocusing on the stone altar and on the little that I know of this nymphaeum. An eeriness clings to the air—of many years and countless histories untold. "Wendeline said Farren came here to open a door for Malachi."

"You are such an astute pupil," she mocks, but then points behind me. "That is the door."

I study the wall of stone and the odd alphabet carved into it in a swirling pattern. For something so old, it is preserved as if etched just yesterday. "What language is this?"

"The language of the nymphs. We cannot read it. No one can, not even the casters. Believe me, they have tried."

The letters are odd, like nothing I've ever seen before, a medley of curves and swirls and circles, some converged, others apart. None run in a linear manner. On impulse, I graze my fingertip across the engraving.

Faint female laughter coils within my ear, as if carried on a breeze.

I frown curiously and retrace the lettering. More faint laughter echoes, a high, playful giggle like that of a response to a tickle. It's joined by others. "Can you hear that?"

"Hear what?" Annika asks.

"Your Highness," Elisaf interrupts in a murmur. "Approaching."

Annika and I turn in unison to see Saoirse gliding along the path toward us with an air of purpose, a flock of four females surrounding her.

My disappointment swells. It wasn't something otherworldly that I'd heard. It was one of them.

"Just what we need," Annika mutters, stepping out of the nymphaeum. I follow her, my pulse racing. Zander told me to stay away from this one. "Oh, look. We were *just* talking about you." Annika's smile for Saoirse is thin as the others curtsy. I assume they are all immortal. There are no ear cuffs to mark them as tributaries.

"I should think you would be more focused on this ghastly murder under your roof." Saoirse's voice is in A chord—high and tinny, with that same pretentious lilt her father uses. "To think, another tributary used to—"

"What do you want?" Annika cuts her off sharply. "You are ruining an otherwise lovely walk through the grounds with your chatter."

I barely stifle my laugh. Annika is nothing if not blunt.

Saoirse's responding smile is smug. "I was giving the others a history lesson."

"*Still* not exciting."

"We have an *outstanding* library in Kettling. Even better than the one in Cirilea."

"Thank you for informing us. I'll be sure to tell Zander, so he can appropriate the best of your collection."

Saoirse's lips tighten with annoyance, either because of Annika's constant interruptions or the clout she casually tosses around. "Anyhow, there is an entire section dedicated to King Ailill and

Queen Isla, some of the texts written by my own ancestors. I was perusing the oldest of them not long ago—"

Annika rolls her eyes.

"—and there was mention of a gift given to King Ailill by Malachi himself. A set of cuffs made from a token to entrap the key caster Farren and suppress her power. They were assumed destroyed when she died." Saoirse's eyes flash to me, then to my wrists. "Those *are* Ailill's cuffs that you are wearing, are they not?" she asks with mock innocence.

"You will address Her Highness suitably," Elisaf says, cordial but with a rare edge to his tone.

She curtsies formally, but her lips curl with disdain.

I hesitate, fighting the urge to check Annika's face for the right answer. Wendeline said most people would have no idea what these cuffs were, but it's not surprising there would be books written about them, or that someone with aspirations for the throne would educate herself. "They are," I say evenly. Lying is pointless when you are caught.

She makes a point of flashing a shocked glance at her friends. "It's odd that the king would feel the need to restrain his betrothed, if she is innocent of the *high treason* she was once accused."

Clever. She's planting seeds of doubt. Her hens will run off and scatter that whisper in every direction.

Annika's eyes narrow. "How dare you—"

"Zander did not require that I wear them. *I* suggested it," I cut off Annika's admonishment. While it might feel good to berate Saoirse, it'll only give whatever rumors she's cultivating faster legs.

Saoirse's eyebrows arch with surprise. "*You chose* to weaken yourself in such a way?"

"Yes." My mind is working fast over my story. We should have had one already. Then again, I wasn't supposed to engage with this serpent. Oddly enough, my heart rate is not spiking with panic as it usually does. Instead, I feel a surge of courage channel through me, much like what I feel whenever I'm reaching for a necklace. "As a testament to my loyalty."

She presses her palm against her chest. "So you *are* admitting that the king doubts your loyalty?"

She deserves an award for her display, and for putting words in my mouth. "Zander does not doubt me for a second. But I'm sure there are those in the court willing to believe *all sorts* of unflattering lies about me, especially those who are trying *desperately* to take *my* throne next to his."

Anger flares in her eyes, as I expected it to with those words. I'm an outsider, a Ybarisan taking an Islorian's seat of power. I tamp down the urge to smile.

The women surrounding Saoirse exchange nervous glances. It can't be a surprise to them or *anyone* in this court what Lord Adley or his daughter are after.

Saoirse lifts her chin. "I haven't heard of someone suggesting such a thing."

Beside me, Annika chortles.

"I guess your sources aren't reliable."

"Dare I say, I think they are quite so." Her gaze darts to my shoulder.

Does she know the truth about the daaknar attack? Or is she trying to con me?

I was proficient at swindling people in my old life. It went hand in hand with thieving—assuming fake identities, gaining people's trust. There was always an endgame with dollar signs. Here, it's about gaining information, about seeing a person's cards without them realizing it. Regardless, the fastest way to force someone to show their playing hand is to bluff. Maybe that's what she's doing.

Unfortunately for her, I have a bit of practice with that as well. "Then I guess they would have also confirmed that an esteemed member of the court was seen with a Ybarisan, and given the *only* source of deliquesced merth would be from the Ybarisans, it would stand to reason that we should suspect that court member of having a hand in poisoning Lord Quill. Isn't that right, Annika?"

Annika's eyes widen, but her blond head bobs. "My brother *the king* was suitably appalled when he heard who was conspiring against him."

"Who is it?" a willowy brunette whispers, and then clamps her lips as if having forgotten herself.

"Oh, we couldn't possibly share names. Not yet anyway." Annika's frown is masterful. "Could we, Romeria?"

I mimic her expression. "No, certainly not until the king decides how he wishes to proceed. And we wouldn't want to take that pleasure away from him."

"Unlike Ybarisans, Islorians do not govern based on hearsay." Saoirse holds her chin especially high, but in her coal-black eyes, I catch the faintest, fastest flicker of something.

"I wouldn't call it hearsay, given it's coming right from the source."

Her eyes bulge with shock before she smooths her expression. "The prisoners have broken their silence?"

I hesitate, wondering how far down this bluff I should go.

"I believe the king has requested your presence at this hour." Elisaf's voice cuts through the tension as surely as if he'd swung his blade through the air. Bells toll in the distance.

"Always a delight, Saoirse." Annika strolls on, and I quickly follow, not daring to steal a glance over my shoulder.

"Did Zander actually want me for something?" I whisper.

"He did not summon you." Elisaf's lips curve. "But I imagine he will want to learn of the trouble you and his sister have concocted."

I replay the conversation in my mind, trying to find holes I might have inadvertently stepped in. "I just wanted to find out what she knows. *And* shut her up."

Annika cackles. "I think I dislike this version of Romeria less than the other one."

"Thanks?" Worry edges into my thoughts. "Is that vein in Zander's forehead going to throb again?"

Elisaf's smile widens. "I imagine so, Your Highness."

Blades clang and shouts ring as I'm sketching Korsakov's left eye —slightly higher than his right, the outer lid drooping thanks to a four-inch scar at the corner. I always wanted to ask where he earned that mar, but I never had the nerve. Korsakov didn't like being questioned.

My ear catches approaching footfalls from the direction of Zander's terrace. Zander normally moves like a wraith; he never makes a sound. But I know without looking that it's him. I've been waiting for him since Elisaf deposited me into my room an hour ago, my anxiety growing with each passing minute as I pondered how angry he might be with me for provoking Saoirse. That I hear his slow, measured footsteps now must be intentional on his part, and it means one of two things—he doesn't want to frighten me.

Or he does.

"How was your walk through the grounds today?" His voice is crisp and laced with irritation, and still it makes my heart skip a beat from nerves that I fear have little to do with my unease.

"Lovely, thank you for asking." If he's angry with me, then my answer will only antagonize him, and yet I can't help it.

He stops at the rail, peering down at the sparring court. "Anything interesting?"

Besides discovering that Malachi expects me to offer myself up to you on your sex stone under the blood moon for all to watch? I fight against the visual that threatens to consume my thoughts. "The swans."

"The swans," he echoes.

"Yes. You know, graceful, long-necked white birds that float." I feel Zander's steady stare as I outline the hump of Korsakov's crooked nose. I've barely thought of the man since I left, and yet when I sat down with pencil and paper, I felt the compelling need to draw his face. A connection to my past life, maybe to remind me of what once was. I can't decide if this situation I find myself in is better or worse.

"That's odd. I was *so* sure you'd say you most enjoyed the part where you fabricated a story accusing a court member of conspiring with the Ybarisans to murder Lord Quill."

At least we didn't have to dance around it too long. "It's the truth, isn't it?"

"This is the Islorian court. We do not deal in truths unless it serves us well." His tone is eerily calm. I think I'd prefer it if he snapped at me. "We have no proof of conspiracy with the Ybarisans. *Especially not* from the prisoners who haven't said a word." He folds his arms across his chest as he towers over me. "But now several members of the court are insisting we bring them forth for a public trial, so they may name the accused, and that court member has fair opportunity to defend themselves against such a heinous charge."

"I assume Adley is spearheading this?"

"That would be a safe assumption."

I set my graphite on the table. "Good. While we're at it, we can bring up what he's doing to the human children in Kettling." I level Zander with a knowing—and scathing—look.

He sighs heavily. "Do you not see the issue with this situation?"

"Besides the fact that the prisoners aren't talking?"

"Yes, besides that one rather significant problem," he says dryly. "After several days of personal attention from Abarrane's temper and blade, *if* they should decide to speak, what do you think they would say? *Who* do you think they might accuse of King Eachann's and Queen Esma's murders?" He looks pointedly at me.

"*Me*? But I'm Ybarisan, like they are."

"And possibly a traitor in their eyes, especially after that compelling speech you gave in the throne room in front of them.

We cannot risk that. So, no, we do not want them to speak. *Ever*. At least not publicly, and certainly not in a court forum."

I curse under my breath. Maybe my conning skills aren't as useful as I convinced myself they would be.

"For someone who has a solid grasp of self-preservation, you seem intent on not surviving."

"But you're the king. *You* decide what happens to me."

"I will lose the faith of many, including Lord Telor, if it becomes obvious that I'm knowingly placing my parents' murderer on the queen's throne. They will not care for my reasons."

"I hate to say it, but I'm beginning to doubt your reasons too."

"That's because you do not understand them, and I am not about to explain myself to you." His jaw tenses. "Your attack on Cirilea proved to my enemies that the royal family can be defeated, even without the strength of an army. It's given them courage. What will happen if something should befall my seat on the throne? What will happen to *you*? Adley has no love for Ybaris. He will not set you free. You will face the fate you are so desperately trying to avoid."

I shudder at the thought of those pyres. "You think Tyree would do that? Name me?"

"I don't believe you two are particularly close, but that could be another of your previous deceptions. I wouldn't put anything past him, especially if he thinks you have turned on your kingdom."

"All the more reason to allow me to talk to him, then. This is what I'm here for, Zander. *Use me*. Otherwise, this charade is pointless."

"I agree, which is why we're going to see him."

I falter, not expecting that answer. "When?"

His attention flashes to my sketch. A curious frown darts across his face, but he says nothing. He collects the capelet I tossed over the back of the wing chair. "Now."

My nerves churn as I stand. I reach for the translucent material in his grasp, but he drapes the garment over my shoulders himself.

"Thank you." I steal a glance at his face to find his steady, unreadable gaze on me as he fastens the gold ribbon. He has an intimidating stare, and it compels me to speak. "I heard you had a library here."

"We do." He hesitates. "Is there something you'd like to read about?"

Everything. The fates, the Great Rift, these mythical nymphs and their magic. "More of Islor's history."

"I suppose Elisaf can take you there." His fingertips graze my collarbone, and the simple, fleeting touch sends a shiver through my limbs.

The corners of his mouth twitch.

"Stop it."

"Stop what?" he asks with mock innocence.

My cheeks flush. "Feeding your male ego. I don't like it."

"Then I suggest you learn how to school those reactions." He offers his arm. "Shall we go to the dungeon?"

After a moment's hesitation, I curl my fingers around his biceps.

CHAPTER TWENTY-TWO

The trip to the castle's dungeon is long and arduous, along a dozen hallways and down a spiral of lopsided stairs that are nothing short of lethal—one side open to a perilous drop and lit by sporadic torchlight. It's as if merely getting *to* the dungeon is designed to kill. I cling to Zander's arm without shame, no interest in finding out how far down that fall would take me.

"Your Highness." A guard bows deeply and then yanks the heavy iron door open with a grunt.

My senses are instantly assaulted by the stench of mold, urine, and rusty metal, accompanied by a medley of low moans.

Shifting out of my grip, Zander's hand settles on the small of my back as he urges me across the threshold. I collect the corner of my capelet and press it to my nose to mask the offensive odor before I retch, and I move forward along the dark corridor. Cells line either side, closed off but for the small, barred windows in the doors. Rattling coughs from deep within make my teeth grind with pity.

What did they do to earn their way in here? Do they deserve it?

I tread lightly down the aisle, not wanting to stir attention and see their wretched faces. Mice scurry along the floors where they meet walls, darting in and out of holes in the stone.

Halfway along, we pass two male guards wearing leather garb similar to Abarrane's. One has three blond braids like hers; the other's entire scalp has seen the sharp edge of a blade. They're her elite Legion warriors, no doubt. They dip their heads and shift to the side but remain quiet as we pass, their expressions yielding nothing.

Zander clasps his hand over my wrist, stalling me. He leans down to whisper close to my ear, "The only advantage we have over him is that he doesn't know where you stand."

An advantage we can lose in a blink. Adrenaline surges through me, and I search for my courage. This is what I was good at—coaxing information out of people who didn't expect my motives. But I was in my element in my own city, a world away—literally. I was a stranger in a swarm of millions, an innocent nobody with a collection of names I could drop to spark either familiarity or fear. I've been off my game since the moment Sofie appeared next to me at that bar, and now I'm pretending to be this guy's sister. I don't know who Princess Romeria was, what she was truly like. Everything we know about her was a facade.

"He needs to think you've found your way here on your own."

I nod, not trusting my voice.

"Last cell on the right."

I leave Zander there, holding my breath as I move on. The deeper I go, the quieter it gets. I count nine more cells before I reach the last at a dead end. I peer into the darkness beyond the barred window, looking for its occupant, but it's pitch-black inside despite the torch glow by the door.

"Tyree?" I call out in a whisper. Nothing. "Tyree—" I gasp as a bloodied male face suddenly appears, familiar blue eyes staring out at me.

"I thought you'd never come." His soiled fingers curl around the bars, the nails bitten to the quick. He peers behind me. Looking for guards or companions. "How did you get in here?"

My heart pounds in my chest. "I still have a friend or two." A lie that he cannot prove otherwise. He looks relatively well. Untortured. "Have they hurt you?"

"*Have they hurt me*?" he hisses, holding up his arm to show me a fresh gash across his biceps. "I wake up to that demon every morning, slicing me with her blade to weaken me."

I wince. "Abarrane. She's scary." Empathy is always a quick way to assuage fear, to put people at ease so they'll talk.

"They took Rodrick and Kieve yesterday, and they haven't brought them back. Are they still alive?" Tyree's voice is low, and he speaks quickly.

"As far as I know." I keep my eyes locked on his, fighting the urge to search out Zander in the shadows. I sense him there, his steely gaze on me, his ears pricked, likely for both information and traces of deception on my part. Zander's right—if I hint that I'm not alone, Tyree will give me nothing. The trick here is to say as little as possible. "I don't have long—"

"You must get us out of here. We have too much work to do yet."

"I'm trying, but it's not easy. They don't trust me."

"It seems you've fooled them into thinking you are a victim."

His words squash whatever shred of hope I might have been clinging to that Princess Romeria was framed. Everything Zander has accused her of, she deserves. "Not all of them believe it."

"But the king does."

"Barely, I fear sometimes."

He leans in, pressing his head against the bars. "You said you had everything lined up that night."

"I did. And then everything went wrong."

"Mother sent word. She is displeased with our failure."

Queen Neilina threw her children into enemy territory to steal a throne. Her son was being hunted and her daughter assumed killed, and yet she's expressing her disappointment? It's all I can do to not shake my head. "She killed our father."

"You mean *my* father and, yes, we both knew she would. The spineless lout would have ended up giving Ybaris to these demons."

I school my expression. *His* father. But not Romeria's?

"We thought you were dead," Tyree says.

"Obviously, I'm not."

"Has Ianca contacted you?"

"Ianca …" I repeat, absorbing that name to memory and making sure Zander catches it. "No." Is that the traitor within the castle?

"She has escaped, along with another. With help from the casters. There were reports that they crossed into Skatrana, so we assume they are on their way here," he mutters, more to himself.

Not the traitor within the castle, then. Someone from Ybaris? I bite my tongue against the urge to ask who this woman is. Princess Romeria would know. "Why would she come here?"

Loud voices carry on the other end of the dungeon block. Someone is demanding to be let through. It sounds like Atticus. It gives me an excuse to glance that way. Zander's silhouette lingers behind the torchlight, but I don't stall there, turning my attention back to Tyree. My window of opportunity to learn something useful is shrinking fast. I move in closer, and the pungent smell of a sour body and foul breath grows stronger. "The vials …"

"Being dispersed as we speak."

My heart skips a beat. "How many have already gone out?"

"Not as many as we'd hoped. We distributed the last of ours in Bellcross. But it is harder than we anticipated, traveling among these demons. They can smell us from across the room."

I don't know if that's a figure of speech, but it's a question for Zander for later. Now, I need to focus. "And you've targeted the tributaries." I keep my voice firm—a statement rather than a query.

"The tributaries, the cooks, the blacksmiths. Anyone willing. They are tired of having their kin taken from them."

Anyone willing. That means this isn't a case of tributaries being targeted, their blood tainted without their knowledge. They're finding humans who will *voluntarily* take the poison. "What happened in Bellcross?"

He shrugs. "We misjudged her. Is it true, what I've heard about the marriage to the king?"

"Yes. Next Hudem."

"So, the fool is *still* enchanted by you, despite everything you've done." He chuckles darkly. "Obviously, he has not tried feeding on you yet."

"No." How does Tyree know about Margrethe's invocation? Unless ... the rumors are right and it wasn't Margrethe's invocation to begin with.

"I must get back to the men."

"Where are they now?"

"Still in the mountains, waiting for my instruction. You *must* get me out of here."

Zander was right. They've found a hiding place north of Lyndel. "I'm trying, but you poisoned Quill, and that makes it difficult. The royal guard is crawling all over this place."

Tyree frowns. "Who?"

"Lord Quill, of Innswick. He was poisoned last night, right here in the royal grounds."

"That wasn't us. We haven't risked coming back to Cirilea yet."

"What about Kettling?" Maybe Adley got hold of a vial in his own city.

He shakes his head. "The river is vast and too well guarded. Who else did *you* give a vial to?"

I falter on my answer. It's a mistake. I see it the moment his eyes narrow. "I shouldn't be down here. This is a big risk."

"Something is off. You aren't yourself." His gaze skitters over my face. "What have they done to you?"

A curse slips through my thoughts. If lies and ambiguity won't work, half-truths might. "It's the invocation. I have holes in my memory."

"What kind of holes?"

"*Big* ones."

Voices in the hall grow louder.

He hesitates. "Then you need to find Ianca. She might be able to explain this."

"Why?"

"Because she's the one who summoned Aoife for you. But after you get what you need, make sure you kill her—"

"Zander, we need to talk!" Atticus's deep voice echoes down the corridor.

Tyree's head snaps in the direction before shifting back to me. I recognize the change in his expression—from caution to complete distrust.

I've lost him.

"He's here, isn't he? Listening to us. *He* brought you here."

The next few seconds happen in a blur.

The space between the bars is just wide enough for Tyree to shoot his forearm through. He seizes the back of my head and yanks me forward. Pain explodes in my nose and left eye as my face crashes into the iron.

"Traitor!" Tyree seethes, spittle spraying against my cheek. But then he releases me with a yelp and stumbles backward. A deceptively small orange flame skips over his pant leg.

Zander is suddenly beside me. "Who helped Romeria poison the king and queen?" he demands, leveling Tyree with a cold, lethal stare.

Tyree smacks his hand against his thigh, trying to extinguish the fire.

"*Who* was she working with inside these walls?" Zander roars, and the tiny flame multiplies, crawling over Tyree like fast-moving bugs, flaring brighter.

"She never told me!" Tyree's teeth are gritted as he struggles to hold back the scream, until the flames have converged and engulf the frayed fabric covering his body. Any second now, his restraint will break, and the bloodcurdling shrieks will begin.

I am instantly transported back to a wooded area outside the city years ago, with a pyre and a woman's relentless screams. "Stop," I croak, my head swirling. Zander will burn him alive in his cell if this continues.

Zander ignores me. "Lord Muirn?"

"A stooge looking for more power," Tyree hisses.

"Adley?"

"Would rather die than trust a Ybarisan!"

The smell of blistering skin turns my stomach. It won't be long before my knees give out and I collapse. I reach for Zander, squeezing his forearm as hard as I can to get his attention. "*Please.* Stop." It's barely a whisper, but between that and my death grip, Zander finally notices me. Something registers in his eyes, and the flames extinguish.

Tyree collapses within his cell.

"Looks like you don't need Abarrane to do your questioning for you," Atticus says from behind us, his nose curled with disgust. The warriors let him through, but they trail him.

Zander's focus is on me, his brow furrowed, and I can't tell if it's on account of my mangled face or the terror that consumes me.

"Brother—"

"What are you doing here?" Zander snaps.

Atticus holds up two scrolls. "Messages from Meadwell and Hawkrest."

"They couldn't wait?"

Atticus squares off against his brother. "No, they couldn't, *Your Highness.*" It's a sarcastic address, Atticus's anger flaring.

Zander's attention turns back to me. My nose is likely shattered, and my left eye is swelling shut, a steady stream of blood gushes down my lip. Yet there's something oddly warm in his gaze.

"Let's get you fixed up," he whispers, slipping an arm around my shoulders in a protective move that I'm in too much pain to shrink away from.

The Legion warriors fall back against cell doors, allowing us room to pass.

"What about him?" Atticus asks, nodding toward the cell.

"He will heal. Eventually."

With a shrug, Atticus leads the way down the corridor. The commotion has stirred the prisoners. Soiled faces peek out from behind the bars, their forlorn eyes on my bloodied face.

"Did you get anything out of him?" Atticus asks.

"Nothing of use," Zander answers without missing a beat.

I wouldn't call what Tyree told us of no use—far from it—but it's a conversation better had when a dozen ears can't listen in.

To the Legion soldiers trailing us out, Zander commands, "Move him to the tower. No one is to see or talk to him unless I am present. Under no circumstances. *No one.*"

Atticus peers over his shoulder, his attention on me now. "Do you wish to parade her through the castle looking like that?"

Zander sighs with resignation. "No."

Atticus nods at the guard as we exit through the main door, but instead of ascending the stairs, he reaches for the panel of weapons mounted on the wall. It swings open with a creak.

Even wrapped in the throbbing pain of my face, I feel a spike of delight at the discovery of a secret passage.

"Tell Elisaf to send for Wendeline," Zander instructs his brother before guiding me in. Behind us, the hidden door shuts with a loud thud, throwing us into inky darkness. The air is dank from lack of ventilation and oddly cool.

"You can't see anything at all, can you?" Zander asks.

"No?" I wouldn't be able to, even if my left eye wasn't swollen shut. *"You can?"*

"I told you already, Islorians are far superior to Ybarisans." He shifts into me. I gasp with surprise as he collects me in his arms, sweeping my legs from under me. "I'd prefer not to spend the day crawling behind the castle walls," he explains, pulling me tight against his chest. "Stay close to me. The passage is narrow."

I curl my body in as we move forward at what feels like a clipped pace.

To be able to see in the pitch-black … it reminds me of Sofie traversing those winding stairs down to her dungeon with such ease. In fact, there are many similarities between them besides that—her speed, the way she moves, her affinity to fire. A thought pricks me. She claimed she could navigate those stairs in her sleep because she used them every day, but what if it had nothing to do with that? She *must* be an elemental, but what else is she?

Could Sofie be like Ailill? An immortal elemental, bound to Malachi? It would explain the way she spoke of missing her husband, as if she hadn't seen him in decades—or longer.

"What troubles you now?" Zander asks.

I hate that he's able to read me the way he does. It makes something as simple as *thinking* dangerous. Part of me is growing tired of hiding my secret from him. Maybe I should tell him who I really am. Maybe Sofie was being paranoid. Maybe she was deceiving me as she did with the truth about the stone.

Or maybe telling Zander will change *everything* for the worst, just when things aren't horrible between us. And they're not, I admit, even given my current excruciating predicament. But I need to understand what I am and what my purpose here is before I trust *anyone* with the truth.

I need to find Ianca.

"Just wondering how often you've watched me in the dark."

His low, deep chuckle vibrates inside me. "Only a few times. And I wasn't the one skulking on your terrace the other night."

"I wasn't skulking," I mutter weakly, leaning the uninjured side of my face against the crook of his neck.

He inhales deeply.

It triggers Tyree's earlier words. "Can you smell our blood from across the room?"

"That is an exaggeration."

"But it's true?"

"Yes."

"What does it smell like?" All I think about is the office in the back of the warehouse, with sprays of blood across the walls and a metallic tinge in the air.

"It's a honeyed scent, with a hint of spice. Like neroli oil from the orange blossom."

"So, it's pleasant?"

He inhales again, as if prompted to do so. "Enough talking. You're in pain."

I *am* in pain. "How did he do so much damage with one hit?"

"You are weaker than my kind, but you are far from weak."

I don't feel strong right now. I focus on my breathing, anxious for any relief Wendeline might provide.

Zander slows and maneuvers me in his arms. A loud click and bang sounds, followed by the grating sound of stone.

I sense us stepping through another doorway, punctuated by the same stone sliding back into place. It reminds me of the church pew in the sanctum, grinding across the floor.

"Do not speak of what Tyree told you. To *anyone*. I must think first."

I hum my agreement as we ascend stairs that I sense are steep and winding. I keep waiting for Zander's pace to slow, his breathing to falter, but there is no sign of fatigue as we go up … up … up.

Zander fidgets with another lever. A clunk and thud of mechanics click into place, and then we're stepping into a bedchamber.

My bedchamber.

CHAPTER TWENTY-THREE

"As good as new. And much easier to manage than some of your past injuries." Wendeline holds up the mirror in front of me.

I scrunch my nose and wiggle it. Aside from a touch of stiffness that she promised would vanish by tomorrow and the dried blood on my lips and chin, no one would ever know that only hours ago, half my face had been shattered by my darling brother.

"Thank you." I offer the priestess a genuine smile.

She returns it, though it's laced with the exhaustion that comes after a healing—her eyelids drooping, the whites of her eyes tinged with red. "You would have healed within a week or so regardless, but I am always happy to speed up that process."

I was eleven when I broke my ankle playing soccer. It took four weeks for it to heal. As much as I am loath to agree with Sofie, this elven body I've inhabited *is* superior to the human one I left behind.

"Sit down and have some tea, Priestess," Corrin orders, pointing to the tray next to the settee and the pot she fetched when Wendeline set to work. "Let's get you cleaned up." Corrin sets a bowl of water on the table beside my chair and begins wiping away the streaks of blood with a damp cloth. Her touch is unusually gentle, her efforts motherly. For once, I don't argue or begrudge the attention, my focus intent on my bed and the secret passage I now know hides behind it. Zander was reluctant to reveal it to me. I don't blame him. How the mechanism unlocks from this side is still a trick I need to figure out, but I am determined.

"I hope the visit with your brother was worth all this." She dabs under my nostril.

"We'll see what Zander thinks." It's the safest answer, and it reveals nothing.

A heavy knock sounds on the door to my suite, followed by Elisaf's voice carrying through the sitting room. "Your Highness, the seamstress Dagny requests an audience."

An audience—as if I'm someone important. Will I ever get used to this?

"What does she want now?" Corrin mutters, pausing in her ministrations to rush for my bedchamber door. "Her Highness will see to Dagny in the sitting room shortly. In the meantime, stop hollering at us like we're animals in a barnyard. You know better," she scolds, shutting the door with a thump. "A bloodied princess would make for delightful gossip, and there isn't a soul in this castle that woman does not talk to on a daily basis." She smooths the rag over my neck and chest.

Dagny can't be *that* bad. "Have you ever tried just *asking* her to keep quiet about something?"

Corrin snorts. "That's like dropping a bale of hay in front of a horse and asking it not to eat. Quickly now, into a fresh dress."

"Your Highness! I have the most thrilling news!" Dagny announces, her knee practically grazing the stone floor in a curtsy as I approach. "The *Silver Mage* has arrived in time for the city fair. I've already sent word, tellin' Odier that I'd be down to his booth in the morn to see the fine silks that were promised. Her Highness must be seein' them before anyone else. I was thinkin' why don't ya come along? You could pick something ya like for those designs of yours. Or for your wedding gown."

"To the market?"

"Yes, Your Highness! First thing in the morn, before the streets get busy. It's the biggest market of the year. Lasts for ten days. People come from all over Islor to enjoy the wares, the delicious food. There are street buskers and actors in costume! The clothier section will be especially hectic."

"I'd love to—"

"The future queen traipsing around with the commoners! Are you daft?" Corrin blurts.

The seamstress's head bobs. "It was a thought. A silly one, of course. Albe always likes to tell me what a foolish woman I am—"

"It wasn't silly at all, Dagny. I would love to go. We'll see if we can make it work." I shoot Corrin a warning glare, to which she lifts her stubborn chin but says nothing.

Dagny beams. "Also, here. I brought you these." She collects a stack of folded cloth from the settee and hands them to me. "Made one in every fine cloth I could scrounge up."

I finger through them. They're capelets, of varying color, material, and style—some heavily detailed with embroidery and lace, others simple and unadorned. I count twelve in total. "These are gorgeous. This is … how did you make them all so fast?" And by hand.

Pink blossoms in her cheeks. "Oh, these take nothin' to whip up. Nothing at all. And I've got me some keen helpers lookin' to learn and eager to have a hand in somethin' Her Highness might wear. But don't worry. I watched their stitchwork like a mother hen, makin' sure it was impeccable. I said nothin' but the best for our future queen."

"I'm sure they're all perfect. Tell them thank you."

Corrin swoops in to collect them from me. "I'll hang these in your dressing room. If there's nothing else, Dagny …" She disappears into the other room.

"Best get back to your gown, Your Highness." Dagny marches away, her hips swinging with her determined steps.

An impulsive urge seizes me. I know this will probably be my only chance. I rush forward, grabbing her arm. "Dagny." I glance over my shoulder to make sure Corrin's not there and then lower my voice to ask, "Do you know anyone by the name of Ianca?"

Dagny's brow creases as she shakes her head. "No, Your Highness. Can't say I do. Is she here in the castle?"

"I don't believe so." If what Corrin says is right, Dagny would know if she was, unless she's using an alias.

She hesitates, her eyes flipping to my bedroom doorway before she asks quietly, "Would you like me to ask around?"

This is opposite to what Zander insisted, but I know in my gut it's the smart move. People may not trust known gossips with sensitive information, but when there's anything interesting or suspicious happening, it's these same gossips people rush to and compare notes, and sometimes those random notes can add up to important details. Like that tributary from Bellcross murdered by Tyree. On its own, it's a tragic case. Adding the context of the Ybarisans circulating vials of poison around Islor, it hints of a deeper plan.

I'm betting on Dagny having more acumen than Corrin believes and connections that I need, but even if I'm wrong, word that Princess Romeria is looking for a woman named Ianca will spread quickly. Hopefully to Ianca herself, if she is in Cirilea.

If she summoned the fates for me as Tyree said she did, then she might have answers to my questions. And I'd rather ask them without Zander around.

"If you don't mind. Discreetly, though."

"Yes, of course, Your Highness. Discretion is my specialty."

I clench my teeth to stop from laughing.

With another curtsy and a glance at my bedroom, as if she senses what I'm asking her to do would not get Corrin's seal of approval, she rushes to the door.

Zander is standing outside, in conversation with Elisaf.

"Oh, Your Highness! I wasn't expectin' you!" Dagny exclaims with a burst of surprise, stumbling to curtsy. "Hope you're havin' a fine day!" She doesn't wait for him to respond, rushing off down the hall.

Her flustered reaction draws a lazy chuckle as he watches her go, and I smile at the pleasant sound. Humans are said to be embarrassingly easy to read, so what could he learn in her pulse just now? Nothing of concern, obviously. If there was ill intent or hatred in her, Zander would know. I suppose I can assume that Dagny was not the one conspiring against the royal family.

But what if no one was conspiring with Princess Romeria? Or at least, not deliberately. Dagny has no idea why I'm looking for Ianca, but she has offered her help because I am to be the queen, and for whatever reason, she trusts that my objectives are good.

What if all of Princess Romeria's scheming was like this? Using people who trusted her for her nefarious goals, without them knowing? What if Zander is chasing an imaginary person?

Zander turns back in time to catch my smile, and his own genial expression holds. With a quick word to Elisaf, he enters my room, strolling purposely toward me. "Wendeline works wonders, does she not?" He's exchanged his white tunic for a black one, probably because the other had my blood all over it. He stops well within my personal space, his eyes roaming my face. "Much better. Except …" He reaches up to rub the soft pad of his thumb back and forth over my jawline, below my ear. "Missed a spot," he murmurs, his voice dropping.

Blood, I assume he means.

I focus on my breathing, hoping my racing pulse doesn't give me away.

The knowing flicker in his eyes tells me that it has.

"I did no such thing!" Corrin is indignant as she emerges from my bedroom to curtsy for the king. Her eyes dart between the two of us, and she clears her throat. "If there is nothing else, I need to see to the kitchen staff. Between the crown hunt and the tournament day, we have our work cut out for us." I don't know how many hats Corrin wears under this roof, but I'm getting the sense that she barks orders and people obey.

Zander removes his hand and I feel the absence acutely. "Is there anything else you need, Romeria?"

"I … no." I swallow against my own fluster. Since when does Zander ask for my opinion on anything?

"Is Wendeline still here?"

"Collecting her strength in Her Highness's bedchamber," Corrin confirms and then marches off.

"Your Highness." Wendeline appears, her hand on the door frame as if to steady herself before moving forward to curtsy.

"No need, Wendeline. I know you are drained. We have much to discuss, and I feel you might be able to help us with some of it." He gestures to the seating area. "Both of you. Please." He says *please,* but I know it's not a request.

She dips her head in acknowledgment and then settles into the wing chair.

I find a spot on the settee across from her. The tension that always swirls around Zander is ever present. Still, those first few moments that he entered were a nice reprieve. "What was so important that Atticus came down to get you?"

Zander's lips twist.

"Seriously?" He still doesn't trust me? "I just had my face broken for *you*."

He sighs. "There are reports of several tributaries found dead in villages outside Hawkrest and Salt Bay. Their throats were slashed."

"Just like the woman in Bellcross."

"Yes," he confirms. "Lord Rengard's letter said she was an exceptionally shy and devoted creature. He couldn't understand why anyone would want to harm her." He watches me closely, and I get the sense he's feeding me a piece of important information, waiting to see if I clue in.

"They misjudged her." I echo the reason Tyree gave for killing the tributary. *A devoted creature*. Devoted to her keeper. "It's because she wasn't willing to poison him. These others must have refused as well."

"Or they figured out what the Ybarisans have in their possession and threatened to speak." He frowns. "But I also must assume that many *are* willing."

"They're tired of having their children taken away." I grimace with new understanding.

Wendeline's curious eyes bounce back and forth between us, but she remains quiet.

Zander drops into the limited space on the small settee, forcing me to shift to make room. Resting his elbows on his knees, he leans forward and studies the priestess until she begins to squirm.

I know that unnerving feeling well.

"Ianca."

She waits a moment and then, as if realizing he is waiting for her to speak, says, "I'm sorry, Your Highness? I do not understand."

"Do you know anyone by that name?"

"Here, in Islor? No? I don't believe so."

"What about in Ybaris?"

She shakes her head.

"An elemental," he pushes. "She's one of Neilina's."

"I left Mordain when I was seventeen, and I never spent time in Argon. *And* I've been here for twenty-eight years. May I ask, what is this about?"

Zander sighs. "It is as we suspected. Margrethe was not the first to summon the fates for Romeria."

My jaw drops. "You already *knew*!" Or at least suspected. And he didn't tell me? I don't know why I'm surprised or angry by this —he's hidden everything else from me, only revealing information as necessary—but my indignation burns.

He ignores my reaction. "Ianca summoned Aoife."

"*Aoife*." Wendeline's eyes widen. "Against Neilina's will?"

"Tyree did not say."

"No. She knew," I interject. "Neilina was disappointed that we failed. Whatever the plan was, she was a part of it, and that must have included what happened with Aoife." I shoot a glare at Zander.

Wendeline seems to consider that. "And Neilina would have had to remove Ianca's collar for her, so yes, I think you are correct." Her gaze dances with thought as it settles on the table between us. "Did he say what precisely they asked Aoife for?"

"No, but I believe it is *also* as we suspected," he says quietly. "Either way, we will not get *any* more information from him."

Despite what Tyree did to me, I cringe at the gruesome memory. "And what did *you two* suspect that you haven't told me?"

Zander stalls on the answer, but then resignation fills his expression. "That you were already a weapon when you arrived here. One that could not be fed upon and could not be turned." His jaw tenses. "And one that I would not be able to resist."

Tyree's dark laughter and words skate through my mind. *So, the fool is still enchanted, despite everything*. "Bewitched," I hear myself say out loud. That was the word Annika used. *Consumed by your beauty and blind to your treachery*. "So it *is* true?" Whatever else Ianca asked of Aoife, she wanted Zander to fall for me, and fall hard.

Zander's intent focus is on the priestess, but I don't miss the way his cheeks flush. He's embarrassed by it. "I would like to know all your thoughts on this. Candidly." It's a request rather than a demand.

Wendeline told me Zander seeks her counsel on many things related to the casters, but it's refreshing to see him burying his arrogance and bowing to others for expertise. Korsakov never asked anyone for advice, and if he asked for their opinion? It was always part of a game to prove them wrong and himself superior.

"If Neilina broke her own decree to summon Aoife for Romeria," she says slowly, "then it is safe to assume whatever she asked for would be detrimental not just to you but to all Islorian immortals."

He smirks. "You mean, like a princess who would kill any of us with the blood that courses through her veins?"

Her eyes flicker to me for only a second. "Yes, like that. Which we must assume Malachi would not appreciate, for you are his creation and seeing you weakened by one of Aoife's creations would anger him." Wendeline frowns. "It is curious, though, that he would answer a summons from Margrethe to bring that same weapon back to life."

"Why would he?"

"He must have another use for her."

I sit and quietly listen to them discuss me as if I'm not here. It's a snapshot of what they must have done for weeks while I was locked up and they were deciding my fate.

"There is always a reason. The fates do *nothing* without a reason." She turns to me, softness in her eyes. "Though Malachi didn't give us back the same Ybarisan princess. He gave us *this* version instead, and I do not believe she means you *any* harm."

"But she is still quite capable of it," Zander says quietly, studying his hands.

"Don't bite me, and you'll all be fine," I retort.

He releases a husky laugh. "I suppose I have the daaknar to thank for that never happening."

Wendeline hesitates, her eyes darting between the two of us. "Aoife was obviously planning on using this union for her own gain, but Malachi must have his motives for wanting a union between you as well."

My heart pounds in my chest. *You're getting warmer.* If I'm right, a literal union of body parts, lying on a stone slab beneath the blood moon, is exactly what Malachi is aiming for.

Worry fills her face. "But if Aoife and Malachi are scheming against each other in *any* way, we have reason to worry, and if Neilina keeps summoning Aoife in her campaign against Islor, I fear what might happen."

Zander folds his hands. "What do you recommend?"

"You could inform her of the truth about her daughter, so she is aware of the risk of more summoning."

"What *else* do you recommend besides feeding my zealous enemy sensitive information that she could somehow use against me?" he counters.

Wendeline's lips purse as she considers his question. "There are those in Mordain who are not devoted to Ybaris and their queen, who believe Mordain should govern itself. Neilina has controlled them for centuries, her fist firmly around every elemental's neck with the excuse that she has everyone's best interests in mind. The people of Mordain and Ybaris have heard a constant drumbeat of the evils of Islor for too long, their kings and queens the ones banging the drum, Neilina worst of all. She has put great effort into convincing Ybarisans that all blame rests at Islor's feet and they must take back their lands. I think it is time they are made aware of their queen's folly."

"Maybe they should stop sending Neilina elementals after they've trained them," I counter.

Wendeline's smile is patient. "They tried breaking free of her rule once. She froze the ports between Ybaris and Mordain and imprisoned any caster found in Ybaris, killing those who resisted her. We lost many during that time. She used those loyal to her to search for gifted babies and train them, believing she wouldn't need Mordain, that she'd find her own elementals that way. This went on for thirty years without Neilina finding herself a single elemental.

"She was so frustrated, she decided to send a message. She started filling skiffs with gifted newborns. Her casters used the winds to help guide them across the Gulf of Nyos, to their capital city." Her face falls. "None survived. After the third skiff of dead infants, they relented and bowed to Neilina once again. She had won. They would rather bend to her rule than risk extinction."

I grimace against the sour taste in my mouth that comes with this ugly history lesson.

Zander leans back. "According to Tyree, Ianca escaped Argon."

She pauses. "That's not an easy feat, from what I've heard of the castle."

"He said she had help. It sounds like she's not alone." He waits for her to speak.

I open my mouth—to add that casters helped her—when Zander rests his hand on my knee, stalling my tongue and my ability to breathe for a few beats.

Wendeline's eyes flash with the display, but she refocuses herself quickly. "Fellow casters likely, though they would need outside aid from servants or the guards. Why they would risk angering Neilina like that ... There would need to be a good reason. And she wouldn't be able to stay in Ybaris. They would hunt her down. I doubt going to Mordain would be any safer."

"Where do you think she'd go?"

"Seacadore. Or here."

I catch the nearly inaudible sigh slip from Zander's lips as he removes his hand from my knee. He was testing her, I realize. "They think Ianca is on her way to Cirilea, and that she might contact Romeria. He insisted Romeria kill her."

Wendeline stares at the pattern in the rug as she seems to absorb that. "We know that Margrethe was in contact with someone from Mordain. If the scribes can reach us, we must assume they can also reach Argon. For Ianca to escape and travel here, to see you, she must know something vital. Something that might involve you." She looks to me. "If Ianca is in Cirilea, it is important you speak with her *before* you kill her. Though I do not recommend the latter. I never would, as you well know."

"I would think seeking out her kind would be the practical move for an elemental arriving in a foreign land, especially one such as ours." Zander watches her closely, and I begin to understand where his suspicions are born from.

So must Wendeline, because she meets his gaze with a sureness that is rare for her when she is in his presence. "I am the highest ranked caster in the sanctum, and I have not offered sanctuary to any elementals."

He seems to weigh her answer. "Do we need to fear her?"

"Can she summon Aoife—is that your question? Not if she is collared. Beyond that, it depends on her intentions. But if she is escaping Neilina's grip, then I suspect not."

He nods slowly. "If she's not with you, then she's in hiding somewhere."

"Do not forget, from Argon to Skatrana, to Seacadore and then *here,* is several weeks of travel. *At least.*"

"So perhaps she hasn't arrived yet."

"Perhaps. *Or* she has, but she is staying hidden for reasons of her own."

"Or she doesn't know if she can trust me," I say.

"There are plenty of rumors to stir confusion," Wendeline agrees.

But what if Ianca somehow knows what I am? I've worked so hard to keep that secret to myself. What if this elemental arrives and unravels it all? What if she sees me as the threat Sofie warned me about and that's why she's coming here? I agree that I need to speak to Ianca, but if there's a way to do it without Zander breathing down my neck, that would be safest.

An impossible feat, likely.

"You may go now, Wendeline. This conversation *must* remain between the three of us." Zander watches her steadily.

"As expected, Your Highness." She eases out of her chair, curtsying first to Zander, then to me.

I point to my face. "Thank you. For patching me up. *Again.*"

"You are certainly keeping me busy." She winks and then departs, leaving Zander and me alone in my sitting room, wedged onto my settee.

Zander's chest heaves with his exhale.

"You don't trust her."

"And you do?"

"Yes."

He peers at me. "*Completely*?"

I stall on my answer. I trust her to heal me and, *I think*, to not hurt me. But I also know she repeats everything we discuss, and her duty is to Zander.

"You are no different than I," he says, as if reading my thoughts. "I know she is honorable, but I do not know if she holds more allegiance for her people than for mine."

"She left Ybaris, though. She came here on her own years ago."

"I'm talking about Mordain, not Ybaris. And for what reason did she leave everything behind?"

"For Margrethe. She saved a baby who would have been killed."

"That is the tale she gave us, yes."

"You don't believe it?" A pinch of betrayal flares with the suggestion that Wendeline might have fed me a false sob story.

"Stings, does it not? To be deceived by someone you find yourself caring for unexpectedly." He pauses. "Do you never sense that she is leading you along a certain path with the information she provides? That she knows far more than she lets on?"

"I don't know?" Everything Wendeline has told me is leading me *somewhere*, but it's because I'm ignorant.

"I'm not saying that I do not believe her on that account, but I also know that Margrethe is not the only one who has received letters from Mordain." He gives me a knowing look.

"Wendeline too? About what?"

"I do not know. If I ask, she will lie to me. It is enough that I know, and she knows that I know."

"How does she know that you know?"

"Because I know." He smirks. "This is a fun conversation."

I smile, despite everything. "Can you read her pulse?"

He snorts. "That woman is a vault. No. Casters are well trained at guarding their emotions. Anyway, the letters she has received are most likely information-seeking and nothing more, but I also do not trust Mordain to have Islor's interests in mind. You heard what Wendeline said. The guild has its own power struggles. There are those who want to break free of Neilina's rule. We know they used Margrethe as a pawn in whatever scheme they are spinning, and I can only assume that letter Wendeline revealed was not the first one Margrethe received. It proves that you are also somehow involved in a plot they have whipped up, fed from old prophecies." He studies his hands. "I fear what role Islor may play in that."

I've learned that Zander is naturally distrustful of everyone, but he's also not wrong. "You don't think Wendeline is on the side of Neilina, do you?" Just the thought brings a pang to my chest.

"If you are asking whether I think she was conspiring with you, no, I do not believe so. She is the one who encouraged my parents to take their repast before the ceremony rather than after. It is because they did that Ybaris's plans fell apart and we are sitting here now. I am quite certain she does not support your mother's ways, but that does not mean she is not working with those in Mordain who have a specific agenda. Someone taught Margrethe how to summon Malachi."

"She taught her everything she knew," I echo. But was it Wendeline who taught Margrethe that skill, or someone else? This mysterious G? Can I begrudge any of them? If Margrethe hadn't broken the rules, I have a feeling I'd be dead in both this world and my own. "I think you can trust Wendeline to do what's right, though."

"I would like to think so, but I no longer trust my judgment when it comes to what I *want* to be true. For now, I must trust her to a certain degree. Her knowledge is invaluable to us." His hazel eyes dart to me before turning away. He hesitates. "I did not like seeing what Tyree did to you." He frowns, as if it bothers him that he would care.

Is that concern tied to this idea of being *bewitched* by me? I bite back the urge to ask. It's clearly a sore spot. "I wasn't a big fan of it either." I touch the tip of my nose, marveling at how perfectly it has healed.

"And *you* didn't like seeing what *I* did to him."

"Setting fire to him? You're surprised?"

"You were terrified. It was as if you've seen something like that before."

I swallow. "I don't know. Maybe I have?"

He studies me. "Are you afraid I would do something like that to you?"

"You've certainly threatened it enough times." He literally *could* have ignited that heavy brocade dress as it clung to my sweaty limbs.

"But I wouldn't."

I want to steer the conversation away from talk of setting anyone on fire. "What are you going to do about the vials of poison?"

"Send men to watch the area around Lyndel. If we can keep the Ybarisans in the mountains, they can't cause too much trouble. But we do not know how many there are and informing keepers that their tributaries may be plotting to murder them will have immortals all over Islor taking matters into their own hands."

"Maybe if you gave them a reason to *not* want to murder their keepers, they wouldn't try."

"Abolish the entire tributary system?" He smirks. "So simple, is it?"

"No, it's not," I agree. I've lain in bed thinking about how, and the only thing I've figured out is that I don't know the first thing about governing anyone. "Maybe start small. Start *somewhere*. But start *now*."

"It's probably best I focus on the more imminent problem at hand."

"Which is what exactly? Quill's murder, Adley's political aspirations, or my mysterious coconspirator?"

"Or what this elemental wants with you." He heaves his body from the settee, stretching when he stands. "What you learned today and what we've discussed, it is not idle chatter. It should not be repeated to anyone. Not Annika, not Corrin. And definitely not Saoirse."

I roll my eyes, though I suppose I deserve that after my stunt by the nymphaeum.

"I should go and ..." His voice drifts as he regards my face again, as he did when he entered.

I can't tell if he's still admiring Wendeline's repairs or if there's something more, but it makes me blush. I clear my throat. "Be a king?"

He scowls, as if catching himself. "Right."

I don't know when I'll see him again. It may be days. I decide to take my chance. "Dagny asked me to go down to the market with her in the morning to look at some fabrics."

"The clothiers down by the port?" His eyebrows arch. "Do you have any idea the thieves and other unsavory folk who linger there?"

"Sounds like my kind of people." There's more truth to that than he realizes.

"They'll give you nothing but a lighter purse for your troubles."

"I have no money, so I'll be safe."

"You have an answer for everything."

I shrug. "It'd be nice to get away from my prison walls for a bit."

His lips twist with thought. "Should I parade you through town again? Empty a bag of gold in the rookery while we're at it?"

"Two bags," I quip, though my brain instantly stirs an image of another ride through Cirilea with Zander pressed against my back, and the flutter in my stomach says I wouldn't mind it at all.

He offers a wry smile but then pushes, "Why do you *really* want to go to the market, Romeria?"

He's too smart or too suspicious, I can't decide. "If Ianca came in on a ship, *someone* will have seen her. And maybe if she hears I'm around, she'll try to make contact. There's bound to be more information among the commoners than here."

"So the future queen wants to wander around town, asking if anyone has seen an elemental caster lately."

"I don't need to announce who I am, do I?" I found a plain navy gown stuffed into the back of my closet that would suffice.

"Any immortal in the crowd will know it's you."

Right. Orange blossoms. "I'll keep my distance."

He snorts, amusement flickering across his face. "I can't wait to hear from Corrin about this."

"She already knows, and she doesn't approve."

"For good reason." His gaze wanders to one of my mammoth windows. "With all the outsiders flocking to the city for the market fair this week, I do not believe it wise."

My frustration swells. I foolishly thought I might be getting somewhere with him.

"Until then"—his eyes flip to my bedchamber—"stay out of trouble."

"Always," I mutter bitterly, reaching for my graphite pencil. "By the way, why did you take my sketch?"

"So the royal guard could be on the lookout for that woman," he calls over his shoulder.

Good luck with that. "Tell me if you find her." I guess that's my answer to who carried me to bed, though I already suspected. I *should* be bothered by the idea that Zander was in my room while I was sleeping.

I'm bothered by the fact that I'm not.

CHAPTER TWENTY-FOUR

I hold my breath as I turn the finial on the bedpost one hundred and eighty degrees.

A click sounds, and one corner of my bed slides out from the wall, stone scraping against stone enthralling even as it raises the hairs on the back of my neck. Outside, the bell tolls marking the midnight hour.

My grin of satisfaction strains my cheeks as I take in the dark and narrow corridor behind it. I had nearly given up. Grabbing a lantern from my side table, its flickering light casting tall shadows around my bedchamber, I gingerly step into the schism.

And yelp at the two familiar faces staring back at me, arms folded over their chests like twin towers of intimidation.

"I believe you owe me ten gold coins," Zander murmurs.

"Surely it's the other way around," Atticus counters. "You didn't think she would figure it out before the clock struck midnight. *I* had far more faith in her. Besides, the bed moved before the twelfth gong."

"Splitting hairs, are we?"

"Shall we call it even, then?"

Zander smirks. "I suppose."

Atticus cocks his head. "She looks guilty."

Now that my initial shock has worn off, my annoyance flares. "You two have been hiding in here all night, betting on how long it would take me to open this?"

They share a glance and then answer in unison, "Yes."

"Well, not *all* night. We assumed you'd wait until well after Corrin's last visit. It's been a tedious hour, though." Zander is in an oddly good mood. "Where are you off to dressed like that?"

Their gazes drag over my long, silky black nightgown—another favorite from Princess Romeria's collection.

"Nowhere. *Obviously*. I was just curious how this worked." I curl my arms across my chest, the cool air within the corridor chilling. "Doesn't the king of Islor and the commander of the king's army have better things to do than lurk in the wall behind my bed?"

"We do, and we're late. Perhaps you can change into something more appropriate."

My attention drifts to their outfits. I hadn't noticed the plain, nondescript black garb, too shocked by their presence. "Appropriate for what?"

Even in the muted lantern light, Zander's eyes dazzle with a mischievous sparkle. "For getting answers."

"You're faster than I gave you credit for," Zander murmurs, peering around the corner of an unassuming door.

"You mean, when I can see where I'm going? Or when I'm not in one of those ridiculous dresses?" I counter, blowing out the lantern and setting it on the ground inside before emerging behind him. The tunic and breeches I found in my closet are fitted but comfortable, the navy cloak perfect to hide beneath. "And let's see how fast *you* are in twenty pounds of chiffon and tulle, and wobbly heels."

"As long as I can keep my sword."

Zander led the way through the dark corridors and tunnels

with the blind ease of someone who has spent years traversing them. I did my best to commit the turns to memory, but I'm not confident that I wouldn't end up lost behind the walls of the castle if I attempted navigating through on my own.

Atticus pulls the door shut soundlessly behind him. The smell of hay and horse dung permeates the air. We've emerged in a courtyard, but it is not the same one as the day Zander paraded me around the market.

Excitement courses through my veins. "Where are we?"

"The eastern stables, outside the curtain wall." Zander is swift on his feet as he moves toward the nearest stall, his cowl drawn up to hide his recognizable golden-brown hair.

A scrawny boy of no more than twelve is talking softly to a saddled horse.

"Silmar."

The boy bows deeply, giving me a glimpse of the gold cuff on his ear. "Your Highness."

Zander glances this way and that, I assume to check for bystanders.

"Sorry, I wasn't thinkin', Your Highness." His juvenile voice cracks over his nervousness.

"Are the horses ready?"

"Just like your guard asked. They're good and strong, but nothin' fancy. This one's my favorite." He pats its haunches. "His name's Tripsy, but I promise he doesn't trip. Don't know where he earned that name. He'll be good for yourself and the lady." His innocent eyes dart to me, and I see curiosity there but nothing more. He doesn't seem to recognize me. It's a nice change. "The one to the left is Spirit."

"She's perfect." Atticus smooths a hand over her chocolate-brown snout before leading her out of the stall by her reins.

Silmar clicks his tongue, and Tripsy steps forward with a soft whinny.

Zander drops several gold coins into the boy's hand.

The boy makes to bow and then catches himself. "Thank you

kindly." He lowers his voice to a whisper to add "Your Highness." He hesitates when he looks at me. "Will milady need a stool?" By the way his face scrunches, I'm guessing he doesn't have one handy.

"No, I'm good." This horse isn't as looming as the black stallion we rode, and I'm not in a ball gown tonight, though it will be the first time I've climbed onto one on my own.

"You put your foot in there." Zander points to the stirrup, smirking. He's finding my lack of skill amusing.

I make a point of rolling my eyes before following the instruction, gripping the saddle as Atticus did. I hoist myself up, smiling with satisfaction as I lift my leg. Only Tripsy decides to take two sudden steps forward, throwing off my balance. Zander is behind me before I tumble, his hands clutching my hips in place.

"You weren't kidding about the riding situation." Atticus snorts as he leads his horse toward the wooden gate.

"Shall we try again, or do you have more insolence you'd like to share first?" Zander's voice hints of stifled laughter.

I throw my leg over and settle in my spot, lifting my chin with indignation, even as my cheeks burn.

He climbs into the saddle behind me. Without the ball gown between us, I'm keenly aware of his thighs pressed against mine. He doesn't make an effort to keep his distance this time as he reaches forward for the reins. "We'll be back in a few hours, Silmar."

The boy scurries to open the gate and allow us to pass through. The click of the horse hooves echo in the silence of the surrounding street.

"He's a bit young to be out here all alone, isn't he?" I ask.

"It's safe enough. Silmar prefers being outdoors with the horses. He sleeps in one of the stalls most nights. If we can stable them without waking him, we will."

"Do you call everyone by their name?"

"That's what names are for, are they not?"

"But you actually know all their names."

"I try to, yes." He pauses. "Should I not?"

"No, you should. I just didn't think a king would keep track of his servants. That's ... nice." Korsakov had nicknames for all of us because they were easier for him to remember.

"It breeds loyalty. Also, when the king knows a servant's name, that servant is less likely to do something they shouldn't."

"So, it's more a subtle fear tactic than being considerate?"

"It's both, but I don't have the luxury of being *nice* simply for the sake of it."

We descend through town at a steady pace. Atticus leads, his head swiveling this way and that, as if constantly on the lookout for threats. We're taking a different route than the one we took with the cavalry, this one leading us farther to the left of the castle.

"You do this often? Take secret passages and ride horses like Tripsy?"

"You have a problem with Tripsy?"

I steal a glance over my shoulder to find him grinning beneath his cowl. If I didn't know better, I'd say sneaking out has invigorated him as much as it has me. "No, but I wouldn't call him pedigreed, compared to the last one we rode together." He looks more like a workhorse skilled at pulling wagons of stone.

"We can't ride one of the royal thoroughbreds through Cirilea without attracting notice. And it's best that Boaz believes us in our chambers, fast asleep."

"The captain of the royal guard doesn't approve of the king sneaking out like a misbehaving boy?" I tease. Elisaf said Zander was known for lurking among the commoners.

He scowls. "I do as I wish."

Ahead of us, Atticus barks with laughter. "Boaz will send the royal guard to shadow Zander while he's *doing as he wishes*."

"And any fool half drowned in a vat of mead would be able to spot them. They are not trained to be inconspicuous."

"And tonight, we need discretion?"

"We need information that I won't get within the castle walls or from my royal sources."

"Where are we going?"

"To Port Street, to see if anyone there has heard about any casters arriving on a ship. Someone must know something."

"Huh. With all those thieves and unsavory folk? I recall *someone* suggesting a similar plan. Who was it, though? Someone intelligent beyond her years, but why can't I remember …"

Zander's deep chuckle vibrates within my chest, and an unexpected flutter stirs inside me. The stone-faced king laughing seemed an impossibility a month ago, and now it is me who has sparked this genuine reaction. "Are you quite finished?"

"I don't know. We'll see. Aren't you worried people will recognize me?"

"There will be as many mortals as immortals. And besides, I will keep you close."

We cross a street and descend along a much steeper slope, and I sense the mood of the city shifting. We've left the quiet residential neighborhood of brick buildings and pitched roofs that surrounds the castle and are venturing into a more industrial area where wooden and metal signs dangle from posts marking various professions. I strain my eyes to read them as we pass—blacksmiths, butchers, wheelwrights, rope makers, glassblowers. Through the windows, I see nothing but darkness, but now and again, I catch the faint glow of light from someone within toiling late into the night.

A briny scent hangs in the air, and I find myself inhaling deeply, as if my lungs crave it.

"It calls to you, even with the cuffs," Zander murmurs, and I detect a hint of awe in his voice.

"I don't know." It could just be the lure of the ocean.

"I'm telling you, it does. Just as that flame calls to me." He points to a lantern that glows beside a sign that reads Currier. In the small display window below is a stretched cowhide. My nostrils catch the pungent smell of rich earth and oils, not altogether pleasant but vaguely familiar of tanned leather.

Ahead of us, torches and lanterns burn like tiny beacons down the hill. "What about all those?"

"Yes." As if to prove his point, every flame within my line of sight flares. It's only for a split second before they return to normal, a blink of an eye, but it steals my breath.

"Quit showing off," Atticus mutters, earning Zander's chuckle.

"What's your affinity to, Atticus?" I ask.

He peers over his shoulder at me. "I don't have one."

I frown. "But I thought all the nymphaeum-born immortals did. Annika does."

"Yes. She stole mine in the womb," comes his wry response. Is there bitterness in his tone? I can't tell.

"Atticus does not need an affinity," Zander says. "He has a king's army to swell his ego."

"Yes. An army that I should be leading into battle instead of escorting my fool brother on some hunt for useless information." He taps his heels against his horse, and it speeds up.

We're moving away from the industrial area now and closer to the water's edge. Raucous voices filled with laughter tickle my eardrums. I assume this is Cirilea's nightlife that Elisaf suggested I experience.

Two royal guard members on horses linger at a street corner. We pass them without slowing. They don't seem bothered by three cloaked figures.

Atticus stops where our lane meets a broader street. We sidle our horse next to him. Straight ahead, the silhouette of an enormous ship stands solemn, its mast reaching into the indigo sky. A sliver of an ordinary, meek moon glows above, and I find myself wishing for a blood moon to cast its brilliant light across the span of ocean.

"We're going this way." Zander steers Tripsy to the left.

I take in the view with unbridled fascination. The street is lined with establishment signs for a myriad of taverns and inns, and judging by the scantily clad women perched on the balconies tempting the crowd with their exposed skin, brothels. Everywhere I look are revelers, some stumbling out of doors from too much drink, others gathered in small groups, their giggles and shouts hinting at an enjoyable night. Mixed with the ocean air are faint wafts of spilled ale and stale urine. Three men stand in a corner with their backs to us, relieving themselves on the side of a building.

A busker sits on a wooden crate ahead, strumming an energizing melody on his banjo for a crowd, the tune and his lively voice blending with the street buzz to create a friendly atmosphere.

When Zander spoke of thieves and unsavory folk, I assumed dark alleyways and cutthroats waiting in the shadows. This looks more like the evening festivities after a city parade.

We stop where several horses are tethered to posts ahead. Zander hops off and guides Tripsy into a vacant spot.

"Is it always like this?" I ask.

"When a large ship arrives at port, yes. And the *Silver Mage* is a large ship. But also, the market fair has brought many to the city." Zander pats my thigh in a wordless gesture for me to dismount. He's doing that far more often as of late—familiar touches, little grazes. The days of being repulsed by the sight of me appear to be over.

I find the stirrup with my foot and ease myself down. Getting off a horse is easier than climbing on, and yet Zander seizes my hips to guide me down. My feet hit the cobblestone and his hands linger a moment longer, tightening their grip, his body nudging me suggestively from behind. Maybe that's just my mind making those suggestions.

Or the bastard enjoys coaxing those reactions from me.

He releases me only to entwine his fingers with mine.

"I thought we were incognito down here. Is there a need to keep up this act?" I lift our conjoined hands.

"I told you I would keep you close."

"You're afraid I'm going to run."

"I'm not afraid, but I would not put it past you. Besides, is this so insufferable?" Humor dances in his eyes.

He knows it's not. "Are you testing me?"

"I'm *always* testing you, Romeria." Quietly, he adds, "And you are always testing me."

Atticus drops coins into a boy's hand to mind the horses, and then we set off along the street, Zander hiding deep within his cowl, his hand a viselike grip around mine, but not unpleasantly so. It's difficult to steal glances from beneath my cover, so I rely mostly on my ears, catching accents like Elisaf's, though thicker. They must be Seacadorian ship hands and sailors, enjoying Cirilea's nightlife before they disembark for the next leg of their journey.

That these Seacadorians mingle freely, that they're not afraid of the Islorian immortals is fascinating to me.

A man and woman spill out of a door, the man's arm slung over the woman's shoulders for support, their laughter hysterical as they stumble across the street and disappear into an inn.

"Where exactly are we going?" I ask.

"To the best source of information in Cirilea." Zander nods to where Atticus holds open a door. The sign above his head reads The Goat's Knoll.

"This is where Elisaf was attacked." I didn't mean to say it out loud.

Surprise flashes in Zander's eyes before he smooths it off. "You retain a startling amount of information." His hand slides over the small of my back. "And that happened outside, in the back alley."

"Not comforting."

"No one in here will touch you."

No one but Zander.

Darkness swallows us whole as we step inside. I take quick stock of our surroundings. The Goat's Knoll is not a place a king and queen would frequent. It's a rustic tavern that smells of body odor, tallow, and ale, lit with just enough lanterns so mortals don't stumble over tables. Two men sit on a tiny stage by the bar, one playing an accordion while the other claps and sings, the bawdy lyrics stirring laughter from those listening.

A woman in a ruffled burgundy silk dress approaches Atticus. "You're late," she scolds in a sultry voice, reaching up to toy with strands of her strawberry-blond hair that rests against her collarbone. The simple act draws my eyes to her plummeting neckline.

Atticus collects her hand and presses a kiss against it. "I apologize, Bexley. We were delayed."

"Hmm." Her violet eyes drift to Zander and flash wide. "Interesting company you keep tonight, Atti." She dips her head ever so subtly, a sign that she recognizes the king but is respecting the discretion he obviously seeks. "Are you sure you would not be more comfortable in my private office upstairs?" Her chest rises with a deep inhale as her eyes rake over me, settling on my neck.

A chill skitters down my spine. She's an immortal, and her thoughts are clear.

"A booth in the back near an exit will be sufficient," Zander says evenly.

She dips her head a second time and holds out her hand. Atticus drops several gold coins into her palm. Only then does she lead us forward.

We walk in single file—me sandwiched between my towering male companions—and I scan my surroundings from beneath my cowl. The crowd is a mix of Seacadorian sailors and Islorian commoners, the women in flirty dresses, the men in splayed tunics. At nearly every table we pass, people are in deep conversation with their companions while sipping from copper mugs of ale. Some wear the cuffs of slaves on their ears, but they appear nothing like the docile, obedient servants I'm accustomed to seeing within the castle walls.

Zander ushers me through quickly, but still, I note curious glances and wide eyes of surprise. He leans in to whisper in my ear, "You were going to keep your distance, were you?"

I resist the urge to elbow him in the gut. He's right. Everyone knows the future queen of Islor is Ybarisan. There is no way for me to remain hidden among these people—a reality that leaves me feeling as exposed as if I were standing naked in front of them.

"I assume this will suffice." Bexley gestures toward a small booth framed by a heavy curtain. Many more like it run along the wall, some curtains drawn closed, others left open to reveal amorous couples tucked away.

Zander urges me in first and then slides in beside me. The wooden bench is small, and his thigh nudges against mine.

Bexley settles across from us. "Atti, are you not going to join us?" she taunts.

"Not this time, Bex." Atticus draws the curtain, closing us into the dark nook.

The flame within the lantern flares, boosting the light. Zander's doing, I'm sure.

Bexley's observant eyes dart from it to Zander and me. She folds her hands on the table in front of her. "Atticus said he had two *friends* who would like to meet me, but I do not believe this is the sort of encounter I was hoping for."

Zander smiles. "Unfortunately not."

"Pity." Her gaze settles on me. "The infamous Royal Slayer is far prettier than I expected."

"Romeria has been exonerated of all charges," Zander says smoothly.

"Yes. For whatever reason," she murmurs, and it is obvious what she thinks of Princess Romeria's innocence.

Zander sizes her up. I doubt he's used to being spoken to with such cavalier distrust, especially by a barkeep who knows who he is. "We have need of information," he says after a long moment.

Bexley sighs. "Doesn't everyone?"

Zander cocks his head. "And who else has been in here looking for information from you as of late?"

"Oh, you know, soldiers, the occasional aristocrat …" She leans forward to rest her elbows on the table, the move stretching her dress so low that a hint of nipple peeks out. "The usual distasteful lot."

Zander doesn't fall for the bait, his eyes locked on her face. "Anything I need to be made aware of?"

She pauses as if weighing how much truth her answer should include. "There are whispers that more of the poison that killed King Eachann and Queen Esma is traveling through Islor."

Zander's jaw tenses. "Yes, we have heard that rumor."

"It is not so much rumor, is it?"

He stares at her. He didn't want anyone else aware of these vials of poison making their rounds. A foolish wish, surely.

I will give Bexley credit—she matches his look, doing no more than blinking once.

"Have you heard of any casters arriving by way of Skatrana and Seacadore in the last few weeks?" he asks.

Her sculpted eyebrow arches. "Casters?"

"Yes."

"Aside from the wind casters that always come with the ship … no."

"Your establishment caters to many Seacadorians, from what I've seen. Would anyone in here be of value in answering that question?"

She toys with a lock of hair. "You mean, like the captain of the *Silver Mage*?"

"Are you saying the captain is here tonight?" Zander asks.

She pauses, licking her lips. I sense a slight hesitation. "The Goat's Knoll is known for its prudence. I'm sure you can appreciate why Kaders would not welcome questions about his cargo, even if he knows it's the king who's asking."

"I do not care who he has been smuggling out. I want to know who he has brought *in*."

"Still, what you're requesting has a steep price."

"And how many gold pieces is required to pay that price?" Zander asks calmly, reaching for the leather satchel tied to his hip. He expected this.

"Kaders is of both Seacadorian and Skatranan blood. He's an especially grim sod, but he *can* be bought with sufficient gold. My fee requires something else."

"And what is that?"

Her eyes flip to me, and her stare is nothing short of predatory. "I've never had the pleasure of tasting a Ybarisan, and she smells delectable."

My stomach drops.

"No," Zander growls, his hand clenching the bag of coin that now rests between his thighs.

Her jaw sets with determination. "Then I don't know that I can help you."

"You are refusing your king?"

"I was under the impression that you were another commoner tonight."

He pauses to study her. "If this captain provides pertinent information, I can arrange for prime seating at the royal repast, and you'll get your taste of Ybarisan blood there."

Delight dances in her eyes. "Not royalty, but I suppose it will do. Give me a moment." She slips out between the part in the curtain.

"Do you trust her?"

"Completely, and not at all." He tracks her swaying hips through the small slit. "Bexley is one of the most connected people in all Cirilea and a friend of Atticus's who has proven herself valuable time and again. She is an ear to the ground—and to the underground."

"But ..." I'm sure I already know where this is going. There's a man like Bexley back home. They call him Mule. He's a little league player with big league aspirations and an impressive network of ears and eyes. When Korsakov wanted information he couldn't readily find, he'd track down Mule. The intel was always reliable, but he knew Mule was also giving it to anyone else willing to pay.

"Bexley knowing what is important to me means that, for the right price, my enemies might also know."

"And knowledge is power."

"Whether you sit upon a throne or you are trying to steal it. But hopefully she shows prudence, given who I am."

I can understand his hesitation. "So the royal repast is officially happening?"

"Yes. There is already talk of it through the city. Immortals everywhere are salivating at the opportunity. But we're down to three prisoners now."

"*Three*?"

"One died today, and Tyree is too valuable to execute, so I will keep him in the tower."

"Someone died during questioning?"

"With the help of Abarrane's blade across his jugular, yes."

I cringe. "Why did she do that?"

"I needed a way out of that little lie you and Annika stirred up with Saoirse. The source of the accusation can't be questioned by the court if he's not breathing."

His words are like a punch to my chest. "He's dead because of me." Because of my bluff.

Zander studies me a moment, as if weighing the wave of guilt surging through me. "He was dead the moment Abarrane captured him. In truth, he got a more merciful death than the others will face. You helped him in that way."

"Why don't I feel better, then," I mutter.

"Would knowing he killed the tributary bring you comfort?"

"*Did* he?"

Zander shrugs. "I do not know, but he was an accomplice, at minimum, and surely he has blood on his hands."

Don't we all. "Why is Bexley so anxious to feed off a Ybarisan, anyway?"

"Because Ybarisan blood is intoxicating. Most Islorians have never had the opportunity to taste it." He turns to meet my gaze. "She can't harm you."

"I know. But it's weird, having someone openly lust over *feeding* on me like I'm a slice of chocolate cake."

"Is it any different from having someone openly lust over you in other ways?" he asks quietly, his eyes dropping to my mouth. We're sitting so close I can pick out the gold flecks in his irises within the lantern light.

I assume he's testing me again, but even being aware of that, my heart instantly races. The air in our private cubby thickens, the sounds of laughter and muted conversation surrounding us heady.

Something drastic is shifting between us, and quickly.

Zander swallows. He senses it too.

But then his attention snaps toward the drawn curtain. "I do not know what methods Bexley will employ with this man, but keep your composure and tell her nothing."

Atticus draws the curtain back, and Bexley slides in with feline grace. Alongside her is a sturdy man of about forty with striking pale-blue eyes and golden skin, weathered, likely by years of sea and sun. He offers nothing, not even a stiff smile, as he eyes first Zander and then me, lingering on my face a beat too long for my liking. But there is no flare of shock, no nervous fidgeting. It doesn't seem he recognizes—or even suspects—who he's sitting across from. That's a welcome relief.

A server sets three mugs of ale on the table—one in front of the captain, the others in front of me and Zander—and then quietly vanishes.

Bexley winks at me. "On the house."

"What do ya want?" The captain's voice is deep and gruff and laced with a heavy accent.

"Now, Kaders, that's no way to behave with my friends," Bexley croons, resting her arm against the back of the bench so she can twirl one of his sun-kissed curls with her fingers.

"Every time you ask me for a favor, I'll wager it somehow ends up costin' *me* more than it does you."

"And I'll wager you don't mind paying the price," she retorts.

His focus drifts down the front of her dress—half her nipples are still on display—but he doesn't respond.

"They have some questions about your passengers, particularly any casters you might have had on board."

"Through Skatrana," Zander adds, his hands folded tidily beside his mug of ale. He hasn't reached for it.

"Aye, I always have a caster with me to keep wind blowin' in our sails and tame those dreaded sirens."

"Not the casters under Seacadorian employ. Passengers seeking voyage to Cirilea."

Recognition flickers in the captain's eyes. It's fleeting, but it's enough that my heart skips a beat with excitement.

But he says nothing.

Zander casually reaches down to fish out a handful of coins from his money sack. He stacks them in a tidy pile between the ale glasses.

"Aye, there was a caster who came into port with me. She stayed below deck and didn't bother much."

"Just one?"

Kaders dips his head.

"What did she look like?"

Kaders's eyes flitter to the stack of coins in front of him before he collects his ale and takes a long, drawn-out sip.

The softest exhale slips from Zander's lips as he digs into his money purse again, pulling out another equal stack.

"Woman with long hair as dark as ink and eyes like green jewels. Pretty thing."

"Did she give you a name?"

Again, Kaders takes a long sip, waiting.

But Zander isn't so quick to dole out more coins this time. He leans forward and through gritted teeth, repeats, "What was her name?"

Kaders glares at Bexley and with a sweeping gesture collects his coins and dumps them into a leather satchel at his hip. He makes to slide out of the booth.

"Must we play this game?" Bexley's sultry voice doesn't fray, even as she seizes the back of his neck with her delicate hand. He's a strapping man, and she's a slight woman a fraction of his size, and yet his shoulders sink with resignation. "My friend has paid dearly for a few insignificant details." Her free hand slips below the table, into his lap, working at the laces of his pants. "I think it's important you give him a few more."

A slow, steady exhale slides from Kaders's lips. "She went by Gesine."

That has to be a fake name. I would use one, if I were her.

"And did she say where she was going after she left your ship?"

Kaders swallows as Bexley shifts closer, pressing her body against him, the hand below the table now moving at a steady rhythm.

I assume this is what Zander meant about Bexley's methods.

"Didn't ask, and my crew stayed away from her for the most part. They're not keen on the casters. They tolerate ours because they bring us smooth sailing. But she was wearing a gold collar around her neck. My wind woman said this one was of a powerful sort."

Zander and I share a knowing look. She's definitely an elemental. It must be Ianca.

"Is there anything else you might be able to tell us about this caster? Anything at all?"

Bexley leans farther in, nipping at the skin below his ear with her teeth.

"You demon woman," Kaders mutters under his breath, his lids growing heavy with arousal. Her responding giggle is unexpectedly girlish, and it stirs a small smile from the rugged brute.

I elbow Zander's side and nod to the coin purse between his thighs, but he shakes his head, his jaw set. My exasperation flares at his stubbornness. We're about to lose Kaders's attention for good, and any information that comes along with it. On impulse, I reach into the satchel. Zander's body goes rigid, but I ignore his reaction, and the awkward location of my hand, and collect a fistful of coins. I toss them across the table's surface.

The sound of scattering gold grabs Kaders's attention, snapping him out of his lustful stupor for a moment.

"Anything else you can tell us?" I push.

Kaders's breathing is shallow. "She was asking about the Ybarisan princess."

"What about her?"

"If the rumors are true that the king still plans to marry her." Once a reluctant victim, Kaders's fingers are tugging at the laces that bind Bexley's dress together in the front.

"I think we're done here." Zander secures his much lighter coin satchel to his hip.

"My payment?" Bexley asks.

"I will ensure you have your seat. You have my word."

"Pleasure doing business with you."

Atticus pokes his head in. "Boaz just stepped through the door."

Zander curses.

"To the right and follow the corridor until you reach the back alley," Bexley says, her rich, violet-blue eyes landing on me where they linger as her lips curl back. Two fangs slide out from her upper jaw, lethal but oddly delicate, their pristine white glimmering like jewels against the lantern's glow.

I struggle to school my expression as my heart races. They're not as unsightly as I first thought. Threatening, nonetheless.

Kaders grabs Bexley's narrow waist and hauls her onto his lap, yanking up the layers of her dress. She wriggles her thighs around his and with his first groan, it's safe to assume he's seated himself in her. They've dismissed their audience entirely.

My cheeks are flushed as I scoot sideways across the bench to exit, but not before I see Bexley gingerly sink her teeth into the side of Kaders's burly neck, earning a second guttural groan from deep within his chest.

Zander grabs my hand and tugs me out just as Bexley begins

to rock her hips. On impulse, I swipe three gold coins from the table on the way and slip them into the inner pocket of my cloak.

Atticus leads the way, ushering us to the right as instructed. We dart along the hall, passing a slew of occupied stalls. By the time we step out into an alley that smells of rotten garbage and urine, I've seen at least a dozen immortals feeding off humans, a few of them in copulatory poses.

"Elisaf said this was a tavern."

Atticus chuckles. "It is."

"If tavern means brothel." And not even a respectable one with private rooms.

"Where did you think we would collect the most pertinent information? Over a loaf of dark rye at the market's bread stand?" His grin is smug beneath the lantern as his eyes roll over me from head to toe. "Was that too much for your delicate disposition?"

"I'm not delicate," I snap. I've stumbled upon more than my share of lewd acts—blow jobs behind convenience stores, hand jobs against the wall at the club, sex within the shadows of a public park or the dingy stalls of the subway restrooms. "I just wasn't expecting it."

Zander gently slips my hood over my hair and then takes my hand. He's wearing an oddly pensive expression. "We need to get back to the horses."

The three of us run along the backside of the buildings, the cats and rats scattering out of our way. We pass two men and a woman tangled in a complicated menage of limbs and flesh. I assume there are fangs somewhere in the mix, but I can't decipher who is doing what to whom without pausing to shine a light on them. Regardless, the sounds they're emitting are ones of seedy pleasure, not distress, and they aren't the least bit bothered by our fleeting presence.

We emerge onto a side street.

"I'll get our horses. You two wait here." Atticus disappears into the night, leaving Zander and me alone.

It's quiet here but people linger, stealing glances at the two cloaked figures standing at the street's edge.

"Royal guard, up ahead." I nod to the two men approaching on horseback, but Zander has already noticed them. He wordlessly leads me across the street and into another alleyway, this one cleaner than the last but narrow, Zander's shoulders nearly brushing the brick on either side. We're twenty feet in before he stops. "This should be far enough."

Far enough that they don't catch the honeyed scent of my Ybarisan blood, he doesn't say.

There's nothing to do now but stand here, in a confined, dark space with Zander looming over me, until Atticus returns.

"I can't believe we're running from your own captain." I feel the bubble of laughter threaten.

"You know how unpleasant Boaz can be." Zander's voice is low and gravelly.

"I've noticed." Thankfully, Zander has kept him away from me. "You like sneaking around down here, don't you?"

"I enjoy the freedom of being anonymous, and unseen." He pauses. "As do you."

It's what I'm used to. It's what I know. I smile into the darkness. "This was fun." I feel more like myself tonight than I have in a long time. "What do you think about this Gesine tip?"

"She could be traveling under an assumed name."

"That's what I thought too, though I wonder what happened to the other caster she was with." I think back to the conversation in the booth. "Kaders knew what Bexley had planned for him, didn't he?"

"Yes." I hear the humor in Zander's voice.

"And he didn't mind? I mean, he wasn't afraid?"

"That is not the first time that has happened to him. And no, he put on a good show for us, but his pulse was racing, and it was not from fear."

"It didn't hurt him?"

"Nothing more than a slight prick at the beginning, from what I've heard."

I grimace, rubbing the spot on my neck where the daaknar sank its fangs into me.

"I'll wager it's significantly less unpleasant than what you experienced," Zander says, reminding me that he has no trouble seeing me in the dark. "A lot of the Seacadorians come to Islor for that type of evening, and it is almost guaranteed in a place like the Goat's Knoll."

"Are you saying they *enjoy* being fed upon?"

"It's a novel idea, is it not? That when the humans are not forced into servitude, this symbiotic relationship between immortal and mortal could be different."

"And you think humans would allow themselves to be fed upon if they weren't forced?" I ask doubtfully.

"Many would not," he admits. "But some would because humans have great capability for compassion. And others would do it if there was monetary gain. The difference is they would have a choice and not a keeper. I realize it is a provocative notion, one that has stirred debates and worries among my kind, but I think it is a notion worthy of exploring because it is what is right. Another way to live and to survive. A better way."

"There were tributaries in there."

"Servants, but likely not tributaries. They serve their keepers in other ways, as house and farmhands, and trades helpers. This is where they choose to come on a rare night off or if they've stolen away from their burdens for a few hours. Bexley charges a fee for the tables, and people use them however they wish, whether it's enjoying mead or mortal. In some cases, the humans charge for access to their veins. Sometimes, as with Bexley and the *Silver Mage*'s captain, they both take enjoyment from it."

"So, they're already living what you've envisioned, then."

"Not quite. They are earning too little in stipends to support themselves. This extra coin allows them to live a little better. Perhaps buy finer clothes, but not more. In a better version of this world, they have their own homes and families and goals, with no keepers to answer to. There would be mortal villages like there are in Ybaris, with mortal lords and ladies. They would not be at the mercy of those who need their blood to survive, and those who choose to sell it would be compensated appropriately."

And the power would shift from the immortals to the mortals in a drastic way.

I can see why Zander is facing backlash for even suggesting such a thing, why those like Adley would oppose it so vehemently. They feel like their right to survive is being taken away.

"You should build a village for the mortals," I say.

"Melt down a few more gold pillars?" I hear the humor in his voice.

"Sure. And pay them more, so they can support themselves. And stop bidding on forced tributaries. If they want to be one, let them apply for the position. Start in Cirilea and show other cities how it can work."

"You're brimming with ideas tonight," he teases.

"What about the keepers of those servants in there? Don't they care that their servants are selling their blood?"

"Those who would care don't hear of it. The marks don't last long, and the servants ensure to use less noticeable spots."

"Like where?"

I stifle my gasp as Zander seizes the backs of my thighs.

"The guards," he whispers, lifting and pinning me against the wall with his body, our cowls joining to create a cocoon. They must have stopped at the entrance to check for any lurkers or crimes within the shadows. It's dark down here, but I know their immortal eyes allow them excellent sight. Two cloaked figures prowling in an alleyway is suspicious.

Unless they're looking for privacy.

I slip my arms around Zander's head to play the part of the willing partner, which, with his waist nestled between my thighs and his hands gripping me tightly, I can't deny that I am.

Tension cords his muscles.

"You know, it would be *a lot* easier if you didn't make your captain hunt for you," I whisper, heat swelling deep in my core.

Zander's exhale skates across my lips. "It would be *a lot* easier if you didn't react the way you do to me."

"I can't help it."

"Neither can I anymore, it would seem."

The headiness that was building in the tiny nook before Bexley and Kaders arrived slams into us like a thick fog that I can't see past.

I'm unsure who moves first, but our mouths find each other within the inky shield of our cowls. Zander's lips are supple as they explore, at first with a hint of hesitancy, but then with the eagerness of a long-anticipated kiss, deepening as his torso presses against mine.

It's nearly as shocking as the first time this happened, though so much has changed between us since. He is no longer a stranger to me, and it would seem he doesn't wish me dead.

But I haven't forgotten what he is.

Curiosity overwhelms me and I slip my tongue into his mouth to drag across his top teeth, looking for the evidence. What would it feel like to have him unleash those on me?

"Do not tempt me," he growls, shifting my body down so his hips fit squarely between my thighs. The heat of his hands clutching my backside burns as he grinds against me. I may not be able to read his lust through his racing pulse, but I can feel the proof of his arousal. He is as affected by me as I am by him.

I vaguely hear a whistle, but I ignore it, deepening our kiss, sliding my hand into his cloak to gather a fistful of silky hair. A second, more urgent whistle follows.

Zander breaks free and releases his grip, settling me onto the ground. Several long moments hang between us, his breathing ragged as he appears to be collecting himself. As am I, I realize, my own breath coming in short, heady pants.

"We have to go." As quickly as that moment between us came, it is over.

I let him lead me out by the hand, my head swirling in a cloud of exhilaration and confusion.

CHAPTER TWENTY-FIVE

My bedchamber is eerily quiet and dark when Zander and I step through the passage. The bell tower doesn't toll through the night, but it must be well after two as stone grinds against stone, sealing my escape route shut. The lone flame flickers in the lantern within my grasp, but it's enough to feed Zander's ability. Candles all around my room suddenly erupt, casting my bed in a warm glow.

He bends to adjust the small area rug at the foot of the bed, the only evidence of my room's secret and of our recent excursion.

Besides this new unsurmountable tension in the air, of course.

The ride back to the castle was silent and riddled with my unspoken thoughts, and I found myself leaning back against his chest for most of it, to which he didn't seem opposed. But now we're here, alone, and I'm unsure of what to expect. Unsure of what I want to happen.

That's a lie. As I study his tall, broad frame and his handsome face, as I think of that devilish smile and those intent eyes and the feel of his hands on my hips and his mouth on mine, and how his willing body ground into me, I know exactly what I want.

And I'm likely a fool for it.

There is that voice in my mind, the one that seeks out angles as readily as Zander does. It sings of victory, reminding me of my purpose here and how much closer I am to achieving it now that he doesn't despise me. But with that knowledge comes an unsettling stir of guilt. I don't want to use him like that.

Zander wanders to the threshold of my sitting room and pauses a moment to scan the shadows before he shuts my bedroom door.

My heart pounds with potent anticipation that I know he can feel.

Are his thoughts as conflicted as mine?

The silence is overwhelming, the need to fill it urgent. "What are you going to do about Ianca?" I ask.

He smooths a hand over the back of his neck. "Give Boaz a description and have the royal guard keep an eye out. There's not much else we can do until she makes herself known. I'm hoping she'll find her way to Wendeline."

Or she'll hear through the castle's grapevine—which surely has tendrils weaving through the city—that I'm looking for her.

"Tomorrow will be a long day." His hard swallow carries in my quiet room. After another moment's pause, he offers, "Good night, Romeria," and strolls toward the terrace door.

Disappointment sparks but I push it aside. "Especially with my trip down to the market with Dagny."

His feet slow and his laugh—a beautiful, melodic music—carries through my bedchamber. "Tonight did not satisfy your curiosity?"

"No, actually. I've been left *completely un*satisfied," I counter, and watch my challenge sink in.

His jaw tenses as he meets my stare.

My stomach flips as he takes several steps toward me.

But then he stops. He inhales deeply. "Whatever this is between us, it is not real. It is the result of a summoning, of Aoife's intervention, and while I was sure that spell was broken after my parents' murder, that may not be the case."

"That's what you think this is? A spell?" What if it is? What if the only reason Zander is attracted to me is because Aoife made it that way, in some sort of cruel trick?

The discontent that comes with that thought is unexpected and staggering.

His jaw tenses. "I will not be a victim to Neilina's plans. I will not be a bewitched king."

"I don't want you to be." I hope he can read the sincerity in my voice.

"And yet every time I see you, this pull grows stronger, harder for me to ignore." His eyes drift over me. "You make me believe that I can accomplish everything I've ever wanted for Islor. Is that a fool's wish too? Is it also part of Aoife's plan?"

"I don't know."

He bites his lip. "I cannot accompany you to the market tomorrow. I have important matters to attend to."

"Elisaf can take me. Please?" I hold my breath.

He sighs heavily. "Elisaf *and* Dorkus. In a royal carriage, with suitable guard, and *early*, before the masses are out."

A flutter of excitement stirs. I can't believe he's agreeing to let me go. "That was the plan, anyway."

"I'm sure it was." He smirks. "I'll prepare Corrin for it."

His hand is on the terrace door when I call out, "Hey, Zander?"

He pauses, and I note how his shoulders rise and fall with another deep breath. "Yes?"

I hesitate. "Did we ever … *you know*."

"Do I?" he teases, but after a moment says, "No. You insisted we wait. You found great enjoyment in taunting me, though." He half turns toward me but then stops himself. The corner of his mouth curls. "You still do."

But I would no longer insist on waiting.

By the piercing look he casts over his shoulder, he senses that. "Sweet dreams, Romeria."

I catch his chuckle as he pulls the terrace door shut behind him.

Darkness creeps toward dawn before my tumultuous thoughts allow me some rest.

"How in the fates ..." A concentrated frown mars Dagny's forehead as she plucks at a piece of straw clinging to her dress. Brushing it away, she returns to her stiff, upright position. Her beaming smile is genuine. It would be contagious, if not for my exhaustion this morning, made worse by Corrin's nattering about all the reasons she is against this silly outing.

"The clothiers should bring their spools of fine silk to the castle for the future queen's perusal!" she exclaimed while shaking me into my gown, a delightful violet silk that swirls around my ankles and pairs nicely with a capelet with silvered embroidery.

"I've never been in a carriage as fine as this, Your Highness." Dagny smooths her stubby fingers over the red velvet interior.

"It *is* nice, isn't it?" When Elisaf led me to the courtyard and I saw the elaborate ebony-and-gold chariot, and the twenty soldiers who would accompany me, I nearly turned back, given the attention this would draw. But Dagny was so excited for the opportunity to ride to the market with the future queen, I climbed in, unable to disappoint.

I've made use of the excursion, keeping an eye out the window and memorizing markers while Dagny babbles. It's a linear path as we navigate our way down to the market, save for two turns. I spy the top of the ominous tower at my right.

She clears her throat several times, dipping her head to peek past the curtain. Elisaf and Dorkus bank either side of the carriage. "I was lookin' into that special *wool* you asked me about. Talked to a few *weavers* I know." Her eyes widen with meaning. "None of them have heard of it, but we'll keep lookin' for ya. Bound to turn up, eventually."

Her search likely won't return anything if Ianca is going by another name, but I smile. "Thank you."

"Of course, Your Highness. Anything for you." She unfolds and then refolds her hands in her lap. "I suppose you must be excited about your upcoming wedding? Not too far off now. I know it would be the second time through this circus for you, and what with the first one bein' tainted by murder and all, but surely this time will go smoothly. You two will be married, and we can finally put all this bloody business behind us."

Unless I somehow find myself in that nymphaeum on a blood moon, in which case I have no idea what new bloody business will be in front of us.

I change the subject. "I never asked you, how old is your son Dagnar?"

"Seventeen! He's a big, strong, strapping lad like my Albe. Handsome, too, if I do say so myself, being his ma and all." She nods, pride clutching her words, more heavily accented when she's excited.

"Will he be auctioned off soon, then?"

Her smile wavers. "Next Presenting Day. I suppose so, yes. It will be a challenge for Albe and myself, to say the least, but it is the way of Islor." She nods resolutely. The distress in her eyes tells a different story, of a mother dreading the day she loses her son to obligation.

My own upbringing began ordinary and loving until it took a dark turn that soured any fond memories. I have little to call upon to draw sympathy from, but I can sympathize as a fellow human. "For what it's worth, I don't think it's fair how you're all forced into the tributary system."

"No, Your Highness, it doesn't seem so, does it?" She hesitates, picking at a loose thread on her dress. "Is it true that the mortals live free in Ybaris? With villages and farms and whatnot?"

I can only answer that because Zander said as much last night. "Yes."

"You know ... lots of folks were wishin' that once you two

were married, they might open up the rift and let some of us through. Don't suppose that'll happen now, even with a weddin'."

Some of *us*. She means the humans. "Were a lot of people hoping for that?"

"Aye. There's no way out of Islor short of payin' a captain a hefty price to smuggle us out. Far more than any of us will ever see in our lifetime unless we rob our keepers. And even then, we're usually caught in the ports on the other side, and if there's anythin' hinting at a cuff in our ear, we're sent back." She nods. "Seemed an omen, a Ybarisan queen comin' to rule. A sign for the change of the times. There's been plenty of talk over the years, about how the king might be wanting to change the way things work. Is that true? Have ya heard of such a thing happening, or is that just rumor?"

Elisaf said Zander hasn't been silent about his hopes for a progressive Islor. I shouldn't be surprised that it's a topic of conversation among the humans. "It's not just rumor."

Dagny's eyes light up. "Wouldn't that be somethin'? We've prayed for it, ya know. Every Friday afternoon in the sanctum and with our morning devotions, without fail. Dagnar could recite the Fates' Prayer when he was a wee one. 'Course it took him some time to get their names right. I doubt the fates minded much, though." She chuckles, her anticipation bubbling.

I realize my mistake. I don't want to get her hopes up. "It's not something that can happen overnight, or even in a few months," I say slowly. Maybe not in her lifetime, I fear, the more I learn. "Dagnar won't avoid Presenting Day."

Her brow furrows deeply as her head bobs. "Aye! Of course! Surely, there are a great many things that must be considered. I wouldn't begin to assume I understand any of it, being the simple commoner that I am," she blusters.

"I don't think you're simple at all, Dagny." She does that often, puts herself down. Somewhere along the line, someone convinced her that it was true. "And you know what? Corrin admitted to me that there's no one else with your talent for stitchwork." I add in a mock whisper, "Don't tell her I told you that, though."

"I wouldn't dare." She giggles. There's a moment's pause before her thoughts and her mouth are working again. "Ya know, people around Cirilea talk a lot. About a lot of things. I heard them talkin' the other day about how you and His Highness walked through the rookery handin' out coin."

I'm not surprised that made the gossip mill. "They look like they could use it." I saw Elisaf with a velvet bag strapped to his hip, and I casually mentioned making another trip through there today after the market.

"Albe and I have been fortunate. I started out as a laundress until the last royal seamstress passed on. Albe's been a herdsman all his life. You know, after our *other* service." She says it quietly, like she doesn't want to admit to their time as tributaries. "Many of those folks in the rookery have run from dreadful situations that I can't imagine." She frowns. "But no king or queen has ever done that before. Walked through the rookery, handin' out coin. Talkin' to people. Actin' like they care."

"Are you saying we shouldn't have?"

"I'm sayin' you *should*. It's good for them. Gives them hope. A lot of folks are scared. All kinds of whispers of unsettlin' things lately."

"Like what?"

"Oh, I don't want to trouble you with their foolishness." She waves off my question with a swat of her hand. "But it's good for the people to see yous both out there. It's *important* for them to see the good in you, Your Highness."

I'm sure she's referring to all the rumors that I murdered the last king and queen. I don't want to tell her that they're not wrong.

The carriage rolls to a stop. Elisaf's boots land on the cobblestone with a thump, and a moment later, our little door creaks open. "We're here, Your Highness," he announces with a gracious bow, holding out his hand to help me climb down.

The morning sky is painted a soft blue, the air a few degrees cooler than I've grown accustomed to. A breeze kisses my cheek as I take a moment to smooth my skirt and scan our surroundings while Dagny disembarks. We've stopped in front of a small shop with a sign that reads Apothecary. I inhale, remembering the horrid salve Wendeline smeared on my shoulder. The faint waft of chamomile and lavender lingers in the air here.

Beyond the shop, the street runs toward the water. Only a sliver of the bay is visible from this angle.

"Would you like my arm?" Elisaf offers, holding it out.

"How debonair. Where is my usual guard?" I tease, curling my hand around his biceps. The leather beneath my fingers is deceptively soft. It feels odd to be holding on to anyone other than Zander when we're in public.

Elisaf leans in to murmur quietly, "I can tell you where he is *not,* which is gallivanting through Port Street with the captain of the royal guard nipping at his heels."

I giggle. "You heard about that?"

"Who do you think arranged for the horses?"

"This way!" Dagny exclaims in a singsong manner, her hips swinging as she marches forward.

Dorkus and eight other soldiers flank us, giving us a few feet of space, thankfully. The rest stay with the horses and carriage.

The market is already teeming with early risers. I feel their surprised stares and hear their whispers of shock as we make our way toward the booths.

"Interesting place, your Goat's Knoll." I level Elisaf with a pointed look.

His responding smile is wry. "It is."

"What were you doing there all those years ago? Enjoying a pint of *mead,* was it?" I ask with mock innocence.

"I was young and enjoying *many* adventurous things. Do you wish to travel down this path, Your Highness? Because I heard of a certain alleyway that was far more interesting—"

My elbow shoots out, aiming for his ribs.

He deftly blocks it with a laugh.

"Was that *actually* a topic of conversation for you guys?" A surge of nerves floods my chest at the reminder of that stolen moment between Zander and me. A moment he deems a mistake, obviously.

"*Everything* Zander does is a topic of conversation for his brother."

"*Atticus* told you the sordid details." Not Zander. I shouldn't be surprised by that.

"Atticus is worried his brother's head is not where it should be. Again."

We've entered the throng where this discussion is no longer possible. I see much of the same in the crowd as I did that day with Zander—servants, tradesmen, farmers, and all types in between that make up Islor's common class of immortal and mortal. They're setting up their products and chatting with those nearby, preparing for a busy day of earning money.

What is it like to be these people, to live outside these castle walls?

The friendly buzz dulls to a simmer with stares and bows. People gather their children and scuttle away from my guards, as if afraid of being caught on the sharp end of a sword. I smile at them, hoping the simple gesture will ease the growing tension that clogs the air as we pass through.

Elisaf attempts a steady pace but is forced to slow as I linger, admiring the many wares. The stalls are plentiful and diverse, with everything from baskets of fresh fruits, eggs, and vegetables to honey and wax, barrels of grain, and cast-iron cooking utensils.

My nose catches an aromatic scent, and I steer us toward a booth where strips of dried salted meat dangle from hooks. But then I remember that *my kind* is strictly vegetarian, and anyone watching might find it odd that the Ybarisan princess is salivating at a meat counter, so I veer past it to the next stall—a table laden with various tarts and wafers and small cakes.

Elisaf leans in to whisper in my ear, "The queen does not graze at the market stalls. The castle has its own kitchen for these sorts of things."

The woman standing behind the table stares at me, her blue eyes wide with shock. Two scrawny children with curly mops of brown hair are tucked into either side of her skirts, the boy resting his head on her pregnant belly, the little girl sucking her thumb. They all wear the telltale cuffs of ownership in their ears.

Something in their haunting gazes holds me in place. "It's a good thing I'm not the queen, then. And besides, the castle's kitchens don't help me when I'm hungry now." I offer the woman a smile. "I'd love something from your table, please."

The woman gives her head a shake and then curtsies deeply. "What would you prefer, Your Highness?" She has a timid voice.

"I don't know." I can only guess at what I see. "What would you recommend?"

"The bread pudding always sells out first. And people like the marzipan turnovers. Your Highness."

"Did you make them?"

She dips her head. "Yes, milady. I mean, Your Highness."

"All of them."

"Yes."

"On your own?"

The dark circles beneath her eyes tell me as much before her nod confirms it. My attention drifts to her swollen belly. She must be near due.

The little boy on her left points to a stack of tarts with a curled finger. "These are my favorite, Your Highness," he offers in a high-pitched voice. His mother shushes him.

"No, it's fine. Let him speak." I smile at the boy, stealing a better look at the puckered skin on his hand. He's been burned. "And why are they your favorite?"

He grins, showing off prominent gaps from missing front teeth. "The fruit filling."

"Those are my favorite too. Can I ask, what happened to your hand?"

He looks down at his feet. "Punishment. For taking an apple. It was fallen on the ground and rotten, but still, I shouldn't have taken it without askin'."

"An apple." Someone permanently disfigured this little boy because he took a rotten apple?

He glances up to his mother, who pats him on the back before turning to me. In her eyes, I see raw anguish. I'll wager she watched it happen.

"Your keeper did that to you?"

He nods. "But I deserved it."

I glare at Elisaf as my rage flares. "I thought mortals couldn't be harmed," I hiss.

"They can't be *killed,* Your Highness. And the definition of *harmed* is murky when there are claims of theft."

A man appears from nowhere. He shoos the children away with a flick of a wrist as if they're flies, but they're already diving under the table. "Your Highness." He bows before me. His shoulder-length hair is as silver-white as that of an elderly person, such a contrast to his warm olive skin as youthful as mine. "I'm honored to see you admiring my delicacies!" His voice carries. He wants to be heard by the crowd gathering around us, held back from getting too close by my guards.

His delicacies. I scan his ear. No golden cuff. He must be the keeper and an immortal, and the asshole who had this little boy burned for eating an apple that was good for nothing but feeding worms. He looks the part, his jacket tailored and fine, his stature full of arrogant pride.

I force a smile. "I was, yes. Your baker is talented."

"Dare I say, she is the most talented in all of Islor. Her apple tarts never last long."

The woman murmurs, "Thank you, my lord," but I note the way she shrinks from him.

And the way he leers at her. She's a pretty woman, probably in her late twenties.

"And you are?" I ask him.

"Lord Danthrin of Freywich," he says loudly. "Your humble servant, of course. Please, help yourself to anything at this table."

"*Anything*?"

"Anything at all. After all, you are to be our queen."

That's right. I am, even if I'm only pretending.

"I'm glad to hear that." My heart pounds with apprehension as a plan formulates. "I would like your baker and her two children."

Gasps sound around us.

Lord Danthrin's mouth drops open. "Your Highness? I do not understand," he sputters.

"You said I could have anything I wanted. We're in need of a baker, and since she is the best in all of Islor, it's only fitting that she should work for me. So, I'd like this woman and her two children to join the royal household." I turn to the woman. "But only if you are interested in that position. I am not forcing you. It's *your* choice. Would you like to come with me?"

She gapes at me a moment, before offering an almost indecipherable nod, casting a sideways glance toward Danthrin but avoiding his gaze.

Beside me, Elisaf settles his hand on the pommel of his sword, as if he's expecting trouble. Or warning against it.

"Do you have a husband who should be coming with you?" I ask gently.

She shakes her head. "It's just us."

I grit my teeth as I look at her belly. No husband and these can't be Danthrin's kids. I'd bet money that he's breeding her. Corrin warned of his type. It only solidifies my resolve.

Danthrin looks like a fish gasping for air. "But surely you understand I meant—"

"Elisaf, would you be so kind as to reimburse Lord Danthrin for his troubles?"

"Yes, Your Highness." He retrieves the satchel of gold coin from within his uniform coat and sets a handsome stack on the table. "I believe that should suffice."

My stomach curls at the thought that I'm effectively *buying* a pregnant woman and her two children, but if it means getting them away from this man, I will digest the sourness with my head held high. "I'm sorry, I didn't catch your name."

"It's Gracen." She looks like she's been slapped across the face and is still absorbing the shock of the blow.

I try to ease it with a gentle smile. "Gracen, one of my guards will escort you and your children to my carriage, where you can wait for me. I have something I have to do first, but you'll be safe."

Gracen doesn't stall another second. "Mika! Lilou!" she hisses.

The two mops of curly brown hair emerge from beneath the table, both sets of blue eyes wide and confused.

"You're taking her *now*?" Danthrin's face fills with outrage. "But it's the start of the market. Who will work my table?"

"I assumed you would. You're excellent at it. In fact, you've convinced me—I'd also like a few apple tarts." I nod to Elisaf, who adds another coin to the pile. "That should buy us as many as can fit in the children's hands, I think. Don't you?"

Whatever hostile response is stirring within Danthrin's mind, he scans the soldiers behind me and the crowd, and he must think better of it. He nods to Gracen, capping it off with a scathing glare.

She sweeps in, handing two to each child before ushering them around the table.

"Do you have all your belongings?" I ask quietly.

She puts her hands on her children's shoulders as she blinks away tears. "I have everything I need, Your Highness."

Mika's mouth is occupied by a tart as one of my guards ushers them away.

I turn back to the despicable keeper, whose jaw is clenched so tightly, he might crack his teeth. "It was lovely to meet you. The king and I will be sure to visit Freywich the next time we have the opportunity. I'd love to see these prized apple trees you guard so *viciously*."

His eyes flash with understanding. *Good.* Yet something tells me it's the least of his crimes.

We continue down the lane, trailing Dagny who keeps peering over her shoulder to beam at me.

But my rage is simmering. The rookery, and now this market. Aside from Port Street—which may ring of sin to some but to me hints of choice—my first tastes of Islor outside the castle walls are as foul as that wormy apple. "Did you see what he did to that little boy? The kid was probably starving."

"A fair assumption."

"He shouldn't have land or a lordship. We should take it away from him. Who gave it to him, anyway?"

"I thought you didn't have any interest in being queen," Elisaf murmurs, a smug smile touching his lips.

"I don't. Zander can take it from him. Who is this Lord Danthrin?"

"A minor lord from Freywich, a town about three hours' ride outside of Cirilea. And now, your newest enemy."

"I'll add him to my growing collection." But unease slips in. "I assume there is court etiquette or protocol I've just trampled over."

"Yes. Very much so."

I hesitate. "How annoyed will Zander be with me for this?"

A secretive look passes over Elisaf's face. "We shall see."

The textiles section of the market is nearest to the water, and vast. Rows of stalls offer cloth stacked in piles and draped from lines. Silks, linens, and cotton billow in the slight breeze, reminding me of sheets drying outside on summer days. There are hundreds of options. Maybe thousands. I wouldn't know how to choose.

Thankfully, between Dagny and Odier, I'm sensing I won't be a part of *any* actual decision-making.

"I want to see your finest silks and linens in your most vibrant dyes. Nothing less will do for Her Highness," Dagny demands, standing as tall as her stout frame allows.

"*All* of my cloth is the finest. My silks? The finest. My linens? The finest. Wools? *The finest*. I have brought the most sublime fabrics with me on this voyage. Cloth that Empress Roshmira herself has requested. You will find nothing else like it among those *rags* over there." The Seacadorian clothier is a heavyset bald man who speaks in baritone, bows with a theatrical twirl of his hand, and does not hide his disdain for his competition. "Nothing but the finest cloth should touch Her Highness's most exquisite body." He offers another dramatic bow, giving me a chance to steal a wide-eyed glance at Elisaf.

"It sounds like we're in agreement, then! Show me the best of your best, Odier," Dagny demands with far more assertion than I've ever heard from her.

"They are all back here, for Her Highness's perusal ..." The two of them disappear into the throng of fabric, leaving Elisaf and me on the outskirts, my soldiers loitering.

"Did you not want to see what he has?" Elisaf asks.

"I don't think my opinion matters here."

He chuckles. "That may be true. Besides, I think someone wants to speak with you."

I follow Elisaf's nod. Bexley hovers at a stall, testing the weight of a material between her fingers, the ginger and gold in her hair glimmering beneath the sun. She rounds the table, her eyes lifting and zeroing in on me for three beats before she refocuses on the cloth.

"Is it safe?" The last time I saw her, she was straddling Kaders's lap with her teeth in his neck, likely wishing she could sink them into mine.

"She would be a fool to try anything, and she is no fool. Regardless, I will be within reach and watching closely. But when someone like Bexley wishes to speak ... you always listen."

So she has something important to tell me. "What would I do without you, Elisaf?"

His smile is easy. "Somehow I think you would manage."

Before Dagny returns, I stroll over to the next stall.

"You make a lot of noise," Bexley says by way of greeting, testing the frayed edge of a silk between her fingertips. "It has spread through half of Cirilea already that the future queen is out buying pastries and servants in the market."

"I've had a busy morning."

"And with such a faithful guard too." Her eyes dart to where I came from. "I remember Eli *before*. He was a regular at my establishment. A favorite of mine."

Eli? "I guess I don't have to ask how you two know each other."

She smirks. "Not unless you're in the mood for sordid details."

"Not especially."

Bexley wears a modest gown the color of pistachio sorbet, no hint of nipple to be seen. Still, she carries herself with an effortless confidence that I admire. No one tells her what to do.

Her sharp focus drifts over my neck, and I know what she's thinking. A shiver runs along my spine. "You wanted to tell me something?"

"I was going to wait until I saw you at the repast, but when I heard you were here, I thought the sooner, the better." She holds up a rich indigo silk against my cheek. "This would be a stunning color on you."

"Careful. You'll give Odier a coronary if he sees anyone else's material touching me."

She tsks. "Dear, dear Odier. He thinks so highly of himself. He would never step foot in an establishment such as mine."

"I don't have a lot of time before my seamstress returns."

She sighs. "Kaders withheld a few details from you last night."

"How do you know?"

"Because that's what happens after Kaders spills his seed. He spills his secrets." She smiles coyly. "I could have pried the information you obtained from him without you casting a single coin, if you'd stayed long enough."

And watched the full sex show, she means. "You're saying I've already paid up front for whatever you're about to tell me."

Her eyes narrow as she studies my face. "I heard you were meek and subservient."

"Rumors are never entirely accurate, are they?"

"Or in this case, not at all." She pauses. "The caster going by Gesine was not alone. She was traveling with an older woman. She also had a collar around her neck, but Kaders's wind woman told him she was a seer."

Wendeline mentioned the seers before. "Did she have a name?"

"I'm sure she did, but it wasn't one that was used. The caster Gesine was protective of her. Kept her in their cabin and wouldn't let *anyone* near, including the wind woman."

I search for value in this new information, but there are still too many holes in my knowledge of this world. "And he didn't say where they went when they got off his ship?"

"No, though they were met by a wagon. The older woman seemed confused, he said."

"They easily could have left the city by now."

"Perhaps, though there are many places to hide within, if you know the right people."

And if there is anyone who knows the right people, it's Bexley.

"I have a favor to ask you," I say before I can talk myself out of it. I can't rely only on Dagny's network, especially not when I have the ear of Cirilea's most resourceful, and I can't wait for Boaz to show up in the throne room with a collared elemental.

Bexley's eyebrow arches. "A favor for the Ybarisan princess that she dared not ask in front of her betrothed? I will not lie, I am intrigued."

"I need you to find these women for me."

Incredulous laughter sings from her lips. "Is that all?"

"Oh, I'm sorry. I thought you would be capable of something that straightforward. Was I wrong?"

She smirks. "Have you questioned the priestess Wendeline at the sanctum?"

"They're not there." At least, not yet.

"You seem so sure."

"And *you* seem to know something I don't."

"I know *many* things you don't." Her lips twist with thought. "What are your intentions with these women? Will it earn me a place on a pyre next to you?"

So she does have thoughts for self-preservation. "I need information from them. That's all. I have no intention of hurting anyone in Islor." In fact, I'm desperately trying not to.

"What you're asking will cost you."

"What do you want?"

Her eyes settle to my neck before meeting mine again.

I swallow against my apprehension, though I was prepared for this the second I asked for the favor. "The king already gave you his answer on that."

"And is the king your keeper?"

"No." Technically, yes.

"I'm sorry, I thought you weren't the meek and subservient Ybarisan princess you once pretended to be. Was *I* wrong?"

She's persistent, which I expected. "You're already getting your Ybarisan blood."

"Yes, at the trough, like a barn animal." Her nose wrinkles with scorn. "I would prefer yours."

I really don't think you would. "Fine."

Her eyes flash with enthusiasm. "Are you saying we have a deal?"

"Yes." Just not one she'll be expecting. For the first time since Corrin insisted on hiding my scars to keep the truth of the attack secret, I can appreciate the benefit of guarding that knowledge. If Bexley knew the truth, I wouldn't have anything to barter with now. "In private, and *only* after you bring me info that leads me directly to these women."

"That is a reasonable request."

"It's urgent, Bexley. The sooner, the better. And let her know the royal guard has the description Kaders gave us. They're looking for her."

She licks her lips. "Is there anything else you can tell me to help guide my search?"

"Your Highness!" Dagny bellows. Beside her, Odier stands with his hands on his hips and his eyes wide with horror, and I realize my fingers are still grasping the indigo fabric.

I release it as if the cloth burned me. To Bexley, I whisper, "One of them may go by the name Ianca."

"That is helpful."

"Be tactful."

"I am not some prattling servant," she snaps, anger flashing in her eyes. "You would not believe the secrets I keep. Secrets that could sink a great many influential people if I had aspirations for playing the games of these fools who call themselves noble."

"I didn't mean to offend you."

She sniffs, but my apology seems to calm her. "I imagine finding her won't be as difficult as getting a message to you without notice. But I will think of a way. And I would suggest *you* be *very* careful who you trust within the walls of that castle."

"Funny. I was told to not trust you."

"And you shouldn't, but at least I will never deign to wear the skin of a devoted ally to hide the fact that I am your foe." She curtsies. "I look forward to seeing you at the royal repast, though for whatever game you two are playing, I hope you and the king can put on a better show than you have thus far."

Mika is hanging out the window, stroking the muzzle of a horse within reach when we arrive back at the carriage.

"I don't believe a stroll through the rookery as you requested is advisable, Your Highness," Elisaf says.

"Maybe not, given our passengers." I'm sure Gracen is feeling as discombobulated as I was the night I woke up on the royal grounds.

"Also, because you've spent all our coin. We wouldn't have much to dole out."

I struggle to suppress my smile at the guards trailing us, their arms laden with bolts of fabrics—*all* of them necessary, according to Dagny and Odier. "Maybe tomorrow, then."

"The king will be pleased to hear it."

I snort. "I'm sure."

Elisaf glances to the nearest guard, and he lowers his voice. "What did Bexley want?"

I falter over the truth. Surely, whatever I tell Elisaf will make its way back to Zander as it has so far. But Zander also insisted on keeping what we learned from Tyree between us. Who is it among them that he doesn't trust? It can't be Elisaf, could it? If that were the case, why would he assign him to my protection?

And yet Bexley's warning has slid under my skin and taken root, and I can't shake this sense of foreboding that she knows far more about my situation than she's letting on. "To make sure I call you Eli from now on." Zander's conspiracy theory is making me as paranoid as him. Still, if Zander wants Elisaf knowing about the seer, he can tell him.

He shakes his head and chuckles, but he doesn't press.

Mika sees me and waves his misshapen hand emphatically, as if we're old friends. It's comforting to know that Danthrin might have abused him but he didn't steal his ability to still be a child.

An idea strikes me. "Do you think Wendeline could help him?"

Elisaf scratches his chin in thought. "It might be too old a wound, but it is worth her looking at. I will call for her to meet us at the castle."

I have a better idea. "No need to drag her all the way out. Let's stop at the sanctum on the way."

"Try that."

Mika holds his injured hand in the air in front of him and extends his fingers as far as he can. While they're not entirely straight, they've certainly improved. He grins.

To Gracen, Wendeline says, "I was able to fix the nerve damage, but I can't do much for the scars. Mortal skin is more delicate, and it's been too long since it happened. But, with some daily stretching exercises, he should have full use of it again."

"Thank you, Priestess. This is more than we could ever have prayed for." She smooths her hand over her swollen belly.

Wendeline tracks the move with a tired smile. "How far along are you?"

"Eight months. This one has been particularly difficult."

Wendeline reaches forward, but then hesitates. "May I?"

With a wary glance my way, Gracen nods.

Wendeline presses her hand against Gracen's belly and closes her eyes. She's been picking at her fingernails since she healed me yesterday. For many hours, I would guess. They're down to the quick, and in one spot, painfully so. That's the sign of a person who is nervous, conflicted.

Bexley's warning has rattled me.

"I've never met a priestess before," Gracen admits. "Not a real one, anyway."

I'm unsure what she means by that, but now is not the time to ask.

When Wendeline opens her eyes again, they're shining. "You have no reason to worry. Your baby is healthy and strong. She will be born soon."

"*She*?" Gracen lets out a breathy laugh. "Another girl. That's … wonderful news." Her smile falters, as if it's not.

A low wail carries through the sanctum, turning the few heads of people who are here for midday prayer. Lilou fell asleep in Dagny's arms on the carriage ride and was content to stay asleep while the sturdy seamstress strolled the aisles, but she's awake now and searching for her mother. "I should get her before she begins to shriek." Gracen heaves herself out of the pew and waddles away. Mika trots closely behind, closing and opening his hand with fascination.

"She doesn't seem particularly thrilled about another girl."

Wendeline's gaze trails mine. "I sense she has seen great hardship in her young life, and she fears her daughters will face the same."

"Not anymore. At least, I hope not." I'm not sure how much better a life she and her family will have under Zander's employ, but I am sure it will be infinitely safer than the one Danthrin offered.

Wendeline stares at me a long moment before startling, as if catching herself. "I cannot believe you marched up to the lord's booth and demanded to take them all."

Neither can I, after the fact. I shrug. "If I'm playing this role, I might as well get some enjoyment from it, right? Hopefully that monster is suffocating in the bed of tarts and pudding cakes he made for himself."

Elisaf is far in the back, waiting patiently; the other guards are outside. But I sense my time here is limited. Too long and I might be testing the lax leash Zander released me on. Regardless, I'll have to provide an explanation for our conversation.

Three priestesses kneel in front of the altar. They haven't moved an inch since we sat down. There are no wary looks, no secretive stares, nothing to suggest they're hiding anyone within these walls.

"Is something the matter, Your Highness?" Wendeline asks.

"I don't know." I've spent years looking at everyone through a lens of suspicion. I didn't want to use it on Elisaf and Wendeline. But maybe that will be my downfall.

I study the priestess intently as I ask, "What reason would a seer have to come to Cirilea?"

She can't hide the flash of surprise in her eyes fast enough. I think that's the trick with Wendeline—she's always given the opportunity to slip on her invisible armor before facing anyone.

But my impromptu visit here with Mika in tow didn't allow for that.

Her reaction brings a conflicting surge of satisfaction, and a sting of betrayal. Bexley was right, and I've been far too trusting. "You knew."

Her gaze shifts to the kneeling priestesses, and then to her peripheral, to make sure no one is behind us. She releases a sigh that seems to carry the weight of a heavy burden from her chest with it. "They arrived two days ago. But I knew they were coming."

"They're *here*?" I glance around us.

"They will not come *here*. They're not foolish."

"Have you told Zander?" The state of her fingernails would suggest not.

"No."

I shake my head. "You lied to us yesterday."

"I shared what information I could." She studies the floor. "Do not think that I am unaware of Zander's suspicions or his contempt for Mordain. I share that contempt. All *I* can do is act in the best interests of Islor and hope that he continues to allow me the grace to do so."

Zander was right to be skeptical of her, but now is not the time for condemnations. "Where is Ianca?"

"Ianca's knowledge is invaluable, and Gesine is a powerful asset, even collared. They did not break free from Neilina's grip and sail here just to risk becoming puppets for someone else. They will find you when *they* are ready, and not before."

"Why are they even here?" I lower my voice, afraid it's carrying. "Is Mordain scheming against Islor?"

"No." She shakes her head firmly. "Not in the way the king would fear. There are events that must come to pass and pieces that must fall into place. They are here so that when that happens, they can guide you forward as best they can."

"Guide me? I don't understand. Guide me through what?" Frustration bleeds into my tone.

The smile she gives me is pained. "The prophecy is there, collecting dust within thousands of years of ramblings, scribed and forgotten. The Ybarisan daughter of Aoife and the Islorian son of Malachi joined together will bring peace to both realms."

"This is all about some *prophecy*?" Wendeline mentioned it the last time we sat here but didn't elaborate. It didn't seem important to her.

"Not some prophecy. *The* prophecy. You and Zander were meant to find each other."

"And what does Zander think about it?"

Her brow pinches.

"You haven't told him."

"I tried, but he will not listen."

"Why not?"

"Because he is not ready to accept it yet. He is still struggling with his pride after what Aoife did to him."

She means the bewitched king situation, I assume.

"Neither of you are ready, but you will be. I can already see it in the way you look at each other." There is urgency in her vague words.

"Ready for *what,* though? You're speaking in riddles." My anger flares. I had enough of those with Sofie. More than anything, though, I've had enough of hiding, of stumbling my way through this mess alone. I've had enough of people lying to me. I've finally reached my breaking point. "Do you even have any idea what I am or why I'm here?"

Her blue eyes search my face. She exhales slowly, as if making a decision. "You are a key caster, and I assume Malachi has sent you here to try to open the nymphaeum door."

CHAPTER TWENTY-SIX

Mika tears down the aisle as fast as his little legs can carry him, oblivious to the etiquette of the holy place. Somewhere else in the sanctum, Lilou wails.

And I feel like Wendeline has casually kicked out the pew from under me.

"A key caster." I stare at the priestess. An elemental with all four elements. *Very rare, very powerful,* she had said. "No, I'm not." She's mistaken. I'm a basic human. A thief.

She smiles. "You forget that I was a tester in my former life. I can see these things."

"You're saying you *tested* me."

"Yes. After the daaknar attack."

I drop my voice until it's barely audible even between us. "And you found affinities to all four elements in me."

"Yes. Caster affinities."

"That's *impossible.*"

"It was shocking," she agrees. "I also tested Princess Romeria when she first arrived here, to see how powerful she was. Covertly, of course. I can confirm she only had an elven affinity to Aoife. And since the fates cannot gift affinities, the only possibility I have come up with is that Malachi somehow bound a key caster to Princess Romeria's body. But there are none anywhere in Ybaris or Mordain, and certainly not one who has never heard of the fates or elemental magic. I don't know where Malachi found you, or how he bound you to her body, but you *are* a key caster. An *immortal* key caster. You can create with your caster affinities *and* manipulate with your elven affinity. There has *never* been another one like you in our realm." There is awe in her voice.

My head swims. "She said she couldn't believe I didn't know what I was," I say more to myself.

"Do you mean the elemental that Malachi used to do this?" Wendeline asks carefully. "So, you *do* remember a life before waking up as Princess Romeria."

I hesitate. It's the first time I've admitted to remembering my life before coming to Islor. "I *am* Romeria. But I'm not from here."

She inhales deeply and then nods. "Seers can see across dimensions and into other worlds. They've taught us that this is not the only world created by the fates, that there are others with different dynamics and paths of history. Places identical to ours and yet opposite, where humans rule and the immortals and casters skulk in the shadows, hiding their existence."

"Yes. That's where I'm from."

A slow smile stretches across her lips. "I want to hear that story one day when we have time. I imagine it will be like nothing I've ever heard before."

The toil that has clenched my insides for so many weeks unravels a touch. I've told someone. Someone *finally* knows my secret. Except ...

"You've known *all along* what I am?" I can't help the accusation in my tone.

"Yes."

"Why didn't you tell me?"

"Because you were not ready to know then."

My eyes widen with a wave of panic. "Did you tell Zander?" Has he known *all this time,* too, and was simply testing me?

"*No.*" She punctuates that with a firm head shake. "He was

looking for a reason to rid himself of you, one that would lessen his guilt for executing someone who had saved his sister. I feared what he would do if he knew how dangerous you are."

"He would have killed me."

"Any one of them would, if they knew. As would the Ybarisans and most in Mordain."

Just as Sofie warned. Oddly, that brings me comfort. At least she was truthful about that. "What about now? Zander, I mean." He doesn't seem on the precipice of driving a dagger through my heart anymore. Far from it.

"There will be a right time to tell him, but it is not yet. He has other things to focus on, and he doesn't need this as an added worry. You will know when that time comes."

I take in the looming statues as the dust settles from the bomb Wendeline just dropped. "I can't feel anything." Except overwhelmed with relief that I can finally talk to someone about this.

"Not with the tokens you wear. The cuffs subdue *all* elemental power and the ring ... is complicated. It suppresses the caster affinities you brought with you, but it helps channel your elven affinity to water, the one Princess Romeria possessed."

I study the white stone. "Sofie gave me a ring just like this one and told me to not take it off."

"She must have an identical one. It is possible. The ring you wear now was Queen Isla's, but it was designed in the likeness of Aoife's ring, well known to the seers. The gold is a token gift from the fate's antler. When I tested you, I had to remove it. There are spells affixed to it that were not there before, that contain your caster affinities. When Sofie bound you to Princess Romeria's form, they must have carried from the ring she gave you to this one. It is remarkable what she did. I assume she did it to protect you until you learn how to use your power."

"But even before. All my life, I had no idea. How is that possible?"

"I do not know. In Ybaris, all children are tested and marked with an elemental insignia that cannot be forged. Sometimes a parent fears their child will show affinities and be taken away, so they find a caster who sympathizes and will mark their child as human when they are not. I did it for a few children," she admits sheepishly. "Sometimes they remain clueless their entire lives. Other times, they discover that they have abilities by mistake. Setting fire to a barn in a fit of rage, bringing about a rainstorm to calm their broken heart."

I pick through my memories. I don't recall anything strange like that ever happening to me. "And what if it's an elemental who is untrained?" That's basically what I am. An elemental with all four elements. I could summon the fates, if I had any clue what I was doing.

Nervous flutters stir with just the thought.

"That is *very* rare, and to have affinities to all four and not know ..." She shakes her head. "I am curious to know what you feel once the cuffs are off and you remove your ring, now that you know elemental power exists."

The walls you've built around yourself to survive are far too thick.

Sofie's vague words strike a chord. That is what she meant. She knew what I was.

Everything I've known all my life, everything I've believed to be true, has been flipped upside down yet again. My mother spoke of witches masquerading as nurses, stealing babies in the night. In a world where humans rule and these other races hide, is that how casters continue to exist? Are casters left to fend for themselves, or is there a place like Mordain?

"I've only ever heard of one such case of a missed elemental," Wendeline says, cutting into my swirling thoughts. "The story of Eloyan May, who had three affinities. It is a well-known teaching in Mordain."

"What happened to her?"

Wendeline shrugs. "She went mad, as they all do. The elements remained dormant, but they were still there, within her, simmering. When the casters found her, she was confused by what was happening, because she was uneducated."

I frown. "What do you mean, they all go mad?"

"All elementals succumb to their abilities once they reach a certain age, usually between their third and fourth decade. An elemental's powers become ineffective, and their minds muddled. They are unable to decipher yesterday from today and tomorrow, fact from fiction. They speak in riddles that are often unintelligible."

I recall something Annika had said. "They get sick."

"Yes. Some call it a sickness. Others call it madness. They become seers, who are as rare as elementals, if not more so, given most do not survive long. Queen Neilina sends her elementals back to Mordain once they've gone through the change. She no longer values them. But the devoted scribes believe seers are invaluable, even with their chaotic ruminations. They can see across dimensions and time, but they struggle to interpret what is happening and where and when, which is what causes much of their confusion. They no longer have a grasp of where their mortal feet touch." A sad smile touches her face. "Ianca went through the change while they were traveling here."

"Ianca's the seer." The older woman who Bexley said is traveling with the elemental.

"Yes. It is why she still wears an elemental's collar."

"But it happened that quickly? This madness, I mean." It couldn't have been more than five or six weeks since they escaped.

"I've heard of elementals going to sleep in the evening coherent and waking up lost. But often, they will complain that they feel something pulling at the seams of their mind, which is a sign the change is nearing."

My mouth hangs as I process all this new information. "Are you saying *I* would become a seer?"

"As a mortal, yes. But bound to Princess Romeria's immortal body, you are safe from what most consider a horrible disease. The toll on the seer's mind ages them rapidly, and they often lose their mortal sight, though they develop what we call divine sight.

They see the fates in their mind's eye, and they've been able to describe them in great detail for the scribes." Her blue eyes settle on the towering statues. "Their succinct visions are what we have used to model the corporeal forms."

The gilded doe has been here.

My father's peculiar words cling to the forefront of my mind, suddenly feeling more important. "Has anyone besides these seers ever seen the fates?"

"The elementals who summon them. Only those considered chosen are granted the gift of looking upon them."

A sinking realization begins to weigh on my insides. The ramblings ... the delusions ... "Men can be elementals." It's not a question.

"Yes. Ailill was one." She pauses. "Key casters are sired by male elementals. Your father would have been one."

My jaw drops.

"Did you know him? Your father?"

"Yes."

"And he didn't know what he was either?" Genuine curiosity fills her face.

I shake my head. At least I don't think he knew. He never said anything. But everything she just told me fits. Elementals age quickly and lose their eyesight. My father's eyes are weak, and he looks far older than his forty-nine years. I assumed it was the harsh life, but maybe that has nothing to do with it. Maybe the cause is something I could never have imagined.

He is not ill. His mind is simply fractured.

That is what Sofie meant.

"What about a traumatic event? Could that cause this change?" Like witnessing a murder in a parking lot.

"I do not know if there has been such a case. The scribes in Mordain would know." She seems to consider it. "I suppose a shock big enough could be a catalyst, especially if they're already nearing their time."

I steady my breathing.

"Many years ago, Mordain was known for using male elementals to breed caster children. The most famous of all—Caster Yason—fathered three hundred gifted children before his change."

"That's a lot of … babies." I censor the far crasser word I'd prefer to use, for Wendeline's benefit.

"There is a statue of him in Mordain's capital, Nyos, standing like a proud bull." She smiles bitterly. "After King Ailill's folly, Ybaris no longer permits male elementals to live. They fear they would not bend easily to the will of Ybaris, and they could not risk another Ailill, tempting the fates so recklessly. But also, they are the ones who create key casters, and once Ybaris learned of how Ailill used Farren to tear the fold, they decided that the risk of allowing a key caster to live far outweighed the benefit, should one ever fall into the hands of Islor again."

"So, you're saying Ybaris and Mordain have spent two thousand years slaughtering babies to protect themselves against a key caster, and yet here I am."

"Malachi has found a way around Ybaris's bid to stifle him from this world, yes. He is attempting to open the door to that nymphaeum again. You *must* not do it."

"Well, *of course* not. Not after what you've told me about Farren and tearing open the fold. But why does he think I can do it if she couldn't?"

She does a perfunctory glance around. "We are not entirely sure, but we think it is because Farren used her power to attempt to pry the door open, instead of taking the altar and allowing the nymphaeum's power to channel through her."

Taking the stone. "Right. *That*."

"Aoife created you to destroy the immortal Islorians. You were her weapon. And Malachi has taken her weapon and morphed it for his means. I can't imagine she will be happy if he succeeds."

"So, I'm a pawn for two scheming gods." I'm a pawn … again. "Why didn't you say anything to me before about what I am?"

"I wasn't yet sure *who* you are. Keeping it from you was the wise choice until I figured that out." Mika runs past again, his childish giggles and a determined Dagny trailing. Wendeline smiles at the boy. "But I think I have a good idea now. And *you* seem to appreciate the danger of *what* you are. Of the harm you could cause."

"Yes, which is why I'm worried."

"Malachi cannot force you to take the stone on Hudem. The fates can't create will out of thin air."

There is small comfort in that. But my situation is growing clearer by the moment. "I'm never returning to my old life, am I?" Even if I could, would I want to? Based on what Wendeline just told me, I would have another ten to twenty years in that body, at most, before it lost its hold on reality. I would end up wandering the streets like my father, ranting about demons.

But Sofie's evasiveness when I asked her what would happen to me after I retrieved this stone tells me all I need to know—there is no going back.

Her smile is gentle. "Whoever you were before, you are now bound to this body, and I suspect what was done cannot be undone. But you are powerful in a way that you do not yet understand. Oh, the things you will be able to do once you learn, Romeria … That is why you must allow Gesine to guide you. And Ianca, as much as she is able, though I fear her time of usefulness to you is limited. But you cannot wield caster magic without training."

"What about you?"

"I will have my own tasks here. And Gesine will be a formidable ally. She studied with the scribes before leaving Mordain. She knows more about seer prophecy than anyone else I know."

It dawns on me. *G*. "The letter to Margrethe. It was from Gesine. You *knew* Margrethe summoned Malachi for me."

"I'm the one who pulled the arrow from your body and helped her drag you out of sight." She glances over her shoulder. "You must go now. We have dallied too long. The king will have many questions about our conversation."

And Wendeline has told so many lies. "What do I say to him?"

"Tell him what you've learned about the seer in the city. He is looking for every reason to trust you, even if he does not yet see it. He has been resisting this lure he feels toward you, but he *will* lose against it. I believe that will happen soon."

My heart stutters. What does *that* mean?

"But if there is a way to leave out mention of *our* discussion, that would be best for the time being. For all our sakes."

"He can read me, Wendeline. He knows when I'm lying."

"You're clever. You'll figure out a way." She smiles. "I know it may appear like a bad thing, but there are positives to that ability too. He will begin to see the real you and rely on you and confide in you. You *must* find a way to trust each other. That is how you will survive what will come to pass. Tell him only what he needs to know, for now. Eventually he will learn that I have deceived him. I will accept the consequences accordingly." She reaches over to set her hand on mine. "But please know this, Romeria. *Everything* I have done has been for the future of Islor that the king wants." She squeezes. "Go now. You *must* go. And tell *no one* what you are."

I leave Wendeline sitting in the pew, her eyes closed as if in prayer.

Corrin is pacing in the courtyard when the carriage rolls in. She marches forward to meet me the second my shoes touch the cobblestone. "Where have you been? I expected you back two hours ago!"

I force down the conflicting swirl—relief, panic, dread—that has gripped me since leaving the sanctum and feign a glib tone. "Were you *actually* worried about me?"

"Hardly," she scoffs. "*Your Highness.*"

I'm beginning to appreciate Corrin. In a place where everyone lies or evades the truth, she's easy to read. "It took longer than expected. Odier had a lot of options to consider, and there were a few delays."

"Yes, well, I'm sure the king will also be ..." Her words drift as Mika hops out and tumbles to the ground. He tucks and rolls before scampering back to his feet. "Why is there a little boy with —" She grabs him by the ear and holds him in place to check the marking on his cuff. "I don't know this house. But why do you have someone's child? What have you done?"

"I found us a new baker."

"We already have one!"

"And now we have two. Corrin, this is Gracen," I introduce as two guards help her out of the carriage, her pregnant belly somehow looking more swollen as she climbs down the step. Dagny follows with the toddler in her arms. "And her daughter Lilou. You've met Mika. They're going to live here with us."

Corrin stares at me as if I've suggested we set fire to the carriage.

"They were with Lord Danthrin of Farywich—"

"Freywich," Elisaf corrects quietly.

"*Wherever*. Anyway, we came to an arrangement that avoided me asking Elisaf to chop off the lord's balls and shove them down his throat. Everyone wins."

Beside me, several guards shift.

I switch to a more conciliatory tone. "Please help them get settled. Gracen could use a few days off, and all of them could use a good meal."

"The priestess fixed my hand!" Mika waves it in front of Corrin.

It's a moment before Corrin manages to wipe the shock from her face. She scowls at the puckered skin. "*This* is better than it was?"

"Yes, milady. I could barely move these two fingers before." He waggles them as proof.

She harrumphs, but her initial bluster has died down. "Best

you get to your suite while I deal with *this*. I'll have your meal brought up shortly, Your Highness."

As much as I'd love to hide in my room, Zander will expect me to tell him what I've learned from Bexley, and if I delay, he'll become suspicious. "Maybe wait on that for a bit." I turn to Elisaf. "Can you take me to the king? I need to speak with him."

He bows. "Yes, Your Highness."

With a wink at Mika, I trail Elisaf, my insides churning.

The sparring courtyard is much larger from ground level than from my bird's-eye view above. At the moment, it's crowded with spectators—Legion soldiers, royal guards, and nobility alike—cheering and hollering at the two men occupying its center.

"You've gotten slower in your old age," Atticus taunts, twirling his blade in the air with ease as he squares off against his brother, the metal glimmering beneath the blinding sunlight. Anyone can see the prince, commander of the king's army, is highly skilled.

"And your mouth has grown more tedious," Zander counters with that unnerving edge of calm that he used with me in the early days.

Neither are wearing armor, and both are drenched in sweat, their white tunics clinging to their muscular forms, several spots of deep red where blood from nicks and cuts have soaked through. They've been sparring for some time, though their breathing shows no sign of labor.

Atticus lunges with a swing and Zander parries, their swords clashing, the clanging metal reverberating through the air. I feel it in my teeth.

The crowd watches with eager anticipation as the king and prince trade blow after blow, rarely slowing to take measure of each other, their boots skimming the sandy ground as they dodge close calls that have people gasping and my own heart stalling at times.

They should be wearing armor. That they are not is foolish and arrogant, even if they benefit from their nature and Wendeline's healing power. But there is something in this exchange that feels overtly dangerous. Maybe it's simply the act of swinging weapons meant to cleave into flesh, but I've watched plenty of duels from above, and none are fraught with the fury swirling around this one. Atticus keeps pressing forward, and Zander refuses to give ground. It's as if each would be satisfied with harming the other today.

Annika sidles up beside me. "Anything exciting in the lower streets?"

I sense perked ears around us. Everyone is listening. "Not particularly," I lie with feigned boredom.

Zander's blade stroke catches Atticus's shoulder, earning my sharp inhale. A bright bloom of crimson stains his white linen, and I hazard it's a deep cut. With nothing more than a hiss, Atticus charges his brother in a burst of anger that has me holding my breath, fearing the idea that Zander might be slain in moments. But Zander deftly blocks the barrage of swings with the same grace and balance that Boaz uses during his morning routine.

I nod toward them. "What's with them?"

Annika shrugs. "It's how they work through brotherly disagreements."

"Must be quite the disagreement."

Zander and Atticus's savage dance drags on, until their chests begin to heave from exertion and Atticus's swings are a little wider but no less ferocious, his handsome face cracking with frustration.

It's Zander's impeccable footwork and angled parries that finally gain him an edge. The moment happens in a blink—easily missed if a person weren't riveted to the battle—with a measured last-minute sidestep that throws off Atticus's balance. Zander delivers a swift kick that Atticus cannot recover from. He lands on his stomach with Zander's sword point against the base of his spine.

The crowd falls silent.

"Do not presume to tell me where to order *my* army," Zander chides, his jaw taut as he holds his blade there for three long beats before relenting. He turns and walks away, marking the end of their duel, his victory clear.

Atticus rolls onto his back but remains where he is, chest heaving.

The moment Zander's attention shifts to me, my heart races with nerves. I don't know how to begin to wrap my mind around the idea of prophecy, but there was a time I didn't believe in magic and monsters and gods. Are the seers right? Were Zander and I meant to find each other?

He approaches with a small smile that must be for our audience's benefit because it does not touch his eyes. In those, I see the weight of whatever has him so bothered.

"How was your morning?" Zander asks through ragged breaths, his gaze roaming my face. His shirt is unfastened around the collar and drenched, but it smells of him, only more fragrant.

"It was interesting." Curious looks touch us from every angle, even as spectators drift away and soldiers collect their weapons and move onto the court. I step forward even closer until we're almost chest to chest and I'm forced to tilt my head to meet his eyes. I reach out to pinch his soiled shirt. A small and relatively innocuous gesture of intimate affection, and yet it feels bold. "Have you ever heard of Freywich?"

He falls into the part seamlessly, his hand sliding against my side, the heat of it burning through material to my skin. "Freywich." He frowns. "Small town near Eldred Wood, I believe." He pauses. "Why?"

"Just curious." Maybe he'll never hear about today's mischief. I reach forward and toy with a loose string on his tunic. A distraction tactic to keep my thoughts shallow and my pulse guilt-free.

But the leveled gaze he settles on me tells me it's not working.

"Can we talk? In private."

Zander's eyes drift to my mouth. Is he thinking about last night as well? "Is it important?"

"It might be." Would he even care that Ianca is a seer and she's in Cirilea? I know he would care that Wendeline has lied about knowing.

Boaz appears at our side, his boot heels slapping together as he halts. "Your Highness, Abarrane and the others are waiting for you in the Round Room." His eyes flicker to me and narrow. He still doesn't like me, and he definitely doesn't trust me.

"I need to refresh and have a word with Romeria."

"But Your Highness—"

"They can wait." He hands his sword to Boaz, and then, settling a hand on the small of my back, leads me into the castle.

"This is the king's chamber." I've only seen it briefly, from the terrace that one night, and my focus was not on the furnishings. My eyes climb over the Baroque-esque sooty-black décor—everything from the walls to the carpet to the heavy drapery. Much like my room, the molding and trim are gilded.

I assumed Zander was walking me back to my suite, but we continued past my door to the next one. When he led me through the sitting room and directly into his bedroom, my mind started spinning various scenarios and thoughts that I should not be entertaining near him.

I'm hyperaware of the enormous king bed centered against the wall.

Zander disappears into another room, and a moment later, my ears catch the sound of bathwater running.

"You don't have a Corrin to do that for you?"

"I have servants to ensure my things are washed and tidied

and the lantern at the door is always lit," he calls out. "But I prefer to do things on my own."

"So do I."

"I've noticed."

On impulse, I reach out to test the softness of his mattress. Feathers like mine, surely. "But Corrin refuses to show me how to turn my bath on, and I haven't been able to figure it out. It's annoying."

"That's because she still thinks you might use it as a weapon if you ever get your cuffs off."

What *could* I do without these cuffs on? If I knew what to do with affinities to four elements and two different kinds of magic—caster and elven—hiding somewhere within me? "Seriously?"

"She's not very trusting, if you haven't yet noticed."

"I feel like I'm breaking through with her, though." Just like maybe I'm breaking through to Zander too.

The door to his dressing room sits open. I wander in and marvel at the countless jackets and other livery, illuminated beneath a candelabra overhead. It smells like him in here—a woodsy scent that appeals to me. Against the back wall is his suit of armor. I stop in front of it to study it closer. It's what he was wearing the night I met him, when he nearly killed me where I stood. I drag my finger along a deep gouge in the breastplate. I hadn't noticed it before.

"A battle-ax, during a war at the Great Rift, the last time your people tried to invade." Zander is suddenly behind me.

I tense but force myself to relax. "I figured you'd want something like that repaired."

"I should. It weakens my armor. But it also reminds me that I am not invincible."

I watch him curiously as he picks through a stack of shirts, pulling out a white one. His golden-brown hair is damp from sweat and curls at the nape of his neck. He could pass for any other man who just finished a workout and is dressing for a day at the office.

Except he's not human, and nothing about our situation is average.

"Did you enjoy your time in the market?" he asks casually, shifting to a section of pants, seemingly unfazed that I'm openly staring at him.

"I did. Yes." I turn my attention back toward his jackets. "What was that about, with Atticus?"

"What do you mean?" he asks, feigning ignorance.

"You two are angry at each other about something."

"A difference of opinion on whose army it is, the king's or Atticus's." He scowls at a frayed seam on the pants he pulled out. "There have been more whispers of plans for attack in the city this week, given the flood of outsiders coming for the fair. Unsubstantiated and without cohesion, but there are enough that we cannot ignore them. Atticus took it upon himself to order more soldiers to camp outside our city walls."

"Aren't more soldiers good in case these rumors are true?"

He sighs heavily. "I suppose."

"So, the issue is not the soldiers, it's that Atticus made the call without asking you. And you decided to ridicule him publicly for it, even though you make it sound like the army is his to maneuver. I heard it just last night. Something about his swollen ego."

"Are you always so blunt with your opinions?"

"You mean honest? I know that's a foreign concept to people around here." I smooth my fingers over the black-and-gold embroidered jacket. The hand-stitched detail is like nothing I've ever seen. The thread gleams as if spun with actual gold, and maybe it is. "This is nice. Have you ever worn it?"

He hangs his chosen outfit on a hook by the door. "Yes. To my parents' funeral and for my coronation. It was made for our wedding. And as far as my brother is concerned, is there a particular reason you're defending him?" His jaw tenses.

"Besides common decency?"

He yanks his soiled shirt over his head and tosses it into a basket in the corner, giving me an eyeful of curved, hard muscle.

"Did you know that upon interrogating one of the lady maids, I found out that you two grew *very* acquainted with each other during his escort from the rift? *Many* late-night games of draughts. Some so intense, he was seen sneaking out of your tent just before dawn, and there was telltale blood found in your sheets. I do not recall any of my games of draughts ending like that."

I peel my eyes away from his body to absorb what he's insinuating. "Are you saying they *slept* together? That *I*"—I point at my body, because it's this body I've inhabited that has done so many unspeakable things—"slept with *your brother*?" I feel the blood draining from my face. "I think I'm going to be sick."

"I doubt that reaction would swell his ego." Zander's shoulders sink. "I apologize. This was my anger speaking. You shouldn't have found out this way. Or at all."

"No, I *should* have. Sooner, probably." I glare at him. "If we were together, he's likely the one who would want you dead." A thought strikes me. "If you died, who would rule?"

"Atticus," he admits. "And I might have believed that theory, if his tributary was not also dosed with this deliquesced merth intended for him. *And* one of your men shot him with a deadly arrow. But no, I do not believe Atticus conspired against me, especially if it meant slaughtering his entire family. He may want to be king, but he would not want to wear a crown drenched in blood. He has too much honor and too much love for Islor." His attention skates over my lavender dress. "He simply couldn't resist taking something that was mine."

Princess Romeria's virginity, apparently. I don't know how much honor there is in that.

"Does he know that you know?"

"I don't believe so, and I'd like to keep it that way."

"Of course," I mutter.

He disappears into the bathing room, leaving me with my hands pressed against my mouth to keep my scream from escaping. *This place and its goddamn web of lies and secrets*! And after today, I am quickly being pulled into its treacherous weave.

The running water cuts off, and I listen to the clank of a buckle, the rustling of boots being kicked off and pants being shed, and a moment later, a body sliding into water.

Despite the swirl of shock that grips me, a heady tension stirs in my lower belly at the mental image those sounds conjure.

"I don't have much time. Abarrane is likely cursing me. What did you need to tell me in private, Romeria?"

He's left the bathing room door wide open. Is that an invitation after last night, or merely efficiency? Or is he testing me? He admitted that he is—always.

At least I have a reason to keep my distance, which makes it harder to read the guilt and panic settled firmly on my shoulders now that I know what I am. "Bexley found me in the market. Kaders left out some details."

There's a long pause. "Can we not talk through a wall? Please come in here."

There goes my strategy.

With several deep, calming breaths, I round the corner and step into Zander's windowless bathing room—a mirror of mine, other than the black stone tub where mine is copper. It's illuminated with a dozen flickering candles, no doubt lit with a single thought from him.

Zander rests his head on the back of one end and stares up at the ceiling, his Adam's apple jutting, his powerful torso on display, the rest of his body hidden below the surface of the water, too dark to catch even a glimpse.

My mouth goes dry. He may be the most desirable creature I've ever laid eyes on. And in this case, it's an advantage, and possibly my saving grace.

Steam coats my skin as I ease in to take a seat in the chair next to the tub. I let myself admire him. I don't take calming breaths or force my thoughts elsewhere. I stare and think of the feel of him in the alleyway last night for those brief moments until my blood thrums in my veins and my body hums with anticipation of it happening again.

Maybe this is another one of his tests, but if it is, I'll win it on my own terms.

His head rolls to the side to regard me.

"Do you normally have an audience when you bathe?" I ask.

"If there is a female in my bathing chamber, she is not sitting in a chair beside me." He smirks. "What did Kaders forget to mention last night?"

"That there was also a seer on his ship."

The amusement slides off Zander's face. "A seer. Here in Cirilea?"

"Yes. She was traveling with the elemental. They climbed into a wagon and disappeared."

A flurry of thoughts fly through his gaze. "I've always wondered what it's like to speak to one."

"It's confusing, sometimes disturbing." I rush to add, "That's what Wendeline told me. We stopped by the sanctum on the way back." But I also know firsthand, another stunning truth I need time to process.

"Did you tell Wendeline what Bexley told you?"

"I figured you would if you wanted her to know." I study Zander's chest intently to try to mask my lie.

He nods. His expression is pensive. "I've heard they can see things that we can't."

Find the gilded doe.

What has my father seen? Something about me, obviously. He said the gilded doe was looking for me. But Wendeline also said their visions aren't rooted in reality.

"What else did Bexley say?"

"Nothing important."

Those piercing hazel eyes shift back to me, and I know that even news of the seer isn't distracting him anymore. He must sense the tension coursing through me with my lies. But which secret is weighing me down more? That I've tasked Bexley with finding Ianca, or that I'm a key caster sent to open a door and possibly tear a dimensional fold that will release a fresh army of monsters, or that Wendeline has been scheming with Mordain because of some prophecy that would see us together?

I do the only thing I can think of to distract both of us from too much consideration. I drag my chair closer, reach for the washcloth, and dipping it into the water, smooth it over his neck.

A sharp inhale slips from his lips.

"She told me not to trust anyone." I smooth the soft material over his collarbones and his shoulders, focusing only on the feel of his body beneath my fingers, keeping my thoughts shallow. It's not hard to do. In fact, it's impossibly easy to focus on nothing but Zander when he's around.

"That's rich, coming from her."

"That's basically what I said. But the more I learn, the more I understand why *you* don't trust anyone." His chest is a canvas of smooth, unmarred skin, perfect in its sculpture. Warm water sluices over it as I wash away all evidence of sweat and dirt and dried blood.

"Everyone has given me a reason not to," he admits after a moment.

"What about Elisaf?"

"Except for him. I trust him."

"Completely?" I echo his question regarding Wendeline yesterday.

"Yes."

"How can you be so sure?"

My fingertip grazes his bare skin against his rib cage, and he inhales deeply again. "Because I am the one who made him what he is."

My hand stalls. "He told me he was attacked by an immortal in an alleyway."

"He was. He'd been in the Knoll that night and allowed someone on his vein. We can only take so much before it becomes hazardous. But then the male who accosted him took more, far too much. By the time I came upon them, Elisaf was nearly gone. I knew he wouldn't survive. So, I used my venom on him."

"But you blamed the attacker for turning him. He was executed for it." Zander is the one who told me that turning mortals was punishable by death no matter what the reason.

"Yes." He studies my face a moment, as if waiting for my reaction to that admission of guilt.

I make a second pass over his prominent collarbones. "I'm sure you had a good reason."

He smirks. "Besides not wanting to die?"

"You were the prince, and Elisaf was attacked. Neither of you would have died."

"Maybe not. But my father would have felt the need to make an example of me. As it was, I had to fight to keep him from executing Elisaf." Zander's eyes shift from their intense scrutiny of my face back to the ceiling. "Humans are the literal lifeblood of Islor. We need them to survive, and the fear that the blood curse will take all of them from us runs deep, all the way back to the days of Ailill and Isla. Turning a human for *any* reason is forbidden by the crown. So Elisaf and I lied, and his attacker received the punishment he deserved."

"And now you and Elisaf are bound by this secret?"

"We're bound by the simple fact that I created him. I am his maker. He cannot help his loyalty. It is ingrained in his being. An odd side effect."

"You're his master."

He snorts. "Don't *ever* let him hear you say that."

"He said you took pity on him after. Helped him survive and made him a soldier."

"We helped each other survive. Another side effect of the venom is the euphoria of releasing it into a vein. It's an exhilarating feeling, and when you give in to it once, it's difficult not to keep giving into it."

"You're saying it's addicting."

"Yes. Addicting. Highly. Another reason why the act is banned within Islor. It took months to get the urge out of my system. Elisaf and I went into the mountains north of Lyndel, under the guise of helping him transition. Really, it was both of us battling our urges."

I feel him exploring my face as I squeeze the cloth and watch the water pour down over his chest. "So, you trust him completely, then."

"More than anyone else I know." He pauses. "And now you know one of my deepest secrets."

I sense the question hanging in the air. *Tell me your secrets, Romeria.*

The relief that I feel with Wendeline knowing is staggering, but I can't assume the reception of my news will be as welcomed by the king, nor will the glaring proof that yet *another* of his trusted people have lied to him.

"You have a cut," I whisper, stalling a moment to study a thin red line across the ball of his shoulder.

"It's already healing."

I slip my hand below the waterline to travel over his abdomen, the ripple of muscle against my palm mesmerizing. I'm exploring far more than is probably smart. His body tenses as I lean forward to reach even farther. "You really should wear armor when you swing around that sword of yours."

He seizes my hand, halting it, his chest heaving with each breath. "We've played this game before, haven't we?"

"I don't know. Have we?" I lock gazes with him. Now that I know what I am, I can never step foot near the nymphaeum on the blood moon, which means I'm never leaving these lands, a reality that has not yet sunk in. What will happen to me? Wendeline thinks I have an important path to take, and it involves this man.

This king, who believes himself under some spell.

Maybe he is.

But how then do I explain what I'm feeling for him?

"Maybe this time, it isn't a game," I whisper.

His shallow exhale skates across my cheek. "Should we find out?" He pauses a few beats and then guides my hand downward, along his abdomen, farther, releasing it just shy of the assumed target, his gaze fixed on mine as he waits for me to make the next move.

Beneath my palm, his taut muscles tense with anticipation. But it's in his bright eyes that I see the truth—he's as confused and conflicted as I am, but he wants it to happen just as badly as I do.

My blood races as I curl my fingers around the hard length of him, the skin velvety soft against my palm. Whatever else he is with me—angry, resentful, frustrated—he cannot hide his attraction.

His head falls back against the tub, a pained look on his face. "I did not think you would do it."

"Did you not want me to?" I slide my hand down as I touch him thoroughly, memorizing the feel and weight of him against my palm. "Should I stop?"

His throat bobs with a hard swallow. "What I want right now is for you to climb into this tub."

"With you?"

He smirks. "If you dare."

I call his bluff, but not in the way he expects.

Kicking off my shoes, I climb into the warm water. Zander's eyes flash wide as he shifts, his legs slipping between mine to make room for me. Water splashes over the sides and onto the marble tile as I settle onto his lap, my violet dress billowing for a second before sinking beneath the surface.

The surprise fades quickly as our mouths crash into each other in a tangle of lips and tongue and teeth and our hands frantically wander as if attempting to touch every inch of each other all at once. I can't help myself. The tip of my tongue slides over his teeth.

With a deep chuckle—he knows what I'm searching for—he yanks off the capelet with a jerk of his fist, tossing it aside. "Those are annoying," he whispers, burying his face in my neck while his hands tug at the top of my dress, slipping the capped sleeves off and dragging the bodice down to my waist.

He pulls me flush against his body, his deft hands gripping my thighs tightly. Mounds of sopping silk bunch between us, but I can still feel him there, pressing against my thigh.

I close my eyes and let my head fall back, and I revel in the feel of Zander's hands searching the material as his lips trace the curves of my breasts with slow, precious sweeps of his tongue.

Releasing a curse laced with annoyance, he grabs hold of my skirt and pulls. A tearing sound fills the dark, heady bath chamber. Beneath the water, his hands explore my bare thighs, then between them, his touch oddly gentle compared to his frustration a moment ago as he caresses and teases and probes. His eyes burn as he watches the enjoyment unfold over my face. "Does this help with your dissatisfaction from last night?" he quips softly.

I rummage for words between shallow breaths. "Yes. Though do you know what would help more?" I roll my hips against his hand, earning his guttural groan.

Tearing the front of my dress the rest of the way, he grasps my thighs and pulls me forward.

My body tenses with anticipation.

"Your Highness!" comes Boaz's deep voice from the sitting room, startling us.

Zander's lips part with a long, slow draw of air, as if he's struggling to regain his composure. "What is it?" he snaps.

Heavy footfalls approach, and my arms instinctively curl around my exposed chest.

"Lord Stoll is eager to speak with you. He's received a message from—" Boaz's words falter when he rounds the corner.

"A message from ..." Zander prompts, as if the two of us aren't in the tub together. There's nowhere to hide, and he isn't the type to duck.

Boaz's eyes flicker to me before shifting away. "From his steward in Hawkrest. There have been cases of poisonings. Six of them."

Zander's head falls back. "So, it has begun."

"The tributaries were caught while trying to run. They are being held, but he needs guidance on how to punish them accordingly, given they are mortal. His people are terrified. Word is spreading."

"I guess that ends that." Zander gently eases me back from his lap and pulls himself out of the tub, giving me an impressive eyeful before he steps out. He leisurely wraps a towel around his waist and exits to dress in the adjacent room.

Boaz scowls at me, my arms still wrapped around my bare chest. "He has not learned his folly," he mutters under his breath before disappearing.

CHAPTER TWENTY-SEVEN

"*This* is the library?" My mouth hangs as my eyes rake over the lush conservatory, alive with mossy trees and weeping vines. Countless lanterns cast a moody glow despite the afternoon sun streaming in from the glass dome above. A stream trickles along next to our stone path, providing just enough space for a few iridescent fish to pass.

"The aisles for books are around the outside," Elisaf explains in a whisper, pointing out the multiple levels above us. "The core is where people come to read, and sometimes to talk."

Several people look up from their books and turn from hushed conversations. A few rise to bow as I pass, their seats in alcoves cocooned by vines and in stylish high-backed chairs that remind me more of a club lounge. They gape as if the last place they expect the soon-to-be queen is in a library.

Four ornate black-iron spiral staircases lead up, one to each floor.

"All these books, and you guys couldn't bring me even one when I was locked up and begging?" I offer Elisaf a flat look.

"*Evil* Romeria did not deserve entertainment," he whispers, humor lacing his voice. "Was there something in particular you are looking for?"

"Yes." If I'm stuck here, I need to arm myself with as much information as I can, rather than waiting for everyone else to feed it to me. "Anything on the history of Islor and the fates."

Elisaf bows and gestures toward the tallest staircase. "I believe we can find something that way."

Nearly an hour later, my arms are laden with books, and he leads me to an elegant chaise beneath a pergola draped in lavender blooms. "I assume this will do?"

I sigh dramatically as I set my stack on a small, round table. "I suppose." The bold flowers cascading down are vibrant shades of fuchsia and sapphire, enormous, and like nothing I've ever seen before anywhere, let alone inside a library. I gingerly reach for a tendril to measure it in my palm, and the petals suddenly snap closed over my finger. I jump back in alarm.

A deep cackle sounds nearby.

"That's one of her favorite games," Elisaf says as we watch Annika stroll past, her arm hooked in a young, attractive man's. A lantern flame glints off the man's cuff.

He's a tributary.

She winks and continues. I guess not all of them have the same qualms as Zander.

"Is there anything else you might need, Your Highness?"

I sink into the seat. "No, this is perfect. *Eli.*"

He pulls his own book from beneath his arm and settles into a nearby chair, a playful smile curling his lips.

Princess Isla of Cirilea was known for her difficulties harnessing her elemental affinity. As a gift to his betrothed, Caster Ailill forged a ring using a token from Aoife, designed with the sentient ability to amplify the wielder's affinity based on need. While wearing the ring, Queen Isla could manipulate water with a thought, making her use of her affinity effortless and effective.

Known to be a devout student of Mordain's scribes during his tenure in Nyos, Ailill forged the ring in the likeness of the one that graces the hand of Aoife, Fate of Water, as seen in the visions from the seers. While never confirmed, scholars believe the undetermined white stone has ties to the ancient nymph.

I smooth my thumb over the odd, dull white stone. The ring matches the one in the illustration. Is that how it came to life the night I searched for Annika in the water? Did its sentient abilities answer my desperate plea for help with the drowning woman at the bottom of the river?

Sometimes the urge calls to me to slide off the ring and see what happens. Now that Wendeline has told me what Sofie did, that urge is stronger. But while I'm wearing Ailill's cuffs, I guess there is no point.

"Filling that devious mind of yours with information?"

I startle at the sound of Atticus's voice. My heart hammers in my chest as he strolls up the path to the pergola. He's cleaned up and changed since I last saw him, lying in the dirt in the sparring court.

Princess Romeria slept with this man.

Was she genuinely attracted to him, or was she simply stirring up trouble?

He is striking, and they spent weeks traveling from the rift to Cirilea before she ever laid eyes on Zander, so I guess it's not the most unbelievable thing to happen, and yet she was heading here to marry his brother, *the king*. Though, I suppose the plan wasn't for a lengthy marriage. It was only supposed to last hours, if that.

But for the two of them to share whatever they did during that journey, for him to then learn she was planning on killing him …

Atticus must hate me.

And I can't let on that I know any of this.

I take a calming breath as I shut my book. "How's your arm?"

Atticus pats the spot with his palm. "It got a little tender loving care from the priestess."

"Wendeline spends her days patching us up."

"Nothing compared to the merth bolt through it six weeks ago. Remember that day?"

"Some parts are a little foggy."

He smirks, but then looks to Elisaf and jerks his head. A sign for the guard to leave us.

Elisaf slides from his seat and vanishes down the path.

Atticus watches him go and then takes his place, leaning back, his powerful thighs splayed, his arm slung over the back of the chair.

He's *far* from unappealing physically, but now that I know what kind of brother he is to Zander, any attraction I could have had to him has fizzled.

I plaster on my best aloof expression. "Is there something I can help you with?"

He cocks his head. "You really don't remember me."

"And what should I remember?"

He picks up one of the books I haven't gotten to yet—a cloth-bound text on Kettling's history—and leafs through it. "My men and I spent weeks escorting you from the rift down to Cirilea."

I know I shouldn't ask, but I can't help myself. "And did you and I spend any time together?"

"Beyond the obligatory? No." Blue eyes flip to me. If I didn't know our secret, I probably wouldn't read anything in them behind the usual mixture of curiosity and wariness. But now that I know what transpired between us, in those scant moments, I see the hints of longing and hurt. Maybe even a touch of guilt.

Princess Romeria fooled him as readily as she fooled everyone else. She could have used him unwittingly to learn of all the things Zander has accused this accomplice of. Did she make him promises?

His focus returns to the book. "I imagine that worked well for you, given you were ferrying these vials of poison. Wouldn't want us to catch on."

This impromptu visit must be about the murders in Hawkrest.

"I just keep playing over and over in my mind how you would

smile and wave, and the whole time, you and your brother had these grand plans to murder us all when we're most vulnerable."

"I'm sorry." There's nothing else I can say.

He tosses the book back to the table and does a perfunctory scan around us, I assume to make sure there are no eavesdroppers besides Elisaf. He's intelligent enough to know my guard will hear the entire conversation, now or later. "My brother is making enemies."

"Isn't that what kings do?"

"Not this many, this fast." He picks at a loose thread on the rose fabric on his chair. "This idealistic dream of his to end the tributary system and give mortals a place in the court and land for villages ... it will never happen."

"Why not?"

"Because it would require overwhelming support from Islorian's immortals, and he doesn't have it. And he underestimates his adversaries' conviction."

"I guess it's a good thing he has such a competent brother leading his army, then."

"Yes. Full of soldiers who need their tributaries as much as men like Adley and Stoll. How far do you think they'll follow before they turn and start fighting for the other side? How far would *you*, if someone told you that you were risking your life in battle for people who wish you to starve?"

"There can be a new system. One of free will and compensation. There are humans who will offer it still, who enjoy offering it. We saw it at the Knoll."

His pristinely white, perfect teeth flash with his mocking laughter. "I see you've been bitten by the same bug." His intense gaze lands on me. "This idea that our king has been entranced by the Ybarisan princess who wants to end Islor's immortals is gaining momentum among the people. Whether it is true or not won't matter soon, but I'm beginning to fear that it is, and it is steering all his decisions. It would explain what stayed his blade that night, why he guards you like a precious jewel." He leans forward, resting his elbows on his knees. "And why he has placed a murderess next to him on the throne."

"You know why. He wants to find out who conspired with her."

"With *her*. Not with you." His lips twist with bitterness. "There was no conspirator within our walls, not in the way Zander has painted it. Not in a way that might lessen your blame. But I'm not sure he sees that. I'm not sure he sees *anything* anymore, beyond his keen focus on *all things* Romeria."

"That's not true." Even with Atticus's chastising words, warmth spreads through my chest.

"What I witnessed the other night in the alleyway—"

"There were guards around, and we looked suspicious."

His flat expression says he doesn't believe a word. He studies his hands for a long moment. "They will *never* allow you to be queen, not after what has happened."

"It's a good thing I don't want to be."

"You two are quite the pair, then, because I'm not sure Zander wants to be king." He slides from his seat and leaves without another word.

I watch him stroll away, his shoulders sagging.

"Did you hear any of that?" I ask when Elisaf returns.

"I did, Your Highness."

"And I assume you know what Zander suspects happened on that escort to Cirilea?"

Elisaf's brown eyes flash to me, understanding in them. He confirms it with a nod.

"So he just lied to my face."

Elisaf frowns. "What *should* he have said? The truth?"

"I guess not." Not if he thinks no one knows of his indiscretion. I sigh. "I don't trust him. I think Atticus wants to be king."

"Of course he does. He is King Eachann's second-born son. He has a claim to the throne, should something befall Zander."

"*Exactly*."

"That does not mean he conspired to take it."

Clearly, Elisaf holds Atticus in high regard, too. "So then what was this visit about?"

"He is frustrated by his brother's choices, and I believe he was taking your measure."

"For what?"

"That, I do not know." He settles into his chair and returns to his book.

But my thoughts wander to my memories. To Tony, contemplating his options as his brother lay dying on the floor. While the big oaf may not have had anything to do with orchestrating Korsakov's demise, he saw the opportunity to rule the crooked little kingdom.

What would a brother do to rule an *actual* kingdom?

"The only time the little urchin stops talking is when he's hiding!" Corrin glowers as she yanks the silk coverlet over my bed. "It took us over three hours and the help of a guard to find him earlier!"

I laugh as I finish off some shading on my sketch. "I assume they're settling in?"

"A family suite in the servants' quarters. Oh yes, I should think so. I have half a mind to lock the room from the outside until she can chase after her own youngins."

"Please don't. I can speak from personal experience when I say being locked in a room for a month sucks."

"You deserved to be locked up," she counters.

"You're right, I did. But they don't. They've been through enough. Did you see her swollen ankles? And how tired she looks? That table was *literally* covered in food that she made herself. Their keeper is a monster. He's likely been abusing them for years. Who knows how many others there are?" Just thinking about that smug face makes me grit my teeth.

"I was helping her into the bath, and I noticed marks on her body. She told me he's been feeding off her and allowing others to do the same. Regularly. That kind of strain on a pregnant woman ..." Corrin shakes her head as she fluffs my pillows.

"See? I think I'd pull up a chair and clap if he were in the death square."

Her lips twist. "I've already had their markers exchanged for the royal ones. She's been trying to get into the kitchen, you know. Said she wants to earn her keep and prove 'Queen Romeria didn't make a mistake.'" She air-quotes that last part with her fingers. "Everyone's calling you queen. I don't know what you two are waiting for anymore. You might as well get married now."

My heart flutters. "Because this isn't real, remember? Zander's on a conspiracy theory kick, and I'm going along for the ride so I'm not locked in a room for the rest of my life." Atticus's words still linger in my mind a day later, a somber echo of what I, too, have speculated, about this possible accomplice within these walls. And if I have questioned, and Atticus has questioned, surely Zander has doubted it too. Yet, he keeps me at his side, stoking flames of discontent among aristocrats who do not wish to see a Ybarisan as queen, let alone one shrouded in such dark whispers as murder.

Corrin snorts and gives me a knowing look that makes me wonder if she's somehow privy to our intimate moment in Zander's bathing room yesterday. That moment, however fleeting, certainly felt real, but I haven't seen a hint of him since. It's as if the vampiric king of Islor is hiding from me. "Dagny said your gown will be ready in time for tournament day."

"Great." The day is approaching quickly.

"If there's nothing else, then? The kitchen is busy preparing for the hunt, and I have plenty to do, including attempting to fix a lavender dress I found in a sodden, torn heap."

I avert my sheepish smile and thrust the page toward her. At least she's not pressing for details on how it happened.

Her forehead creases as she collects it. "This is *me*," she states with surprise.

"Yes."

Her perpetually hard eyes soften as they scour it. "I've never had a portrait of myself. Thank you, Romeria."

It's the first time she's ever used my name. "And thank *you* for your help with Gracen and her kids. I know it was probably a lot to dump on you, but I couldn't leave them there."

She slowly rolls the paper. "I will admit to regretting my initial reaction, after I learned more about their situation," she says quietly.

"Is that an apology?"

"From Corrin? Impossible," comes Zander's voice from behind me.

He stands in the doorway of my terrace. Nervous excitement rushes through me at the sight of him, and at the flood of memories of our last encounter. Somehow, he becomes more attractive every time I see him.

I attempt a cavalier attitude as I say, "Now I know why you moved me so close. It's so you can show up unannounced, *any time* you please." It won't be long before my racing pulse gives me away, if it hasn't already.

"Your Highness." Corrin curtsies and then, with a smirk my way, departs.

I set my pencil down on the coffee table and steady my breathing as I regard the king, wearing his usual simple tunic—today in white—black pants, and black jacket, tailored to a carved body I've seen and felt unclothed.

Will we pick up where we left off?

Just the thought makes me dizzy.

Zander strolls in, stops at the threshold to my sitting room, and leans against the door frame casually, his arms folded across his chest. "Could Corrin's apology have anything to do with a certain baker and her soon-to-be *three* children you confiscated from their keeper?" he asks evenly.

"You've heard." Is he angry? I can't tell. He's guarding his reaction well.

"I believe you threatened to have Elisaf maim Lord Freywich, and quite viciously."

"Not to his face," I counter. "He tortured that little boy, he's been breeding Gracen, *and* Corrin just confirmed he was loaning her out—"

"You did the right thing," he cuts off my rant.

A wave of relief washes over me.

"Those are exactly the kind of immortals who have gotten away with their cruelty for too long."

"Yes." I falter, waiting for the "but that's not how we do things in Islor" lecture. After a few beats, I realize it's not coming. "So, that's all?"

He frowns. "What do you mean?"

"I figured I'd get at least one threat of a whip out of this."

"Again, with this whip," he mutters.

"But you're not angry with me?"

"My life would be *so much* easier if I were." He sighs heavily. "Come with me."

I eye his outstretched hand with equal parts wariness and thrill. "Where?"

"To divest me of more of my gold for the people. A favorite pastime of yours, apparently."

"Thank you, Your Highnesses. Thank you. May the fates bless you." The woman with the liver-spotted hands that I remember from our last trip through the rookery curtsies deeply. The man behind her—I assume, her husband—leans heavily on his cane today. I recall the torn shoes he wore last time. They've been replaced since by a fresh pair. But I note the bandaging above his ankle.

"Can I ask what happened to your leg?"

"Just an infection, Your Highness. I'm sure it's nothing to

worry about. It'll run its course." He waves off my concern with a smile, followed by a wince as he leans.

"I'm afraid of what that course may be." Especially when the man is already in this state. "Have you been to the priestess at the sanctum?"

"I didn't think we … I meant …" His gray eyes dart to Zander as he fumbles, "I don't want to be a bother."

I read his reaction to mean Wendeline's services are not available to people of the rookery. I suppose it makes sense—she can only tend to so many—and yet her talents are being used to patch up sword fights for immortals with unnatural healing abilities when people like this man are suffering. My anger flares.

"Go in as soon as you can and ask for Wendeline. Today, ideally. Tell her Romy sent you."

"You should listen to her. She's pushy. She's liable to come back tomorrow and check," Zander adds with a smirk.

The man promises he will, and they hobble off back to their shack.

We've reached the end of the rookery. In my grip is one of two velvet bags holding the meager remains of the gold we emptied into the palms of humans cast aside by Islor's cruel system. It doesn't feel like nearly enough.

I pause for a moment to take in the water. Dilapidated skiffs creak and thud softly against the rickety docks to the rhythm of the waves. The approaching sunset bathes the bay in shades of coral, auburn, and gold, the colors bleeding into the evening sky. Despite their squalid circumstances, I envy these people for their view.

While we quietly linger here, laughter and revelry carry from the busy city streets, hinting at the influx of people who flood the gates each day for the market to peruse the wares and enjoy the vibrant atmosphere. Corrin said more come in anticipation of the tournament day.

The sounds of hooves against stone draw my eyes down the

street. More soldiers on horseback trot along. Cirilea is crawling with the king's army. Their uniforms are not the polished matching armor of the royal guard, but a varying medley, men pulled from various lords to serve at the king's behest. Or Atticus's, according to Zander's bitter words the other day. At the helm of this cluster is his brother, sticking out in his shiny gold breastplate.

One of the men says something, and Atticus barks with laughter.

"He gets along well with them," I note, even as my body tenses with an odd mix of confusion, apprehension, and guilt. Whatever happened between us, it was not *me* who was a party to it.

"He is a strong leader. I hazard many of them would follow him into the depths of the Great Rift. They respect him greatly. He does not take sacrificing their lives easily, nor in vain."

Who, once upon a time, slept with your future wife. Despite everything Princess Romeria did, that must burn Zander's pride. "He came to me yesterday, in the library."

"I heard." Zander's sigh is soft.

"He doesn't agree with this charade."

"Yes, he's told me many times."

And yet Zander does not appear concerned by his brother's continued disapproval, whereas that sharp prick of worry keeps jabbing me. But maybe disagreements are routine with siblings. I don't have any experience with that. Or maybe it's what it means to be king. Disapproval or not, those closest to you will always fall in line and play their roles.

Atticus sees us, and with a quick word, peels away from his group and steers his horse toward us. "Your Highness," he offers cordially, dipping his head toward me. His black stallion is identical to Zander's, and the pair of them loom over us.

"Anything of concern in the market?" Zander asks smoothly.

"Plenty of drunks who would cut themselves down with their own weapons before they could cause any harm."

"Let them."

Atticus smirks. "My thoughts exactly." Whatever tension swirled between them on the sparring court yesterday seems to have evaporated.

"It is best we return to the castle. Darkness comes soon." Boaz dips his head in deference to Zander, even as he attempts to coax him. He has been scowling since I stepped out of the castle. It does not take a genius to see the captain does not believe the king's time is well spent in the rookery.

"You're welcome to go ahead with Atticus." Zander grips my waist to offer support as I hoist myself onto the horse. Even in my dress and heels, I'm beginning to get the hang of it. In seconds Zander is in the saddle, roping his arms around me to collect the reins, and setting off along a street that isn't familiar to me, one that heads uphill, away from the castle and the market and everything I've seen of Cirilea so far.

I take it all in with curious eyes and the unexpected contentment of Zander's strength against my back. "They're following us," I note, glancing over my shoulder to see a line of the royal guard snaking along behind us.

"Of course they are." I can't tell if he's annoyed by that.

The street we're on tapers off to a dirt road, and then something more akin to a path as the horse's powerful legs propel us onward and upward, through bramble and broad, leafy trees that I need to duck from in places. And then the path suddenly opens to a clearing and a cliff. Beyond is a seemingly endless ocean; behind is a view of the valley below, peppered with tents for the king's army.

Zander hops off the horse and then guides me down with gentle hands.

"What are we doing up here?" In the far distance, I can just make out the outline of a ship. Closer to us are a few small skiffs. Fishermen, hoping to catch a meal in the calm water before nightfall.

Zander's eyes scan the water. "I come here to think sometimes."

I walk cautiously to the edge, marveling at the steep rock face. Far below, waves hurtle themselves at the stone.

From this angle, I spot Boaz and his men standing idly on the path, waiting and watching, but not pestering. Giving him space. If Zander comes here to think, it's likely to brood. He has plenty to brood over lately.

"What are you going to do about those murdered by the tributaries?"

"The only thing I can do. Execute them. They murdered their keepers. I hear they have not even feigned innocence. We need to make an example of them to deter others." His jaw tenses. "They are already on their way here. They should arrive on the day of the tournament, in time for a public execution before the crowd."

I grimace. "A big day of death." Six mortals plus three Ybarisans.

"More than you realize, I am guessing. We have not executed a mortal in Islor since King Rhionn's time. We either send them to the rift to keep the border guard nourished, or we use them for immortal children to practice on when they come of age, to learn how to control their feedings."

Mention of children makes me think of the sparring court, of the little girl giggling as Zander scooped her off the ground. "When do Islorian immortals come of age?"

"The cravings first being around six. We're wild and greedy little things. It takes time to learn how to control our needs. It's usually after you accidentally kill your first mortal. I remember mine." He smiles sadly. "Her name was Erskand. She was a bread maker who stabbed a soldier when they came to escort her daughter to Presenting Day. The soldier lived, of course, the daughter was auctioned off to a lord, and Erskand died at the hands of a child. Or rather, to his teeth and unrestrained appetite. She fought me, which only made things worse."

I flinch at the visual. "And you still feel remorse for it."

"Every day," he admits softly. "Your lady maids were both sent to the rift. I do not know if they still live."

Punished accordingly, Elisaf had said.

"I am also enacting a new law that states any mortal who poisons an immortal through the act of repast will be sentenced to death, and any mortal who delivers a vial of this poison to the royal court will receive one hundred gold coins and absolution of any crime for possession."

"That's smart. The gold coins, I mean."

"It'll sway some, but not all. Ybaris has given the mortals a gift and a weapon, and once they realize what it is, there are those who will seek it out and make the best use of it."

"What are you talking about?"

"The tributaries who poisoned my parents are in the sanctum. We don't have an alchemist caster, but Wendeline has been testing them regularly. It has been many weeks since that night, and yet the merth still hums in their veins."

"So anyone who feeds off them would die, even now."

He nods somberly, his jaw tensing.

I process what he's saying. *Oh my God.* "It's like having an immunity," I say, more to myself. Or a vaccine. A thought strikes me. "Do you think that's why the daaknar died when it bit me?" Did Princess Romeria drink this poison?

"We cannot ingest it. Wendeline tested that too, on an immortal sentenced to death for his crimes. He died just as dreadfully as my parents and Lord Quill. And merth is as toxic to Ybarisans as it is to us, so I have to assume you did not consume it. Then again, you freed Annika from raw merth cord with your bare hands, which is an impossibility, so you tell me, Romeria."

I shake my head. I don't know. What I *do* know is that there are a lot of mortals who would want to get their hands on this poison, for revenge or protection, or both.

"With regard to these prisoners, I cannot give them to the soldiers or the children. There is no other way to punish them, and we do not keep people in the dungeon that don't serve a purpose."

"Who knows about this immunity?"

"No one but Wendeline and us, but that will change soon."

And when it does … fear will take over, above any moral decency among these Islorian immortals. The keepers will put them all in chains. "How many vials of this stuff do you think they brought over?"

"You came with five hundred soldiers. Each could have carried several vials, but we did not find any on them. There were also the supply wagons." He shakes his head. "Who knows how many were in there?"

"But she thought she could seize the throne and then kill off the immortals by inoculating as many humans as possible with this poison? She thought she could do all that with five hundred men?"

"Plus whatever help *she*"—Zander casts a look my way —"corralled from within. It was a bold plan, I will admit, and perhaps it wasn't to seize the throne but rather simply to remove Ailill's heirs, so we would be a weaker target for Neilina to overtake. Your men remained camped outside the city wall before the wedding. During the night, they could have shuttled the wagons for safekeeping up in the mountains, until Neilina attacked with her army. We may never fully understand those plans.

"But even a handful of vials here and there has the potential to cause considerable strife within Islor, as we're seeing. It will stir panic, and keepers will strip away what few rights the mortals have in a bid to keep themselves safe."

"What about Adley? He can't appreciate the idea of this threat of poison any more than the others."

Zander scowls. "The worm tongue is still busy, poisoning the water and swaying people from within. I do not wish to think about him tonight." After a moment's pause, Zander reaches over and curls his fingers over my wrists. The smooth obsidian cuffs that have no visible seam click open.

My mouth gapes.

"I put them on you. I can take them off." Zander slips the cuffs into an unseen pocket. He watches me intently. "What do you feel?"

I slide my hands over my bare skin. They're naked without them on. "What *should* I feel?" According to Wendeline, nothing of my caster magic while I wear this ring.

"A pull. Deep inside here." His fingertips press against my chest, just above the swell of my breasts. It's an intimate gesture, especially with the flash that stirs of his mouth on my body, but he doesn't take it any further.

I search for something—anything—that might resemble this pull he describes. "I don't feel anything."

He frowns. "Perhaps it has something to do with being brought back to life by Malachi. Maybe he somehow severed your ties to Aoife. I will admit, I do not understand the workings of the fates."

That can't be true. Wendeline tested me and found all four caster elements *and* my elven affinity. It *must* have to do with the ring, but that is not something I want to test now, in front of Zander.

I hesitate, smoothing my palms over my wrists again. "Why did you take the cuffs off?"

His shoulders sag, and his attention drifts toward the sea. "What am I to do with you, Romeria?"

He asked that exact question once not so long ago—though it feels like an eternity—when I lay in bed, recovering from the daaknar attack.

I don't understand why he's asking it again now. "Have I done something wrong?" *Again?* Is this about climbing into the tub yesterday?

"You've done *everything* wrong. You are hotheaded, you speak out of turn and do the opposite of what we agreed to, you antagonize me as if you have no fear of consequence. You continue to lie and deceive me. Your heart bleeds too much for the plight of mortals, and you seem willing to challenge *anyone* who doesn't bleed the same." He sighs, his hazel eyes settling on me, a brilliant kaleidoscope of gold in the setting sun. "You do everything wrong, and yet everything *right*."

My blood rushes to my ears as I process his raw words, as he reaches for my wrists, collecting them within his hands.

"I took these off because, for all the threats to me and to my throne, I do not believe you are one anymore." His fingertip pushes back a stray hair that flutters in the wind. In his stare, I see vulnerability and pleading. The same look I saw that night when he begged me to tell him it was all a mistake. "Please do not prove me a fool again."

The knots in my stomach coil tighter, threatening to cut off my ability to think. I could be the biggest threat of all. To him, to Islor, to *everyone*.

The urge to tell him, to unload this burden that grows heavier with each day, rushes me in an overwhelming wave.

I *need* to tell him. Before I let this go any further, he needs to know what I am.

I open my mouth, willing the words to come out.

I am a key caster, and Malachi sent me here to unlock the nymphaeum.

"Boaz is likely cursing every fate under the sun. We should head back." Zander guides me to our horse.

My burning confession gets lost somewhere along the ride home, curled within Zander's arms.

CHAPTER TWENTY-EIGHT

The lantern flames dance as if with a renewed spark tonight. Perhaps it is the swell of patrons circulating through the royal grounds, their worries of poisoned tributaries seemingly far from their minds as they laugh and converse and disappear into the depths of the gardens.

I feel the seduction in the air, too, as I lean against my terrace's stone railing, a heady anticipation thrumming through my limbs. A quick glance over my shoulder ensures Zander isn't sneaking up behind me.

With shaky fingers, I slip my ring off.

And hold my breath.

Nothing happens.

I frown with dismay. Wendeline was wrong. I don't feel any—

A twinge stirs somewhere deep in my chest. At first, I think I'm imagining it, but then it grows, radiating outward, expanding along my arms and legs, crawling up my neck and along my spine, until my entire body vibrates with this energy that is both foreign and familiar, like the adrenaline rush I'd feel when reaching for a necklace or slipping a watch off a wrist—except magnified by a thousand.

It's distracting and uncomfortable.

And exhilarating.

Wendeline was right. I can feel my affinities now.

I shove the ring back on my finger and the odd surge quells almost instantly. Relief overwhelms me and I laugh as I peer down at the ring in my hand. If I had to feel that all day, every day, I might lose my mind. Sofie knew what she was doing when she bound whatever spells she cast to this body.

What will *I* be able to do with these powers?

"The gold is said to be a gift from Aoife to an elemental, a piece of her antler." Zander's footsteps against the stone rouse my pulse for an entirely different reason.

I keep my eyes forward as I struggle to calm my racing heart. "I read about it yesterday. It's sentient." Whatever that means.

He comes up behind me, his height looming as he settles his arms on the railing, caging me in. "I heard you plan to drag Elisaf to the library again tomorrow. He *hates* the library."

I love the library. I'm becoming more adept at guarding my words, and yet it's harder to keep them in. I *want* Zander to know who I am, to get to know the real me.

His breath skates across my neck, stirring gooseflesh over my bare, sensitive skin. "My mother gave the ring to me to give to you. It's supposed to help you channel your affinity to water. I suppose you sensed its importance that night in the tower, even if you didn't remember why." Zander pinches the lace on the lapel of my robe between his thumb and index finger, as if testing the material. His fingernail drags along my skin, sending another shiver skittering through me. "But if you've somehow lost your affinity, then it is nothing more than a trinket."

The tie on my robe unravels with Zander's soft tug, and it distracts me from thoughts of my deception. He slips one side off, revealing my nightgown and the scars across my shoulder.

A prick of self-consciousness goads me to shrink from Zander's inspection.

"Don't," he whispers, leaning in.

I close my eyes and revel in the feel of his lips against my injured skin as he traces each unsightly claw mark as if it's the most beautiful part of my body. "What is happening?" I hear myself ask.

He pauses mid kiss. "Wendeline believes there is a reason you returned the way you did. She said that perhaps what Malachi did to your memory was a blessing to us all, that it's a second chance."

"A second chance for what?"

"For me to forget the Romeria of yesterday, along with all her cruelty. And for the Romeria of yesterday to forget her hatred for what she does not understand. And even though I know there is something you continue to hide, I am fighting against this constant aching pull I feel toward you." He adds quietly, "Fighting and losing. So let us not play this game of pretend anymore. At least not for tonight."

My robe slips off to pool on the cool stone terrace floor. He cradles my chin in his hands. "And let me see if I can find that affinity of yours, wherever you've buried it deep inside." His kiss is soft but assured this time—unlike the hesitant and the frenzied ones of the past—and I allow myself to melt into it, my core thrumming with eagerness as I press into the hard planes of his body.

He slips a hand over the small of my back and directs me through my terrace door toward my bed. Halfway there, his hands gently slide the straps of my nightgown off my shoulders. I pause long enough to allow the material to fall to the floor. I hadn't bothered with undergarments since I was preparing for bed, and my heart shudders with nervousness at the feeling of being bare in front of Zander.

But the rustle of his clothing comforts me. I won't be alone in this for long.

Steeling my courage, I turn and settle on the edge of the mattress in time to watch him kick off his boots and shuck his pants. His tunic has already been cast aside.

"Son of Malachi, indeed," I murmur, taking in his impressive size.

He smirks. "Where did you hear that? Son of Malachi?"

"Not important at the moment."

"I suppose not." He sets his dagger and sword on my nightstand, within easy reach.

I frown at them. "Do I have something to worry about?"

"From me? No." He moves closer, and I prepare for his weight, but he surprises me by dropping to his knees. "You have nothing to worry about from me. Ever. I couldn't hurt you, even if I wanted to."

"You *did*—want to, I mean. Have you forgotten? Has Malachi taken your memory too?"

He smirks. "No, though I *am* suitably distracted." His palms slide up my thighs, stirring heat in my lower belly, his gaze tracing my face, my neck, my breasts, my abdomen, before moving back up. "But I no longer feel the desire to look backward. I only want to look forward, with you."

Thick lashes frame eyes that beseech with their honesty. This gentleness is a jarring contrast to the other versions of him I've been treated to—everything from loathing to indifference. But now this, a vague professing of what?

I don't know what I feel for Zander, and our dark past isn't something that can be easily forgotten, but I don't want to discuss it at the moment, not while the king of Islor is kneeling before me, plying me with seductive words.

I part my thighs.

His eyes drop and flare with heat as they take me in, and when I weave my fingers through his hair, around the back of his head to guide him forward, his dimpled grin makes the one from the throne room that day seem a frown.

"Not timid indeed," he murmurs, his shoulders settling in between my thighs, his palms pressing against me.

I gasp at the first swipe of his tongue and fall backward onto the bed, reveling in his skill as he lowers his mouth on me. This isn't my first time experiencing this, and yet it feels as though it is. My body hums as anticipation builds, my fingers coiled around the soft strands of his hair, my leg hooked around his shoulder and my hips moving against him, striving to get closer.

Vaguely, I fret that my cries might be heard through the open terrace doors, or all the way to Elisaf's ears on the other side of the sitting-room door, but that worry slips away with all my other thoughts, save for the way my body comes undone beneath Zander's skilled mouth.

His lids are heavy and his lips swollen as he crawls onto me, dragging my satisfied body up with ease to center me in the bed.

"Did you find my affinity down there?" I tease, my mind sluggish in the afterglow.

"No. But I know where to keep looking." His teeth scrape across one nipple, then the other, sending shivers through me and down to my sated core. He doesn't linger long, fitting his hips in between mine. Our foreheads touch. "I think maybe Wendeline was right, and Malachi did give us a gift," he whispers, pinning my arms above my head.

I absorb the feel of our bodies against each other, no piles of chiffon and silk between us. "I think you might be right." And despite my anger with Sofie, she saved me from a much different path. I can't yet find my way to thanking her, though.

I open my mouth to remind him that we need a condom until I remember that his kind can't reproduce outside of Hudem, and do condoms even exist here? At least I don't think I have to worry about diseases.

The thought brings a smile to my face as I curl my hips into his, my body amply prepared and craving the fullness of him. Zander slides into me with a smooth, skilled thrust, burying himself deep inside, drawing my moan.

He stalls a moment, holding my gaze as he leans in to press a long, slow kiss against my lips, and then his hips begin moving above mine in a steady rhythm, with the same grace as when he dances with his sword, every muscle beautifully taut with tension and yet appearing to exert little effort.

My body responds, slick and undulating and aching with need, my legs hooking around him as I match his tempo. He leans in to kiss me and doesn't pull away again until we're both shuddering against each other, our cries surely carrying into the night.

I wake to the feel of someone fumbling with my ring.

My body tenses with panic as I quickly take stock of the situation. Zander is next to me in my bed, his hot, bare skin pressed against mine. He's merely toying with it, I note with relief, not trying to slide it off. Now that I know what happens when I remove it, I know I can't function without it.

"Good morning." His voice is gruff with sleep.

It *is* a good morning. Sun streams through the windows, promising another bright day. The terrace door still sits wide open, allowing the sound of steel clashing against steel to drift in from below. And I'm lying next to this man—this immortal—who I find myself drawn to in a way I can't describe.

I don't know if I've ever felt this content in my life.

"I was just thinking about the day I gave this to you," he murmurs, his finger stroking the white stone.

"Really? Is this what we're doing? Lying naked in bed and reminiscing about you with another woman? This is fun," I tease dryly. "You know what would be even *more* fun to discuss is which *male* tributary you'll be using the next time you have a need."

He rolls onto his back with a groan and a stretch, the sheet sitting precariously low on his taut abdomen, highlighting the rigid length below.

My thighs clenches with anticipation.

"And you assume the act would be strictly platonic because it's a man?"

My eyebrows arch in surprise.

"My preference is for females." He slides his head on his pillow to study me. His golden-brown hair is full and mussed and sexy. "And I wouldn't." He swallows. "Not if this is real."

"This is real." At least it is for me.

He reaches up to stroke the wayward hair off my face. "Whatever Aoife might have done … I will be a better king with you by my side. I will be the king that Islor needs. It becomes clearer to me with every day that passes."

Flutters stir in my chest even as my trepidation grows. Would he still say that if he knew what I was?

"You don't want to be queen?" he asks quietly.

"That's not it." Though I've professed it many times, I'm beginning to see the good I can do here. The urge to tell him the truth is overwhelming, but my dread holds me back. Just a few more days of this, at least. More time so I can prove that he has nothing to fear from me. "Atticus said they'll never allow it."

"They have no choice. These noblemen have gathered power they have no right to wield. That changes now. They do not have a say in who I marry or who I love."

An ache stirs in my chest with his words.

Concern carves into his face. "But what if *she* comes back?"

I assume he means Princess Romeria. I trace his hard jawline with my fingertip. "I don't think you need to worry about that."

"No?" His sleepy, docile eyes roam my face. "How do you know?"

"I don't for sure, but I think you're stuck with this version for good." It's the closest to the truth I can give him. "But *if* she does come back, please do me a favor and kill her."

He snorts. "I think Corrin will before I get the chance."

"Speaking of Corrin, she's going to storm in here any minute."

"No, she won't. Elisaf will warn her off."

"You assume he knows what happened in here last night?"

Beneath the sheets, Zander's hand grazes my hip and my belly, before shifting lower, between my legs.

His penetrating touch pulls a deep moan from my lips, unbidden.

Zander's gruff laughter carries through the chamber. "Yes. I'm going to assume he knows."

The cloud cover and threat of rain brings with it a damp chill in the morning air. I huddle within my cloak as our company travels across the bridge at a steady canter, heading for the crown hunt. Beneath the grace of daylight and calm, I can appreciate the detailed masonry and the span of the construction, requiring five yawning barrels to reach from one side of the river to the other.

An eerie sense of déjà vu courses through me, and my attention drifts to the shoreline where I dragged Annika to safety. I vaguely remember slick mud that night, but now there are only patches of lush, clover-laden grass. It was in that same place that I was seconds away from being stabbed to death by the man whose thighs hug my hips.

We leave the bridge behind and follow the road into the dense forest, and I think about how dire things were that night and how drastically they have changed. And how drastically they still will, likely. My life is here now, a Ybarisan among the Islorians. As their queen, if Zander's bedroom whispers translate into reality.

But also as one of these key casters—a creature that no longer exists in this world, and that many will demand die, if Sofie and Wendeline are right. I have to assume they are.

At some point, I will have to tell Zander. What will he say, knowing his queen could bring ruin to his kingdom? Is that news better received before or after the wedding ceremony?

I have struggled to find guilt over Princess Romeria's misdeeds, but these lies are all my own.

We reach our destination a half hour later, as the dense forest opens into a clearing.

I try not to gape. "All *this* to chase a wild pig?" Elegant marquee tents in shades of ecru, green, and gold stand in a line, servants sweeping through with platters of food and pitchers of drink, preparing for the king's tardy arrival. Soldiers in full armor mill around the horses at the outskirts. String music and laughter carries. Somewhere within are Lords Sallow and Telor, and unfortunately, Adley.

"The crown hunt is tradition, just as the tournament day, and I wouldn't discount nethertaurs as mere wild pigs."

"I'm sorry, a nether-*what*?" This is the first I'm hearing of such a beast.

A smirk laces Zander's voice as he explains, "A residual of the sort of beast Caster Farren released when she tore the fold. It is three times the size of a boar and far more grotesque. They go to ground for years, only surfacing every few decades. We've killed many but can't seem to rid ourselves of them. There have been rumors of one in Eldred Wood as of late, devouring stag and boar. The gamekeepers found three half-eaten mortals a few weeks ago. Nethertaurs prefer immortals, as do most of the beasts that were released," he adds as I grimace.

"Though, I suppose those mortals deserved what was coming to them for poaching in the king's forest, but it is still a cruel way to go. If we are lucky, we will rid ourselves of the creature on this day, before it vanishes again."

"And when you say 'we,' you mean *you*, right? Because I'll be waiting by the food table while you go chase your monsters." I was still picking at a bowl of sour red berries when Corrin chased me to my vanity, scolding me for my late night "activities" that were causing me to drag my behind this morning.

His chuckle warms me. "I requested paper and graphite to keep you busy. My horse moves faster with a single rider, anyway. As an aside, you will need to learn to ride on your own soon. As much as I enjoy being able to do this"—his hand slips inside my cloak to skate over the bodice, giving my breast a gentle squeeze —"a queen must be proficient in something as basic as equestrianism."

"I *want* to learn." My thoughts are elsewhere, though. His mention of Farren knocks on a door I feel the urge to nudge open. "How many of these beasts were released when Ailill used that key caster?"

"Hundreds? Maybe more. I don't know that there was ever a count. We have a whole section in the library on the various creatures. The nethertaurs were the most docile. There were others, like the winged scaly beasts that pillaged entire villages in the night, breathing fire and consuming entire herds of livestock. The last of those was killed by Mordain eight centuries ago."

Dragons, surely. "But there are still beasts here, two thousand years later?"

"The dredges of them, yes."

I hesitate. "Sounds like Farren caused a lot of problems for everyone."

"Which is why key casters no longer exist. It is the only thing Ybaris and Islor ever agreed upon."

I take deep, calming breaths and focus my thoughts on the bustle ahead to try to keep the gnawing anxiety at bay.

"Bring me more wine," Annika demands, waving her mug in the air.

"Yes, Your Highness." The servant sets a plate of fruit compote and hard cheeses at my place.

"Thank you," I offer. Meanwhile, I'm trying not to salivate at the succulent platter of smoked ham and roasted game bird in front of us, the smell wafting through the main tent.

The mousy woman with the button nose and brown doe eyes startles as if surprised I'm looking at her, let alone thanking her. With an almost imperceptible nod, she scurries away.

Annika leans over. "Why do you do that? Thank the servants for delivering your food to you?"

"You mean, show common manners?" I throw back before I

can stop myself, and with too much bite. I've been studying the nobility around the enormous U-shaped table, lined with eucalyptus and willow branches and laden with food and drink, so I can better emulate them. However, the more I see, the less I want to do with *any* of them. The way they wave their goblets in the air to have them filled, snap their fingers to beckon, bark when servants aren't running ... And it's not just a few, it's all.

It's one thing to slip into a room and impersonate someone for an evening. I can't play one of these people for the rest of my life, which is a decidedly *long* one.

Annika cocks her head, genuinely intrigued. "But they're servants. What drives that impulse inside you?"

Because I come from a world where this behavior is not acceptable, I want to say. Except that's not entirely true. I suppose I can't fault her entirely. If history books and cinema have taught me anything, it's that the days of kings and queens were like this. Then, it had nothing to do with immortal versus mortal and everything to do with rich versus poor, nobility versus commoner.

And while the society I'm from has evolved, there is still a caste system, and it is blinding when you happen to be a street kid who slips into elite parties to steal jewels. I've seen fingers snapped and noses upturned, service staff treated like part of a room's functional décor rather than fellow humans. I once watched some rich prick make a bartender cry because she put too much lemon in his drink, all while the club's manager prostrated to offer his condolences for the heinous error. I've seen enough to know that you put too much ego and entitlement under one roof, and basic decency wanes.

Unfortunately, in Islor, crying over too many lemons is the least of these mortals' hardships.

Regardless, I need to guard my behavior carefully around these people, so I don't draw more attention than I already do. "What is the priestess doing here?" I watch the woman with wiry white hair hover by one of the tent entrances. Aside from Wendeline, the casters I've seen in the sanctum and walking the royal grounds at night are climbing in years, the youngest of them surely close to seventy. How much longer before they all expire?

"She's bait." Annika carves off a chunk of meat, and after dipping it into a yellow mustard, pops it into her mouth with a satisfied moan. "The nethertaur is drawn to caster magic. She'll go with them to lure it out."

My jaw drops. "She agreed to this?"

Annika waves away my horror. "She'll be fine. There will be dozens of them out there to fight it. Zander and Atticus slayed the last one together without any help."

I hide my grimace with a piece of cheese. Speaking of Atticus … I search out the commander of the army—and apparently Princess Romeria's secret lover—and find him off to the side with Adley, his brow furrowed as he listens to the Lord of Kettling. Whatever they're discussing, it's Adley who steers the conversation, his jaw rigid as his lips flap with quick, angry words.

As suspicious as Zander is of everyone else, I wish he would be more suspicious of the one who stands to gain the most if he died, who has already proven himself willing to take what isn't his.

Atticus's blue eyes flicker in my direction, as if he can sense my gaze. I shift to study my plate, but it's too late to hide the fact that I was spying on them. "Do you know where Zander went?" He ducked out ten minutes ago.

"Probably to the royal tent to prepare for the hunt."

I set my napkin on the table. "I think I'll go find him."

"And help him dress? Or *un*dress?" Annika teases around a mouthful of stewed vegetables, her eyes carrying a knowing glint of humor.

"That's your brother you're talking about," I remind her and smile with satisfaction at her grimace as I head for the exit.

"Your Highness." The mousy servant appears with a small plate in hand carrying a sweet apple tart, much like the ones from Gracen's stand. She curtsies. "I heard you like these." Her voice is soft, meek. I'm noticing that about all of them, though. Corrin and Dagny are unusual in that regard.

Word of the incident in the market must have spread among the servants. "Thank you." I collect the plate.

"If Her Highness would please wait a moment." She darts away and is back in seconds with a fancy, rose-colored parasol. She steps out into the drizzle, the umbrella open and waiting for me.

"What's your name?"

"Bena, Your Highness." She offers a small curtsy.

"Thank you, Bena. I can take it from here." I collect the handle from her.

She frowns with consternation, as if the idea that the queen should hold her own umbrella is unfathomable. "But—"

"Stay here, where it's dry. I'm only going over there. Honestly, it's fine." I breathe a sigh of relief as I trudge through the trampled grass, happy to be away from them all and eager to see Zander. It's a blessing that he has hidden me from these people for as long as he has.

The king's tent is the smallest but most elaborate—a silver-and-gold, bell-shaped construct meant solely for him, its peak at least twenty feet in the air.

Unfortunately, my path there isn't clear.

"Eating and running?" Atticus stoops to slide beneath the parasol—which I suspect won't offer much protection soon as the deluge worsens—and collects the handle from me. His broad shoulders consume most of the space.

"I'm not hungry." I take a step back and find myself halfway in the rain again. He may have been with this body, but he wasn't with *me*.

"Yes, hence the plate of food in your grasp." Atticus steps closer to shield me, his blue eyes scanning my face. "The nobility think their future queen doesn't want anything to do with them."

That's because I don't. "People like who? Adley?" I meet his steady gaze. "He has your ear."

"I tolerate him because I must, at least for now, as does my brother. As do you, if Zander plans on following through with this idiotic notion of marrying you."

"And why exactly is it idiotic?"

"Must you ask?" He cocks his head. "It's obvious Neilina did something to get in his head as far as you're concerned. He tripped all over himself before, and he's doing it again. I see he's even removed your cuffs, something he was adamant he would not do." He nods toward my bare wrists.

"And I'm sure he's told you I can't access my affinity." I've tried several times over the past few days, with cups of water and while soaking in the bath. Each time, nothing has happened.

"And you've *never* lied before." He smirks. "In all my years, I've never seen my brother behave so carelessly. He's not thinking straight. He's not seeing what's right in front of him."

"You're right. I don't think he's seeing the threat in front of him," I hiss, his insinuation that Zander could not care for me flaring my anger.

Atticus sighs. "I don't mean to offend you, Romeria. But there are too many reasons to not put you on that throne, regardless of feelings. The east will not cooperate and Adley's supporters grow."

"Then get rid of him," I say, without really considering what it means to say that within this world, and it's not a pink slip. I glance around to make sure no one overheard that, but we are alone out here, in the rain.

"Spoken like your mother," he murmurs wryly. "Having Adley executed will only cause more tension and Islor is already rife with it."

"Well, I guess it's a good thing Zander has the devoted support of his commander to make sure they all fall in line with whatever he decides, *isn't it*? A commander and *brother* who would *never* betray him?"

His eyes roam over my features, stalling at my mouth but only briefly before flittering back to my eyes. "Why do I feel like you're accusing me of something?"

"Because you're paranoid?"

"Do I have a reason to be paranoid?" he asks evenly.

"*Do* you?"

"What game is this we're playing now?" He frowns curiously. "Do you know something I don't?"

I hesitate. Was Zander wrong? Did Princess Romeria and his brother *not* have an affair on the trek from the rift to Cirilea? I poked at the topic in the library and thought I saw the truth within his eyes, but was I only imagining it? Maybe Atticus is innocent of everything, and I've been loading a gun and leading him to the firing wall unfairly.

I'm keeping too many secrets.

A flare of reckless bravery swells inside me. I can't help myself. I meet his scrutinizing stare and say, "I doubt it's as fun for you as draughts was." Whatever that even is.

My taunt has the desired effect. Stark understanding fills Atticus's expression in a wave of shock.

I use the moment to duck away, abandoning him with a parasol in hand. By the time I reach the gold-and-silver tent, the rain has soaked my gown. The guards wordlessly pull the tent flap back to allow me in.

Zander stands like a statue as a servant fastens a buckle at his side. I assumed he would be wearing a full suit of armor, but he's dressed like a warrior with layers of studded black leather beneath a few sleek-looking armor plates—at his shoulders and forearms, across his chest, at his knees.

He looks lethal.

"Are you not hungry?" he asks.

"I'll eat later," I murmur, collecting the opulent details of the royal tent's cozy interior as I wander in. The grass floor is hidden beneath layers of carpets with rich colors and patterns. One side is furnished with tufted settees and velvet armchairs, while a long rectangular table sweeps across the other side. A map of Eldred

Wood is stretched out next to a cache of polished weapons. It reminds me of Sofie's bodyguards' collection. There are blades of varying size and menace, some straight backed, others trailing in curved points. "You're going to use *all* of these?"

"Not all, but many."

I nibble on the tart as I give the arsenal another long look before shifting to the topographic map of the forest. It's vast, covering an expansive area of west Islor, and detailed, illustrating the many rivers, lakes, rapids, and rocky elevations among the dense wood. "What are all these painted stones?" Markers of some sort.

"Green for the animal carcasses found, black for the mortals."

I grimace at the cluster. "So, you know where to find this nether thing?"

"The nethertaur?" He smirks. "Yes, the general area. It's deep within the woods. We'll draw it out."

"I heard how." I give him a pointed look.

"Priestess Clyda will not be harmed. Thank you, Basil." He offers the servant the briefest smile, but it's enough to remind me that Zander doesn't behave as the other nobility do. Fortunately.

"You're going to be careful, right?" I have no idea what this beast is that they're hunting, but if it's anything like a daaknar ... Plus, Adley will be on the hunt with them, armed with weapons. Concern pinches my heart for the man I've shared a bed with for the past several nights.

"As careful as a pack of fools hunting down an otherworldly beast." Atticus strolls in as Basil slips out. Boaz and Elisaf trail him. "We should depart soon, to make the most of the daylight." My stomach tenses as he heads toward the weapons table—toward me—with his typical arrogant stride, his gaze steady and unperturbed, as if I didn't just drop a bomb on his head. He must realize how I know. Zander is going to be furious with me when he finds out, but at least I have my answer.

"Gully's Pass or Hollow Falls?" Zander asks, too far away to sense the tension whirling inside me.

"Gully's Pass is safer for the horses." Atticus stops on the other side of the table, directly in front of me.

I avert my attention to the map to search those two locations. "Safe is good."

"Safe is what we *all* want." Atticus tests the weight of a bow.

I hesitate but finally look up to find somber eyes on me.

"Regardless of mistakes I have made in the past," he whispers, "I will *always* protect my brother. I *swear* it on my life, and on Islor. You believe me, right?" The sincerity bleeding from a voice that normally dances with wry humor is startling, and I find myself nodding numbly. Whatever Princess Romeria and the prince shared, I can see now it was not loathing for Zander.

"Let us finish our attack plan," Boaz pushes, drawing a finger across Gully's Pass. "We will enter here and ..."

Attention thankfully drifts to the map, allowing me the chance to sneak away. Several *karambits* gleam on the table. I only know what they are because one of Korsakov's guys carried that knife and the idiot sliced his own radial artery open. They had to rush him to the emergency room before he bled out.

I pluck the closest to me from the table. Tucking it into the folds of my dress, I innocently shift to the settee with my apple treat and hide the blade beneath the corner of the rug.

With a weapon for safekeeping, I collect the paper and graphite from the table and busy myself with a sketch of the king's handsome face until Zander announces it's time for them to leave.

I frown at my personal bodyguard, who has strapped a small arsenal to himself. "Elisaf's going with you?"

"Yes, Elisaf has been pacing outside bedroom chambers and minding a princess around the clock for weeks. He needs a break and is going to join the fight," he mocks with a grin, answering for himself in third person.

"Fair enough." I raise my hands in surrender. "But what about me?" I look meaningfully at Zander.

"Do I still need a guard to keep you in line?"

"Well, *no*, but …" *What about Saoirse and the others*? I want to say. Surely, she's just waiting for the opportunity to pounce.

He leans in, slips a finger beneath my chin, and tips my head to lay a languid kiss against my lips. "Don't worry. None of them will come anywhere near this tent with Abarrane here."

"*Abarrane*!" I hiss. "Why her?"

"Because she *must* be receiving punishment for *something*, though she does not yet know what." The Legion captain materializes out of nowhere and steps from behind a room-divider screen to my left. How long has she been here?

"We will see you in a few hours. Play nice." Zander disappears into the drizzle, along with the rest of them.

"Be careful," I murmur as an afterthought. My dread swirls at the thought of an afternoon with a woman whose résumé boasts torture techniques. At least I won't have to deal with any ambushes, though. I eye her warily. "I'm sure you could still catch up with them if you leave now."

"Why, when I could spend the afternoon here with the Ybarisan princess who aims to be our queen?" Her braids tumble off her shoulder as she stoops to collect the hidden blade from beneath the rug.

The blood drains from my face.

"This is quite the choice to pilfer from the weapons table. You'll stab yourself within minutes." Her lips pull back with a wicked smile. "Shall I show you how it works?"

"What are you, a newborn foal? Fix your stance." She swats my calf with the flat edge of her sword, making me jump. "Shift your left foot back to strengthen your balance and bend your knees."

I follow her instructions, ignoring the fact that I'm in a gown.

"Now, jab."

With my fingers curved around the blade's handle in my palm, I make a sweeping motion with my arm.

"Not bad. Back to position. And again."

We've been practicing this one move since the hunting party left, interrupted briefly by Annika who, upon seeing my company, quickly fled. That earned my babysitter's grin of satisfaction. I think she prefers to be feared.

Despite my tutor's abrasive nature, I find I don't mind her teaching style.

"You are getting sloppy," she mutters, nodding toward the settee. "Take a rest."

I drop the knife onto the table with a groan—my arm aches—and flop into my seat. "Aren't you going to ask me what I intended to do with it?"

"I *know* what you intended to do with it. *Nothing*," she sneers as she paces. "You are surrounded by enemies who did not want you on the throne before the attack, and their hatred has only grown. You saw an opportunity, and you took it. It is what I would have done in your place, too, so perhaps you will not be entirely useless."

I think that's a compliment, but I don't want to assume anything, especially coming from her. I hesitate, afraid I'm going to regret this. "Would you be willing to teach me how to fight?"

She spins on her heels to face me. "*You* want to be trained as a Legion soldier?"

"*No*. I would just like to be able to defend myself."

"I do not train for defense. I train for war. I train Legionaries."

"But you just trained me with *that*."

"That was not training," she scoffs, roping her braid around her fist. "That was a simple lesson because I was bored. It would be a waste of my time. I doubt you could fend off a puppy."

"I could if you trained me. Zander already mentioned ..." My voice fades as I watch her eyes flare with rage.

"*No*. I do *not* train princesses, *or* Ybarisans." Her tone bleeds with scorn.

I hold my hands up in surrender. "Okay, fine. Zander said you were the best of the best, so I just thought—" Shouts sound from outside. They're soon followed by shrill screams.

Abarrane moves for the tent's flap, her sword drawn. I grab the karambit and follow her out into the rain.

The quaint meadow has tumbled into chaos. Two of the bell-shaped tents have collapsed, and servants are fleeing the main rectangular tent where one side has caved in. The screams from inside are earsplitting and steeped in fear.

"What's happening?"

A second later, a beast leaps out from the tent's opening, a man's limp body dangling from its maw, and I have my answer.

CHAPTER TWENTY-NINE

"*Stay here.*" Gripping the hilt of her sword with both hands, Abarrane eases forward in a crouch with stealthy steps, a predator stalking its prey—except she is a petite female warrior, and the prey is a massive creature on four powerful legs. Its shoulders reach ten feet in the air, and its back is coated in blue-tinged scales, the rest of its sinewy form in matted, oily fur.

It swings its unsightly head toward us, and I shudder under its intense stare. A sickening crunch sounds, and the man's body falls from its mouth in pieces to land in the grass like debris. It lifts its upturned snout in the air. It's sniffing, much like the daaknar did that night when it was scenting Annika.

With a deep roar, it charges.

My heart is in my throat as I watch it gallop forward, its jutting tusks curved like the blade in my hand and twice the length, ready to gore anything in their path. The bloody sheen coating them proves it already has.

Several soldiers with swords approach cautiously, while others hang back. Two fire bolts at the beast's back using crossbows. They bounce off its scaly armor like toothpicks.

"If your affinity is anywhere within you, I suggest you find it now," Abarrane hisses.

I assume she means my elven affinity. "I haven't been able to!"

"Then you will surely die today." She shifts her position and readies herself to meet the beast head on. It's moving too fast, and she's too small. There's no way she'll be able to stop that thing, and when she fails …

A surge of adrenaline and terror seizes me as I grip the handle of my weapon, which seems even more pointless and puny than the one I stabbed the daaknar with.

Abarrane dives away from the beast's thrusting tusks but is back on her feet in an instant, swinging at its haunches. Her blade slides across the back of its hind leg, spraying inky-blue blood.

It roars in agony and spins to lunge at her again. She deflects it with her blade and darts out of the way, stabbing at the beast's side as she rolls. It snaps at the air, showing off a mouthful of fangs that make the daaknar's seem paltry.

I watch in horror as it catches Abarrane's shoulder with its tusk, cutting through flesh and bone. She lets out an agonizing screech—I have a good idea of the pain tearing through her insides right now—but she swings her sword against its neck, using the momentum to pull herself free and stumble away. She makes it five paces before she falls to the grass.

With another sniff of the air, it shifts its attention to me.

I'm paralyzed as it stalks forward. Clutching my tiny blade, I know I can't outrun this thing, and my meager lessons won't save me.

My elven affinity to Aoife. To water.

I need it *now*.

As if in response, the gold begins to burn against my skin. My heart races. Finally, it senses I *need* help.

Annika said I could have used the river that night to defend myself instead of saving her, but there is no river here, and I wouldn't know how to use it if there were. No one would teach me.

The nethertaur is a mere thirty feet away now, gaining speed despite its wounds. The trampled grass reaches up and lashes out at its legs, as if attempting to coil and tangle, to slow. It's Annika, I realize, using her element as she runs this way, yelling something that I struggle to hear over the blood rushing in my ears.

"Use the rain!" I finally make out.

The rain. I peer up at the crying sky. "How!" The only way to stop this thing is with a comparable beast.

The next few seconds seem to move in slow motion.

A surge of adrenaline bursts from somewhere deep inside me, and then I watch as the raindrops pull from every direction, taking shape as they rush toward the nethertaur, forming a body and legs and a head, until a duplicate of the beast but made of water charges forward.

I'm doing this, I realize. This is me, manipulating an element.

They collide head-on, the water beast exploding on impact and the nethertaur collapsing in a daze, long enough that Abarrane hobbles over to embed her sword between its eyes. After a few twitches, the beast stills.

I bend at the waist, waiting for my heart to slow and my shock to settle. For a moment, I'm sure I'm about to hurl. I stopped it, though. I used this elven affinity I can't even find, and I stopped one of these otherworldly beasts.

A bubble of delirious laughter rises in my throat.

Abarrane limps toward me, her face a ghostly white, wiping the inky-blue blood from her blade onto her pant leg. "Fine," she huffs. "I will consider training you."

"Why would the nethertaur leave the depths of the forest and come all the way here, into the meadow?" Zander paces around the tent. "Especially when we had a caster to attract it?"

"I do not know." Wendeline is perched on the settee, her eyes bloodshot from healing as many as she could. Four soldiers and six servants were killed by the nethertaur, another five were mauled—two far beyond the priestess's skill. The few female aristocrats remained mostly unscathed, save for a few cuts and scratches. A wicked part of me was disappointed that I didn't see Saoirse's body among the heap thrown into the wagon, but I heard she leapt onto a horse and galloped away at the first sign of trouble.

Bena was among the perished. When I saw her body, I cried.

A messenger raced out to carry news to the hunting party of the attack. They arrived back to camp a half hour later, the horses' mouths were frothing from exertion, Zander's and Atticus's faces pale.

Zander won't accept Wendeline's answer. "It went from tent to tent, as if searching for something. Or someone. Why would it do that when we had the only caster in the forest? That was intentional for that reason."

"Maybe it sensed Clyda had been here."

"We would have crossed paths and drawn it away."

"There is another possibility." She swallows. "There may be traces of Margrethe's caster magic on Romeria. It could have *somehow* sensed that."

"This long after?" he asks doubtfully.

"I am no expert in the nethertaur, so I cannot say for certain. But it's the *only* reason I can think of." Wendeline's eyes flicker to me briefly.

Other than the truth. The beast could sense *my* caster magic, tucked behind whatever firewall Sofie created and bound to this ring. It came out of the forest's depths to find *me*. Bena—and all those other people—died because I was there.

I tamp down the guilt. Zander must not know. Not yet. "The important thing is that it's dead, right?" Its reeking carcass was loaded onto a wagon so that it may be hauled through Lower Market Street as a prize.

"Yes, I suppose." Zander pauses, and a slow smile curls his lips. "And it was the future queen of Islor who defeated it. That is something to celebrate."

The last thing I feel like doing is celebrating. "I had help."

"Merely a finishing strike. Come." He curls an arm around my worn, frazzled body. "You need to be at the head of that parade."

"Stop fidgeting."

"I haven't moved an inch. Ow!" I wince at the sharp poke from the pin Corrin slid into my hair.

"That was the last one." She steps back to admire her creation —a complex weave of braids and coils that pulls half my hair back while leaving the rest tumbling over my shoulder. "Go on, take a look at yourself."

I ease out of my vanity chair and stand before the full-length mirror, shifting from side to side to appreciate the dress Dagny dropped off late last night, flustered and bleary-eyed, as if she hadn't slept. The stitchwork is pristine, the fit flawless, the style poised and yet sexy.

If I'd known what I would be wearing it to, I would have asked her to make me a sack.

"I've done my best," Corrin declares. "If the king is not pleased, it will be because you chose a style that is entirely out of fashion."

"Since when does the king pay attention to women's clothes?"

Corrin harrumphs.

"Besides, doesn't the queen set trends?"

"So you *are* willing to play the queen now?" She smiles smugly.

I enjoy playing *his* queen, the one he comes to at night, the one he wakes to in the morning, unclothed and welcoming. It has been that way every night since our first together, our evenings fraught with passion, our mornings lazy and sensual repeats, before he slips out to tackle his day of kingly duties and Corrin barges through my door.

I just can never play his queen in the nymphaeum, that relentless voice in my head reminds me.

I *need* to tell him.

And yet every time it's on the tip of my tongue, I bite it back, afraid it will ruin what we have.

I stretch my leg out, watching the slit part and the gauzy material cascade around my thigh. Sexy stilettos would suit this dress, but there is nothing of the sort in Princess Romeria's closet or, dare I say, anywhere. Still, we managed to pair the dress with gray satin-and-leather heels that don't match the color but complement it nicely. Together with the complex weave on my head, I hardly recognize myself.

I don't know if it'll be strong enough armor to face a day of death. "You've done well, Corrin."

A knock sounds on my closed bedroom door.

"That must be the king, here to escort you."

My nerves stir.

"Remember, chin up, back straight at all times," she coaches.

But it isn't Zander waiting for me. It's Dagny.

"Oh, Your Highness, I just had to come and see you before you were off." Her grin is wide as she takes me in from head to toe, her hands clasped at her ample bosom. "Isn't she breathtaking?"

Even with my swirl of trepidation about bearing witness to today's events, my smile for the effervescent seamstress is genuine. "You are a marvel, Dagny."

"Oh." She waves away my compliment. "I'm just fortunate enough to dress the future queen. I brought you another capelet." She pulls the fold of fabric tucked under her arm and thrusts it into my hand. "I heard it's supposed to cool off tonight something fierce. Thought you might need it. The silk was a gift from a friend at the market." Dagny's eyebrows rise knowingly. "It's been made 'specially warm."

I recognize the silky indigo material within my grasp immediately. It's the one Bexley was intent on when she told me about the seer.

"She can't wear a capelet with *that* dress," Corrin scoffs, shaking her head. "How utterly silly she would look."

"Oh, fates, you're right, Corrin. You're always right. I'm a daft woman," Dagny blathers, ringing her hands. "Might as well keep it, though. Perhaps you might find use for it." She winks at me.

No, Dagny isn't so daft after all. "Thank you. I appreciate it." My heart thumps. Bexley said she would find a way to pass along information, and she has—through my seamstress. Dagny might not be the most clandestine with her hints, but they easily pass over Corrin's scrutiny.

"Anything for our future queen." She curtsies and with one last pointed look at the capelet, she ducks out.

I study the clothing in my hand. It's thicker than the others. She's layered it. And the stitchwork is far sloppier than Dagny's handiwork. Too sloppy. Dagny didn't make this.

I tuck it under my arm. "Corrin, is there any more of that pressed apple juice you brought me this morning? It was *so* sweet."

Her forehead wrinkles in thought. "I'd have to check the kitchen."

"Would you mind?"

"I need to make my way down there, anyway." She collects the empty tray from my first meal. "I'll be back shortly."

I wait to hear the sitting-room door shut before I dart to my dressing room with the coverlet. Wiggling my finger through a space in the shoddy seam, I tear into it, pulling the material apart.

A small slip of paper is tucked within.

Market Apothecary. Who you seek waits for you there tonight.

My insides twitch with anticipation as I read the scrawl.

Bexley found Gesine and Ianca, and I know where the apothecary is. I can get there on my own if I have to, I'm sure of it.

But maybe it's time to tell Zander.

My perked ears catch the sound of the exterior door shutting. I shove the torn coverlet and note in a corner, and with a breath to steel my nerves, I march into the sitting room, adrenaline thrumming in my veins.

Zander's eyes rake over me as I approach, from my hair all the way down to my shoes. My skirt splits open with each step, exposing my leg to my hip. His eyes flash wide at the sight.

I do my own admiring, though. Today, he has chosen an especially exquisite jacket in ink-blue satin, fitted to his body and fastened from neck to waist. It's adorned by metallic swirls and floral vines. It pairs with my outfit nicely.

"That is the dress Dagny made for you?" he asks evenly. The softer, passionate Zander I found in my bed is tucked away, leaving me to contend with Islor's cool and composed king again.

But I've also come to enjoy this dance between us.

"She did. Corrin was so sure you wouldn't approve, given you're a connoisseur of women's fashion and all." I can already see that he does approve, though, in the way his eyes flare with heat and his lips part.

He releases a long, slow exhale. "It's adequate."

My eyes widen with surprise.

The corners of his mouth twitch. "I didn't think you the type to fish for compliments."

I stop in front of him. "Oh, but you're wrong there. I *love* compliments. *And* reactions."

His gaze scrolls over my body again, stalling on the slit. He slips a hand through and up my thigh, his skin hot against mine, settling against my bare hip. A groan escapes him, likely at the confirmation that I'm not wearing anything beneath. "That *is* quite the gown."

"It *adequately* covers everything it needs to cover."

"You like to harp on things when you are annoyed. You look *more* than adequate today."

"See? Was that *so hard*?" I inhale sharply as his touch shifts further into the slit, to tease my sensitive flesh, instantly stirring need. But he pulls away abruptly, that mask back in place. "It is going to be a long day. Let us get through it before I show you my reaction."

I feel his promise between my thighs.

He offers me his arm, which I eagerly accept. Tension radiates through his body, cutting my playfulness short. I don't need to ask what bothers him. It's the repast, it's the public execution of the tributaries. It's everything that is wrong with Islor.

Elisaf greets us outside the door and bows deeply. "Your Highness, you look radiant."

"Well, that's a much warmer reception than my *betrothed* had for me," I mock.

"Don't encourage her," Zander mutters. "Though, I hope she can retain this level of giddiness through the day."

A servant sets a plate of the tiny Seacadorian grapes in front of me and scurries off.

From my left, Annika reaches over and grabs a bunch for herself before I can swat her hand away. "Why do you think I was adamant to sit next to you?"

"My charm?"

She snorts.

"I heard you like those." Zander's attention roves the crowd and then the jousting competition in its midst below. The execution square has transformed from the dark and loathsome space that terrorized me from my tiny tower window. It's far larger than I realized, encased on all sides by bleacher-style seats that climb many feet into the air. Around the perimeter are the black-and-gold banners marking Islor and Cirilea, their heavy brocade fluttering in the mild sea breeze.

It is more an arena than a square, and every seat is occupied—nobility in the front, commoners in the back. The afternoon sun beats down on the gathering, its rays glimmering off ear cuffs like sparkling facets of a diamond, picking out the mortals.

I pluck a vine off the plate. "And *I* heard they were a rare treat, hard to get." Thankfully our partition—higher than others—is adequately shielded by canopies. It also screens my view of the ominous gray tower above, where Tyree rots away.

"There are perks to being queen, and one of them is having whatever you want, whenever you want." Zander's arm is casually stretched across the back of our chairs, but his face is hard, his mood somber. He's not enjoying any part of the pomp and excitement from below. It could be because of what's yet to come, or it could be because he's lived through far too many of these events.

I, on the other hand, can't help but be enthralled as I listen to the crowd roar, and I watch with anxious anticipation as soldiers take turns competing.

"Whatever I want, whenever I want?" I pull grapes off one by one with my teeth, allowing myself thoughts of taking Zander in my mouth last night, hoping the lustful rush of my pulse might spark a reaction.

He watches the move intently. It's a moment, but the corners of his lips twitch.

I force my attention back to the view below. Atticus is there, the commander of the king's army, his armor resplendent in the afternoon sun as he slaps the backs of his soldiers, both the winners and the losers. He has avoided me since the day of the hunt. It's a relief.

I search the countless faces in the stands. Adley is there, of course, sitting next to Saoirse. Farther away are Telor and Sallow. I imagine I will get to know them soon enough. Bexley sits with the nobility. She's in a black satin gown, its V-neckline reaching down toward her navel, revealing the swell of ample breasts—a strange choice for a tournament day. She's watching me intently. Even from here, I can see the predatory glint in her stare. She has plans for me, and my neck, now that she's delivered on her part of our deal. She's going to be thoroughly disappointed when she learns the truth.

I push aside the shred of guilt I feel for the deception and dip my head, a silent thank-you.

"What is that about?" Zander asks.

"I'll tell you later." I don't see myself as having a choice for much longer, given we'll be leaving here to spend the night together. But now is not the time, given his sour temper.

A servant in a black uniform darts in with a sweeping bow to deliver two chalices brimming with an amber-colored liquid.

Elisaf collects them from us and wordlessly takes a sip, then another. After a moment, he sets them down with a murmur of "exceptionally sweet" and shifts back.

He's checking for poison.

"He risks his life like that every time you have a glass of wine?" There's incredulity in my voice.

"Since you brought poison with you to Islor, yes. If it hasn't already been tested by another." Zander pauses. "Would you rather he didn't? Have you tired of me *already*?"

I shake my head. "I'd rather Elisaf not be the taste tester."

"You'd have someone *else* risk their life, then. Abarrane, perhaps?"

I glance over my shoulder to where the warrior stands with her hand angled toward her hilt. Even with her shoulder bandaged, she looks coiled to attack. "I'd rather *no one* did."

"Tell that to your former self. She seemed intent on murdering us all."

I give up on lightening his mood, shifting my focus to the games.

The sun has dipped below the horizon when the last victor bows —a burly soldier whose weapon of choice was a spike-riddled mace. His opponent is carried off on a stretcher. He's not the only one today. I fear some of these challengers are beyond Wendeline's talents.

And yet the spectators clap and cheer and scream with every brutal round, as if this is purely for entertainment.

"It is time," Zander murmurs.

I tense when the first of two wagons is pulled in by brawny

workhorses, three wooden crosses erected on each, the prisoners already tied and waiting. I remember wondering before why the pyres, why not a guillotine or a simple blade? But seeing their reverence for Malachi's flame everywhere I look, I think I understand now. He is their creator.

Still, I abhor it.

Even more, I abhor the impatience that hangs in the air.

Zander's body is taut with tension when he stands. A hush falls over the crowd, as if everyone has been waiting for this moment.

The wagons make a slow parade around the arena floor.

"People of Islor," Zander begins, his deep voice carrying through the entire arena—at least it seems that way. "A plague scourges our lands in the form of a poison, the same poison that took our beloved King Eachann and Queen Esma. We are hunting it down and will prevail against it. Unfortunately, there are Islorians among us who have given in to malice. We cannot allow that. They must pay for their crime of murder with their lives."

Murmurs erupt in waves.

The wagons roll into place, and I force myself to take in the six tributaries who were swayed by dreams of freedom from their forced duties.

My stomach drops.

Four of the prisoners are children, the oldest no more than fifteen.

"Zander." I rise, the impulse to stop this display overwhelming.

"I see it," he says through gritted teeth.

Two women are with them. Their mothers, likely. All wear masks of fear, though in varying degrees. The two boys—maybe thirteen—hold their chins high in a show of bravery, but the dark stains running down their pants tell a different story.

"Where is Lord Stoll?" Zander calls out, his voice overly calm, icy.

A man in fine livery who was standing in the square steps

forward to bow. These are servants from his lands. "Your Highness."

"I was told you were submitting six tributaries for punishment. Why are there four *children* before me?"

"Your Highness, because they've murdered their keepers."

"And *how* would anyone know that they have this poison running through their veins?"

"Well, I … yes, I agree, that is an issue," he falters before clearing his throat. "But it doesn't change the fact that these mortals took poison with the intention of killing someone. They'll do it again if given the opportunity."

"You mean, the immortals who were taking their vein against the law?"

"Yes, but they're old enough to know what they were taking …" Stoll's voice drifts under Zander's lethal stare.

"As far as I'm concerned, those immortals—*any* immortal who doesn't abide by the law of the tributary system—deserves the punishment they received."

A murmur rises, but it's quickly followed by hushes for silence.

Zander turns to the prisoners. "Do these children belong to you?"

The women nod emphatically. The one on the left pleads, "Please, spare them. It was us. We put it in their drinks. They didn't know."

"But *you* did."

Their heads bob.

Zander's jaw clenches. He likes to think on issues, and he wasn't given that opportunity because the lords fed him a story of wicked and defiant tributaries, and then wheeled them out, tied to crosses, ready to burn.

My shock has shifted to rage. "They did what *I* would do if these were my kids," I hiss under my breath, loud enough for Zander to hear. They had a chance to stop them from being fed upon by monsters. It's what many parents would do. My disgust swells as I grip Zander's forearm. "You can't do this. This punishment isn't right."

He meets my eyes as if searching for an answer as a henchman nearby holds a flaming torch. "And what would you have me do? Cut them loose? People do not yet realize that the poison lives in their veins for good, but when they do, they'll do worse to them than this."

"I don't know, but *this* punishment is wrong, and you know it." My mind spins over a solution. How would this be handled in my world? "Send the adults to the dungeon. Or for labor at the rift. And send the children to Seacadore. Pay Kaders to smuggle them out."

His eyes are wild and desperate. "And if they come back?"

"Why would they *ever* come back here?" I mutter, but something Wendeline said strikes me. "The casters mark the humans in Ybaris to confirm they've been tested. Have her mark these people. If they're crazy enough to want to come back, it'll deter them."

He seems to consider that for another moment. "Release them *all*." The three words echo in the yawning silence, but it's quickly drowned out by an uproar. Outrage splays across the faces of the nobility as the ropes are cut with swords and the prisoners are ushered down the steps. They cower together, their faces streaked with tears.

Among others in the crowd, there is a mixture of everything from shock to relief to disappointment. Atticus stands below, peering up at us, his jaw clenched. Another of his brother's decisions that he does not approve of. Or maybe it's my influence that he can't accept.

I smooth my hand over Zander's back, hoping the small, silent gesture offers him even a minor shield against the noise.

Zander's hand lifts in the air, and silence falls again.

"These prisoners will be escorted to the dungeon until I decide the best punishment for them. But for their crime of ingesting a poison meant to harm, these prisoners will be branded." He nods toward Wendeline.

She stalls a moment, appearing flustered by the unexpected request. I imagine she thought her days of marking humans were over. But then she rushes forward, her white-and-gold gown flowing behind her as she pauses before each prisoner, collecting their hands in hers, earning a wince of pain, as if whatever she's doing hurts. Wendeline reaches the end of the line and turns toward Zander to bow.

"Let us all see the mark of a tainted one!" Zander calls out.

The prisoners look at each other and then hesitantly lift their hands in the air to show the circle with two interlocked crescent moons on the fleshy part of their thumbs, the outlines glowing in Wendeline's caster magic.

A cold wash of familiarity courses through me. I've seen that mark before, tattooed on the hands of the People's Sentinel. "What is that symbol?" I whisper.

"I do not know, but whatever it is, I'm sure everyone will have heard of it by next Hudem."

There's a stir in the crowd as Lord Adley steps down from the stands and strolls confidently into the center of the square.

Beside me, Zander's molars grind.

"If I may, Your Highness—"

"No, you may *not*," Zander barks. "You will not be given a platform to spew your lies and your schemes any longer, Lord Adley."

Adley's eyes narrow in defiance.

But Zander promptly dismisses him as if the Lord of Kettling is nothing more than a nuisance. "Lead the prisoners to the dungeon, and if a single hair is harmed on their heads, every guard in the escort will visit this square at dawn, and those pyres will be used." He looks pointedly at the men with swords as the six mortals follow them out on wobbly legs. "I need this night over with *now*," Zander mutters under his breath, waving a hand to his left.

A parade of soldiers marches out, the three Ybarisan prisoners sandwiched between them, shuffling forward in a line.

I inhale sharply. They're wearing nothing but the fetters around their ankles and wrists. When I saw them last, they were filthy and bloodied. They've since been bathed and healed, save for the eternal slash across the arm to subdue their elven affinity. They've been prepared.

I struggle to hide my sneer. I guess the immortals can't feed off grimy bodies.

All three walk forward with their chins held high, as if the fact that they're marching to their public execution—naked—doesn't faze them. Maybe this pales in comparison to what Abarrane did to them. I steal another glance over my shoulder to catch her private smile as she observes.

People are watching me as readily as they watch my condemned Ybarisan brethren. I keep my gaze forward as the men are forced onto three tables, their arms and ankles shackled to each corner. Piles of timber of varying lengths have been stacked beneath, kindling for a fire.

The priestesses move in quietly for their task of keeping the Ybarisans alive.

"For the crimes of murder, conspiracy to commit murder, and conspiring against the crown, you are receiving the penalty of death by royal repast followed by pyre. May the fates have mercy on you." Zander's voice is wooden. "As an honor to those of noble blood, we offer first sampling to them."

A line of nobility scamper forward from the crowd, some faces I recognize. Adley is not among them. He is busy spouting words in Atticus's ear, his expression tight and his gestures sweeping.

Atticus stands stoically and listens, his face stony. I can't begin to read him.

The nobility look like eager children as they flock, each finding a corner of a prisoner. Even from this distance, I can make out their fangs as they elongate. The Ybarisans visibly tense as teeth sink into their flesh, and my stomach curls. This is nothing like the night I witnessed Zander with that tributary. That was tender and considerate and personal.

This is savage.

And it's not just a few. The lineup grows, snaking around the tables and pyres. There can't possibly be enough blood for them all.

"*This* is why Ybaris calls them demons," I whisper under my breath.

Beside me, Zander tenses.

And then the first scream ricochets through the square.

CHAPTER THIRTY

It's a domino effect, from the first aristocrat to the last who fed at the trough. The Islorian immortals feeding on the Ybarisan prisoners crumple to the dirt-covered ground, writhing in pain, their backs arched, their teeth gritted in agony.

"What is happening?" Annika whispers, her voice filled with horror.

"They took the poison." Realization sweeps across Zander's face.

"I thought they couldn't," I say. "I thought merth would tear them apart. It *is* merth. Isn't it?"

Zander's eyes snap to Wendeline. "That's what I was told."

Bodies thrash and people scream in horror, scurrying away as if whatever afflicts the nobles is contagious. The relentless screams—so many of them—set the hairs on my neck on end. The priestesses look toward Wendeline, who shakes her head. She can't help them, she's saying.

And in the center of it all, the three Ybarisans strapped to the tables laugh.

My head swims with dizziness. "There has to be something we can do," I hear myself say.

Zander hesitates. "There is." His jaw clenches as he steps to the edge of the railing.

An enormous ball of fire erupts around the three tables and the victims. People scatter even farther. The cries of agony cease almost immediately.

Zander is using his affinity, and this is not a parlor trick. By the countless hanging jaws, this demonstration proves he is far more powerful than anyone realized.

The crowd watches as scorching flames burn for another few seconds and then, just as suddenly, the fire cuts out, leaving nothing but a pile of smoldering corpses, the smell of charred skin and an eerie silence, as everyone absorbs the shock of what they just witnessed.

A deep, wicked laugh sounds from high above, carrying across the stillness in the square.

"Praise be the future queen of Islor!" a male voice sings.

It's Tyree, in the tower.

"One drop of her blood to end your curse forever! One drop to free all!"

The color slips from Zander's face. "Fates, it isn't merth that they're taking. It's *your* blood. How did I not see this?" Again, Zander's eyes dart toward Wendeline, and the accusation is clearly there.

The pained wince she offers says everything.

She lied to him about that, too.

What other deceptions has she spun?

My face burns as I feel the heat of countless stares crawling all over me. "I didn't do this," I croak, though no one hears my words. I steal a panicked glance Annika's way. She knows I'm innocent. Those close to me know.

Zander turns to me.

"*I* didn't have anything to do with this." I feel compelled to remind him of that, given the conflicted look in his eyes. He *must* be able to read my confusion and my horror, can't he?

"It won't matter," he says quietly.

Numbness washes over me. "What does that mean?"

"Yet again, we find ourselves here. You did not learn the first time, brother!" Atticus bellows, shifting into the center of the square. The flames from the torches glint off the gold in his armor. "Your betrothed suggested this royal repast, and now we know why."

My mouth drops in shock. This was Adley's idea. I didn't even know what a royal repast was. Atticus knows that!

He walks a slow circle, addressing the crowd. "Twelve of our lords and ladies have been slaughtered in a single vicious swoop because our king can no longer see the danger standing right beside him, despite how many times I've warned him. He would put a queen on the throne with blood running through her veins that could poison us all if given the opportunity."

He points to the smoldering mess. "*This* is no surprise. It was not the high priestess who killed the daaknar, but the Princess Romeria, when the beast sank its teeth into her."

Gasps sound from every corner of the square.

"What is he doing?" I hiss.

Zander's jaw tenses. "Seizing an opportunity."

"But your king continues to lie and deceive, protecting a woman who came here to destroy us." Atticus's face is grim as he turns to Zander. "I fear you are leading Islor down a path it cannot recover from. I am sworn to protect you, even if that means I must protect you from yourself." His voice is strong and commanding as it carries across the arena. I imagine it's the same as on the battleground. "As King Ailill's heir, and an heir to the throne of Islor, I *cannot* allow this foolishness to continue any longer. You will relinquish your seat immediately."

"You have no authority to do this," Zander says, his voice oddly serene.

"And what will you do to stop it from happening? Burn the city to the ground just so you can keep a crown you have no interest in wearing?"

Time seems to hang as the two brothers lock gazes and unspoken words pass.

"You may be firstborn, but you have proven that you do not belong up there. Not anymore. And I will do what you cannot." Atticus's chest rises with a deep inhale. "Guards! *Seize her*!"

Is this happening? Again? "He can't do this, can he?"

Zander's eyes shift to the soldiers moving in. A flash of shock skates across his face when he sees Boaz leading the charge. "Abarrane!"

"The Legion is with the rightful king of Islor, Your Highness." She punctuates that with a fleeting bow.

Zander yanks his sheathed jeweled dagger off his hip and presses it into my hand, curling my fingers over it. To Elisaf and Abarrane, he orders, "Get her to her rooms and hold them off. I'm right behind you."

I stare at the weapon in my palm until Elisaf grabs my arm.

"Come. It's not safe for you here anymore."

I clutch the dagger's hilt as we run.

Everything seems to move in slow motion and yet warp speed. My mind is caught in a fog, the sound of blades clashing all around me. Abarrane and the Legion cut down charging soldiers as if they were farmhands swinging shovels. Somehow, we make it from our seats in the tournament square to the royal chamber stairs.

"Hold them off!" Elisaf orders to Abarrane, not slowing to ensure they listen. We dash for my suite.

Corrin is pacing around my sitting room when we reach it. "I was in the kitchens when I heard the yelling! There are soldiers fighting everywhere. *Who* would attack us like this with all the king's army in place?" she demands, but her normally resolute voice carries a tremble.

"I'm afraid it *is* the king's army that has attacked. And the commander is leading the charge," Elisaf says, his lungs showing some strain.

"I didn't know about the poison! Atticus knows that!" I cry

between ragged breaths. I've never moved so fast in my life.

"It does not matter. He is using this to his advantage."

Shouts ring from somewhere far below.

"I warned you, didn't I!" My indignant rage bubbles. "I warned you both that he couldn't be trusted, and you didn't listen to me!"

"I did not think he would do this." Zander charges in, a smear of blood that isn't his own on his cheek. A haunting shout carries up the stairwell, one of agony, of likely a final breath. "Atticus has claimed the army. Some still fight for me, but they will not last long. There are too many. We need to leave *now.* Even the Legion can't hold them off. Abarrane knows where to meet us."

"Why is Boaz against us?"

"Because Boaz is for the crown, and he clearly no longer feels I am fit to wear it." He nods toward my dress. "Change out of that, quickly, unless you feel like running in it."

Corrin and I rush to my closet. Her fingers work frantically over the hooks and buttons. I peel off the delicate material, leaving it in a heap as I don my tunic and pants.

Zander appears in the doorway just as I'm yanking on my second riding boot. Corrin is on her knees, furiously tying the laces. "Are you ready? We need to get out of the city immediately. We will meet Abarrane out near Eldred Wood."

I curse. "I need to go to the apothecary first."

"For what?"

I hesitate. "Bexley found Ianca and Gesine. They're waiting there for me. She sent the message this morning. I was going to tell you after the tournament."

"What message?" Corrin gasps as she remembers. "You've been scheming again! And with *Dagny,* of all people! I *knew* you were up to something." She stabs the air between us with her finger. "I warned him not to fall for this new—"

"It's not what you think!" I yell over her tirade.

"Why am I not surprised by this?" Zander shakes his head. "Wendeline has lied and manipulated us in far worse ways than I ever anticipated, and now you want to seek out *more* of these treacherous casters from Mordain?" His anger rises with his words. "That spectacle out there could have been avoided had she told us what this poison was. We would have known to check the Ybarisans. This is what she wanted. Islor in shambles."

"But I don't think it is." Whatever her reasons for deceiving him, Wendeline said everything she did has been for the future of Islor that Zander wants.

"And what do *you* know about what is and what isn't, Romeria?" he seethes. "*All* of Islor will be hunting you—the immortals, to ensure your death; the mortals, for your blood. No, the absolute *last* place I'm taking you is to more casters."

"But I *need* to see Gesine," I push through gritted teeth.

"Explain to me why?" he demands.

Wendeline said there would be a time to tell him, and I would know it. With his kingdom crumbling around him, I don't suppose this is it. Yet I'm afraid that if I leave Cirilea tonight, I'll never get the answers I need to survive in this world. "Because I'm a key caster, and she can teach me how to use my affinities."

Corrin gasps.

Zander's face pales. "You can't be."

"And yet apparently, I am. It's a *very* long story that we don't have time to go through right now, but I need to get to the apothecary. If you don't want to take me, fine. Just get me past these walls, and I'll get to it myself."

"You won't last an hour on your own. I don't know how you'll survive, even with me," he murmurs absently, pushing his hands through his hair, sending it into disarray.

"I *need* Gesine to help me understand what I am. *Please*. Don't worry, I'm not going to open any doors or tear any dimensional folds. I'm not going anywhere near the nymphaeum on Hudem."

Zander's eyes are clouded, his thoughts somewhere as he processes this. "The nethertaur sensed you. That's why it came to the meadow."

"Yes." There is no other answer but the truth.

"How long have you known?"

"Since the day I went to the market with Dagny. Wendeline knew after the daaknar attack, when she tested me."

"The market ...," he echoes, and I sense where his mind is veering—to all the intimate moments and opportunities I had to tell him. And I didn't.

"I'm sorry. I was told you'd kill me if you found out—"

Elisaf charges in. "We *must* go now."

A switch seems to trip in Zander's head. He turns to Corrin. "You will come with us?"

"I would only slow you down. Besides, I have a household to take care of, Your Highness, including three new members, soon to be four."

Gracen and her kids. What have I unwittingly dragged them into?

Zander's jaw tenses. "I do not have time to stand here and argue. Atticus knows you are loyal to me."

"And he also knows I maintain this castle's operations better than any other could," she says haughtily. "I will keep things in place until your return." She nods as if confirming that decision, but in her eyes, I see a mixture of resignation and fear.

Zander sees it too. "Do not risk yourself needlessly. If he presses, give him whatever information he demands." He bows deeply. "Until my return."

"I will buy you as much time as I can. Stay safe." She looks to me. Her face remains wary, but her curtsy is uncharacteristically deep. "Both of you."

"How does Atticus not know about this passage?" I stumble over a crumbled stone, nearly dropping my lantern.

"Because it's called the king's alley for a reason. Only the king has seen it since it was constructed *many* centuries ago," comes Zander's muted response. "Four kings have used it. Ailill,

Rhionn, my father, and me. My father led me through it, and his father led him through it, and so on. And while Atticus deigns to play king in my absence, he will never know of its existence."

Instead of unlocking the passage at the bottom of the winding steps as Zander did last time, he led us beneath the steps and along a hidden path I had to crouch to pass through while the men had to crawl. Now we trek silently along an endless corridor that reeks of mildew, the skeletal remains of dead rodents crunching beneath our boots, as we flee into the night with stockpiled provisions—mainly weapons and gold.

That the king of Islor had his own go bag like the one I stowed in my apartment for a quick getaway is not lost on me.

"Imagine how differently things could have gone had you only been honest with me," Zander muses.

"I was afraid you would kill me!"

"Yes. Spend the night wrapped in a woman and then rise to execute her in the morning. That sounds like me."

"Sounds like that night in the tower."

Zander stops so abruptly, I plow into his back.

"And while we're on the subject of being honest, you knew Atticus wanted to be king. He brought all those soldiers, loyal to him, into the city. Was it for protection, or was it so he could overpower you?"

"Possibly both," He admits, continuing forward.

"How could you *not* see what he would do?"

"Because he is my *brother*! And because it seems I cannot see *anything* clearly when you are around."

"So this is *my* fault? Even though I warned you not to trust him?"

He sighs. "I think we're past the point of blame. But I wager Ybaris got what it wanted."

"Who poisoned Quill? Was that also Atticus?"

"I do not claim to know anything anymore. Whoever the culprit, they did so to keep people afraid of the Ybarisan princess set to be queen. Atticus has been seen with Adley and the others. I don't doubt now that they have been whispering in his ear notions of claiming the throne, convincing him of the righteousness of it. And then today happened, and he saw his chance. It could not have been more perfect, really, though it seems the priestesses have had their own hand in plotting, independent of everyone else. It does not matter anymore, does it?"

Atticus's accusation loiters in my mind. "Do you even want to be king?"

"No, I do not," he admits, shocking me with his resolute answer. "Which is why I must be." He pauses. "So this story you fed me, about not remembering anything—"

"A lie. My name is Romeria Watts. I'm from New York City, where mostly everyone is human and there is no talk of fates and casters and immortals. An elemental named Sofie tricked me into helping her save her husband, only to stab me in the chest with a token horn from Malachi. I woke up in this body, which is exactly like my own body, with people accusing me of murder."

Behind me, Elisaf curses.

"Except you're not human. You're a key caster."

"Apparently, but I had no idea. I don't know how it all works. I never felt *anything* until I took this ring off the other day."

"You tried to tell me," Zander says, more to himself.

"Yes. But that didn't work out well for me." God, it feels like a concrete block has been lifted off my chest.

"And how are you supposed to save Sofie's husband?"

"I don't know exactly, but I think he might be imprisoned in the Nulling." Sofie said Elijah was trapped somewhere and it sounded like Malachi was the one who sent him to that place. When the fold was torn, the monsters who escaped were from the Nulling, sent there by the fates. It would make sense then, that the two are the same. Though, the last time I saw Elijah's body, it was in a stone coffin in Belgium. "Malachi sent me here to try to open the nymphaeum door, which I obviously am *not* going to do. And I'm not going to help Sofie. So that leaves me with learning how to be a key caster."

"Until people find out what you are. As if they didn't already have reason to kill you," Zander mutters.

"How do you know you can trust Gesine?" Elisaf asks quietly. They're the first words he's spoken to me since we crawled through the tunnel.

"I don't, but if they wanted to kill me for being what I am, they had a thousand opportunities to do it."

Silence drags on as we trek along the path. I ache to know what's filtering through Zander's mind right now, but he isn't saying anything.

We arrive at the end of the corridor and meet a solid stone wall that I've come to learn means nothing in this world of secret passageways.

"How close will this bring us to the apothecary?" I ask.

"A few blocks away." Zander puts his finger to his mouth for quiet. He listens for a moment, before reaching above his head to press on a block. A telltale click sounds and the wall moves out.

And the tiny thrill skates through my mind. I was made for this kind of world.

"Your childlike fascination with these things continues to amuse me," he murmurs, obviously sensing my reaction.

"I was a thief in my former life, so sneaking in and out of places was sort of my thing." It feels oddly liberating to admit that.

Zander shoots an incredulous look my way before we step into a cramped room full of dust-covered crates. "It's a storage cellar," he whispers. Moving for a wooden door, he pushes against it. And curses.

"Padlock?" Elisaf asks.

He nods. And then falters. "We will have to move quickly once we leave here, as soldiers will begin scouring the city, if they aren't already. I will get you to the apothecary and then, if this Gesine is who you think she is, then that is where you and I must part ways." In the glow of my lantern light, his hazel eyes carry a myriad of emotions I can't discern. "I haven't thought clearly since the day you marched into my life, before or after the attack. If I am to take back what is mine, I need *all* my wits about me."

I swallow against the ball that swells in my throat. I'm not sure what is more startling—that I'll be alone in this strange world, or that a man I've come to care for deeply is abandoning me at a time when I need him most.

But I'm used to being abandoned by those closest to me, and I'm not about to beg him to stay.

Pausing a moment to listen for passersby, he barrels through, splintering the wood. We step out into an alleyway. The lower streets are deserted, save for the odd figure that darts from one corner to the next. No royal guards sit on horses, no market revelers linger. Yet I feel eyes on us as we move along, silent and hidden within our cloaks.

None would guess that it is their king and the Ybarisan princess, fleeing in the night.

Up ahead, the apothecary is dark, its windows shuttered by thick curtains.

"She said tonight?" Zander stalls in the shadows.

"Yes." My eyes scour the corners around us, every nerve ending on edge. Movement in an alley catches my attention. A figure in a black cloak. They shift into the cast of the lantern just long enough for me to catch the strands of strawberry-blond hair before shifting back. It's Bexley. She knew I would be here. After what happened in the square, she can't be here for my side of our deal. She's either here to see me off, or to kill me.

The side of the curtain moves.

"There's someone inside," I whisper.

"Yes. I saw that."

As one, we cross the street.

"I will keep an eye out." Elisaf disappears into another shadow. There are so many to slip into in this world.

We're four feet from the shop when a click sounds, and the door creaks open an inch.

Disquiet grips me.

Zander slips in first, his hand clutching the hilt of his sword. The surrounding lanterns flare, and I assume it has something to do with his affinity. I'm momentarily envious.

"Shut the door behind you," a serene female voice says.

I do as instructed, throwing us into darkness.

"I sense the flame burning inside you, King of Islor. You are powerful for an Islorian."

"As I'm sure you are, even with that collar around your neck, High Priestess," he says, equally calm.

My eyes frantically search for a hint of what Zander sees.

A faint glow erupts in the room, a ball of light that floats in the air, swelling until it illuminates a woman in a charcoal-gray cloak, with long, inky-black hair and pale-green eyes, just as Kaders described her. A simple gold collar encloses her delicate neck.

"It is unnerving, the unique skills of your kind. It will take time to become accustomed to it, though I will say I am enjoying my newfound freedom in your land." Her piercing gaze shifts from Zander to me. She bows deeply. "I am Caster Gesine, Your Highness. We knew each other once, but I see now that Wendeline was right, and I am no longer a familiar face. You are Romeria, but not the one who left Ybaris."

My heart skips a beat as I search the shop for the older woman. I see nothing but walls of shelves lined with jars and mirrors reflecting my face back at me. "Where is Ianca?"

"She is safe outside of Cirilea. The journey here was long and took its toll on her, but she is anxious to meet you. Wendeline said you did not know what you had in your old life."

I shake my head. "I didn't believe in any of this."

"Did Aoife curse me?" Zander interrupts. "Did she weaken my mind by binding my heart to Romeria?"

I clench my teeth against the sting of that question.

Gesine's green eyes flitter between the two of us. "We can discuss what she did when the time is right. I think you will see soon that it does not matter."

"You speak in riddles," he growls.

"It may seem like that." She nods to my hand. "That ring. Remove it if you will. I would like to get a sense of your power for myself."

Zander watches me intently as I slip Queen Isla's ring off my finger. That heady thrum of power begins crawling through my body almost instantly, intensifying with each passing moment.

"Remarkable." Awe blossoms over Gesine's face. "It is unpleasant for you?"

"*Very.*" I don't know how to describe this sensation. It's a mix between the prickling, tingling buzz of pins and needles in my limbs, and a surge of adrenaline through my veins.

"That feeling will dull when you learn how to contain it."

"Thank God for that," I mutter. In the shadows behind Gesine, I spot an unfamiliar woman's face staring back at me. I startle, and seeing that it's a reflection in a mirror, spin around to look behind me. Only Zander is there.

I turn to face the mirror again, my wariness edging in.

I reach up to touch my cheek.

The woman in the reflection does the same.

I touch my nose.

She does the same.

"Oh my God," I whisper, clutching at my neck as waves of shock engulf me.

The floating orb brightens, shining more light.

I take in the stranger looking back at me, with her angular face, her pale-blue eyes, and her heart-shaped lips. The only similar thing to both of us is the color of our hair. "This isn't my face." Or my voice.

"An illusion," Gesine confirms. "The caster bound that to the ring, as well. To give you some semblance of familiarity, and make the transition into Princess Romeria's body easier."

"To help me." This was Sofie's version of *help,* along with the spells to stifle my caster powers. She thought of *everything*.

"I would suggest you slip the ring back on for now. Until you learn how to contain what stirs inside you, you will not be able to focus on much of anything else, and we have a journey ahead of us."

Within seconds of the cool gold band encasing my finger again, the purring adrenaline quells. I glance up to see my familiar face in the mirror once again. The one constant that I've known all my life.

It's the only thing I have left.

A single knock sounds on the door, and Elisaf ducks in. "Soldiers are moving in. We have only a moment."

"We must move with haste, then." With a sweep of Gesine's hand, the counter slides aside to reveal a gaping hole beneath and the tip of a ladder.

I push aside my bewilderment at her ability to do that. "The last time I followed an elemental somewhere, she sent me to this godforsaken place and put me in this body."

Gesine dips her head as if to acknowledge my anxiety. "My *only* purpose here is to guide you in what already is."

Do I believe her? I don't think I have much choice. I can't stay here, and it's clear I'm not welcome to follow Zander.

I look to him now.

"The Legion will be waiting for me." His eyes drift to my mouth, and something unreadable passes. "This is where we part ways, Romeria Watts of New York City."

"Right." Where he was once a stranger to me, now I am one to him, regardless of the nights we've shared. An ache stirs in my chest, but I set my jaw. "Goodbye."

His jaw tenses.

"You have misunderstood," Gesine says. "You *both* must come."

"No," Zander and I counter in unison.

"She is not safe anywhere around me, and we have different paths," Zander adds quietly.

"Your path is the same and must be taken together. Romeria, I'm sorry, but the old is now destined with the new, and there is no going back. There is only forward." Her eyes show sympathy.

I nod. I knew as much.

She shifts her attention to Zander. "The seers have seen the end of the blood curse, and it is at the tied hands of the Ybarisan daughter of Aoife and the Islorian son of Malachi. Is that not what you wish?"

"Yes, I have seen it too. So did everyone sitting in that square today. I know what Romeria is, and *that* is not how I want to change Islor. Not by killing my people." Bitterness flares in his voice.

Her responding smile is gentle. "That is Aoife's way, but that is not the *only* way."

"And what will you get out of this? Do not tell me you have risked yourself for the sake of Islor."

Her fingertips skate over her golden collar. "Freedom for my kind, eventually. Perhaps I will see it before my days come to an end. Perhaps not."

Shouts ring outside. Elisaf steals another glance from the curtain. "We no longer have another option." He points toward the opening in the floor.

With a deep sigh, Zander nods.

One by one, we climb down the ladder. My boots splash in murky water that smells of sewage. Torches reveal a dank tunnel that leads into darkness.

With another wave of Gesine's hand, the counter drags itself back into place, hiding our route. Her sleeve falls with the movement, revealing an emblem that shimmers with a golden glow.

I point to it. "What is that?"

"My affinity to Aoife." She pulls her sleeve up and holds her arm out, allowing me a chance to study the mark—a circle encasing a golden deer that spans the width of her forearm. There are two more circles in a line above it, only smaller, one with a bronze bull, and the other with a silver butterfly. "I have affinities to three elements, though my ties to water are much stronger than the other two."

"Find the gilded doe," I whisper. Is this what my father meant? Find Gesine?

"We will take this tunnel to the rookery where there is a skiff waiting to sail us outside the Cirilean border."

"I *must* meet my soldiers in Eldred Wood." Zander's voice offers no negotiation.

"And then we will head north together, to the Venhorn Mountains."

Elisaf groans. He's clearly not fond of that plan.

"You know what lives in those mountains." Zander gives Gesine a pointed look.

"I do. If we cannot sail to Seacadore, then it is the safest place in Islor for us until Her Highness has been adequately trained."

Zander turns to me.

I show him my back. I haven't forgotten that just five minutes ago he had plans to leave me.

His soft sigh carries. "We will get you there. I cannot promise we will stay."

Gesine presses her lips together and then nods.

"How have you learned to navigate my city so quickly, High Priestess?"

I bite my tongue and refrain from reminding him that it is no longer his city.

"You have more allies than you realize." Gesine smiles at me. "As do you, Your Highness. Many allies and many who wish to see you as their queen."

My mind swirls. "Please. No more Highness. No more queen. No more Princess Romeria." I've had enough of it all. "It's just Romy."

"Very well, Romy." She dips. "You will return to this place and bring hope for the people. But we must go *now*." A moment later, as if she could sense it coming, wood splinters somewhere above.

We flee Cirilea, the exiled king of Islor and I running side by side.

And yet worlds apart.

CHAPTER THIRTY-ONE

Sofie's stomach was a twisted ball of anxiety and fear as she rose to watch the Fate of Fire circle the coffin, his narrowed eyes on the still forms. This was not normal. Malachi never paced in such a way. "Has something happened?"

Malachi traced Romeria's cheekbone with his lengthy index finger. Even in death, with the token still embedded in her flesh, her body remained perfectly preserved. He refused to allow Sofie to remove it and bury Romeria's corpse outside beneath the oak tree. "She knows what she must do."

Sofie's heart skipped a few beats. "And she will do it?" Romeria would finally claim the immense power radiating inside her to tear the Nulling's fold? Her hopeful gaze landed on her husband's face. With the door to the nymphaeum opened, Malachi promised to unite them. Here, or in Islor, it mattered not, if she and Elijah were together.

Malachi's lips unfurled in a fiendish smile. "Eventually, she must. She will have no other choice."

ACKNOWLEDGMENTS

These last few months spent in another world with Romeria have been thrilling and scary, and I'm so glad I took this chance. The story has brought back my love of writing at a time when I needed it most. Writing is a lonely endeavor and yet no book ever reaches readers' hands without help. I'd like to thank the following people for their help:

Jennifer Armentrout, for encouraging me to "scratch that itch" and venture back into fantasyland.

Jenn Sommersby, for your talent with this beast and your patience with my many tics. As always, you were a delight to work with.

Chanpreet Singh, for working your magic to catch all the little errors that slip through the cracks.

Hang Le, for nailing this cover (and every cover you tackle for me.)

Nina Grinstead and the team at Valentine PR, for your passion, help, and expertise with spreading the word.

Steph Brown and Justine Wood from the Bookish Box, for giving this book some extra attention through your awesome book subscription box.

Stacey Donaghy of Donaghy Literary Group, for the laughs, the support, and the eagerness (and the angry naked cat GIFs.)

Tami, Sarah, and Amélie, for keeping Tucker's Troop alive and a fun, safe place to be.

My family, for delivering plates of food to my cave and tolerating me even when my thoughts are on another planet.

ABOUT THE AUTHOR

K.A. Tucker writes captivating stories with an edge.

She is the internationally bestselling author of the Ten Tiny Breaths, Burying Water and The Simple Wild series, He Will Be My Ruin, Until It Fades, Keep Her Safe, Be the Girl, and Say You Still Love Me. Her books have been featured in national publications including USA Today, Globe & Mail, Suspense Magazine, Publisher's Weekly, Oprah Mag, and First for Women.

K.A. Tucker currently resides in a quaint town outside of Toronto. Learn more about K.A. Tucker and her books at katuckerbooks.com

CPSIA information can be obtained
at www.ICGtesting.com
Printed in the USA
LVHW092251110222
710756LV00002B/171

9 781990 105159